Charles Collins is the pseudonym of a first-time author born and raised in West Yorkshire where this novel is set. Charles currently works in the construction industry for a company predominately involved in house building. He and his wife have three daughters living and working in other parts of the UK. Charles is a keen supporter of the Rugby League, a lifelong fan of the Leeds Rhinos.

Having spent forty years working in construction, this middle-aged man decided to write a crime fiction novel for no other reason than personal enjoyment; his eclectic taste in music is reflected in the lead characters' choice of songs liberally sprinkled throughout the novel. The writer hopes you, the reader, gets as much enjoyment from reading this story as he did writing it.

This work is dedicated to the author's wife and three daughters; their support has been so important in the production of this novel. The time and space afforded to the author is and will always be gratefully appreciated.

Charles Collins

RETRIBUTION

AUSTIN MACAULEY PUBLISHERS™
LONDON • CAMBRIDGE • NEW YORK • SHARJAH

Copyright © Charles Collins (2020)

The right of Charles Collins to be identified as author of this work has been asserted by him in accordance with section 77 and 78 of the Copyright, Designs and Patents Act 1988.

All rights reserved. No part of this publication may be reproduced, stored in a retrieval system, or transmitted in any form or by any means, electronic, mechanical, photocopying, recording, or otherwise, without the prior permission of the publishers.

Any person who commits any unauthorised act in relation to this publication may be liable to criminal prosecution and civil claims for damages.

This is a work of fiction. Names, characters, businesses, places, events, locales, and incidents are either the products of the author's imagination or used in a fictitious manner. Any resemblance to actual persons, living or dead, or actual events is purely coincidental.

A CIP catalogue record for this title is available from the British Library.

ISBN 9781528912822 (Paperback)
ISBN 9781528960274 (ePub e-book)

www.austinmacauley.com

First Published (2020)
Austin Macauley Publishers Ltd
25 Canada Square
Canary Wharf
London
E14 5LQ

The author acknowledges and thanks all those who helped and assisted in the proofreading stage of this piece of work, his wife, their three daughters and Liz, a close friend, not forgetting the team at Austin Macauley, he will be forever grateful for their unbiased opinions and comments, thank you.

Songs and artists featured in the novel in the order they are referred to:

Songs/Artists

Riders on the Storm The Doors
Double Trouble Lynard Skynard
That Don't Make It Junk Haley Tuck
Cocaine JJ Cale
5446 That's My Number Toots and the Maytalls
Rotterdam The Beautiful South
Get It On T Rex
Jobseeker Sleaford Mods
16 Sells From a 30.6 Tom Waites
Jubilee Street Nick Cave and The Bad Seeds
You Think I Don't Know (But I Know) Charles Bradley
My Conversation Slim Smith and The Uniques
Run Through the Jungle Creedence Clearwater Revival
Big Shot Dr John

Chapter 1

Year: 2005
Matthew Tanner was 61 years old when he died, shot in the back of the head, no warning, fast, clinical, professional. It's very unlikely that he heard the gun shot or felt the pain of the bullet passing violently through his skull. It is, however, highly likely that in the hours immediately before death, he was feeling happy, even elated at the success and audaciousness of the venture he and his compatriots had recently conducted. The heist, or as he saw it the rescue, a liberation had been years in the planning, days in the execution and hours since its complete success. The raid in the Bosnian capital Sarajevo had gone well, just as planned; gold bullion, hidden for nearly 100 years, had been found, freed and now resided in the false bottom of the truck parked next to his felled body.

In a dense secluded forest, somewhere within the state of Bosnia, Matthew's life, had been abruptly cut short, all that remained was his collapsed corpse lying face down on the dry rutted earth. As his body twitched its final reflexes of life, blood slowly oozed from the exit wound high in the centre of his forehead and began to spread gently away.

Hearing the shot, a man jumped down from the cab of the truck.

"What the fuck! Tommy?" screamed Davy Watts as he looked in disbelief at the body of Matthew Tanner laying prone on the ground the plume of blood spreading away from his head, staining the dust a dark, almost black red. With both arms raised, Watts pushed the man standing over the felled body so hard his quarry also fell to the ground, two bodies on the ground, one dead, one alive.

Thomas Henry Smythe (aka Tommy Smith), the self-proclaimed leader of this band of men, had already holstered his Smith and Wesson before Watts could see the gun, conscious not to appear trigger happy. Smythe lifted himself back onto his feet, Watts stared at Tanner's body the next few seconds would determine whether this, Smythe's pre-planned action, would be a success.

Then as expected, the fourth member of the gang, Frank Jessop, joined in the condemnation of Smythe as he too jumped down from the truck after hearing the gunshot and witnessing Watts' reaction. In his broad Yorkshire accent, he shouted,

"Oh my god, that's it, we're well and truly fucked now. When the Bosnian coppers turn up, we'll be locked up … forever! Shit, shit, shit … you dozy bastard, Tommy."

Smythe had to appear to be in control, even relaxed, to give himself the best chance of getting the other two men to accept the situation. In truth, they had no choice. In as calm a voice as he could muster trying to control the effect of the adrenalin pumping hard and fast through his body, he explained,

"I told you both before we came out here, if this job was successful, Tanner was going to go to the press with this little escapade of ours. We would lose all the gold, he was gonna write a book about it, for fuck's sake and even if he didn't name us directly, it wouldn't take a Sherlock Holmes to find out who we were. We all agreed, even him," he shouted pointing to the corpse on the ground; the other two turned their heads to look once again at the dead man. That gave Smythe a split second to take a deep breath, to stay in control. "No publicity, that's what we all agreed, but we knew that Matthew had different ideas. We agreed that nobody needs to know the real reason for this trip or what we've got in this truck, other than the four of us, we agreed to keep all of this quiet."

"How the fuck can we keep it quiet, Tommy? Someone will have heard the shot," questioned Watts, his barrel shaped body making a threatening stance now standing directly in front of Smythe, his fists clenched. It wouldn't just be a push this time.

"There's no one within ten miles of here. The Bosnian army use this forest for military training, gunshots sound regularly around here," replied Smythe moving one step back away from Watts in a way calculated to be subordinate. "I noticed about a mile or so back, there was an area of sapling trees, and you both know from your experiences in the TA that new planted woodland is not used for military exercises and that's the same here. We will dispose of the body there; we've got plenty of tools in the truck."

"How do you know it's the same here?" said a calmer more collected Davy Watts.

"This forest belongs to a Bosnian logging company, they allow the army to use it but their business is timber and I don't think they would be too pleased if spotty young squaddies were running around, blowing holes in their precious commodity of young fast-growing trees, do you?"

Jessop responded with childish sarcasm, "What happens when they harvest the trees?"

Smythe took another deep breath, he'd hoped for this reaction, sensing he was beginning to win the argument and could begin to relax the adrenalin rush was beginning to subside.

"Those trees won't be harvested for another ten years; I researched it long before we came out here. The ground is soft; the area was the site of a mass war grave before they filled it and planted trees two years ago. In ten years' time, if a body is found, they'll think it was one that was missed previously. With no identification, the remains will probably get buried in an unmarked grave in a cemetery somewhere. Matthew has no living relatives in England and after all, he's Eastern European by birth, with no living relatives here either, no friends other than us, no –"

"Yeah and one so called friend just put a big hole in his head … the poor bastard," interrupted Jessop.

"Yes, I'm his best pal, was his best pal, I'm the one that has to live with this and if either of you decide to tell the authorities, there's nothing I could do to stop you."

"Oh, nicely put, Tommy, you arrogant fuck," said Watts as he again began making menacing steps towards Smythe. "Me and Frank are now accomplices, we'd lose all that 'stuff' in the back of the truck and we'd end up in the same boat as you, without our share. Hell, it's not just my future in that gold but my wife and kids as well, if it all goes tits up now, I would never forgive myself."

Smythe felt a sense of satisfaction begin to grow in his chest, Watts was the first to mention family back home, it was now only a matter of time before he and Jessop would relinquish their objections in favour of a quiet life of wealth and financial comfort at home.

"No, what I mean is …"

"Save your breath and excuses for yourself, Mister Smythe, or should I say retired Sergeant Thomas Henry fucking Smythe of the Yorkshire Regiment of the Territorial Army, sir," scalded Jessop as he made a mock salute. "The same Sergeant Thomas Henry fucking Smythe who saw action in Northern Ireland and the Gulf where he was decorated for bravery. Oh, yes and he saved the life of one Francis Jessop a Corporal in the same regiment. Well, if I go along with this, consider the debt I've owed you since 1990 well and truly paid. When we get back home, I never want to see you again," he shouted.

"As you request, Corporal," their discussion ended there.

Listening to Jessop and Smythe, a light bulb switched on in Davy Watts mind. "You've been planning this for weeks, haven't you, Tommy? You devious bastard. Matthew Tanner was never going to survive to write about this … was he?"

"I'm not going to deny it, Davy, that twat was going to tell anyone and everyone about this venture of ours," announced Smythe, venom in his voice. He pointed once again to the corpse on the ground as if to verify his claim. "He never listened to me, never considered my concerns, we all risked our lives on this job and he was going to tell it all in a book, a novel, for fuck's sake, to prove his ability as a researcher and a story teller … we would have been left with virtually nothing but a small percentage, a finder's fee that's all."

Davy Watts was now more enraged than before, he moved close up to Smythe, the two men stood toe to toe, staring, it was Watts who spoke next in loud voice almost shouting.

"You involved us in your plans without our knowledge, you didn't trust Frank or me to keep our mouths shut, did you, Tommy? Don't bother to deny that either … well, that's it as far as I'm concerned, when we get home … if we get home … don't come round my place no more. And! For your information, as far as I'm concerned, a share of a finder's fee, no matter how small, would have been okay with me. I was just happy doing the army stuff again with my mates, like old times … d'ya get it now … eh? Sergeant? The gold means jack shit to me. A man is dead and you murdered him in cold blood … you're an evil bastard, Smythe. Don't for one second think you can sneak up on me or Frank like you did with Matthew … I'm gonna watch his back and he's gonna watch mine … we're mates, I trust him, he trusts me."

The silence that followed was deafening. Watts took a breath and then in a much calmer tone said, "Let's get on with this, Frank." He turned and started walking to the back of the truck, Jessop followed and glared wildly at Smythe as he walked past him.

In the misty dusk of the Bosnian late summer in dense woodland, the three men dug a deep hole in the ground without any words spoken between them; the work was undertaken seamlessly, teamwork at its best. When the grave was finished, the naked body of Matthew Tanner was lowered into the pit. The soil arising from the dig was placed and compacted, as best they could, the excess was spread around over a larger area. When finished the scene appeared to have changed very little and they all knew that by late morning the following day there would be no evidence to represent another dead body discarded in this area of Europe. As previously intended, they continued on their journey through the forest for 50 miles or so to a location at the edge of the vast woodland where the forest met the river, their campsite for the night.

In the twelve years or so that have elapsed since this incident, it's quite possible that the decomposed body of Matthew Tanner has been found but without any form of identification, it is probable that, today, it lies decaying in one of the many official unmarked graves in that war ravaged region of Europe, a soldier perhaps, from one side or the other, no headstone, no loved ones named, no eulogy and no one to mourn his passing. However, in another country in Europe, there are, today, three men living who were present at his demise.

***

Matthew Tanner was born Armon Cabrinovic, a Bosnian Serb. Born in 1944 during traumatic times for Eastern Europe, but thanks to the remarkable strength, both physical and mental, of his mother, and then the devotion of his stepfather, from who he takes his Western European surname, he rose to become a well-respected University Lecturer specialising in European History. He researched and wrote prodigiously about his subject with five books published in his Serbian name. If you were inclined to look, you would probably find two or three of these books residing in most of the University Libraries in England, they are recommended reading for students of Modern History. Not all his research found its way into published print and neither was the research always fact based. He had a penchant for writing fictional stories around historical happenings and expanding them into novels, but didn't believe his works would be considered publishable so they didn't get any further than an archive box in his study. Except that is for one particular strand of historical research that he had been working on for almost a decade, it had serious potential as a fact-based novel, according to several publishers, one publisher had offered a £20,000 advance. His characterisation, he always considered, was his weakness but in this particular novel that was not the case. The fictional characters were, after all, based on living characters, his best friends, all strong personalities in real life, ex Territorial Army, the '*go get 'em*' type.

The novel was complete except for the final chapter, the discovery that proved his historical research and the heist that liberated the booty from where it had been hidden since 1911. The epilogue to the novel would be the return of 200 bars of gold bullion to its rightful recipient, the Serbian nation.

Matthew intended to finish his work on his return from the escapade depicted in the novel, but alas, that wasn't to be. His naivety, perhaps, or his complete focus on the historical implications of his research and the kudos that it might bring him professionally, made him blind to such human failings as avarice and revenge that would subsequently lead to his murder.

The soon to be completed novel rested in the form of a hard copy manuscript in the offices of a publishing company based in Leeds. The work was in the form of diary references used to provide the background for the novel, and fifty thousand words of story that depicted how gold hidden for nearly a century came to be found and what its original intended use was prior to its liberation by a historian and three friends. The manuscript had been deposited in 2001 with Proudman Press with strict instructions not to break the seal on the envelope containing the hard copy until the final chapter could be added.

In 2017, the manuscript was found in an archive room by a work experience student whose thankless task it was to copy, catalogue and electronically file all the unpublished manuscripts housed in the archive store, prior to the company moving premises. It just so happened that this particular student had ambitions to read Modern History at University after her A level exams and recognised the authors name appended to the envelope containing the manuscript, the wax seal had become brittle and snapped as she moved the package. Her curiosity got the better of her and she decided to make a copy for herself, her intention was to use it purely for research. She knew she wouldn't be able to quote from the manuscript or mention it as a research article, she would be prosecuted for theft if found out, she later catalogued and scanned the manuscript for electronic filing.

In September of 1995, Armon Cabrinovic aka Matthew Tanner, Senior Lecturer and Head of the History Department at Leeds University, formally accepted an invitation to visit the University of Sarajevo to help in the rebuilding process of the university's library damaged by Bosnian Army mortar bombs during the five-year siege of the city. The siege had ended some six months earlier after prolonged international pressure and UN negotiations. Armon had been courting this invitation with his Bosnian Serb contacts since the ceasing of hostilities needing a formal invitation from the Bosnian Authorities to secure his passage through the UN peacekeeping lines surrounding the city. His intention was, on the face of it, to help his Eastern European History colleagues in the post siege restoration project, however, he had another reason for his visit. On his arrival, he purposefully and quickly settled into a routine of working late in the Library, and as expected, he was often left alone in the building at night. This gave Armon time to undertake his other research and two years later, he returned to the UK where he began to set out a strategy that would, unbeknown to him, end with his untimely and unceremonious death.

Now, twelve years have elapsed since those events in a forest in Bosnia, they are a distant memory for those involved and a complete mystery to everyone else, however, that was about to change.

Chapter 2

Year: 2017

Driving towards Leeds on a late January morning from his home in Carlton, Detective Inspector Jaxon Wolfe found the traffic to be unusually ponderous. Heavy traffic at this time of day was to be expected but, on this particular morning, it seemed as though every vehicle in Yorkshire was heading for Leeds City Centre. Wolfe had purposefully delayed his journey from home to have breakfast with his daughter, Isabella, before driving her to the bus station in Carlton to catch the school bus. The traffic queues during the morning rush period always gave rise to feelings of frustration. Wolfe had on several occasions toyed with the idea of popping out the portable blue flashing emergency light housed under the driver's seat, '*slapit on the roof 'ala' Kojak, get to Leeds in no time,*' he thought, but that would be considered misuse. In an attempt to break out of his gloom, he loaded a CD into the dashboard slot.

Outside the car, a low mist stuck to the road like dry ice, cold, very cold, minus 3 degrees, dismal, depressing, but the difference with the microclimate inside Wolfe's car was stark, 22 degrees, he felt as warm as toast. The CD began to play but was suddenly interrupted by the ringtone of the integrated phone system. He recognised the number displayed on the dashboard screen as the Leeds Headquarters of the West Yorkshire Metropolitan Police Force based in the city centre. He guessed who might be trying to contact him.

"Good morning, WPC Middleton, DI Wolfe speaking, how are you today?" he answered in a cheerful tone in contrast to the gloom outside his vehicle.

"I'm fine gov, but it's much worse for some poor soul."

"Oh … OKAY there's me trying to be cheerful and you shoot me a statement like that … better give me the details."

"Well, that's how it is sometimes … PC Broughton responded to an emergency call an hour ago and arriving at the scene, confirmed the discovery of a body … in a cave … his description, not mine." She paused, perhaps waiting for a response, but there was none so she continued, "Workmen on moorland about 20 miles to the North West of Leeds moved a boulder and there it was."

"Mmm … in a cave?" responded Wolfe. "Bizarre and a bit suspicious."

"Pete and forensics are already at the scene."

"Okay, what's the exact location, Pam?"

"Carlton Moor, next to the Blackhill Hide rocks."

"That's a five-minute drive from my house," he replied trying not to express anger.

Middleton paused for a second,

"Yeah, I know, gov ... the Acting Chief overheard PC Broughton calling it in and insisted that DC Halford respond first," she explained. "Don't forget you have a meeting here with the chief at 11am, so I assume you're on your way in?"

Wolfe replied, "Him ... his bloody timekeeping and meetings, he lives in a different world to the rest of us. Tell the Acting Chief that Pete Halford called me and asked me to attend, and make sure Pete knows it too!"

"Okay, sir, will do."

With the hazard warning lights flashing, he spun the car round, executing a perfect U-turn in the less than perfect driving conditions and headed back on the A650 towards Carlton. No need for the blue flasher, there was very little traffic heading in that direction.

The low visibility hindered the journey; a drive that would usually take ten minutes took more than twice that length of time.

Blackhill Hide is an outcrop of rocks high on moorland above Carlton. Jaxon Wolfe was born in Carlton and very familiar with the area, he played in and around the rocks as a young boy during summer school holidays that seemed to last forever.

Wolfe reached the final leg of the journey with a sigh of relief, Moor Pasture Road takes traffic from the centre of Carlton up to rocks at Blackhill Hide and beyond to the suburbs of Leeds. He accelerated the car up the steep road to his destination on the moor top, the growl from the engine increasing as it raced up the hill and then it seemed to diminish as the long bonnet of his roadster pierced through the swirling befuddled mist into the crisp blue skied brightness as he drove high above the roof tops of suburban Carlton.

The beauty of the scenery that greeted his escape from the clinging haze instantly reminded him why he lived in this particular part of West Yorkshire. To the left, the Wharfe Valley from above the mist now looked like a long thick strand of cotton wool covering the river that squeezed its advance to freedom on the East Coast between rolling green and brown hills. To the right and high above his eye line rested the Blackhill Hide rocks, huge, solid ever present, yet, a strangely fragile outcrop of pre-historic rock puncturing the moorland around it. Visible from miles distant, the rocks have attracted tourists from far and wide since Victorian times. Nowadays, local climbers practice their skills here before attempting more challenging assents.

'Riders on the Storm' played through the car's audio system from the CD, Jim Morrison crooning 'there's a killer on the road' brought Wolfe sliding back to the job in hand and on cue, he joined in with the vocal 'yeeahh ...' bringing his Z4 to a halt next to a vehicle he recognised. Hitting the stop switch on the dashboard, the engine turned off and 'The Doors' were unceremoniously halted in mid song. Silence erupted inside the car and Wolfe stared for a few seconds at the extensive views across the Dales, however, this didn't compensate enough for the fog, and the slow-moving traffic conspiring to make him more irritable and grumpier than usual. Opening the driver's door, an icy blast of air hit his face.

"Bloody hell, it's chuffing freezing up here," he said to nobody in particular whilst swinging his right leg out through the open door groaning and hauling himself upwards.

"You're getting too old for that type of car, boss," was the comment directed his way from the open window of the car he'd parked next to.

"Sod off, Halford," he retorted bending low enough to look through the open passenger door windscreen of DC Peter Halford's standard issue saloon.

"What I drive is my business, Pete. Anyway, at least, I managed to get my arse out of my car, where as yours is still stuck to the car seat. Come on, the dog needs to see the rabbit!"

The young DC, not long out of uniform, reluctantly manoeuvred himself out of his vehicle then reached onto the backseat of his car to collect his overcoat. Walking round the car, he began fastening the garment around his tall skinny frame to keep out the cold. Halford's gelled hair glistened against the sunlight as he looked over and past DI Wolfe's shoulder, then he tipped his head towards vehicles parked on the other side of the car park. Wolfe responded to the signal and followed his gaze; he recognised amongst the vehicles a car belonging to Professor Arnold Higgins, a Senior Pathologist with the Local Council and two white vans used by the Scene of Crime Officers together with a police patrol car.

"Must be particularly interesting if Arnold Higgins is on site," said Wolfe.

Halford pointed to a white canvas tent a hundred yards or so from the car park edge and announced,

"The body was discovered up there by workmen clearing an area for a new footpath." Then lifting an open pack of cigarettes to his mouth, he nonchalantly clamped the next available smoke between his lips.

The whole area seemed dwarfed by the mighty Blackhill Hide rocks, horseshoe shaped around the hollow where the Blackhill Giant used to rest in inclement weather, or so the myth would have it. The moorland spread out from the hollow entrance down to the car park. It looked ugly brown, a matted carpet of dead bracken storks punctured by cold grey rocks of all shapes and sizes, broken fragments of the huge rocks overshadowing the whole area, randomly scattered by some ancient great force, the dwelling giant perhaps, intending to throw them into the River Wharfe down in the valley to make a splash. Wolfe had spent all his childhood and most of his adult life in Carlton, he had no wish to live anywhere else. He was jolted back from his thoughts by Halford.

"SOCO are up there getting first look, Prof. Higgins said he'd give us the nod when we can have a butchers," he paused to take a drag on his cigarette.

"Only one copper at the car park entrance, Pete?"

"Yes, PC Robertson, the other uniform in attendance, escorted the ambulance through the fog to Airedale A and E."

Confused, he turned to his deputy. "Ambulance! What happened?" the hard-inquisitive look in his eyes made Halford quickly retrieve a notebook from his coat pocket.

"The workman that discovered the body … err … Arthur Bolton, was obviously shocked by what he saw, falling and hitting the back of his head, knocking himself out," flicking over the page he continued,

"So, his workmate, err … Thomas Green, ran over to the pub," Halford pointed in the direction of the Blackhill Rue Hotel on the opposite side of the road, "and raised the alarm."

"No mobile phone?"

"That's the question I've been asking myself, boss."

"I'll come back to that later. Is Bolton badly injured?"

"Paramedics in attendance said he'll need stitches and a check-up following his concussion, that's all."

"Who did the man Green call first?" Halford turned and looked at the ground.

"Errr, 999, I assume."

"Don't assume, bloody find out! It might be important."

Halford looked suddenly worried about what he might have missed.

"Pete, from what I know thus far, we are dealing with a suspicious death and to me, that says don't accept anything that doesn't look right, and more importantly, don't make assumptions. Facts, Pete, that's what we deal in, facts. Find out who this guy, Green, called first on the hotel phone and tell me before you file a report, but right now, let's get a look at the body." Wolfe started walking with purpose towards the crime scene tent. Halford stepped hard and fast to catch up to his superior officer.

"Boss, forensics might not be ready for our size tens inside their tent yet."

"Sod forensics, I need to see what that workman saw …"

Wolfe led the way as the two men walked from the parking area onto synthetic matting laid on the ground that lead towards the crime scene tent. The nearby gravel footpath used by visiting public, walking to and from the Blackhill Hide rocks, stretched away in the opposite direction, and was being cordoned off with metal poles and day-glow tape by a policeman, mumbling to himself about having to perform such menial tasks.

"PC Broughton, that's important work you're doing there, do it properly or you will soon find yourself on a mountain bike chasing knocked off Corsa's driven by teenagers wearing hoodies!" Wolfe said in his best authoritative voice.

"Yes, sir," came the reply from the burley constable with whom he'd been drinking, joking and socialising with two nights previously at an off-duty event, celebrating the retirement of a popular desk sergeant.

"This your idea, Pete?" Wolfe said pointing to the matting they were walking on,

"Yes, gov, I know it's a long shot, there must be thousands of tourists walk all over this area every year but you never know, we might find evidence connected to the corpse."

Patting him on the back, Wolfe remarked, "We'll make a decent cop out of you, yet."

Halford smiled, it made up for the earlier mistake, he was first to the crime scene tent and opened the entrance flap for his senior officer to enter before him.

"Morning," announced Wolfe

"DI Wolfe, how the devil are you today?" remarked the grey haired doctor of forensic science in a jovial manner without turning to look at the person that he was addressing.

"Not too bad, Arnold, bit early in the morning for this, I hate having my beauty sleep interrupted."

"Ha, lost cause there, Jaxon ma boy," said Higgins still not turning to look at him. "Cosmetic surgery wouldn't be able to fix that so sleeping won't work."

The other two personnel inside the tent began to snigger.

"When you've finished taking the 'mickey', perhaps, we can get down to business," replied Wolfe, a little embarrassed that his old friend had managed to get a laugh at his expense.

Dressed like his two colleagues in light blue synthetic overalls, shoe covers and gloves Arnold Higgins is more than twenty years older than Wolfe with a full head of grey hair on top of a gleeful wrinkled but jocular face that always reminded Wolfe of an old-fashioned music hall comic laughing with his audience.

The two detectives were able to stand upright, unusual inside most crime scene tents; they surveyed the scene in front of them. Each man was handed a pair of blue synthetic shoe covers and gloves to wear. Although it was bright outside, floodlights had been set up, and mounted at head height on stands to illuminate the area in and around an opening between two large boulders. As a result, inside the tent was warmer than outside, a stale but sweet musty smell hung in the air that Wolfe couldn't distinguish. Blue plastic sheeting covered the floor and most of the irregular higher surfaces inside the tent. Light reflecting around the tent gave the appearance of a sci-fi film set completely alien to the surroundings outside.

"Okay, detectives, step carefully towards me, you'll have to crouch down here so you can see into the void," prompted Higgins in his deep part Welsh, part Yorkshire accent.

Wolfe led; Halford followed and did as instructed bending down awkwardly, making their way to the opening where an arc light was focused, a distance of 15 metres or so. At the opening, they both hunkered down and looked into the void beyond. Wolfe immediately had to catch his breath, Halford was obviously surprised as he looked over his boss's shoulder.

"What the fuck … why is …"

"Have respect for the dead, constable," reprimanded Wolfe. "Look at the scene for a few moments before you say anything more."

In sync, they lowered themselves further into seated positions on the ground sheets next to the forensic scientist.

The view that greeted their gaze was probably the most peculiar sight both men had ever seen. The fully grown figure of a naked man was clearly visible no more than two metres into the void, sat bolt upright with a straight back like a petulant child told off for slouching. His leathery reddish skin contrasting with the floodlit background of green moss and lichen giving a posed, almost sculpture like appearance. The right hand of the corpse was resting on the right knee, natural yet composed, the position of his head, however, looked unnatural, chin lifted, neck stretched and face pointing towards the ceiling of his coffin cave but with eyes closed as if in contemplation.

In unison, Wolfe and Halford followed the dead man's blind gaze towards the top of the cave, bending their heads down almost touching the ground. The arc light couldn't penetrate too far, so blackness was all they could see. The left side of the corpse just visible was in shadow; left leg stretched out in front of the body and left arm hanging down by his side. Except for a slightly bloated belly, the man's physique showed well-defined muscle structure, giving the impression of a man in reasonable physical shape. The sound of trickling water could be heard deep inside the cave, and the heat from the floodlights was causing the lichen to emit a light mist of vapour and an odour, now more pungent, but the same smell Wolfe detected when entering the tent. The vapour moved around the corpse within the cave, creating a very sinister vision before it evaporated as it moved towards the entrance. Something suspicious had occurred to provide this very unusual scene but Wolfe couldn't help thinking that this man had an air of peacefulness about him.

Halford's expression was one of stunned silence, eyes wide open and jaw dropped, he'd clearly never looked upon anything quite like this. There again, Wolfe thought to himself, *'I've never encountered anything quite this bizarre either.'*

"You can speak now, Pete, if you want."

"How the hell did he get in there? Who, what, why ... did someone put him in there, was he alive, was he dead?" Halford took a breath. "Surely, he didn't go in there of his own free will, and he's naked, where are his clothes, bloody hell, where do we start with this and what is that smell ... the smell of decay?"

"All very relevant, Pete," said Wolfe relieved that Halford had stopped ranting. "Now let's confirm the obvious. This here is the body of a naked male and judging by his physique, I'd say no older than mid-thirties when whatever happened to him brought the poor bastard to this hole in the ground ... and no that is not the smell of decay, it's the damp lichen on the rocks warming up, giving off an odour." Wolfe then turned his gaze to Higgins. "This is a little out of the ordinary?"

"Not a normal occurrence, I'll grant you that."

"I need your initial thoughts, Arnold ... and I know those would be completely off the record and no official report or comments can be made until your forensic investigations are complete but I need something, anything, that can get me and the force moving on this," he wasn't trying to hide his concern in his voice.

"Your thoughts are the same as mine, Jac," confirmed Higgins. "Male aged 25 to 35 years old, judging by his physical appearance. I'm assuming he didn't enter this place of his own accord," pointing towards the corpse he continued, "look at his pose, and the way his legs and arms are bent, almost naturally arranged, he was probably incapacitated or had died shortly before being placed in here. Sitting him down and arranging his limbs like that would be near impossible if rigor mortis had set in and this fellow is now set hard. I think it would take more than one person to drag him in the cave, he must weigh around 14 stones, too much for one person to handle and set him up in the position we see him in now."

"Arnold, he appears so relaxed in that seated position, no signs that I can see of any physical trauma, no blood stains that I can see, no visible bruising and no immediately visible evidence of foul play. Are we assuming too much to say that he wouldn't have entered this cave of his own free will?"

"No, I don't think so, look at that rock over there," Higgins nodded towards a large boulder used to block the cave entrance before being moved by the workmen.

"How would he manage to close himself in? That stone must weigh ten times his body weight, the workmen who discovered the corpse used a mechanical digger to move it."

"So, dead on entry or just incapacitated, what do you think?"

"Dead. If he'd managed to move, I'm sure he would have tried to get out and, therefore, he wouldn't be ..."

Wolfe completed his sentence, "Sat down ... point taken."

"We'll check for marks on that boulder but I doubt we'll find any," said Higgins. "Now let's progress this a little further. Look at the man's buttocks, they're not yet fully flat against the seat and no visible evidence of bodily fluid leakage, so on that basis, I will also assume he hasn't been here too long and he died somewhere else." Anticipating an interruption, he lifted his hand to stop the question, "A day or two, Inspector, that's all. We've had constant freezing temperatures in this region over the past week which might increase my estimate by 24 hours, that's all. That's why there's no smell of decay," Higgins nodded at Halford in confirmation. "He's frozen solid, however, he'll begin to thaw under these lights. I reckon, we'll soon be able to lift him straight off that rock without him sticking to it."

"Uhh!! Too much information," said Halford with a grimace.

Wolfe took over, "We need to identify him, find out his known movements. So, what about fingerprints or better still a DNA profile?"

"Both, give me four or five hours for the fingerprints and I'll get them e-mailed to your office, but I'll need two or three days for the DNA."

"Well, let's hope his prints are on our database, maybe he's got previous. If he hasn't, it's going to make identification that much more difficult." The two detectives turned and made clumsy movements towards the exit.

"Thanks, Arnold," said Wolfe.

So as not to appear ungrateful Halford responded similarly, "Yes, thanks."

Standing up outside the tent, Wolfe arched his back and let out another groan lifting his head skywards. His head lowered he now took in the view, the rolling peaks and valleys of the Yorkshire Dales bathed in bright low winter sunshine created dramatic shadows stretching into the valleys, the heavy morning mist was beginning to evaporate as the temperature increased under the cloudless sky. *'Beautiful,'* he thought. *'But just scratch the surface and you never know what horrors can be found.'*

After a couple of minutes of silent thought contemplating how to take the investigation forward, Wolfe acted, first calling to Halford who was now in the car park talking to PC Broughton. Responding immediately, Halford jogged towards him, his instructions were to make inquiries at the Blackhill Rue Hotel, check with the manager, and get formal statements from staff and residents regarding anything suspicious or unusual that might have occurred over the past week in the area. In particular though, find out who Green called first. Wolfe told Pete to be discrete and not to mention in detail what had been discovered.

Checking the time with his wristwatch, Wolfe pulled his mobile phone from the inside pocket of his jacket. *'Twenty minutes before my meeting is due to start with Haigh-Watson, he'll be in his office now, no doubt,'* he thought whilst calling HQ. *'He'll be expecting me to knock on his office door soon. Well, he's got another thing coming.'*

After one ring, Angela Grafton the receptionist answered,

"Morning, DI Wolfe, the chief wants a word and has told me to put you straight through to him when you call in."

"Angela, put me through to Constable Middleton first and she can then transfer me to the boss after I've spoke to her."

"You'll get me into trouble, Detective."

"Tell him I pulled rank on you."

"Yeah, like that'll work," Angela said sarcastically. "See you soon, Jac."

Wolfe was put on hold until,

"How's it going, gov?" said Middleton. "What's the situation out there?"

"The situation, Pam, is that I want you and a PC of your choice to get over to A and E at Airedale General as soon as possible." Wolfe explained what he wanted her to do, he trusted her competency, and knew that if he kept her informed and involved, she could be relied on and would always report directly back to him before anyone else. He concluded with,

"Right, Pam, put me through to our leader, I know he's been waiting for me to report in."

"Sure, I'll contact you on your mobile when I've interviewed Bolton and Green," she put Wolfe on hold again.

Then, "Detective Inspector Wolfe, I expected you in the office this morning. As an Inspector, you should be controlling investigations from HQ, not out in the field. Bear in mind, DI Wolfe, that you were reinstated in your previous rank on your return to full time duties because that is proper procedure but your rank is open to review in a few months and this is not the first time I've had to remind you of your duties."

Wolfe held his mobile phone away from his ear and faked a yawn, he'd heard the Acting Chief Constable rant this way before. Suddenly, there was silence, Wolfe let it hang in the air, then replied,

"Sir, as we have discussed recently, we are very short staffed, I didn't want a rookie detective on scene without an experienced officer guiding him. We both know that the initial assessment of a scene is the most important part of any investigation and I made a judgement based on the information that DC Halford had reported in."

"Okay, DI Wolfe, you've made your point, so you were called to the scene on Carlton Moor?"

"Yes, sir." Once again, silence for a second or two. "The body of a man has been found on the moor near Blackhill Hide, in a situation that is both weird and bizarre."

Acting Chief Constable Marcus Haigh-Watson listened intently as the detail of the scene discovered on Carlton Moor was described to him. When he'd finished his briefing report, it came as no surprise to Wolfe when Haigh-Watson said,

"Remain at the scene, Inspector, I'll be there within the hour, and don't let forensics move anything until I've had a look and tell that forensic pathologist that's an order."

"Yes, sir!" That was that, the line went dead, call ended.

Wolfe wandered back down to the car park and was scowling at his mobile phone when from behind him, he heard Arnold Higgins say, "Fancy a coffee, Jac, I'm having a break."

"Sure," he let the forensics expert catch him up and they walked together to Higgins car.

"Haigh-Watson wants you to hang around until he gets here in an hour or so and not to move or disturb anything until he's had a look … and that's an order, Doc," Wolfe informed him with a wry smile.

"He's a pompous twat," retorted Higgins. "Thinks it's a two-minute job analysing a scene like this, he doesn't
know the first thing about forensic investigation. I'm going to be here all day, be lucky if I get a lunch break."
The smile on Wolfe's face widened and he let out a stunted laugh as he was handed a steaming cup of coffee. He took a sip of the hot liquid.

"Doc, there's whiskey in this coffee … from your stash of malt?"

"Don't be silly, young man, that would be an unacceptable waste of a perfect elixir," Higgins snorted. "No, it's some blended rubbish given to me as a gift, mixing with coffee is all its good for."

Together, they drank their alcohol-laced coffee sitting on the open tailgate of the SUV staring towards the moor.

Bathed in bright sunlight, the large grey rocks guarding the entrance to Blackhill Hide shone, quartz like, on the moor top but it was the bleached white crime scene tent that drew their gaze, a beacon grasping their quiet attention, both men pondering what had happened to this poor fellow that meant the discovery of his body interred in a tomb in this Dales beauty spot

Chapter 3

Acting Chief Constable Marcus Haigh-Watson is one of the highest-ranking police officers in the force and now overseeing the fourth largest police force in the country. The current Chief Constable of the West Yorkshire Police Force is due to retire from duty in a year or so but he is currently on suspension from duty, gardening leave as it is referred to by his assistant. The fact of the matter is that the Acting Chief Constable is in control of the force while the in-post chief is under investigation for gross misconduct, a charge he is vehemently opposing. Haigh-Watson is working in the senior role and is expected by those in the know to be an automatic replacement for the outgoing Chief. Certain perks are bestowed upon him to reflect his rank and superiority. To members of the public, the most noticeable evidence of this is a chauffeur driven Jaguar with all the latest technological gizmos attached. His employers would prefer that he use this car on official business, however, he decided to drive his own car to the crime scene this particular morning.

In the dimly lit basement car park of the West Yorkshire Police Force Headquarters in Leeds, chauffeur Eddie was surprised to see his charge walk past him towards the area of the car park reserved for personal vehicles, and in a panic, he said in a voice which echoed and reverberated off the cold concrete walls louder than he had intended,

"The car is ready and waiting, sir, I'll just get the keys."

"No need, Eddie … taking my car this time," he replied without turning to look at the chauffeur.

Haigh-Watson strode with purpose across the car park floor and due to a perfectly fitted made to measure police uniform covering his slightly overweight and slightly podgy physique, he cut a very imposing figure. He always walked with his back straight and head held high which made him appear taller than his meagre 5ft 10in. Beneath a peaked cap, another symbol of his high rank, his round clean-shaven pale face was expressionless, cold grey eyes not moving from their focus straight ahead, activating the remote-control device from his jacket pocket as he drew closer to the vehicle.

Eddie stood and watched as the interior of the Range Rover hidden in a dark corner of the car park suddenly illuminated and the headlights flashed. Realising the Chief was in a rush, Eddie moved quickly back into his office and pressed a wall mounted switch to open the roller shutter door that gave entrance to the car park. As the large corrugated metal door clunked, clanked and rolled upwards, natural daylight sprayed with increasing intensity into the basement void, conquering and enveloping with ease the luminance emitting from artificial lights. The door was fully elevated before the Range Rover had time to manoeuvre into a position to exit the basement.

With an engine roar, the expensive SUV moved at speed out of the car park up the ramp into the late winter morning sunshine until all that Eddie could see from his position were the brake lights glowing as the car stopped to find a gap in the city traffic.

"Wouldn't need to stop if I was driving," Eddie shouted from his glazed screen office cell. "I'd have the siren on, that would soon get those office workers out of the way."

"Where's he off in such a hurry?" asked the spotty junior attendant as he watched the roller shutter descend.

"Probably forgotten his sandwiches," said Eddie sarcastically walking to the elevator, thinking about the cup of tea he was shortly going to drink in the canteen. He would now take it easy until the chief returned or until the end of his shift, whichever was sooner.

Haigh-Watson drove with tempered aggression until calming down enough to make the phone call he needed to make. Ten minutes later, Anita had been informed and had reluctantly accepted that their planned evening together would now have to wait for a few days. The rest of the day and over the coming weekend, press officers, local media and official briefing meetings would occupy most, if not all, of his time, therefore, no opportunity for the R and R that he had carefully planned for this weekend.

The mist was burning back as the day pushed towards midday and when the Range Rover turned into the public car park below the Blackhill Hide Rocks overlooking Carlton, a perfect dry, crisp and bright mid winter's day greeted his arrival.

Wolfe spotted the arrival of the 'top brass' whilst talking with PC Broughton outside the crime scene tent. Holding the entrance flap of the tent open, he peered in and in mock salutation said,
"Doc, salvation has arrived, in a big fuck off 4x4, I'll go and brief him on the situation so far, see you in five."

Higgins shouted a response but Wolfe didn't hear it sufficiently enough to make sense of it and nor did he particularly want to.

Haigh-Watson was climbing down from the driver's seat as Wolfe got within earshot.

"Good morning, sir."

"Is it, DI Wolfe?" was all he got in reply as the Chief started walking at pace towards the crime scene tent. Turning and quickening his pace, Wolfe caught up to him but was unable to prevent him from walking within the cordoned off taped area that was intended to be isolated from use.

"Sir, that area hasn't been scanned for forensic evidence yet."

"This is a tourist thorough fare Inspector, any evidence gathered here will be purely circumstantial hundreds of people will have trampled all over this area within the last week."

Wolfe frowned in disgust but watched carefully the path he'd taken towards the tent covering the crime scene.

"Morning, Doctor Higgins, what have we here then?" was all he heard before the tent entrance flap closed behind him.

Turning and motioning to the duty constable, Wolfe watched and waited as PC Broughton, from his position at the car park entrance, moved towards him.

"Cover that area there with matting," sweeping his hands to mark out the area walked over by Haigh-Watson.

"Yes, sir," replied the PC.

Wolfe walked briskly along the designated route to the tent and entered to find Haigh-Watson and Higgins crouched down pointing towards the corpse.

"Decomposition hasn't started yet; this body hasn't been here long, two maybe three days at the most," Higgins was saying.

"So, death occurred within the last week," said the chief as he looked over his shoulder to see Wolfe entering.

"Glad you could join us, DI Wolfe."

"Sir," he replied.

Higgins continued, "Possibly, but death didn't occur here, there's no evidence of loss of blood or other bodily fluids here."

"How do you know there's been a loss of blood?" interrupted Wolfe.

"Well! Whilst you were out, I had a good look around the body and awkward as it was, I couldn't find any dark patches on the body that would indicate pockets of dried blood within where blood would have settled, therefore, he has obviously lost a lot of blood, but there's no evidence of bloodstains here. More importantly, there is a very small open wound in his back just below his left kidney."

"A knife wound?" interrupted Haigh-Watson

"No, more a puncture wound rather than the incision of a knife," said Higgins. "Whether this wound resulted in death cannot be determined here; an autopsy obviously will give us a better understanding. Also, we can just see a small tattoo on his left upper arm a Leeds United amber and blue shield with the letters LU tattooed twice underneath it."

"LU, LU, ah Lulu!" replied Haigh-Watson. "So, he's a football fan with a passion for a famous 1960s' Scottish bird," he continued not hiding his sarcastic tone.

"Preferred Dusty Springfield myself," said Higgins.

"Leeds United Loyal Union," interjected Wolfe. "A fans organisation, some might say, but some might also say more interested in off field antics than team support. He might be on our database."

"Right then," said Haigh-Watson trying to be authoritative but actually sounding pompous, "A man with experience like yours, surely, you can offer an insight into what has occurred here."

"First of all, Acting Chief Constable," said Higgins indignantly. "Even with my vast experience and believe me it is vast, it would be against my ethical code to make any judgements based purely on visual inspection, an autopsy and full written report will indicate my findings officially."

"And how long will that take?"

Higgins took a deep breath; Wolfe knew this was for effect.

"At least, seven working days, so next Thursday at the earliest."

"Mmm ..." muttered Haigh-Watson as he manoeuvred himself awkwardly towards the tent exit his legs unnecessarily bent, he would have been able to fully stand up and motioned to Wolfe to follow him. Then outside in the bright sunshine, he purposely chose the higher ground, straightened his back and said to DI Wolfe, still taller than his superior officer despite the difference in ground level between them,

"You and that so-called Doctor go back a long way, don't you, Inspector?"

"Yes, we've worked a number of cases together," curious to know where this conversation might be leading.

"Good, put all the pressure you can bring to bear on him," and raising his voice he continued, "I want that written report on my desk Monday morning before 10am and if that means he has to work through the weekend, then so be it." Haigh-Watson began walking towards his car along the correct route this time, Wolfe knew to accompany him.

"Possible contract killing?" questioned Haigh-Watson.

"Maybe ... but rival hooligan gangs involved in contract killings? I don't buy that, chief."

"Mmm ... confirms what I was thinking."

Haigh-Watson nodded his head and Wolfe replied without a pause,

"Why try to hide the body? A contract killer would just do the job and go, without a care as to where the body would be found. Maybe, the corpse was transported here or was being taken somewhere else and something happened."

"Pure speculation," added Haigh-Watson. "However, I think we can discount any speculation that he may have gone in there on his own, killed to order is my hunch and then hidden."

"I'll have the database searched for known LULU members, there may be references to known associates and even family members," concluded Wolfe.

When the two reached the Range Rover, Haigh-Watson opened the driver's door.

"I was hoping to go away this weekend to the lakes for a bit of ... relaxation, but I expect the press will want a statement before Monday," said the Acting Chief sounding almost melancholy.

"Chief, I fully intend keeping the press at bay until next week. If they want anything before then, why don't we get our press office, sorry, Media Liaison Department, to issue one of their standard statements. That way, it gives us more time to make our investigations without hacks breathing down our necks."

"Media liaison is an important aspect of police work nowadays, Inspector, and you know it's a particular requirement of mine to keep the media on our side, so don't be so flippant about their involvement." Haigh-Watson stopped and looked directly at Wolfe. "However, perhaps, keeping the press at arm's length over the weekend might not be a bad idea," he paused. "Okay, Inspector, keep me informed, I'll have my mobile with me, leave messages if I don't answer, concentrate all your efforts on this one, there's something strange and sinister about this case, see if you can make some progress before Monday."

"I'll need more personnel, sir," he replied, more in hope than expectation.

Haigh-Watson lifted himself into the driver's seat and then responded,

"Take the constables you've seconded already and chose a detective from the pool, those not working on high profile cases, but that's all, Inspector, we're stretched thinner than tissue paper at the moment." He started the engine but before driving off, he called through the open window of the driver's door. "Keep me informed every step of the way, DI Wolfe."

"Have a good weekend, sir, I'm sure the wife and kids will be pleased?"

"Yes well ... mmm," muttered Haigh Watson, "It's a lad's weekend actually."

"Oh, I see ... well enjoy, sir," he managed to say before the Range Rover drove away.

Before he had reached Carlton Town Centre, Haigh-Watson had concluded one more phone call and now on his second call was re-arranging his liaison with Anita in the Lake District. He then found a layby on the road to Keswick where he stopped to make yet another phone call, but this one didn't involve Anita Coombes, his mistress and ex madam of a well-known establishment in Leeds. It was to his wife, he would be staying in Leeds over the weekend due to workload and wouldn't get home to Bristol until the following week.

Within seconds of the Acting Chief Constable leaving the scene, Halford appeared from the Blackhill Rue Hotel walking towards the crime scene and noticing Wolfe, he brushed his forehead with his right hand and flicked an imaginary bead of sweat on the ground, and smiled. When he was close enough to be heard, Wolfe said.

"Waited for him to leave, did you?"

"Well, I didn't want him asking questions before I spoke to you."

"So ... go on then, tell me what you've got?"

Halford pulled his notebook out of his trouser pocket, straightened it and looked at the notes he'd made.

"According to the landlord, at about seven o'clock this morning, Green came running in, out of breath and demanding to use the phone, he wanted to call an ambulance." Halford looked at Wolfe, but there was no reaction so he continued, "The proprietor, Mr Greg Hughes, confirmed that he picked up the phone and immediately dialled 999, and asked for police and ambulance, and he gave the location as the Blackhill Rue Hotel on Carlton Moor. He also heard Mr Green say that there was a body on the moor and that his workmate had fallen over injuring his head, and was now unconscious and bleeding from the head wound. Then he gave the number on the restaurant phone to the emergency service."

"Did Green leave the pub and wait outside for the ambulance?"

"He did, but after the ambulance arrived and the paramedics were attending to the injured workmen, he came back into the bar and made another call from the phone at the end of the bar." Halford looked up from his notebook and lifted his left arm in a way that made Wolfe realise that Halford had anticipated his next question. "After Green had left to wait for the ambulance, Hughes went upstairs to keep an eye on proceedings from one of the upstairs rooms and didn't see Green re-enter the building but heard him talking on the phone a few minutes later, so went downstairs but by the time he got back to the bar, Green was hanging up the phone."

"So, we've got no idea who Green was talking to?" said Wolfe.

"Well, Hughes told me that Green apologised for not asking to use the phone but needed to contact the office. Hughes assumed he meant his employer, just to let them know what had happened and before Green hung up, heard him say he'd call again from the hospital to let them know how Arthur was."

"Can you confirm that he did call his employer, Pete?"

"Well, the last number dialled on that phone was that of a company called Hennersy Contracting. I called, and they confirmed that Green and Bolton are employees of theirs," said Halford ending the briefing there. Wolfe was silent in thought and Halford decided not to speak until spoken to.

The silence was broken by Wolfe's mobile phone, the opening riff to Double Trouble by Lynard Skynard; he looked at the screen first before answering.

"Hi, Pam, what have you got for me?"

"Gov, I've just interviewed one of the workmen," explained Middleton. "Name of Thomas Green, his workmate, Arthur Bolton, has been rushed into surgery so we won't be able to speak to him for a while. Green told me that they were preparing to start work on diverting a ditch on the moor and needed to move a large rock out of the way with their JCB to gain access. Bolton was supervising whilst Green operated the digger, then when the boulder was moved, Bolton looked into the hole behind, let out a scream and jumped backwards, tripped hit his head on the bucket of the excavator and fell to the ground. When Green got to him, he was mumbling, saying there was a body and pointing towards where the boulder had been ... still there, gov?" inquired Middleton.

"Yeah, still here, Pam," replied Wolfe.

"Green told me he took off his yellow jacket, rolled it and placed it under Bolton's head, and that's when he noticed blood was escaping from a gash in his head, so he decided to call an ambulance and ran down to the Hotel ... Blackhill Rue?"

"Yeah, it's just over the road from here," interrupted Wolfe.

Middleton continued, "But not before having a look at what had spooked Bolton. What he described, gov, beggar's belief, the body of a naked man sat in the cave? Enough to spook anyone I would have thought."

"You'll see the photos later, Pam, don't worry, you won't miss out."

"I asked him why he went to the pub to raise the alarm. Didn't he have a mobile? Yes, he said, but it was in the pocket of his high-vis jacket that he had used under Bolton's head, he didn't want to disturb him."

"Have you managed to check that, Pam?" enquired Wolfe.

"Yes, gov, but not that he knows. WPC Jones checked the pockets of the yellow jacket that he used as a cushion under Bolton's head, it was brought into A and E by one of the paramedics whilst I was talking to Green. She's just told me that there is a mobile in one of the pockets and it's fully charged."

"Get the number, Pam, and apply for a call history."

"WPC Jones is sorting that as we speak."

"Well done, include all of this in your report, don't hang around there too long because by the sound of it, the injured guy isn't going to able to make a statement for a while yet and besides, we now know how the dead guy was discovered." Before ending the call, Wolfe added, "Pam, you're now officially working on this case as a member of CID so its plainclothes until otherwise instructed. However, it will mean cancelling any leave you've booked in for the foreseeable future."

"Thanks, sir, I appreciate that," the call ended.

"Nothing wrong with Green's mobile," said Wolfe turning and walking back towards the incident tent. "Seems we have a plausible explanation as to why he didn't use his mobile phone," the comment directed more to himself than anyone who might be listening. Wolfe was met at the tent entrance by Higgins.

"Arrr ... Jac, I'm sure you'd be intrigued to know that the young unknown within is starting to give up a few of his secrets." Pausing for a quick breath, he continued, "A right handed main line drug user, the inside of his left arm littered with needle marks, Rigor mortise fully set, therefore, I can confirm he must have died no less than 48 hours ago and due to the lack of bodily excretions, I can confirm that he did not die here."

"Thanks for the heads up, Doc … just one thing. Rigor normally sets in within 24hours after death, why can't you be more precise about that?"

"Temperatures consistently around freezing for the last two days here on the moor, therefore, Rigor mortise would take a bit longer to set in, might be able to narrow it down further once we get him back to the lab and analyse the liver temperature against the known air temps, best I can do right now, young man."

Wolfe patted Higgins on the shoulder, "That gives us plenty to work with, old man, thanks. I'm going back to the station, Arnold, I'll drop by your place about six'ish for an update, okay?"

"No later, otherwise, catch me in the Unicorn."

Wolfe and Halford turned, and walked towards the car park.

"Pete," said Wolfe.

"You said the '*last*' number dialled on the pub phone was to his employer?"

"Yes, gov," then there was a pause, they looked at each other.

"But what about the one before that?" they said together.

"I'll run a trace as soon I get back to the station," said Halford.

Chapter 4

During the drive back to Holland Walk Police HQ in Leeds, Wolfe's thoughts gradually turned from the corpse found on Carlton Moor to the death of his wife three years previous. Why wasn't he, a police detective able to solve the mystery of her death? The guilt he felt resulted from the realisation that over a period of time, he expected, even demanded, subconsciously, that the hurt would get less, maybe her god was punishing him with guilt for believing that time was all that was required to bring freedom and peace of mind, closure.

The random nature of his wife's killing had haunted Wolfe like a constant headache interrupting his sleep patterns and entering his daytime thoughts without authority. The lack of hard evidence, any evidence really, meant that no one has been convicted of her death which, over a period of time, had pushed him to the brink of a mental breakdown that in turn was only placated by alcohol. Had it not been for the threats from his teenage daughter, Isabella, that she would go and live with her grandparents in Spain, *"And forever, you selfish bastard,"* he would probably be a fully blown alcoholic ex detective trying to survive on his own, suicide in a drunken haze his only remaining ambition. His daughter's final outburst cut deep into Wolfe's raw exposed emotions, an instant sobering effect. He spent the next 18 months in counselling and rehabilitation that, eventually, allowed the police service to offer him his old job and rank back if he wanted it. His superiors were sceptical about the success of this decision but he had to be given the chance to pick up the reins of his previous tenure. Wolfe had served more than twenty years in the police force, the latter half spent in plain clothes and the last four spent at the rank of Detective Inspector. He was considered by his subordinates and superiors alike as the model policeman. He had a bright future many thought, some even hoped, he would make Chief Inspector at the very least. That optimism evaporated when his wife was unlawfully killed.

Married to Maria, a solicitor, they'd first met in Wolfe's favourite restaurant, his favourite because Maria worked as a waitress there to help finance her way through Law School. The establishment, situated on Greek Street in Leeds, was owned by her father, a man of Anglo Spanish origin. Jaxon Wolfe married Maria De-Sanchez two years after her graduation, a year later, Isabella was born.

Wolfe lost his wife and Izzy lost her mother on an inauspicious mid summers' day. Maria Wolfe was shot dead in a drive-by shooting incident in the early evening of that fateful day in July. The conclusion of the criminal investigation that followed stated that Maria was probably not the intended victim. It also concluded that the bullet was possibly intended to kill someone else, perhaps, a solicitor colleague of Maria Wolfe who was representing a gang member accused of the murder of a rival gang leader. To this day, no one has been arrested in connection with Maria's death, the main suspect, well known to the police, had a cast iron alibi for that date and time.

Maria had been working late, and was due to meet Jac and Izzy in Leeds before going to the cinema with a meal at the family restaurant in Greek Street scheduled to follow. Wolfe and his daughter had received text messages from Maria telling them she would be late, not unusual, in fact, almost expected, based on past experience. Father and daughter were wise to this occurrence, and would regularly make arrangements for an hour earlier than necessary and, consequently, they were hardly ever late for the theatre or cinema.

On call that evening, Wolfe had received the message that someone had been shot in a district on the outskirts of Leeds City Centre, the same district where his wife was now an associate lawyer for a firm of solicitors. Wolfe and his daughter immediately returned to his car, and with a blue light flashing, made their way towards Headingley. He hadn't immediately recognised the street name he'd been given because he was more intent on listening to Isabella complaining that her mother wasn't answering her mobile phone but shortly before he arrived at their destination, his car was intercepted by a motorised patrol blocking his route. Wolfe was forced to stop, the driver of the patrol car got out and ran towards Wolfe's vehicle, Traffic Sergeant PC Halford, back then in uniform was accompanied by a WPC who made her way to the passenger side and opened the door, asking Isabella to get out. The evening dusk half-light was illuminated by numerous flashing blue neons, artistic in their appearance, hypnotic in their repetitiveness. At this point, Wolfe realised that the unanswered mobile phone calls and the incident he was racing to attend were connected but no amount of coincidental thought could prepare him for what he was about to be told. The victim at the centre of the incident was Maria Wolfe, his wife, Isabella's mother. He looked back at the car to see Izzy's head drop into her hands, her shoulders shaking and shuddering as she stood outside the car, the arms of the WPC wrapped around her.

"No, no, nnnnnnnnnooooooooo …" hollered Wolfe.

Confusion and disbelief raced through Wolfe's mind, adrenaline surged through his body with dramatic effect. The PC holding him back, stopping his progress was strong but Wolfe reacted swiftly and powerfully against the restraining force being exerted on him by twisting the policeman around, pushing him off balance and freeing himself, the traffic cop fell backwards onto the hard road. Wolfe was able to run with purpose and sped along the road racing as fast as he could. Other police officers and onlookers seemed to him to be frozen in time, he turned to his right into the car park of Simpson De-Lange Solicitors still running, not at all breathless, he was suddenly halted in his progress by three constables. Wolfe couldn't get past them but he caught sight of something over the shoulder of one of the men and, immediately, his whole body went limp. Laying on the ground, the lifeless body of a person he instantly recognised as Maria, lying still on the black surface of the car park. Maria was less than ten feet from her car, face down on the cold hard surface, plip key for her car in her right hand, laptop bag gripped in her left, a pool of blood had spread out from under the left side of her body. Wolfe wanted to take hold of her, embrace her in the hope that she would wake up in his arms but he was forcibly stopped from approaching any closer, he wouldn't be able to touch her, he knew this but he fought to do just that until he was exhausted. Then, uncontrollably and through a mucus filled mouth, he spat out sobs and screams that seemed to nullify and dim the bright blue flashing of the lights from a series of emergency vehicles parked close by, Jaxon Wolfe couldn't hear or see anything other than his love, lifeless, dead.

That night, Wolfe and his daughter sat on the sofa at the family home, his arms wrapped around her in fear that she too might disappear if he let go. Wolfe didn't sleep; Isabella slept for an hour having cried into submission. He felt completely helpless, what could he do to console her?

When she awoke in the early morning, she cried again until she could shed no more tears. Wolfe had contacted Maria's parents and his father to tell them what had happened to Maria, more tears, sobs and the inevitable question, why? Wolfe couldn't answer, he was asking himself the same question constantly. Three generations devastated by the same single event. Jaxon Wolfe had been able to positively identify his wife but was not given leave to touch her.

The following day in the mortuary when forensics had concluded their work and before the pathologist began his, Wolfe was able to hold Maria, she was cold, freezing cold, he cried again knowing how much she hated feeling cold, she used to be so warm … always warm.

Maria Wolfe was an investigative solicitor whose cases sometimes crossed over with her husband's investigations. On more than one occasion, Maria acted for Defence Lawyers, defending clients being prosecuted by the West Yorkshire Police Force. Never a harsh word was spoken between them and, at the end of the working day, work related conversation was hardly ever entered into.

Although the case of Maria's death is still open, it is not being actively investigated and is only referred to for cross checking against similar new cases.

Maria Wolfe's body was released for cremation four weeks after her death, during which time, Wolfe had been discovered on several occasions by his daughter and police colleagues in a state of drunkenness either in his home or in his local pub. He managed to stay sober for the funeral, then broke down in tears whilst delivering a eulogy for Maria, but the following day, Isabella came home after visiting her friend to find him so drunk, that when he tried to stand up, he fell, hitting his head on a coffee table, drawing blood. He spent the next day in hospital but discharged himself in the late afternoon and went to his local pub to get drunk again. It came as no surprise to family and colleagues when in desperation at her father's state, Isabella left home to live with her grandparents in Spain where she spent that summer holiday. She would call her dad once a day from her mobile phone but didn't always receive a response.

 Three months later and after Izzy's outburst, Jaxon Wolfe visited a close friend of Maria's, Ella Forbes, a psychiatrist operating her practice from a surgery in Carlton. He walked to her surgery from a pub he'd just been evicted from after falling off his bar stool and not having the ability to reseat himself, he'd thrown the stool over the bar where it smashed into an optic unit, sending several bottles of spirits crashing to the floor. He then proceeded to chastise the wooden convenience for his own inability to sit on it. He cursed, "Call yourself a stool … you're just firewood, ya fucking piece of trash." The landlord had no option but to evict Wolfe and ban him from re-entering his establishment again until sober. Wolfe staggered through Carlton that afternoon, took a deep breath before entering The Unicorn but before he got to the bar he heard one of favourite songs being played on the Wurlitzer, 'That Don't Make it Junk' written by Leonard Cohen but covered in this version by Haley Tuck. 'I fought against the bottle but I had to do it drunk.' Wolfe felt a sudden surge of sobriety and in a completely subconscious response to hearing the song he turned around walked out of the bar making straight for Ella Forbes surgery two streets away in Moor View.

The incident with the bar stool made Wolfe reflect on the stupidity of this and previous actions, and in his state of sobriety, he found himself off loading all his pent-up emotions onto Ella. She had, on numerous occasions, made contact with his daughter asking her to try and persuade her father to make contact. Now that she had finally got the opportunity, she made sure Wolfe got the full and immediate support of her professional expertise. Although obvious, Wolfe himself had to accept that his response to Maria's death had nothing to do with his emotional loss, more that he saw the law enforcement authority, the Police Force that he was part of, as incompetent and ineffective in finding her killer. Probably more relevant was the fact that he believed himself to be incompetent as a Detective Inspector; he had let his wife and their daughter down professionally. Where was the point in continuing with his chosen profession if he couldn't even protect his own family from the results of violent criminal activity? Drinking had initially allowed him to reminisce on his life with Maria but soon these thoughts were overtaken by resentment targeted mainly, but not exclusively, at himself and his police colleagues. Visions of Maria lying dead on the ground were all that occupied his thoughts when he was sober but drunkenness allowed him to blank out these visions and replace them with the floating abandonment of nothingness, and he wanted to stay with this vision only, it was easier than seeing her dead. Pure denial and selfishness were the root causes of his melancholy state.

Under Ella Forbes treatment, Wolfe began to regain self-respect and managed to stop drinking so heavily, except for one relapse, the anniversary of Maria's death. Izzy and Ella had together expected this return to self-recrimination, and through regular counselling from Ella, but mainly due to Izzy spending more time with him whilst living with the family of her best friend in Carlton, they managed to avoid any lasting regression to past alcohol induced behaviour. The West Yorkshire Police Force internal medical support team were involved, at Ella's request, with the intended result, that 24 months after Maria's death, Jaxon Wolfe was past fit to return to full time duties, subject to regular evaluations.

Back on the force full time, initially seconded to the fraud squad had settled Wolfe down into a routine and, although his wife seemed ever present in his thoughts, his recuperation and acceptance of the situation had now come full circle. Wolfe was transferred back to his previous position in CID Serious Crime Squad a year later. Isabella had moved back into the family home with him, he hardly ever misses her phone calls and he has become quite adept at text messaging. Wolfe and Izzy agreed that each day, they would involve Maria and Mum in their thoughts and conversations, not that they might forget her but just to know that, spiritually, she was still with them.

***

Wolfe arrived at his desk three storeys above ground level in Holland Walk a building close to Leeds City Centre where the West Yorkshire Police Force had recently established its new headquarters. He connected and turned on his laptop, and sent an e-mail to his team requesting a meeting in the incident room at 4pm, giving himself time to have lunch and deal with his e-mails. An hour later, he was enjoying his cheese salad lunch whilst listening to his iPod through earphones,

"Lunchtimes are for relaxing and thinking about the tasks ahead," he told his workmates, but actually he just preferred to be alone and undisturbed during his lunch break.

His iPod was set to shuffle, JJ Cale was singing Cocaine, he began thinking about the body found on Carlton Moor. What had this poor soul done to deserve such an inauspicious end? His death was almost certainly murder, was it drug related? Then, without logic, Wolfe's thoughts turned to the time he first heard this song, as a young teenager browsing through the vinyl records in the Virgin Records, long before Richard Branson went global. One of the hippie looking guys behind the pay desk slipped JJ Cale's Troubadour album on the turntable and immediately cued up this track. After the first few bars, Wolfe was hooked. 'Sometimes, songs hit you like that and now decades later,' he thought, 'I'm still hooked on *Cocaine!'* He grinned and looked around to see if anyone was watching. No one was.

The young Wolfe certainly didn't flourish at school socially or academically but his love of music was a constant companion and he shared his knowledge with anyone who was interested. His obsession resulted in an ability to use research to fuel his interest in bands and genres, old and new. This stood him in good stead later in life when age and confidence brought success academically at a college for further education where he gained access to a career in the police force. Wolfe was 20 years of age when he enrolled at Police College where his ability at fact-finding and research helped him progress. Two years earlier, however, he would not have contemplated such a career after being arrested with a friend on suspicion of dealing cannabis outside a nightclub. The police were working on a tip off backed up by a rather generalised description of the individuals, both were searched and small amounts of the drug were found. Together, they spent 18 hours in the cells before the actual culprits were arrested and positively identified the following day.

Now at the age of 42, Jaxon Wolfe is a conscientious hardworking and popular detective with almost twenty years' service within the police force. Standing 6ft 2in tall, he always cuts a smart silhouette with a physique that a 30-year-old would be proud of, a result of three evenings a week spent at the local health club and one evening a week, playing five a side football with his pals.

Returning to his 'gold fish cubicle' office, Wolfe, brushed the fingers of both hands through his black hair and then stroked his close shaven beard with his right hand before sitting down behind his desk. His physical features were attributed, so his mother told him, to his Irish roots. She was born in Eire moved to England to work in the textile industry where she met and married Wolfe's father in the early seventies.

He opened up his laptop computer, once again he had time to catch up on his e-mails before the incident room briefing; Wolfe had seen junior officers busy putting together the photo display boards for the 4pm briefing. An e-mail arrived from a friend confirming the kick off time for tomorrows five a side clash with a team from the White Heart pub in Carlton, this would be the first local derby of the season. The White Heart versus The Unicorn was always a closely fought affair. Although indoor football was a sport he enjoyed participating in, Wolfe, together with his football team members, favoured Rugby League as a spectator sport. With the exception of one team member they were all Leeds Rhinos supporters, season ticket holders and avid watchers of the sport of Rugby League.

Acting Detective Constable Pamela Middleton opened the briefing, outlining events that took place after the emergency call was received until the arrival at the scene of DI Wolfe, at which point, she handed the presentation over to him.

"The photos you see before you were taken this morning; they show the naked body of a deceased male. The body was discovered by two workmen on Carlton Moor near Blackhill Hide. The men were undertaking repair work to a nearby ditch. They removed a large boulder which blocked the route of their excavator, revealing a small cave and clearly visible within was the body in the situation as you see it in these photographs. The man is assumed to be aged 30 or thereabouts and it is also assumed that he was placed here after he died. The victim's body exhibits the sign of a wound to his lower back in the kidney area left side, our forensic investigation will, I hope, reveal more about this."

As if to make sure everyone understood exactly the area of the body he was describing, Wolfe turned to his right with his left hand placed on the similar area of his own body. "We are treating his death as suspicious based on my discussions at the scene this morning with the Senior Pathologist. Our best estimate is that the body has laid insitu for at least 24, possibly 48 hours. This investigation may well progress officially to a murder enquiry. Pay particular attention to photo No. 5 which shows a close up of the deceased's left arm indicating needle marks. From which we can assume drug use, heroin possibly and photo No. 6 which is a close up of a tattoo high on the victims left shoulder, Leeds United Loyal Union, he may be known to us." Wolfe paused, then asked. "Any questions so far."

"Sir," a young PC seated in the middle raised his arm.

"Yes PC?"

"Mills, sir," replied the constable.

"How do you know the victim was dead before he was placed in the cave, sir?"

"Take a closer look at photo's No.10 and 11 after the briefing, and you will see that there is no evidence of a struggle by the victim to escape, nor is there any evidence of him being bound or gagged. At this stage, constable, we have to assume that if the victim was not incapacitated, he would surely have tried to get out." Looking directly at the young PC then scanning the room, Wolfe continued,

"Now, until we get further information from forensics, I don't want to make any other assumptions and, therefore, at present, we are not saying anything to the press. In fact, I want a press blackout on this matter until further notice. If any of you receive contacts of any kind from the media, direct them to Detective Middleton who will deal with their enquiry." Wolfe glanced at Pam Middleton, he hadn't mentioned this with her before the briefing, she frowned and smiled sarcastically at him.

"Firstly, we need to identify the victim, so those of you with contacts, informants or knowledge of known drug users, make a mental note of the victim's features and those with previous involvement with football hooligan cases, check for known LULU members. We need a name!" Pausing again, he looked at his female colleague and said,

"DC Middleton will now confirm some admin issues to you all and confirm the time of the next briefing meeting." With that parting comment, he moved away from the display boards towards the exit and tapped Pete Halford on the shoulder as he walked past tilting his head in a follow me gesture. Middleton started her closing statement before the two men had reached the door to leave the room,

"Thanks, DI Wolfe. Please note that from today's date, all leave for those here is cancelled until further notice."

A communal groan of disapproval came from the gathering of police officers.

"Didn't take long to get ya feet under the table did it, Pam?" The rhetorical question came from someone in the centre of the gathering.

Upon hearing this Wolfe was about to turn back to the briefing to defend his colleague.

"Leave it boss," said Pete resting his left hand on Wolfe's upper right arm, "she can handle it, she'll make mincemeat of that lot."

"Yes, and while some of you spend your spare time in the pub getting pissed," she stated in her best controlled and low key, not letting this bother her, voice. "I've been studying for my detective exams and when I was asked to stand up to the plate, I did. Now if any one of you feels that this investigation is not for them just let me know cause there are plenty of other officers ready to fill any vacancies." The room fell silent.

"Okay well that's told them," Wolfe remarked as he proceeded towards his office, Halford following smiling to himself.

"Good now I'll continue," Middleton stated into the silence. "Overtime pay will be available, subject to senior officer approval and agreement to the shift work rota I have posted on the main notice board. Further briefing meetings will take place every day at 2pm here in the incident room, those on rota should make themselves available and e-mails will be circulated to the whole team at 5pm every day. This first briefing is now concluded."

In his office, Wolfe and Halford stood either side of the desk.

"Pete, have a chat with PC's Broughton and Robertson, they were first on the scene, make sure their reports are thorough, I don't want Winker Watson accusing this section of loose or sloppy report writing. I'm confident this will be a full-blown murder inquiry by morning and I don't want some smart-arse defence lawyer using loose reporting as an excuse to get a not guilty verdict." Wolfe took a breath.

"Pete, that's not my only concern about this case."

"Hmmm," interrupted Halford. "Had a feeling something else was bothering you."

"Most murders, if that's what this is, which it will be, are committed by someone known to the victim, even a close relation and obvious clues to that fact are often found at the scene but this is different. It's got the look and the smell of a contract killing, and that, Pete, worries the hell out of me."

Halford then continued without any hesitation,
"The victim was moved after death and hidden where perhaps, it was not intended to be found? Therefore, premeditated and it would have taken at least two adults to move the body from one location to another. There was also a JCB on hand to shift the boulder, I assume they hotwired it, that machine looked quite old. The victim's body must have been transported, he was found close to a car park." Halford paused.

Wolfe took over,

"So, was it intentional to leave him where he was found this morning or did some unforeseen circumstance happen that meant he was dumped in haste?" This time, there was silence between them until Wolfe said,

"That's it Pete, that's what's bothering me, he was dumped in haste, but it must have taken a while to put him in that cave and then move a boulder in front of it, even using a JCB."

"Okay, boss, so …" Halford sat down opposite Wolfe, who began walking slowly towards the office door and then when he got close, turned to walk back. This was the routine Wolfe would frequently adopt when he was thinking out loud. Halford had heard about this ritual but this was the first time he'd witnessed it.

Halfway through the second circuit, Wolfe started to speak,

"A vehicle carrying at least two men and one dead body, possibly a transit van of something similar, corpse hidden in the back, it's heading across the moor to a destination … as yet unknown, using the moor road instead of the main roads. Then the van breaks down, it's late at night … perhaps," Wolfe hesitated but kept pacing the office. "They can't abandon the vehicle and walk into Carlton … cause someone might stumble across it, a police car, maybe … and us cops are inquisitive bastards … no, far too risky … they have to get the body the hell out of there, hide it. It must have been at night because they had time to deal with the situation; any approaching traffic would be easily seen before a vehicle saw them, headlights at night, dead giveaway of approaching traffic plenty of time to hide behind a rock, loads of them up there. They get the van off the road … into the car park … that's it! They were heading east because they were able to roll down into the car park … it wouldn't have been possible to push the vehicle uphill, in a westerly direction, the gradients too steep." Wolfe paused for breath, Halford felt that he should say something but Wolfe held his arm out towards his constable, hand pointing up in a don't say anything gesture.

"Pete, have a look at the area East of Carlton, say a ten mile. No, wait, five-mile arc from the town centre, then tomorrow morning at 9am, meet me at the Blackhill Rue Hotel on the moor top. I want to have a word with the owner. From what you told me earlier on, I think he's a bit of a nosey so and so, maybe he heard something during the night a few days ago."

Halford nodded and wrote a few words in his notebook whilst Wolfe sat down at his desk. Halford didn't move, Wolfe suspected there was something he wanted to say.

"What is it, Pete?"

"Well, boss …"

"Yes."

"Contract killing means organised crime, that's scary stuff."

"Don't get carried away by thinking too much, let's just investigate this with what we've got without jumping to conclusions, Pete."

"You mentioned contract killing, not me, all I'm doing is putting –"

"Two and two together, and getting five," interrupted Wolfe.

"Check through missing persons reports, national data base, going back three months for anyone matching our guy,"

"Can't a junior officer do that, boss? I'd be better doing more –"

"Important work," interrupted Wolfe who gazed deeply at his constable without blinking. "This is important work, DC Halford, that's why I want you to do it. You've seen the victim, therefore, any description similarities will jump out at you and someone else could miss that."

"Okay, boss," said Halford lowering his gaze to the desk between them.

"Get back to me before the end of today's shift, Pete."

Halford closed the office door behind him leaving Wolfe alone in his cage looking out on the team assembled to investigate the case; he needed a lead that would shed some light on the case.

***

Wolfe looked up from his laptop and noticed that his office seemed suddenly darker. The clock on the wall showed the time to be 6.15pm. As if in disbelief, he checked the bottom right corner of his computer screen, sure enough, quarter past six. He'd been working on his laptop solidly answering e-mails and filing reports. The last report was the closing statement relating to a series of armed robberies undertaken in Leeds, Manchester, Birmingham, Edinburgh and London. A strange case of robbery with threatening behaviour, a show of hardware, sawn off shot guns in the main, committed by a group of individuals confirmed by their descriptions at each incident as wearing the same disguises. Six individuals, two of them confirmed by their physical appearance, figure hugging cat suits, as women. The problem with these robberies was that there didn't seem to have been anything taken. No one was injured and on the one occasion, the Birmingham heist, an elderly gentleman seemed to suffer from a seizure brought on by anxiety, the whole gang helped him to relax and waited until paramedics arrived to administer aid, only fleeing the scene when it was confirmed that the old man would be okay. All the robberies were executed in banks operated by different companies in five major cities and on each occasion, the thieves gained access to the vaults containing individual safe deposit boxes. The banks were very reluctant to release deposit box owners' names to the investigating officers. When names were finally released, the owners confirmed their contents were intact, nothing missing. The problem facing the West Yorkshire Police Force was that evidence gathered with regard to stolen goods was purely circumstantial, so all they could hope to secure was a conviction for threatening behaviour, hardly worth the effort to gain a conviction in court. However, Wolfe mussed that it was his duty to find and arrest the gang, if only to discover the reason for the so-called robberies. The strangest element to this case was a piece of A3-sized paper was found fixed to the wall in each main vault with the identical computerised message printed on it that read: 'betrayal has its' costs'. Owners were interviewed by their regional police forces but, to a man, they would not comment on the statement as if it had nothing to do with them, nothing had been stolen, the statement had no significance. In a Leeds City Centre bank, the name of a prominent business woman was written on a piece of paper and left in a safe deposit box, as if targeting this specific person. Interviewed by WYPF the person named denied ever owning a safe deposit box and had no idea why their name had been stated as the owner and the bank records backed up that statement. The individual cases are still open but only the WYPF are actively investigating any of these robberies. Unfortunately Wolfe knew that without any new leads in the case it wouldn't be sanctioned for further resource spending.

There was a knock and the door to DI Wolfe's office opened, in walked DC Middleton closely followed by DC Halford.

"What's this, a deputation?" Wolfe said sarcastically.

Middleton was first to speak,

"We think we have a positive ID on the Carlton Moor victim."

"Okay, let's have it."

"Matthew Brookes, a 31-year-old, distinguishing features match. Leeds United supporter, got previous for possession, arrested two years ago, outside the Elland Road stadium, on a charge of possession with intent to sell but we couldn't make it stick, charges were dropped. The last entry states that –"

"Who was the investigating officer?" interrupted Wolfe.

"Errr ... DI James Phillips."

"Ah ... my replacement during the ... err my ... dark times."

"Yes, sir, he's with South Yorkshire now," she replied sharply.

"Mmm. Okay, sorry, Pam ... it's annoying when people interrupt, please continue."

"Matthew Brookes last reported as a patient at the Newbury Clinic near Wetherby, since then, nothing. Next of kin on the report, Mrs Charlotte Marks, his sister, that's it, sir."

"That's good, Pam, I assume you're following this up and trying to track down his sister?" complimented Wolfe.

"Got someone working on that as we speak," she acknowledged.

"Arrange a visit and I want you to accompany me when we have an address."

Wolfe turned his attention to Halford, "You got news for me as well, Pete?"

"Two, possibly three, destinations for where the perps may have been heading. Panorama Reservoir on the outskirts of Carlton, Marston Quarry near Keighley and possibly the River Wharfe East of Carlton, in Bolton Woods, the Strid as it's known, fast flowing water, very dangerous." Halford waited while Wolfe mused on his response.

"The reservoir I know where it is ... it's secluded enough, especially at night, weigh the body down it would, eventually sink into the silt at the bottom, could stay there for years, decades even. Trouble is, there are plenty of houses close to the reservoir, they'd run the risk of being noticed. The Strid ... too risky I think, not easy to get a van close enough, they would have to carry the body quite a distance and no guarantee the body would stay out of sight, the river in that area is very unpredictable. The body might get washed up downstream soon after being thrown in. No, I think we should consider for now that this poor fellow ... Brookes, was potentially destined for the quarry. Is it still a working quarry?"

"Yes, it is and there's something else. Hennersy Contracting, Bolton and Green's employers are currently taking regular deliveries from the quarry for a project in Skipton." He let this statement hang in the air before saying,

"Maybe, there is a connection, Green, Bolton or someone else, perhaps."

Wolfe nodded in agreement, but then was distracted by Middleton turning over the papers in her hands that she had just referred to.

"Boss, last known employer of Matthew Brookes, two years ago, Hennersy Contracting!"

"Promising, very promising. Home address for Brookes?" inquired Wolfe.

"Granary Wharfe, Leeds, an apartment."

"Not cheap property in that location ... better get a search warrant sorted. We need to take a look inside. Well done both of you, we're off and running on this one," concluded Wolfe. As he stood up, his laptop chimed indicating shut down.

"Pete, first thing tomorrow, drive from Hennersy's offices to the quarry, take a look around, see if it's feasible to make a delivery out of hours, know what I mean?"

"Okay, boss, what if someone wants to know why I'm there?"

"There's been a spate of stolen vehicles, joy riders but no cars found, could be dumping them in the quarry … how's that sound?"

Halford nodded.

"Pam, you and I get the short straw, we'll visit Mrs Marks … tomorrow morning. Tell her the bad news, better get a police councillor to attend, say half an hour after we get there. If you're struggling to find the name of a councillor, I'm sure I can furnish you with one or two." Wolfe smiled, the irony wasn't lost on Middleton and she let out a chuckle.

'It's good he can react like this now,' she thought to herself. Halford didn't understand the humour, Middleton had to explain later.

"Oh, Pete."

Halford turned before opening the office door. "Yes, boss."

"We're almost running on empty with regards our staff resource for this investigation so brief two uniforms and order them to visit the Blackhill Rue Hotel to interview the manager … err, what's his name?"

"Greg Hughes," confirmed Halford

"Yeah, him, ya never know something may come of it. One more thing," he added, "check the JCB used by the workmen, it must have been parked there overnight, in the car park probably."

"Okay, and I'll find out if it's possible to hotwire, although most plant these days are fitted with trackers, maybe this one is too old?"

"Mmmm," Wolfe muttered.

"Can trackers be bypassed or was a key used, a master key maybe?" asked Halford.

"See what you can find out tomorrow Pete, but now it's time to go home, we're off duty," Wolfe announced as he followed the other two out from his office, turning off the light and closing the door.

On his way home, Wolfe thought about dropping into the Unicorn for a pint and a chat off the record with Higgins but decided time with Isabella was more important, and knowing Izzy, she would be swatting hard for her up and coming A level exams, and probably would have completely ignored the fact that she needs to eat. He was wrong. When he arrived home, she had a dish of pasta with smoked salmon accompanied by a bottle of chilled white wine waiting for them to consume. Father and daughter talked until midnight just like they used to with Maria, it felt good, Maria would have approved. Jaxon Wolfe slept well that night without interruption but then felt guilty the following morning because he couldn't remember dreaming about Maria.

Chapter 5

The next morning, Paul Anthony Smythe stepped out over the threshold of his large neo-Georgian home and squinted as the bright sunshine hit him in the face, he arched his back and looked up at the blue sky.

"What a beautiful day," he said to himself as he started to walk towards the detached garage.

The house had the benefit of elevated views to the north above the mist that engulfed the Wharfe Valley again that morning. Situated on Panorama Drive to the western outskirts of Carlton, the house enjoyed lavish views of the moor directly to the south as it rose gradually away in the far distance. Large coniferous trees lined the perimeter of the rear garden except for a section at the end of the garden where a gate gave access directly onto the moor and a distant view to the east of Blackhill Hide.

Turning back to face the house, "No kiss goodbye?" he said in a tone readily recognisable to his live in partner standing at the door.

"I gave you a kiss in the house," responded Charley. "Are you counting them now?" she questioned nervously.

Placing, with deliberate stealth, his briefcase on the ground, Paul stepped back towards Charley. She took a deep breath, she knew what was coming and felt there was no way she could avoid it. With gentle but firm precision he placed his right hand around her throat and upon contact Charley became instantly pliable, enough to hide her trepidation, he pulled her towards him slightly tilting her head to one side. He kissed her firm, hard and powerful on the mouth in a way that he had started to do recently. A change in attitude towards her that she had thought was pressure of work but lately it had become a standard ritual that she hated much more now than she'd found it exciting when this treatment of her had first started.

"Darling, I know you don't want me to go," Paul announced as he released his hold, "and much as I'd like to sample your treasures here and now, I have to be in Bristol in five hours and it's likely to be busy on the roads ..."

Charley found confidence to interrupt, "Then you're going to London and won't be back home until next week sometime?" tempered enthusiasm locked in her mind.

"It's the business I'm in Charley, it's got us this house and lifestyle."

Paul kissed her on the forehead with surprising tenderness, turned and collected his briefcase on his way to the garage. He aimed the remote key at the garage door which obediently began to open, revealing two very expensive automobiles, a Mercedes SL55 AMG and a Porsche Cayenne Turbo SUV both Metallic Silver, valeted to showroom condition. The headlights of his chosen carriage, the Mercedes, flashed responding to another remote-control device, the boot lid opened wide and Paul placed his slim line briefcase next to a small holdall he'd placed there the previous evening for his overnight stays. After closing the boot, he opened the driver's door, took off his jacket and hung it behind the driver's seat before sitting in it. With the ignition key in place, he pressed the conveniently labelled 'start/stop button' and the vehicle fired into life its V8 engine roaring like a caged animal. Paul preferred to relate the sound to the vision of a Second World War fighter plane primed and ready to do battle. Fastening the seatbelt across his torso, he selected the auto function for the gear box, disconnected the parking brake, dabbed the accelerator and the car moved from its standing position out of the garage. Waving he drove through the open gated entrance onto Prospect Drive and drove towards Carlton. Charlotte watched as the garage door began to close, she turned and walked into the house.

As she turned after closing the door Martha, the matron like housekeeper, au pair and general maid held Charlotte's five-year-old daughter Samantha proudly by the hand. Sam was dressed in her school uniform and ran towards her mum from the direction of the staircase.

"We're both excited about school today. Sam has told me all about her new friends," announced Martha.

"Yes, I'd like to meet them," said Charley dropping onto one knee and holding her arms out towards Sam. "Who is your best friend?"

"Mummy, all the girls are my best friends," said Sam giving her mum a quick hug before trotting off in search of breakfast cereal.

Less than an hour later, Charlotte had showered, dressed and Sam was ready for Martha to take her to school.

By the time Martha returned from the school run, Charlotte was sat at the home computer in the study, checking her e-mails. She'd begun to daydream about how her life had changed in the last three years from widowed mother at 29 years of age to a 32-year-old living in a large house on the border of the Yorkshire Dales. The sudden death of Alfred, her husband and father of Samantha, came as a shock and had it not been for Paul, she may well have had to go back to lap dancing for a living.

Alfred Marks was a seemingly successful businessman based in Leeds, supplying precious metals and stones to the jewellery industry. He committed suicide, slashing his wrists and bleeding to death in the bath of a hotel bedroom in Harrogate. A typed and signed letter addressed to Charlotte was found on the dressing table of the hotel suite. Alfred's suicide note stated he had run up debts through gambling and bad business decisions, there weren't enough assets left in the business to pay them off. The ignominy and stress of bankruptcy was too much for him to bear, only suicide would bring back his self-respect, his honour.

Charlotte was informed that banks and gambling corporations wanted their share of his remaining assets, and as a result, she had to sell the family home, leaving her without financial means to support herself and her two-year-old daughter. Paul Anthony Smythe had introduced himself to Charlotte as Alfred's landlord for the jeweller's shop he rented in Victoria Quarter. At the funeral Paul offered his help to Charlotte if she should need assistance to dispose of items within the shop or find someone to take on the business. A few months after Alfred Marks had been laid to rest Paul had dealt with the debtors, managing to save some of the value in the Marks family residence and Charlotte, Samantha and Paul had moved together to their new residence in Carlton. Charlotte Marks considered herself to be very fortunate, but …

The knock on the door of Charlotte's study broke her daydream.

"Charlotte, would you like a cup of tea before I go?" asked Martha as she poked her head round the half open door.

"Yes, I think I'd better, Martha. I was almost asleep."

"Oh, I'm sorry."

"No, it's okay, I should be wide awake at this time in a morning," replied Charlotte.

Ten minutes later, Martha returned with a pot of tea, cup and saucer and a plate of biscuits, she placed the tray on a small coffee table in front of a two-seat sofa. Charlotte asked Martha to join her.

"Sit down, Martha, and have a break," her tone hinted at pleading rather than a request.

"Okay," replied Martha. "I'll go get a cup."

The two women, now ensconced on the sofa, stared into the south facing garden stretching out before them, bathed in low sunlight numerous shades of green to brown were created contrasting with the dull mottled flattened bracken of the moor beyond. The low late winter sun gave an almost spring like feel to the landscape, a taste of things to come.

"It's on days like this I can't help thinking how lucky I've been over the past few years," began Charlotte. Martha had expected one of Charlotte's musings about the past; she'd done this on several occasions before. "Then when I start mentally praising my luck, you know, meeting Paul so soon after Alfred died. Sam and I living in a place like this, she's started at school and I'm able to concentrate on my cooking, and Paul just understands. You know, he's told me that when Sam is settled in at school, I've to look for a place in town, you know, a little shop to sell my cakes and pastries; he'll pay for a yearlong lease, see how well it goes."

"Ah, that's great, your cooking is first class you should take Mr Smythe up on that suggestion, the baking and cooking you do would sell really well in Carlton," said Martha with as much sincerity as she could gather from within herself.

"Oh, I intend to …" Charlotte paused as if caught in two minds as to what to say next. Then, "It's just I don't want to tempt fate, I felt just as happy with Alfred but then he …" She sniffed as if about to break into tears. "Well, you know, Martha … you know the story … suicide in a hotel bathroom, and afterwards, all that stuff about him being a gambler, owing money all over the place and hiring call girls."

"There, there, now don't go getting upset about the past, cos that's all it is, the past. Take a deep breath, drink the tea and eat one of these biscuits you made," Martha lifted the plate of biscuits from the coffee table and held it in front of Charlotte.

"Yeah, you're right … Sam is happy at school, isn't she?"

"Oh, yes, always smiling when she talks about school, she has lots of friends, no worries there."

"Sorry to burden you with my problems … well, they're not really problems, are they? Compared to a lot of people, I'm well off and I know I should be grateful for everything I have." Charlotte sat up a little straighter on the sofa and finished her cup of tea. "I'll continue to type the recipes up for those pies I cooked yesterday." She stood up, walked over to the desk and opened her laptop computer.

Martha said encouragingly, "I'll bet in a few years, you'll be publishing a book with those very recipes. You'll have a best seller."

"One step at a time, Martha," Charlotte smiled to herself as Martha cleared the cups and saucers away, and left the room whilst munching on one of the leftover biscuits.

She was halfway down the corridor when she heard Charlotte say,

"Martha, my brother hasn't called at the house recently, has he? Whilst I was out, maybe, I haven't heard from him for a couple of weeks. He usually calls me on my mobile, at least, once a week."

Martha stopped in the hall, looked at the floor, then head up, she concentrated on her answer,

"No, Charlotte, I'm not aware of him calling here or on the phone recently."

"I've left numerous messages on his mobile but he hasn't responded. I hope he hasn't got himself into trouble again, that would be such a shame, he's done well since rehab," Charlotte was now in the hall. "I think I'll take a drive up to his apartment in Leeds."

Martha quickly placed the crockery near the kitchen sink and turned back tracing her steps back to the hall.

"No, you stay here, Charlotte, press on with those recipes, you'll feel better when they're done." And as she reached where Charlotte was standing, Martha gently took hold of her by the shoulders and guided her back towards the study. "I'll call in at his place. Mr Smythe has asked me to take some folders to the office, he was supposed to drop them in this morning but forgot them."

"I didn't hear him ask," said Charlotte confused but accepting.

"No, Mr Smythe called me on my mobile … when I was taking Samantha to school. There are a few bits of shopping I need to do as well. If I go now, I'll be back in plenty of time to collect Samantha from school."

"Paul really shouldn't put on you in this way, Martha; you're a nanny and housekeeper not an errand boy as well."

"Housekeeping involves making errands and besides, it's no trouble." She made sure Charlotte sat at her desk then continued, "You and Mr Smythe have been so kind to me. You bought me the car so I had transport to get me from place to place, it's the least I can do."

Charlotte felt more like getting on with her work now, she felt energised. *Amazing what a cup of tea can do,* she thought as she realised how much she depended on Martha.

Martha Styles just seemed to appear one day. Charlotte couldn't remember ever mentioning to Paul about employing a nanny for Samantha, but there she was, one rainy Saturday morning at the house, saying she was there for her interview for the post of nanny and housekeeper. A woman in early middle age with an hourglass figure wearing a low-cut blouse that showed off her perfectly formed cleavage, a mid-tanned complexion, attractive facial features, bright eyes, and red lips that gave the impression she was very confident about her appearance and attractiveness. Charlotte originally thought her overall appearance was purposeful and that just about any heterosexual male between ages of 25 to 50 would find her very alluring, just as she would want. As it turned out, she was ideal, perfectly suited for the role that didn't really exist until she arrived. Martha was an immediate success with Samantha and now she was part of the family, well, that's what it felt like to Charlotte. After all, Martha now has a bedroom in the house for when she occasionally stays overnight. Charlotte didn't consider asking Martha her age but she thought she must be in her early forties. Charlotte had mused about this from time to time but the subject never seemed to be a talking point. She also mused that, perhaps, Paul had an ulterior motive and that he might actually be having an affair with her but this was laid to rest when Martha admitted in tearful honesty that she was, in fact, gay, a lesbian and that she found Charlotte incredibly attractive but not her type, so the relationship soon became more matronly and acceptable to Charlotte.

Martha was soon driving away from Carlton towards Leeds to undertake her 'errands'.

"Errand boy, that's what she thinks of me. Well, let me tell you, little miss spoilt bitch, if things go to plan, I'll go soon … never to return and I'll be living a life of luxury … somewhere hot," she said to herself picking up her mobile phone, blue toothed to the car, she punched in a number then threw it down on the passenger seat.

"Hello," said a hard voice through the cars speakers.

"She's asking if I've heard from her brother."

"Is she now?" said the man at the other end of the conversation.

"Yes, Tony, she is, so what the fuck do I do about it?" she shouted.

"Martha, calm down, that little shit of a brother of hers got what was coming to him. It was an accident but that said we had no other choice, did we?"

"Of course not, if only he'd handed the stuff over."

"Yeah well it's not the fact that he was taking photos of me in Geneva, it's the others in the photos, they would be more easily identified than me. Anyway, the drugged-up junkie won't be talking to anyone now, so she will have to deal with it and you with her."

"I know, I know, Tony, sorry I just wanted to let off steam. She is so caught up in her own little perfect world it makes me sick."

"It only makes you sick because she has the life that you want," said Tony. Martha thought she heard him let out a snigger.

"You bastard, it's my life she has and you know it, that's what all this is about. What we've been working towards for five fucking years?"

"Is that it, Martha dear?" in his best patronising tone. "Are you finished? That attitude isn't helping."

"Yeah, that's it," followed by a second or two of silence. "Just frustrated that's all."

"Where are you now?" he asked.

"On the way into Leeds, driving through Headingley," she replied.

"What about you?"

"M1 south of Sheffield," he added. Then she told him about the false errand she had to perform in Leeds and that, on the way, she would call at Brookes' apartment.

"Okay, do what you said you were going to do, call at his apartment, make sure someone sees you. Then do the delivery as requested and other stuff you have to do to keep up the illusion, okay?"

"But what do we do if she gets the police involved? You know, file a missing persons or something," Martha sounded concerned, worried.

"Nothing," he replied. "But she will need you even more if that happens. Now, if you're feeling frustrated, take a little time out and get one of your internet pals to arrange a little party, it's worked in the past." He could almost feel Martha relax at this comment.

"Yeah, ya right, it's been two weeks since the last one, that's what I need, a right good f …" Suddenly, she remembered something she'd wanted to say last time they'd spoke. "Hey, I slipped two of those little gems into a guy's drink last time before we got to the party. Well, he almost pole vaulted into the place after I'd given him a fluff up in his car," she let out a dirty giggle to emphasise her delight at the effect she'd had on the man who'd been the subject of her attentions.

"Martha, you're insatiable."

"No, just free to do what I like and it feels good," still smiling, she was grateful that Tony always managed to make her feel better; she started feeling randy, her temperature rising in all the right places, she let out a sigh.

Tony, sensing something, said,

"Don't get carried away now, Martha," he warned, "don't think about getting your talons into Charlotte Marks' man, it won't help matters."

"He's a wimp, an excuse for a man, took a sneaky look at his weapon the other morning …"

"You cheeky bitch."

"I've got bigger nipples," she started to laugh out loud. Tony joined in. *'Funny,'* he thought, *'she always manages to put me in a good mood.'*

"Stay loose," he said, then the phone line disconnected.

"Loose! That's my middle name," she said with a grin.

Charlotte Marks had just started typing up one of her recipes when the doorbell rang. She looked through the hall window as she walked to answer the call, there was a car parked in the drive. She'd been concentrating so hard, she hadn't heard the car arriving. Opening the door, she saw a man and a woman standing outside. She could tell by their disposition that they were there on official business. The woman looked familiar.

"Mrs Marks, Mrs Charlotte Marks?" asked the man. Suddenly, a torrent of anxiety washed over her, these are police.

"Er … yes, what's happened?" she managed to say through a dry open mouth.

Wolfe was initially caught off guard by her response but continued as he had intended.

"I'm Detective Inspector Wolfe and this is Detective Constable Middleton, we're from the West Yorkshire Police Force, may we come in?" They both presented ID cards.

"Oh, my God … please … yes, come in … is it Paul? No, not Sam. Where is Martha … oh she's not here … she's out …"

"Mrs Marks, please shall we sit down?" asked Middleton and noticing an open door into what she assumed was the lounge, she guided Charlotte gently into the room and eased her into a sofa so she could sit next to her. Wolfe closed the front entrance door and followed the two women.

"Mrs Marks, do you have a brother … Matthew Brookes?" he asked as he sat in a chair opposite the sofa.

"Oh, is Matt in trouble again?" Charlotte instantly began to relax.

"Not exactly, Mrs Marks … I've got bad news, I'm afraid and there's no easy way to say –"

Middleton interrupted before Wolfe could take a breath to continue,

"Charlotte, the body of a man fitting the description of Matthew was found yesterday morning on Carlton Moor."

"He's dead?"

Middleton nodded.

"My God, how … was it a car accident? Where is he now … I must go to him," she began to raise herself from the sofa. Middleton gently held her back.

"Charlotte, DI Wolfe needs to ask you some questions first." She glanced at Wolfe.

Taking her cue, Wolfe said, "Charlotte, can you remember when you last saw Matthew? Please take your time, we fully understand this news has come as a serious shock to you."

A few moments passed, Charlotte seemed to take stock of the situation and then said in a calm but nervous voice,

"I saw Matt about two weeks ago. I called to see him at his flat in Leeds, we had a chat, a cup of coffee. I took some of my biscuits for him to try. I've been phoning him since but there's been no reply. I just said to Martha this morning that I haven't heard from him. Oh no, she's going to call at his flat to see if he's there … I'd better tell her not to go, where's my mobile?" Once again, she tried to stand, then she just burst in tears sobbing uncontrollably.

"Martha?" Wolfe asked.

"Errr, my … our au pair … I must tell her what has happened."

Middleton glanced at Wolfe as she again gently restrained Charlotte, this is what she was waiting for.

"Charlotte, don't worry about Martha, we'll send someone over to his apartment. DI Wolfe needs to make a phone call. Is there somewhere private he can go?"

Through sobs, she pointed to the open door.

"The study across the hall," she said.

Wolfe left the lounge and walked into the study, his mobile to his ear.

"It's Wolfe," he said quietly. "Put me through to PC Mills." Wolfe looked around the room while he waited, his attention drawn to a photo on the desk.

"Mills here, sir, I've checked the address you gave me. The property belongs to a Mr Paul Smythe," he spelt it out to make sure. "S.Y.M.T.H.E."

"How long has he owned it?"

"Almost two years."

"Thanks … Andrew … it is Andrew, isn't it?"

"Yes, sir, that's correct … well, Andy actually."

"Right, Andy, I want you to find out all you can about Mr Smythe, be discrete, just internet stuff at this stage, check police files as well. Also, find out what you can about an Alfred Marks, he should be on our records, he was a suicide victim three years ago, according to DC Middleton, e-mail me a short report."

"Already checked on Alfred Marks, sir," said Mills a little sheepish. "The name Charlotte Marks came up with a hit on the system … and Alfred Marks, her husband, came up. Yes, he committed suicide three years ago, police were involved because he was found in a hotel bathroom, wrists cut, he was in debt to the tune of half a million. Hardly anything left in the estate when the debts were paid off."

"Well done, any record of who he owed money to?"

"Yes, sir," replied the young PC. "We have a note on file, but its only one contact and he was only owed £50,000 or thereabouts, no mention of any more debtors … which is strange," he muttered more to himself than Wolfe.

"Who's the contact that mentioned?"

"Errr, a Henry Mateland, otherwise known as …"

"Toots," interjected Wolfe.

"You know this person, sir?"

"Yes … he is, or should I say, was a snout of mine a few years back." There was silence for a second or two. "I'll explain later … have you got a known address for him, constable?"

"On file here … updated two years ago … Oakwood, North Leeds."

"And Alfred Marks owed him £50 grand?"

"According to the file note … yes sir," replied Mills.

"Bloody hell, he's come up in the world … east Leeds small time wheeler dealer, mainly weed … at least he was last time I met him."

"You knew he was a drug dealer, sir?" said Mills with undisguised disgust.

"Don't get ya knickers in a twist, PC Mills, cannabis was a class C drug then as it is now. He had good contacts and helped the West Yorkshire Police put hardened drug dealers behind bars … heroin, cocaine, crack and more besides he even testified in full view in a high profile murder trial, helping us to convict a gang leader and half a dozen of his henchmen responsible for the deaths of children and adults. That gang leader's now done eight years of a minimum thirty-year stretch and apparently, he's now some guy's bitch in high security at Wakefield, a broken man doing penance for his crimes. Toots is harmless, a community stalwart … last I heard."

"Sorry, sir, I didn't realise."

"That's okay, Mills, policing isn't black and white, there's a lot of grey but, sometimes, you have to take a view on whether the grey is closer to white or black … Toots is definitely on the white side … although he's actually black!"

"Sir?" replied Mills, now confused.

"Text me his last known and postcode for Toots and I'll pay him a visit," instructed Wolfe. "And get that report on Paul Smythe a.s.a.p. Once again, well done." Wolfe disconnected the line.

The sound of someone crying, wailing, interrupted his thoughts all of a sudden. During his conversation with Mills he'd been staring at a photo on the desk in front of him without thinking and the crying made him instantly forget why he'd thought the photo interesting.

Wolfe walked back to the lounge where he found Charlotte Marks bent forwards now sitting in an armchair, head in hands sobbing and being consoled by Middleton as best she could whilst she sat awkwardly on one of the arms. She looked straight at Wolfe as he entered the room and nodded. Charlotte Marks had described the tattoo her brother had on his left arm and, more importantly, a scar under his right ear, the two distinguishing marks Wolfe and Middleton believed would provide them with sufficient proof of identity prior to a positive ID of the body after the autopsy. The investigation could now move on and although painful for the relative, the apprehension of the perpetrator of this crime was paramount and that would be better achieved with speedy positive identification of the victim.

Wolfe sat down on the sofa, he'd have to wait to continue with his questions and while doing so, was taking stock of the ornaments and framed prints adorning the room, well, he assumed they were prints. The lounge was large and looked out through a sizable conservatory that gave view to a pleasantly landscaped tiered garden with ornamental trees planted at purposely positioned focal points. Wolfe found himself thinking that the garden he was viewing would have been perfectly acceptable to Maria, perhaps, only the inclusion of some miniature Seville orange trees in the glasshouse would have been the difference if Maria lived here. Once again, he was broken from his concentration but this time, it was the fact that he realised he was staring at an enlarged copy of the same photo he'd seen in the study.

Next to a large cast stone fire surround were stained timber shelves almost as high as the ceiling and on the lower shelf rested the framed photo that had attracted his attention. The five men depicted in the photo looked happy albeit obviously posed; four of them were wearing military uniform, three in similar olive green and brown camouflage outfits, and the fourth crouching in front was wearing what appeared to be, simply because of its style, an outdated solid green uniform with a crest positioned over the left breast. The fifth member of this ensemble was wearing civvies, in this case, jeans, shirt and jacket but standing to one side, his face, slightly in shadow, was indistinct but drew the viewer's eye because his presence spoilt the composition. *Maybe that was what was intriguing about the smaller photo in the study,'* thought Wolfe. *'Bad composition.'*

"Sir, I'm going to make Charlotte a cup of tea, would you like a cup?"

"Yes, please," he said without thinking, his concentration broken again.

Middleton stood up with Mrs Marks and guided her to the sofa where she sat down next to Wolfe.

Wolfe noticed the streaks of mascara below her eyes that emphasised the bags under, swollen by trauma, she was dabbing them with a tissue but this only served to spread the black patches. Charlotte lifted her head and blew her nose, then when she'd wiped the base of her nose, she turned to Wolfe and said,
"I do apologise, Inspector, you must think me such a wimp, I ..."

"On the contrary, Mrs Marks, I fully understand what you are going through. I had the same experience in relation to a very close friend of mine a few years ago," Wolfe suddenly realised he hadn't intended to say anything but it just came out.

"Please call me, Charley ... a family friend, Inspector?" she said through a sniff.

"Yes ... you might say that." *'Enough*,' he thought. *'Must get off this subject.'*

They looked at each other, smiling and Wolfe decided now was a good time. "I need to ask questions about your brother and they might be difficult for you to hear, let alone answer and I apologise in advance for any discomfort that might bring."

"What ... more than I've already been through?"

"Maybe, Mrs ... err, Charley ... I'm sorry."

"That's okay, you're doing your job and that's fine by me."

Wolfe decided to make a start, "Charley, was your brother, Matthew, a drug user?"

"He was ... I mean, he used to be. Three months in rehab and before that, a month in a clinic in Hertfordshire, and he's been clean for more than a year now."

"What were the drugs he was using?"

"He got really bad with heroin about three or four years ago, and before that, it was cannabis and alcohol, but it was heroin that made him a nightmare to live with."

"You lived with him then?" inquired Wolfe.

"No, I didn't but I saw the effect his addiction had on his girlfriend, it drove her to leave him and move in with a friend of his, and I think that only served to make matters worse ... I'm not blaming her for his addiction, he brought that on himself. Matthew was always easily led, the drug thing started out as peer pressure but, eventually, it turned to a dependency that his friends were able to resist or grow out of but he lacked the will power to do the same. One by one, his friends left him and, eventually, Beth left him. Beth was nice, I liked her, she wanted to settle down, she wanted children but Matthew was only interested in the next hit."

"Heroin is an expensive drug, where did he get the money, was he in employment?"

Charlotte paused and looked hard at Wolfe.

"He couldn't hold a job down until he left rehab but if you're thinking he stole money, then you're so wrong. Matt didn't need to steal to pay for his habit. Three months after graduating from Durham University, he won on the lottery and after he'd given some of it away to our parents, me and a few friends, he still had –" Wolfe's impatience got the better of him and he interrupted her which made her look sharply at the detective.

"How much did he win?"

"Half a million, or thereabouts, so you see, he had the funds to fuel his habit, all he had to do was go to a cash machine and draw his money out, when he could remember his pin number, that is. He would ring me on his mobile if he couldn't remember his pin number because I could always remember it … 2.6.82 … my birthday." Charlotte's head dropped, her hands covering her face. Wolfe moved to console her just as Middleton entered the room bearing a tray with three cups of tea and a few biscuits on a plate. Charlotte looked up as the tray was placed on the coffee table.

"Hope you don't mind but I saw the barrel of biscuits on the worktop and I thought you might like one," she said to Charlotte.

"Not for me, but please help yourself," she said pointing to the glass urn packed with biscuits. "You too, Inspector!"

Wolfe waved his hand to decline.

"No, I insist, Inspector. I'd like your opinion, my baking, my recipe … well, Mum's base recipe with my additional ingredients … actually, to be perfectly honest, it's an old base recipe … Victorian, I think, but I refer to it as Mum's recipe in the book."

"Oh, you write cookery books then, Mrs Marks?" inquired Middleton.

"There's a publisher in Leeds waiting for me to complete my recipes and I have a deadline to …" Charlotte paused and started to weep again. "My God," she sobbed. "What have I said? How could I … think of me when he's … he's … dead … Oh my God, what would our mum and dad think of this?"

"We'll contact them, Charlotte, if you wish?"

"No, they're no longer living," Charlotte was looking straight at the woman detective. "It's just that they always thought he'd get himself into trouble."

"Did Matthew not get on with your parents?" asked Wolfe.

"Dad disowned him many years ago, couldn't cope with the drink and drugs, and when Matt came up on the lottery that very nearly pushed Dad over the edge. He refused to accept the money Matthew sent him following the win, in fact, Dad even wrote to Camelot demanding that they hold on to the money until he proved he could stay clean. Dad died of a heart attack soon after, Mum died last year, brain tumour but they both thought Matthew would end up overdosing or something, they wouldn't be surprised at all."

"Charlotte," said Wolfe a little concerned that the reality of the Matthew's death, although not official, was not connected to a drugs overdose. "We do not believe that your brother died of a drugs overdose." He let silence dominate the air for a couple of seconds. "His death is suspicious; we are convinced that he was unlawfully killed."

"You mean, murdered, don't you? But who would do that, Matthew didn't have enemies? He was very likeable; I mean, his drug addiction and even the heavy drinking just made him more likeable, he didn't get violent or abusive, on or off drugs, he wasn't your typical junkie, he was just irresponsible, always smiling, he thought the whole world was cool, no one was bad, just full of 'people who were too uptight', as he put it."

"Did he tell anyone, other than family, about the lottery win?"

"Not that I know of. In fact, it was the responsibility of the win that pushed him into rehab, he wanted to use the money to set up his own housing charity, he has … there is still more than £450,000 in the bank, I know because I checked last week. Having not heard from him for a while, I became a bit suspicious and checked the account, no withdrawals for more than a week and the last one was fifty quid, hardly enough for a single hit."

"With your permission, we'll check the account."

"No problem," she said and gave further details to Middleton.

"Okay, Charlotte, can you think of anyone or any reason why Matthew would come to harm?"

"No, Inspector, I can't."

"Did he have a job?"

"Yes, until three or four months ago, he was working as a driver, a chauffeur sometimes I think."

"Who was his employer?"

"I don't know … I'm not being very helpful, am I?" Charlotte looked and sounded embarrassed.

"Is it that you can't remember or that he just didn't tell you?" enquired Wolfe softly.

"I did ask … he just avoided telling me, there always seemed to be something else he wanted to talk to me about. He avoided telling me … maybe on purpose, I don't know." Charlotte was now even more embarrassed and her cheeks began to redden.

"That's okay, Charlotte," consoled Wolfe. "I avoided telling my girlfriend what I did for a living until the day I was the responding officer to a 999 call and arrived at the bank next to her father's restaurant in full uniform whilst she was waiting at tables. She saw me, went bonkers, we got married six months later."

Charlotte smiled, "Thanks … you didn't have to tell me that … but you did."

As she leaned forward to take hold of her cup of tea, Middleton looked at Wolfe over her and mouthed, 'ohhhh,' followed with a sarcastic smile.

Wolfe ignored the jibe but did feel a sudden pull of attraction towards Charlotte Marks, a feeling he hadn't felt in a long time, but then, once again, guilt hit him like a punch to the midriff. He had to put closure between Maria and himself, life, his life had to continue. Suddenly, he noticed that Middleton and Charlotte were staring at him.

"Errr, Charlotte," he said.

"Please call me Charley, that's what everyone else calls me," she announced in a sweet almost childlike manner.

"Okay Charley," said Wolfe in a boyish tone.

"What about you Inspector," she asked, "what is your first name ... if you don't mind me asking?"

"Jaxon, spelt J.A.X.O.N ... but most call me Jac ... J.A.C."

"How unusual, but all the same interesting," she mused turning away from him whilst swivelling her hips towards him.

Later, DC Middleton couldn't stop herself from poking fun at him during their drive back to HQ.

"Wow, she's got the hots for you Jac spelt J.A.C."

"Charley," he said quietly composing himself. "Why did your brother have a job, surely, he didn't need to work?"

"Matt said he worked because he enjoyed driving, and that driving gave him responsibility and a reason not to succumb to the temptations of idleness that could lead to drugs and alcohol. Matthew wouldn't drive under the influence. In fact, I remember a couple of months ago, he was sat here with me when he took a phone call and he said, without any sense of embarrassment, that he 'wouldn't be able to drive for a least three days because he was already high on dope, and that he intended going on a bender that evening and God only knows where he'd end up come tomorrow'. You see, Jac, Matt knew he had a drug problem but thanks to rehab, he seemed, to me, at least, that he could control it."

"Charley, the scars on his arms clearly indicate main line drug use," said Wolfe in raised authoritative voice.

"He told me he was off heroin last summer when he was discharged from rehab," Charley replied in a judgemental tone.

"Okay ... I accept Matthew was a reformed addict ... to a certain degree," Wolfe raised his right hand to stop any potential argument. "Do you know who his supplier, his dealer was, Charley?"

"No, I don't for certain but a couple of times I did overhear conversations he was having with someone about collecting a ... wad? Which I assumed to be cannabis and not heroin, he was quite open about it, never embarrassed that I might be listening."

"Did you ever hear a name mentioned?" asked Wolfe with more impatience and growing frustration.

"I'm trying to remember, Inspector ... I know it's important ... I've got it ... Toots!!" she announced. "As in Toots and the Maytalls, a 1970s' reggae band from Jamaica."

Wolfe frowned, twice within an hour that name had been mentioned, just coincidence? He looked at Middleton, she was writing the name down in her notebook. What was bothering Wolfe most though was the fact that Charlotte Marks knew of Toots and the Maytalls. Once again, silence was the loudness that broke his thought.

"Charley ... err, Mrs Marks, I think we've finished with our questions, for today. We've arranged for a bereavement councillor to visit you here and I believe, she may be waiting outside."

Middleton took the hint, stood up and left the room walking towards the front door.

"I'll be okay, Inspector, no need for a councillor, but thanks."

"I can't insist that you talk with our councillor but, at least, meet her and take contact details … please?"

"Okay," conceded Charley.

After the bereavement councillor had been introduced, the two detectives left the house. Wolfe realised that in his thoughts, he was beginning to feel empathy towards Charlotte Marks, he knew what emotions she was going through now and where those emotions might take her. He hoped she was stronger than him.

"Women cope better with bereavement than men, don't they, Pam?" questioned Wolfe as they drove away from the house.

"I'm sure we all cope differently with loss whether men or women," as she glanced at him from the driver's seat. "Let's give her closure, because that's what she'll need more than anything, we must find out what happened to her brother!"

"Yep, you're right … head for Oakwood, I want you to meet an old friend of mine."

Chapter 6

Henry 'Toots' Mateland lived in a leafy suburb of Leeds that overlooked the public parkland area of Roundhay around which the Victorians built houses that offered those who could afford it, the ability to live and indulge in their favourite pastime of walking. Roundhay Park was and, still is, one such area where the Victorian public could walk at ease through park and gardens, with its naturally elevated position above the congested stifling atmosphere of Leeds City Centre allowing the privileged few a taste of clean unpolluted air. The contrast in air quality is much less pronounced nowadays, however, property ownership in this suburb of Leeds is still high on the desirability scale. Roundhay Park is, after all, a local amenity and, above all, a local treasure.

The address given to Wolfe by PC Mills was Oakwood Road which overlooked the periphery of the Park. The house was one dwelling at the end of a Victorian terrace, sturdy and strong, an epitaph to a bygone, never to be forgotten, generation.

"Bloody hell, he's come up in the world," admired Wolfe as Middleton drove the car onto the driveway of a property named and numbered 5446 Oakwood Road.

"No, I don't believe it … the house number…the significance of Mills text didn't register but……wow". exclaimed Wolfe.

"It's just the house number … part of the postal address, surely," said Middleton.

"Oh, yee of little knowledge, it's the number of the house, yes, but it's also the title of a Toots and the Maytalls song … '5446, that's My Number.' When I first heard the song I thought it was a reference to the slave trade when African slaves were given numbers rather than names because it was easier for slave traders to identify them, but in actual fact it's Toot's Hibbert's inmate number when he was jailed for petty crime as a youngster."

"Who's Toot's Hibbert?"

"Oh dear," sighed Wolfe … "He's the leader of the band … Toots and the Maytalls."

"I see … you learn something new every day," replied Middleton sounding indifferent but not really meaning to. The imparted knowledge had little to do with the reason they had entered the driveway of this property. Middleton parked the unmarked police saloon in front of the house, as she and Wolfe exited the vehicle, the front door to the house opened.

"You'll need a search warrant to get any closer, so unless you've got one, you can both …" announced a large black Caribbean man stood where the entrance door used to fill the space. Suddenly, he was silenced and began to walk slowly down the stone steps from the elevated entrance. At drive level, he stopped and opened his long almost endless arms.

"Jakssann … Wolfmarnn, it's a pleasure to see you, old boy," he said in a pronounced Jamaican accent with obvious English gentry overtones.

Wolfe and Mateland embraced like long lost brothers. As they broke, Wolfe spoke first, he thought he saw the beginnings of a tear in the big man's eyes.

"Looking good, Toots," said Wolfe as he stood back.

"All the better for seeing you, boss."

"I never got the chance to thank you for attending Maria's funeral."

"She was a beautiful creature, a wouman of style and sof…isti…cashan," he stated in his forced Jamacian twang perfect in every way … well, except for her choice in men … but then no one's that perfect." At this, Toots began to sob, this strong colossus was now shaking with emotion.

"Yes, you're quite right, no taste in men at all … I miss her so much … although I see her every day in here," Wolfe tapped his temple.

"Apologies for not being in touch, big man," he continued.

Sniffing back the tears, Toots replied, "Apology accepted, old boy."

"Stop calling me old, I'm younger than you, ya stupid sod."

At this, Toots stood back, took a deep breath.

"Not that stupid! Look at this place I have here, all bought and paid for … and legit as well. Hey, where I my manners? Come in let me show you around."

"But we don't have warrants," replied Middleton, in a tone that didn't hide her sarcasm.

"Wow! She's a cute one, Jac, better watch ya step with her." He turned and motioned to Wolfe to follow him into the house. "Your ass…is…tarnt can make tea, I assume?"

"Oh yes, she makes a good brew." Wolfe looked over his shoulder, Middleton was miming words at Wolfe but the only word he took any notice of was 'off'.

"The house number Toots? That's something else man."

"Yeah, I drove passed here a couple a year's back, saw them putting up the sale sign, by the end of that same day the sign came down. I just had to buy it Jac. The day we moved in I put a ghetto blaster on the top step here and played 5446 on replay for about an hour."

"That must have made an impression on the neighbours."

"Oh yes," Toot's enjoying the memory, "but we're all friends now," he finished with a loud laugh as the pair stepped over the threshold.

The hall, immaculately decorated in a modern minimalist style, was wide enough to position a leather sofa against one wall, with a small coffee table in front, without encroaching on the natural corridor or impeding access to the wide ornate staircase. Wall mounted up lighters emphasised the impressive ceiling height. Catalogues on the coffee table re-affirmed the business being undertaken inside; Toots Mateland was a travel agent. Exotic white sand beaches featured on the front covers of the brochures.

"This way, sir and madam," announced Toots as he ushered them through an open door to the right of the hall. "Please take a seat … can I get drinks for you both … tea, perhaps? No alcohol whilst on duty, I assume."

"Tea, milk, no sugar for me," said Wolfe sitting.

"Me too," huffed Middleton as she also sat down in a modern leather office chair, it immediately felt comfortable.

An array of demountable displays, again depicting long idyllic secluded beaches framed with Palm tree foregrounds stretched up from individual floor mounted bases, these covered one side of the large room, a grand antique desk behind which was parked a leather office chair similar to the ones in front finished off the colonial appearance. The desk only served to emphasise the wide expanse of the tall Victorian bay window, through which could be seen the driveway where Middleton had parked the standard issue Mondeo, it looked lost, out of place, without purpose.

Toots moved and manoeuvred his meaty frame into the chair on the opposite side of the desk, as he sat, he reached for the phone on the desk.

"Tesa, I have two guests with me. Can you bring in two teas and a glass of water for me, please? Thank you." Replacing the handset, Middleton thought she saw him wink at her. "Now then, officers, what can I do for you?"

Wolfe was first to speak, "Quite an impressive setup you have here, Toots."

"Tourism is big business, especially the Caribbean, set this little venture up a few years ago. I specialise in holidays to suit all, business is booming, man."

"All legit and above board, I assume?"

"Of course, ABTA registered," he replied as he pointed to a framed certificate on his desk.

"Everything in here looks like it's demountable … ya know, for a quick get away!" Middleton interjected continuing her sarcastic tone.

Ignoring the comment, Toots replied in his best English accent, "Seems we may have got off on the wrong foot, detective …?" as he smiled at her.

She responded, "Middleton, DC Middleton."

"Ahh … so good they named you twice," Toots held out his hand. The invitation appealed to Middleton and with a smile she reached across the desk to shake his hand. She was surprised at the warmth of the greeting and the controlled strength of the large Jamaican.

"You're right, of course, detective, every Saturday evening, I take down the displays and store them. This room doubles up as a cinema for friends and family at the weekends, new James Bond movie this week."

"How is your mum, Toots?" Wolfe said as he remembered the widowed Jamaican immigrant, he first met more than fifteen years ago.

"The old girl's doing fine, lives in the apartment on the second floor," replied Toots raising his index finger to point at the ceiling. "Not at home at the moment, out with the 'Derby and Joan Club' on the Park, afternoon Ti Chi they call it, oldies make shapes in the open air is what it looks like to me … fit as a bloody fiddle … at 78! She'll outlive me."

"This is a large place for just you and mum, Toots."

"Not just me and her. I have a partner, and she has two kids, a boy and a girl."

"You've settled down, my friend. Congratulations, I'm pleased for you."

"Yeah, I needed it, she's a lovely lady and the kids … they're the best."

A knock on the door interrupted their discussion.

"Come in, Tesa," responded Toots.

A dark skinned stunningly attractive young woman entered the room carrying a tray of drinks. As she placed the tray in the middle of the desk, Toots announced, "Tesa is my partner's daughter. Tesa, I'd like to introduce you to Detective Constable Middleton and Detective Inspector Jaxon Wolfe from the West Yorkshire Police Force."

Wolfe stood hand extended towards the young woman, his face almost split in half by the smile. They shook hands, she very gently, he too harsh, he thought.

"Pleased to meet you, Tesa."

Middleton stood and reached over brushing away Wolfe's contact.

"Pam Middleton, Tesa ... how are you?"

"Oh, I'm very well, indeed," she replied in solid middle England accent that contrasted with her complexion but in a way made her even more appealing to the eye if that was possible.

"Are you here to book a holiday?"

"I don't think so, Tesa," said Toots before either could reply.

"Oh, I see ... well, I'll leave you to discuss your business with Henry." And with that, she turned and left the room, watched by all three.

Wolfe and Middleton resumed their seated positions; Wolfe decided now was the right opportunity.

"Toots, does the name Matthew Brookes mean anything to you?"

"Wow, straight to the point, Inspector, just like old times ... yes, the name Matthew Brookes is known to me ... you wouldn't be asking me if you didn't think I knew him, now, would you?"

"When did you last see him?" Middleton asked boldly.

"Three weeks ago today, to be exact," Toots looked directly at Middleton to emphasise the exactness of his statement.

Wolfe jumped straight in, "When is he due to fly out?"

"Tuesday ... early morning Leeds Bradford to Amsterdam then onto Princetown," his matter of fact reply took both detectives by surprise. "He's a regular customer but is treated the same as all my clients, a one-week reminder is sent and a final reminder three days ago, copied to me automatically, I got that message this morning along with four more passengers on the same flight."

"Mr Brookes was overheard asking you for a wad two weeks ago."

"Ah and you think, because of my previous dealings with class C drugs, that I'm supplying him dope." Then silence with a stare that could melt concrete.

"Well, are you?" said Middleton a second or two later.

"No ... and I'll tell you why: First – I don't deal any more, haven't done for over two years. Second – Matt Brookes goes to Jamaica for a fix and I arrange with my brothers over there to have a wad ready for him when he arrives. Third – Matt Brookes is loaded, he pays cash and is able to purchase the best stuff, he is discrete and only consumes, and he doesn't deal because he doesn't need the money."

"Matthew Brookes won't be catching that flight next week ... he was found dead yesterday morning."

Henry Mateland stared in disbelief at Wolfe, silence engulfed the room, Wolfe waited for a response ... eventually it came.

"That is shocking ... very sad news ... my God he's only thirty years old." Then a sudden realisation hit Mateland light a bolt of lightning.

"Thanks to you, Jac, I know enough about police work to realise that you're here talking to me because his death is suspicious, and you've found or been told that there's a link between Matt and me, so ask your questions ... I'll answer."

"How would you describe Mr Brooke's behaviour the last time you saw him?"

"He was excited, ready for two weeks in the sun. Chillin' in the Caribbean was his favourite pastime."

"Normal behaviour for him, would you say?" inquired Wolfe.

"Yes … but now I think about it, there was one comment he made … let me get this right … he said he was going to quit his job and the holiday would help him decide what to do next. 'Was the driving getting too stressful,' I said. 'No,' he said, 'I just don't want to work for that outfit anymore.'"

"What do you think he meant by that?"

"I took it to mean that he'd been asked to do more driving and, perhaps, he thought it was excessive … I'm not sure what I thought really."

"What sort of driver was he?" asked Middleton.

"Flash car driver mainly, more a chauffeur, I suppose … I didn't really ask. What I can tell you is that he turned up here now and again in some very expensive machinery, Ferrari's, Maserati's, Range Rovers and a Roller once … one of those huge two door things, it looked brand new to me."

"Don't suppose he said who …"

Toots shock his head without waiting for Wolfe to finish his question.

"And I never asked," he said.

"Sounds like his employer … imported cars," announced Middleton.

"You know … that thought crossed my mind and I mentioned it to his sister … Charlotte … Charley … thinking I could invest because I'd heard it was a lucrative business importing luxury motors. That's when she told me that he didn't need to work at all, he was a very wealthy man and that he only worked to stop getting bored. Odd thing though … she always paid … with her credit card … whilst he sat next to her."

"So, you've met his sister then?" asked Wolfe his eyes wide.

"Wow … Wolfe man … she obviously made an impression on you!"

Middleton couldn't help but smile.

"Yeah, yeah, yeah," responded Wolfe wishing to brush over Toot's remark. "Did she ever question how much he was spending?"

"No, never. In fact, she insisted I organise a chauffeur driven private hire for the whole of his stay with a mobile contactable driver … and that wasn't cheap."

"She was keeping tabs on him then," said Middleton.

"Well, now you mention it, I suppose, she was … yes, but he's a recovering addict and I just thought she wanted to look after him, protect him from falling back into harder drugs."

"So, his addiction wasn't a secret then?"

"Of course, not, they both talked openly about it, maybe it was his way of controlling it, after rehab … ya know, people deal with addiction in different ways, you certainly couldn't say he was in denial."

"Do you think he might have relapsed and gone back to heroin?"

"I would say that was highly unlikely. He seemed to me to be very happy. I can tell you from experience he wasn't high on anything last time he was in here … just tired … in need of some R and R is all."

A pause in the conversation allowed Wolfe to ask, "How often did he go to the Caribbean?"

"You took ya time getting to that question."

"Don't get clever, Toots … just answer the question," retorted Wolfe.

"If he was bringing stuff back and selling it, I'd know. I still have contacts and word would have got to me … knowledge keeps me safe."

"Toots, do this properly ... answer the question ... not what you think is implied by the question."

Toots nodded more in respect than deference. "He travels with my company twice a year, each time he has spent a month in the Caribbean around February and September."

"What if you didn't know he was importing ... what if your contacts weren't aware, Toots?" Wolfe said with a hint of condescension.

"The price on the street would go down, Wolfe man, you know that," said Toots defiantly.

"Could he be distributing somewhere else ... where you don't have contacts?"

"Maybe, but that's dangerous ... and I don't believe he's tough enough to get involved in a turf war ... and to my knowledge, there's nothing shaking in Yorkshire."

Middleton jumped in, "What about London?"

"Oh dear ... you're just out of uniform, aren't you, Detective Middleton?"

"Absolute suicide," interjected Wolfe trying to save her embarrassment.

"London is sewn up tighter than a ducks butt at 50 fathoms, he would be hung, drawn and quartered ... his dismembered body left in bags outside Scotland Yard, they wouldn't care," announced Toots.

"Okay, Toots ... I'm going to ask a favour."

"Yes!"

"You don't know what the question is?"

"Yes, I do ... will I go to the airport to see if anyone checks in as Matt Brookes?"

"You got it."

"We can't trust him," announced Middleton.

"Actually, I'd trust him with my life ... and besides, a police officer would stand out like sore thumb."

"I'll arrange a surprise courier service to the airport for someone on the same flight, with me as driver. Alright, Jac?"

"Perfect."

DI Wolfe and DC Middleton stood, and both shook hands with Henry Mateland. Wolfe turned before leaving the room. "Oh, just one more question, Toots."

Mateland and Wolfe locked eyes. "Well, one more it is, old boy."

"Did Alfred Marks owe you money?"

"Not that I'm aware of Jac."

"So, you knew him then?"

"Oh yes and if anything, I owed him money." At that, Henry Mateland flashed his left wrist at Wolfe on which was strapped a very elegant gold watch. "I bought numerous pieces of jewellery from Alfie over the years, this watch was the last item I bought from him and Clare, my partner was given a gold necklace on loan ... see if she liked it before buying it. Two days later, I went back to his shop to buy it and it was closed. I found out a couple of days after that he'd killed himself ... very sad." He continued, "Jac, come round on Saturday evening, I'll mix up a few Jamaican cocktails." He said with a wink, "Talk over old times and watch a movie?"

"Very kind of you, Toots, but I promised Izzy I'd take her for a meal on Saturday night," replied Wolfe trying not to sound like he was lying.

"How old is Isabella now?"

"17 going on 30 ... if you know what I mean."

"Yeah I think so difficult to live with but impossible to live without, I'll bet?" said Toots as he patted Wolfe on the back whilst exiting the house.

"Keep in touch, Toots, call me Tuesday when you return from the airport."

"Sure thing, Jac!"

As soon as Middleton started the car, and began manoeuvring the vehicle out of the drive and onto Oakwood Road she said,

"Surely, you don't trust him to help us, for all we know, he might be involved in Brooke's death?"

"He's solid, Pam, as I said," Wolfe explained in a calm but assertive tone. "However," he continued. "I want you and Halford overseeing the check-in desks and passport control at the airport, but Toots mustn't know you're there, I need him to believe we trust him."

"Oh, I see ... so all that mates stuff in there was phoney?"

"No, not at all. I would trust him with my life! But we have to cover all bases so you will be behind the scenes checking live CCTV ... because he'll clock you no matter what disguise you tried! Pete will be out front at passport control acting like airport security."

Chapter 7

Saturday morning, Wolfe and his daughter ate bacon sandwiches, and were talking about what they were going to do for the rest of the day. Izzy said she would go to Leeds shopping with a couple of friends, Wolfe would do the general shopping then meet a couple of his friends that afternoon in The Unicorn. They agreed to call each other early evening and decide in which restaurant they would eat, however, that was all the arrangements turned out to be, just arrangements. Late morning, Wolfe answered a phone call.

"Arnold."

"Jac, I have some news regarding our mutual friend."

"Matthew Brookes, you mean … age 31 … once again, Doc, you were right on the money there," praised Wolfe.

"Mmm … that's as maybe, I can confirm that he was definitely murdered and that a very amateurish attempt was made to cover it up with drug use."

"Wow, that obvious?"

"Not initially, but when I got the body back to the lab, I ran several toxicology checks on samples of his blood, there was heroin in his system but it hadn't travelled more than a foot up his arm –"

"He was dead before he injected," interrupted Wolfe.

"Exactly … heart had stopped functioning before the injection and therefore, the only conclusion … third party involvement."

"So, any idea on what actually killed him?"

"Well, yes … but pure supposition at this stage. However, after the autopsy on Monday morning, I'll be very surprised if I can't confirm a heart attack brought on by severe trauma." Higgins paused. "Remember the puncture wound to the small of his back?"

"Yeah, I remember you pointing that out."

"Well, it turns out there were two, one either side, my guess is punctured kidneys brought on the attack; this young man suffered, Jac … suffered needlessly –"

"Hang on a second, Arnold," interrupted Wolfe. "What do you mean 'suffered needlessly'?"

"I checked the concentration of heroin in his system with the equipment in the lab and subject to independent checks, I can tell you that the concentration of heroin in his arm, was so high that it would have killed him almost as soon as it hit his heart. That's what I mean about amateurish, why kill him and then inject him with such a high concentration of narcotic?"

"Were both his kidneys punctured?" asked Wolfe.

"Yes, I scanned several X rays and they show that each wound was deep, one of them deep enough to puncture right through his left kidney … very traumatic."

"Intentional, do you think?"

There was suddenly silence; Wolfe had time to move his phone in front of him to check if he was still connected.

"That's it …" came the response eventually. "That's what was concerning me, was it amateurism or something else?"

"Make sense, Arnold … I'm getting a little confused."

"Okay, okay … calling you and speaking out loud rather than just thinking or even talking to myself has added another theory that just might work."

"Spit it out, Arnold," replied Wolfe, sounding more impatient than he had intended.

"Okay … the two puncture wounds! The diameters of the holes where they break the skin are much smaller than you would expect to find from a needle attached to a surgical syringe, the holes aren't much larger in size than human hair, it was the dried blood and bruising that caught my eye."

"Acupuncture needles, perhaps," stated Wolfe.

"No, not acupuncture, the wounds go much deeper than you'd expect from acupuncture … the cold war in the '60s and '70s … spies and all that … a weapon called a spear was the favourite tool of many an assassin. The spear was made of high tensile steal, around 150mm long, one end bent back on itself to form a ring and worn by the assassin over the middle finger, so that with a clenched fist, the weapon would stand proud … outward."

"I've never heard of such a weapon."

"Lethal at close quarters … swift and devastating when used by an expert. Puncture through clothing without obvious trace, human muscle and organs could not offer any resistance to the impact of such a weapon. However, the effectiveness is only guaranteed by the expertise in its use, in short, the assailant would have to know where best upon the body to strike with such an instrument."

"You're talking about a hitman," replied Wolfe.

"Yes, possibly … certainly someone who knew how to use a spear."

The two men paused their conversation to muse a short while, it was Wolfe who broke the silence.

"So, we need to find out more about Matthew Brookes, was he murdered due to something he knew, someone he knew or had he information that somebody wanted." Wolfe paused in thought then continued,
"I think another meet with his sister might be in order. Thanks for the information, Arnold, I'll see you Monday. I assume, I'm invited to attend the autopsy?"

"Of course, Jac, you are more than welcome, see you Monday."

Higgins was about to hang up when Wolfe said,

"Yesterday … on the moor … Winker Watson asked me if I thought it might be the work of a hitman. I said I doubt it … there'll be no living with him now."

"He was just guessing, Jac. Still, you're right; he'll be prancing around like a rooster when he finds out."

An hour later, Wolfe was once again, standing outside the house on Panorama Drive, Carlton where Charlotte Marks lived. The door opened before he could ring the bell and a well-built buxom woman stood in the opening like a nightclub bouncer.

"Can I help you?" she said.

"Yes, I'm Detective Inspector Wolfe from the West Yorkshire Police Force, I've called unannounced but I was hoping to talk to Charlotte Marks if that is possible."

"Would you mind waiting here, Detective Inspector? I'll see if Mrs Marks can see you," she replied as she walked back into the house, leaving the door open.

Unlike his last visit, Wolfe was able to take in the full expanse of the frontage of this property whilst waiting and in doing so, he had to step back from the porch.

"Wow, this is one big house," he said to himself, not realising he'd been overheard.

"Yes, it is, Inspector," said Charlotte Marks. She was standing in the porch wearing a figure hugging white printed T-shirt over skinny jeans with a pair of high-heeled pixie boots that emphasised her long slender legs. The sheen on her long brown hair reflected the low sunlight and framed her face; big green eyes and long lashes, high cheekbones and a light tan completed the appearance.

'Wow again,' but this time he just thought it.

"Mrs Marks," he stuttered slightly, whilst trying not to stare. "Were you on your way out? I didn't mean to interrupt your day."

"No, it's okay, Inspector, please come in."

Wolfe followed Charlotte into the house then through the hall and into the lounge, trying not to focus on the perfect symmetry of her backside as her hips worked up and down, her back straight, shoulders high and her head perfectly positioned, a picture of pure elegance.

"Please take a seat, Inspector," she turned in front of the sofa they had sat on yesterday.

"Mrs Marks …" said Wolfe as he sat.

"Charley please, Inspector, or at least Charlotte. Have you forgotten already? I made the same comment yesterday?"

"No … errr … Charley … I didn't forget, but please don't take this the wrong way when I say … you were very concerned about your brothers demise yesterday but you don't seem as concerned today."

"I am … I mean, I was very close to my brother." She sat down next to Wolfe. "And that's why I won't let myself get emotional like yesterday, Inspector. If he saw me crying as I did, he would tell me off, tell me to grow up, grow a backbone, people come people go, life starts life stops, get over it! My brother was a lovely man but he had my mum and dad's attitude to life … deal with it … cause if you don't, life will deal with you."

Wolfe thought for a few moments trying to work out whether this was just another phase in Charlotte's reaction to her brother's death or a hard arse attitude carried down from her parents.

"Charlotte, I'm here to ask a few more questions. These are off the record and you don't have to answer them, but I will have to ask them at some point in our investigation, and I'd rather ask them now."

"That's okay, Inspector. oh sorry, I can't keep calling you Inspector, it's too official and besides, you don't look much like a policeman today … dressed in civvies … do they still say that in the police force?"

"Yes … they do! But it tends to relate to uniformed officers. But you're right, jeans and an open neck shirt is … are, I suppose, my civvies." Wolfe replied feeling relaxed. "Jac as I mentioned yesterday is fine with me."

'This woman's now got me acting like a besotted school boy,' he thought as his pulse began to race. *'I haven't felt like this since I first met …'*

"Something wrong, Jac?" asked Charlotte.

"No ... sorry Mrs errmm ... Charlotte."

"Is my name that easy to forget, Jac?"

"No, no ... it's just I haven't been so readily open like this with anyone for a long time, it's unusual and it feels strange ... almost alien."

"Well, Jac ... can I get you a drink? It might help you relax and after all, you're off duty!"

"Yes, Charlotte, I'm off duty but I'm driving, therefore, I'm going to have to –"

"Jac," Charlotte interrupted. "You don't strike me as the kind of man that would sit and watch a girl drink on her own ..."

"Okay, I'll have what you're having," Wolfe replied with exasperation, he'd had enough of this banter and needed to get to the purpose of his visit.

Charlotte stood and whilst walking out of the room, she said, "I'll be back in a minute then you can start your interrogation."

"No, I'm not interrogating you ..."

She didn't respond, she'd left the room smiling to herself.

Wolfe stood then sauntered around the room looking at the photos dotted around, once again, as yesterday, his attention focused on one particular photograph, that of the five men, four dressed in combat fatigues and one spoiling the composition in the foreground dressed informally. When Charlotte returned, he was, once again, seated on the sofa studying intensely the framed photo removed from the shelf.

"Martinis," she announced. "The perfect drink for a Saturday late morning, wouldn't you say, Jac?"

The drinks were put on the coffee table and Charlotte sat down on the sofa sitting upright, no hint of a slouch. Wolfe adjusted his seating position lifting himself up so their eyes were level.

"What is so intriguing about that photo?"

"Oh sorry," apologised Wolfe pathetically. "I hope you don't mind me looking at it ... I'd better put it back."

As he tried to stand, Charlotte put her hand on his upper arm. He sat back whilst looking at her hand gently resting on his arm then his gaze lifted to stare into her eyes, green, appealing, deep and for a split second, he felt that he could completely disappear into them.

"That photo belongs to my partner, Paul." She lent in so close to Wolfe that he could feel her breast pressed against his arm as she pushed the photo away to the far side of the coffee table.

A distracted Wolfe not thinking just wanted to keep asking questions, "What was the reason for the photo?" he asked in a blubbering tone and no sooner had the words left his mouth he felt stupid and embarrassed.

Charlotte now distracted by Wolfe's question averted her gaze from him back to the photo.

"Oh ... err, Paul told me that it was a celebratory photo, just before they went to somewhere in Europe, something to do with helping to re-build a library I think after the end of a civil war, but I'm not quite sure." Charlotte replied then added, "I could call him if you like?"

"No, that won't be necessary," Wolfe ignored the framed photo on the coffee table and decided to continue asking questions about Matthew Brookes. First, he lifted the Martini to his mouth and took a small drink, it helped to calm his blushing.

"Very nice, Charley."

"Oh, thank you," she said as she twisted a little closer to Wolfe, "for the compliment on the drink and for calling me Charley that feels much better."

"Was your brother in any trouble that you were aware of?"

"What do you mean by … trouble?"

"Matthew has previous for selling drugs, albeit the last such recorded offence was over five years ago; he also had a drug habit and, as I'm sure you are aware, one fuels the other. He must have mixed with a few characters that maybe you considered to be … shall we say, unsavoury or unscrupulous."

"Well, I wouldn't know, he didn't confide everything in me."

"Charley, you controlled his finances, you must have, formed an opinion, let alone made sure you met most of his contacts."

"Most of his contacts … yes, but not all."

"Charlotte Marks, don't treat me like a fool. Toots Mateland told me you were there every time Matthew paid for a flight to Jamaica and you had to authorise his expenditure."

"Yes, I am … the trustee of his money," Charlotte's gaze dipped to the floor. "It was his money not mine but I promised my mum before she died that I would make sure his habit didn't run away with him … and I think I've failed, I let my brother and my mother down."

"No, Charley, you didn't fail anyone," as soon as he said it, he regretted it.

"Oh, my God … he was killed, you think he was murdered … why … he wouldn't hurt anyone … he was a very gentle man … weak, perhaps … but he wouldn't hurt a fly."

"We can't officially confirm this but we are increasingly coming to the conclusion that yes, he was murdered."

"Oh no … No! Why … why?" Charlotte covered her face with her hands and leaned into Wolfe.

He instinctively wrapped his arm around her and allowed her to rest her head on his shoulder for a few seconds before asking,
"Have you checked Matthews' account recently?"

She lifted her head, sat up, reached for her glass and lifted it to her mouth. She took a long sip, then said, "Yes, I checked his account yesterday after you and your colleague had gone. Then, once again, this morning and it's all as expected, Jac. I'm the only one with access to the account, Matthew can't, couldn't withdraw money from it. He got an allowance based on the interest generated from the capital."

"You said yesterday that this pot of money came from a lottery win?" asked Wolfe as he reached for his drink.

"Yes, that's right, half a million or thereabouts. He bought tickets twice a week up to winning … stopped buying tickets after that. He went into rehab less than a month after winning the money."

"How come you were looking after the money for him?"

"You think I'm manipulating him for my own benefits, don't you, Jac?"

"I have to ask the question, Charley, we have to consider all options."

"So, I'm now a suspect," said Charlotte in disgust.

"I have to ask, it's a process of elimination made more relevant now that I know how much money your brother had in the bank."

"Excuse me, Inspector, I'll be back in a minute," Charlotte wasn't trying to hide her anger as she stood up and left the room.

Wolfe felt a little bemused, the line of questioning was to him fairly obvious and needed to be explored. Charlotte returned in less than a minute carrying a red folder which she handed, almost threw at him.

"There you are, DI Wolfe, in that folder is a copy of the winning ticket a list of the pay-outs for that draw, letters signed by Matthew that gave me power of attorney over his financial affairs, letters to and from the tax office, and bank statements." Charlotte paused.

"If I didn't raise the query now, I would –"
"I thought you were off duty, Jac," she interrupted.
"Yes, I am but …"
"Sorry, Jac. I know you have to ask awkward questions and now I realise that a Detective is never 'off duty'."

"How did this arrangement happen?" asked Wolfe as he thumbed through the folder.

"I was the first-person Matthew contacted after he realised he'd got a winning ticket, even before contacting Camelot. At first, he didn't want the money, he'd just come down from a high and saw the winnings as temptation, he didn't want to go back to heroin dependency. The capital gives him" she paused, "sorry … gave him almost £2,000 a month, he got this allowance as a standing order of £1,500 per month and if he required more money, he would ask me, and …"

"Did you ever refuse him additional funds?"

"Yes, once or twice … because when he asked, he was either drunk or high on weed. When he was sober, I asked if he still wanted the money but he couldn't remember asking, let alone what he wanted the extra money for."

"So, when he was serious about wanting extra money, you didn't complain?"

"No … as I said, it was his money."

There was silence for a moment or two whilst Wolfe thought about what to ask next.

"Why did he find it necessary to work, to have a full-time job? After all, it appears to me he didn't really need the money," he asked.

"To pay the rent on his apartment in Leeds and because he didn't want to be alone, he felt more confident, more in control if he had responsibility."

"Who did he work for?"

Again, silence whilst Charlotte considered her response.

"For the past couple of years or so, he worked for a courier firm." She paused. Wolfe didn't interrupt he could see she was concentrating and he didn't want to break her train of thought.

"I don't know the name … he may have told me but I can't remember and before that, he worked for a building company, err … Hennersy, I think they were called."

"That's very helpful; we'll contact Hennersy on Monday."

"But what will 'they' be able to tell you about Matthew's death, you think they had something to do with it?"

"We need to build up a profile of Matthew's habits and routines, and no better place to start than his work colleagues," concluded Wolfe. "Now can I ask one further question? Then I'll go and let you get on with your weekend."

"Oh dear, no … my weekend hasn't got much going for it at all … I'm on my own for most of today and most of tomorrow … I'm supposed to be working on the recipes for my book but all I can think about is poor Matthew … he was a wonderful brother, a lovely man … all I've got planned for the weekend is to get drunk and look at photos of Matt."

"Is there no one to keep you company?"

Charlotte replied with a sigh, "My daughter left earlier with the nanny to go shopping into Leeds for a present for her friend's birthday party, then she's going to the party, won't be home until the evening and my partner is on business in Bristol and London." She looked suddenly vulnerable, almost pathetic, thought Wolfe, but he also realised that although this was an unofficial interview, reference might have to be made of this meeting in court if they were to convict a perpetrator as a result of these discussions, any reliance on her statements here today would refer to her state of mind at the time, and alcohol fuelled conversations could and would always be challenged in court. Therefore, he mused to himself she'll have to be interviewed formally at another time … so he made a decision.

"Charlotte," he asked. "I'm feeling a little hungry and occasionally, at the weekend, I take Saturday lunch at the Grumpy Olde Man wine bar on The Grove and today is one of those occasions … would you care to join me?"

Suddenly, her eyes lit up like diamonds. "That would be wonderful, yes, I'd love to join you, just allow me a minute to check my makeup and get my coat."

Waiting in the car outside the house, Wolfe wondered what the hell he was doing, he was about to embark on a social gathering in a public place with a suspect in a murder enquiry. Although that wasn't really the reason for his concern, more the fact that he felt he was cheating on his wife by merely meeting with another woman. "Don't be so bloody pathetic, Wolfe," he said to himself as Charlotte emerged from the house wearing a figure-hugging leather bomber jacket over the white T shirt, skinny jeans and high heels. She locked the door and strolled over to Wolfe's roadster like a model working a catwalk. Wolfe just stared. "My God," he said to himself. "She's gorgeous."

As Wolfe drove towards Carlton, he asked Charlotte several questions relating to Matthew's last employer, and established that courier also meant chauffeur and delivery driver, cars mainly, very expensive ones, sometimes, collected on the continent and delivered to his employer's clients in the UK. He also confirmed Henry Mateland's statement that as far as Charlotte was concerned, Alfred Marks didn't owe him any money and that Mateland had insisted on paying for the necklace shortly after Alfred committed suicide. Neither could Charlotte find any evidence that Alfred owed money to betting syndicates or banks but had to sell the shop in Leeds and the house in Moortown in order to pay off the debts claimed by various organisations after court injunctions were brought against her in relation to her late husband's financial dealings. The whole thing was confusing to Wolfe, what evidence was used against Alfred, after his death to show that he owed money. Wolfe decided that should the opportunity arise, he would investigate these matters, but first, there was the suspicious death of Charlotte's brother to concentrate

Chapter 8

The portly bespectacled receptionist/security attendant had just swallowed a mouth full of his cheese and tomato sandwich, and was looking forward to his shift ending in five minutes, he would lock up the building for the night, and call in at the local pub for a pint on his way home. Just then the entrance door to the 'UnLock-NLoad' storage depot opened and in walked three men. They had walked through the door in close single file but were now three a breast and walking slowly towards him, the man in the middle being propped up by the other two. The man in the middle was recognisable to the attendant, he'd entered the building before, but the other two were strangers. The two props were well dressed in black two-piece suits, one wearing a contrasting blue open neck shirt, the other completed the black effect with a black polo neck sweater under the suit. Both were wearing dark glasses under short cropped hair, one jet black, gelled and combed back, the other just short, natural no added product. As soon as they reached the desk, the man in the middle coughed and drops of blood fell onto the desktop, he looked dishevelled, his face red as if he'd been in a fight, watery eyes that offered nothing but complete resignation.

"Sorry, Sam," he said as more blood splattered the desk. "These two gentlemen here are my business partners, we're here to collect some things from my container." He handed a plastic card with a bar code on it to the attendant who scanned the code, looked at the computer screen down to his right then from under the desk, he produced a bright yellow plastic disc that he handed with the plastic card back to the blooded man who was coughing more desperately and losing more blood.

"Mr Jessop," said Sam. "Shouldn't you go to the hospital?"

"Shut the fuck up, fat man," was the menacing response from the blue shirted brawny bouncer like man, in an accent that Sam couldn't place, but he realised that whatever had happened to Mr Jessop, might happen to him if he wasn't careful. So, he nodded to show he understood the implication of the remark.

"Let's not make things any worse for Mr Jessop ... eh, Sam?" said the other man in a softly spoken voice, he was much slimmer but well-built with a defined physique. "Now be a good fellow and do as my colleague says without any further comment. We are going up to the ... err, the third floor," he said as he looked at the disc he'd taken from the injured man.

"Oh, and go and lock the front door. There's a good fellow". The soft-spoken man offered in a pronounced English accent "We don't want or need interruptions, don't think about calling the police either. I want you to stand at the front door and look into that car outside. My other colleague in the car will be able to see you then, we'll be back soon, Sam, don't worry, all is good."

No words were spoken between the three men as they walked towards the lift. When the doors opened, the injured man groaned and sank a little further towards the floor but held up by the other two, he was dragged in as the doors shut. On the third floor, the injured man was forced to sit outside a large sliding door marked 33 as the other two used the disc to release the electronic lock and push the door aside.

"On the right-hand side, bottom shelf four metal boxes, unlocked, that's what he said, boss," said the burly man wearing the blue shirt as he waited outside to keep an eye on their captive.

The storage facility was large enough to hold a medium-sized family car but, surprisingly, empty except for several pieces of furniture, a few framed pictures or paintings loosely covered with bubble wrap, vehicle parts and an engine that were all stacked at the far end of the store. As described, there were three shelves on the right hand side, ornaments and general household matter spread untidily across them but, as expected, on the middle shelf, mid-way into the container were four metal boxes similar in size to large safe deposit boxes found in banks. The soft-spoken guy opened them all one after the other and on every occasion, a bright yellow glow was reflected from the stainless-steel lid onto his face. A set of sack barrow wheels leant against the side wall which he commandeered to move the now closed metal boxes. Although heavy, each box was lifted and eased onto the base plate of the barrow with little more than a grunt.

Using the sack barrow the boxes were wheeled out of the storage container, the sliding door was shut, the injured man forced to his feet and all moved into the lift once again. Down three floors, they passed through reception where the yellow disc was thrown over the reception desk and it could be heard hitting the solid floor behind. Sam was asked to move from the front entrance back to his usual spot behind the reception desk, escorted with a look from the thuggish one that said, 'don't do or say anything because you might end up like Jessop here'.

Sam saw the boot of the black Range Rover he'd been staring at open and when the rear kerb side door was opened by the man supporting Jessop, Jessop was bundled into the car behind the driver. The metal boxes were then lifted into the back of the vehicle, the sack barrow thrown roughly on top and then the tailgate shut. The big four by four reversed back made a 90-degree turn so its headlights, on full beam, glared intensely into the building, making Sam squint and cover his eyes. The vehicle then sped off in the direction of Leeds town centre. As soon as the vehicle was out of sight, Sam called the police.

Chapter 9

Wolfe and Charlotte had parted company at around 8pm the previous evening. They'd been joined by Wolfe's daughter, Izzy and her friend, Jemma, at around 6pm. It was a slight embarrassment to Wolfe when sometime later, he overheard Jemma ask Izzy,

"Is she your dad's new girlfriend?"

To which Izzy had replied,

"I hope so ... she's lovely."

Wolfe wasn't sure if Charley had also overheard the conversation but it was at that point he'd decided this particular social gathering should come to an end. Twenty minutes later, he ushered Charley into a taxi home. The long kiss on the lips and the embrace that happened before she entered the vehicle, witnessed by daughter and friend alike was accompanied with hoots of approval. Fortunately, neither Wolfe nor Charley heard the noise coming from inside the bar.

After washing the car on the Sunday morning, Wolfe was preparing a roast dinner for Izzy, Jemma and himself whilst listening to 'The Beautiful South, Rotterdam' through his iPod and piping it through the house in an attempt to wake the two sleeping beauties.

Then his mobile phone rang. "Wolfe speaking."

"Sir, it's PC Mills."

"Hello there, constable. To what do I owe this intrusion into my weekend off?"

"Yes ... sorry, sir, I'm aware you're not on duty."

"So why the intrusion on my private life, constable?" Wolfe was being mischievous without reason, he just felt that way out, interrupting his music listening pleasure always made him think, *'Why now? You could have at least waited till the track had ended.'*

"A body has been found in a car in a car park in Leeds City Centre." Mills waited for a response but none came. Wolfe fell silent, but why he wasn't sure, a sudden churn in his guts had stopped his reverie dead.

"The registration on the vehicle has been matched to a Frank Jessop."

Once again, Mills waited and this time a response came.

"Constable, is the name Frank Jessop supposed to mean something to me?" said Wolfe trying to sound enthusiastic.

"He's the Managing Director of Hennersy Contracting, I'm looking at a profile of the company on the internet and it's the same company that those two guys who found the body on Carlton Moor worked for. I remember searching this company at the time ... anyway, I thought, I'd call you, rather than the duty officer ... hope that's okay with you?"

"Oh, my God," said Wolfe as the sudden realisation of what he was being told hit him like a thrown brick.

"Yeah, that's quite okay, constable. Who's on scene now?"

"Two patrol constables, sir," replied the PC.

"You get yourself out there now, constable err Andy, cordon off as much of the area as you can, get someone to take over from you at the station, and get hold of DC's Middleton and Halford, and tell them to meet me out there. I'll be there as soon as."

"Sir!" came the recognised reply to an order.

Wolfe responded. "Andy, send me the link to the website for Hennersay?"

"Will do."

"I suggest you call Pam Middleton first, you'll probably catch two birds with one stone … if you catch my drift? Well done, Andy," he ended the call.

Forty minutes later, Wolfe arrived at the car park serving the Horizon Shopping Centre in Leeds City Centre. The car park entrance was cordoned off by police vehicles and uniformed officers, Mills had done well. Wolfe was immediately allowed through the barriers. After parking his car, he was informed by a beat officer to go to the second level, but first he went to the car park attendant's office.

After speaking with the attendant upon entering the stairwell, he was immediately hit by the cold stench of urine, he thought holding his breath would help prevent the putrid smell penetrating his senses, but it was too late. He ran up the concrete stairs to the second level. Opening the door, he could see Mills talking to another officer as they stood next a black Range Rover.

Mills turned and walked towards Wolfe. "Apologies, sir, for interrupting your weekend, but I thought you'd want to know immediately."

"No problem. Let's have a look at what we've got."

The two men walked towards the vehicle. Wolfe asked if forensics had arrived, he was told they were on their way. Mills also updated Wolfe on how the vehicle was discovered by the attendant shortly after his shift started.

"Are you sure he's dead?"

"Yes sir, didn't open the driver's door because his head is leaning against it, I was worried that he might fall out and I didn't want to contaminate the scene. There's no evidence of breathing, no condensation on the window."

"Okay Constable."

Sunlight bathed the bonnet of the SUV, the remainder was in shade, it looked sinister, the rear blacked out windows adding to the effect and when Wolfe arrived at the passenger side, that sinister appearance was confirmed by the sight of the body of man slumped over the steering wheel leaning to his right, head against the driver's door window. Upon closer inspection, he could see fragments of blood and sinew splattered on the inside of the windscreen. The person inside had been shot in the back of the head at very close range.

"Is it unlocked?" Wolfe asked as he stared through the windscreen, suddenly noticing his own reflection looking back at him.

"It is now, we found the key on the floor over there," replied Mills as he pointed to a darkened corner of the car park. "We've cordoned off the area and bagged the plip key. I've unlocked the doors with it but haven't opened them, we … I mean I, wanted to wait until you arrived, sir."

"Well, we'll wait until forensics gets here."

Wolfe and Mills walked around the vehicle, carefully avoiding anything laying on the concrete floor. They were about to crouch down to the floor to look under the vehicle when the door to the staircase opened, first Middleton appeared then Halford closely followed by Higgins and his young assistant, both carrying large black leather cases.

"Jac, what have we here?" said Higgins as he strode purposefully towards the Range Rover.

"Vehicle found here this morning by the car park attendant, there's the body of a man inside, he's draped around the steering wheel, shot in the back of the head."

"Oh, my God, what a mess," said Jenny Walters, the junior forensics officer as she looked through the vehicle's front windscreen.

"Jenny, it looks like he's slumped against the driver's side door."

"Okay, we'll go in through the door behind the driver," she replied in a middle England accent.

Higgins had already walked around the back of the vehicle and opened the front passenger door. "Jac, definitely deceased, killed here shot in the back of the head," he shouted from within the vehicle as he stretched across the passenger seat.

"Through the driver's head restraint … I can see powder burns and singeing around a hole at the back of it," announced Walters as she leant into the vehicle through an opened rear door.

"Shot through the head by someone sat behind, execution like, I'd say, Jac?" asked Higgins.

"It certainly looks that way," accepted Wolfe now leaning through the other rear door.

Whilst the forensic team continued with their initial examination of the scene, Halford was despatched to formally interview the car park attendant.

When Wolfe called into the attendant's office earlier he'd looked at CCTV footage from 5am when the car park opened.

Mills and another PC were again searching for evidence in the wider area of the car park floor. Wolfe and Middleton stood close to the vehicle, Pam watched in silence as the forensic team did their work whilst Wolfe looked closely at his mobile phone and said,

"Pam, there's more than one connection here to the body found on Carlton Moor on Thursday."

"What's that, sir?"

"Look at this," he handed his phone to Pam.

"So this is a business profile of Frank Jessop … yeah it looks like the guy in the Range Rover," she added quizzically.

"Notice anything familiar about him?"

"No."

"Remember that photo I was looking at in Charlotte Marks home? The guys dressed in army fatigues?"

"Yes."

"Well, he could be one of the men in that photo, very similar features. There are two framed copies, one in the lounge and one in the study. I want you to go to her house and ask if we can borrow one of them, get names and as much info as you can in relation to those in the photo. I think the Brookes murder and this here are linked;

don't tell her that, just say we're continuing with our wider inquiries into her brother's death."

"What if she say's no?"

"Tell her it's a personal request from me and if that don't work, we'll have to warrant it."

Middleton looked at Wolfe with raised eyebrows.

"Don't ask, Pam, and keep that last comment to yourself please. Go now, we'll meet tomorrow at HQ."

Wolfe considered his next move very carefully although he didn't really have a choice in the course of action, but he did have a choice in what to say and that was what required careful attention. With purpose, he lifted his mobile phone within view and scanned through the contacts menu until he arrived at the contact he wanted to use. As expected, he had to leave a message.

"Sir, DI Wolfe here. I apologise for disturbing your weekend, another body, a male murder victim has been found, this time in a multi storey car park in Leeds and I believe, from the evidence currently obtained, there is a connection between this latest killing and the body found on Carlton Moor on Thursday morning. That person is now confirmed as Matthew Brookes, a 31-year-old, who used to work for Hennersy Contracting and the second person found this morning is ... or should I say, was MD of Hennersy Contracting. I'm continuing as lead investigator on both investigations. I will give you a further update on your return tomorrow."

Whilst the body of Frank Jessop was being removed from the vehicle, Higgins reported his initial findings to Wolfe with his usual matter of fact emotionless delivery, not unusual in his line of work, in fact, utterly expected.

"Shot in the head at very close range through the head restraint on the driver's seat, instant death, he wouldn't have felt a thing. Having said that it would appear from facial injuries, not consistent with a bullet through the head, that this chap was battered and bruised prior to death, he may have been involved in a fight but there are no marks to the knuckles on either hand therefore I think he may have been assaulted ... beaten up. We can see the bullet lodged in the front windscreen pillar, we'll remove it soon for examination. I'm certain it's a 4mm from a hand gun ... we should get an idea of the make of gun that discharged it when we get the bullet back to the lab."

"This has contract killing crawling all over it, doesn't it, Arnie?" stated Wolfe.

"That's for you to determine, Jac, my boy," replied Higgins. "All I can tell you is how this chap was killed. However, there is one assumption I'm prepared to share with you ... the killer used the head restraint as a silencer, didn't want to risk unwanted attention and give time to make a clean getaway."

"Yeah, that crossed my mind too," Wolfe added as he looked at the high corners of the ceiling to the car park, "the cameras on this floor, according to car park attendant, are not working, they're scheduled for repair ... seems a bit convenient that, don't ya think?" He pointed but didn't wait for an answer, "So no CCTV on this floor ... but CCTV at the entrance shows the Range Rover drive in and it looked like the victim was driving. So I'm thinking, killer in the back seat, car drives past the cameras at the entrance, drives up here, quick assassination and then the killer ... well, he gets the hell out of Dodge, straight to the street into the centre of Leeds and off. Probably picked up by another vehicle."

"Now that, Jac, is an assumption. There's no evidence that the killer is male!"

"No, you're right there, Arnie. I'll leave you here to do your job, call me if there's anything further you want to report." Wolfe turned and walked towards the exit then reaching it, he turned to say, "Don't forget … midday tomorrow for the report on Matthew Brookes. That doesn't give you much time after the autopsy in the morning but I'm sure you'll manage it."

From over his back, Higgins waved an arm above his head. Wolfe didn't see the response; he was already through the staircase door and making his way out of the car park.

Chapter 10

Wolfe arrived home early evening, having spent seven hours of his day off beginning another investigation into another murder. This time, there was no doubt that murder had been committed, violent in its nature, clinical in its execution. Entering the house, he was greeted by his daughter Isabella.

"Hi, Dad," she said as she kissed him on the cheek. "Jemma and I prepared dinner; we've eaten ours and Jemma's gone home, she wanted to say thanks for allowing her to stay over last night. I told her you were busy and that she could stay whenever she wants."

"Oh, she's welcome anytime," replied Wolfe as they walked together into the sitting area adjacent to the kitchen.

"I'll warm your dinner now if you want, Dad."

"Yeah, I've hardly eaten all day."

"Pam called in earlier and left this package for you." She handed him a flat brown A4 envelope that had his name hand written on it in a script he recognised as that of DC Middleton.

Wolfe had begun eating his meal before he opened the package; it contained the photograph Middleton had been dispatched to obtain from Charlotte Marks earlier in the day but this time the photo was without a frame and names were printed across the bottom margin of the print, previously obscured by the frame. The names were listed along two lines the top line identified left to right names as David Watts, Thomas Henry Smythe, Francis Jessop and the line below identified the person crouching down in front as Matthew Tanner. A date was handwritten next to Tanners name, 21st May 2005. As Wolfe had noted before they were all wearing army fatigues but Tanner was wearing a different camouflage pattern to the others more sand coloured tones than the other green and brown colours and upon closer inspection he noticed a flag emblem over the left breast pocket of Tanners outfit. The other person in the left foreground spoiling the composition was not named. Wolfe turned his attention to this section of the print and studied it more closely. The frame had concealed from view a large proportion of this person dressed in jeans and pullover with their back turned to the camera and head turned to the left slightly in profile. His concentration then switched back to the main group and in particular the man identified as Jessop. He was satisfied this person was, without doubt, the man found shot in the head earlier that morning. His focus now concentrated on the background of the image looking for clues as to where this photo might have been taken but there appeared nothing obvious only dull white, standard studio background he assumed.

He was staring so hard he hadn't heard or noticed his daughter standing over him; she was also concentrating on the photo.

"I think I know who that is!" she announced as she pointed to the uniformed man in the foreground.

"What?" exclaimed Wolfe a little startled as his concentration broke.

"Say that again." His left hand covering the margin at the base of the photo.

"Yeah, I think it's him" Izzy looked closer and studied the image. "Yep I'm sure it's Matthew Tanner but that's not his birth name," she replied. Wolfe lifted his hand and checked the name, although he knew she was right.

"What do you mean not his birth name?" Wolfe turned to face his daughter and she pulled a chair next to him from under the table to sit on.

"Yeah, Mrs Williams, my History teacher, was always quoting from his books using them as a reference for interpretation of events in Modern European History." She looked at her father, his gaze was full of questions but he couldn't speak, Izzy decided to backtrack a little to offer some explanation.

"My History A level concentrates on European History, they call it modern but in actual fact we study from 1850 to the present and Matthew Tanner." She pointed to the figure in the photo. "Researched extensively that period of History in Europe, he's a lecturer at Leeds University. Mrs Williams studied under him for her degree, she believes he is working in Eastern Europe now. He wrote several reference books on the subject but not under the name Tanner, under his Serbian name, Arm ... on Cab ... rin ... o ... vich. I think that's how it's pronounced. They're excellent books with lots of background information based on his own research and documented evidence, he's considered to be the leading authority on this period and even when I use other research material, it's not uncommon to see his name quoted as a reference."

"Izzy, how can you be so certain that it's him?" Wolfe pointed to the figure in the photo. "You were six when this was taken."

"Ah, yes ... well ... ya see ... a few weeks ago at Proudman Press, they asked me to box up a section of old manuscripts ... and ... I know I shouldn't have done it." She paused for a second. "But the seal on the envelope had cracked, the papers inside just fell on the floor, and that's when I saw the name and this photo, or a copy of it anyway." Another pause, then a sigh followed by a whimper, "I realised pretty quickly that it was the draft of a historical novel written by Matthew Tanner ... so ... I ... I copied it, I thought it might come in useful for exam revision. Nobody paid me any attention when I copied it. There was a copy of a letter from Proudman Press in the envelope, they offered a £20,000 advance, that's how impressed they were. If they find out, dad, I'll get the sack and they'll prosecute me for stealing."

"Okay, okay let's not worry about that yet," said Wolfe, trying to be protective. Izzy was about to break into tears, tears of embarrassment not guilt.

"Does anyone else, other than me, know that you've got a copy of a manuscript that belongs to your employer?" said Wolfe instantly returning to detective mode.

"No, just you and me," she started to weep.

"Izzy, calm down," Wolfe put his arm round his daughter and whispered to her. "Where is the document now? I need to read it, it might have a bearing on the investigation."

Izzy waited a few seconds then without a word, went to her bedroom, collected an A4-sized envelope and returned to the kitchen.

She extracted the document from an envelope and placed in front of him, the cover was a copy of the letter sent by Proudman Press to Matthew Tanner at an address in Headingley outlining the terms and conditions of a proposed £20,000 advance payment. Proudman Press would have exclusive rights to market and publicise the book wherever they wanted for a percentage of any future profit.

Father and daughter sat at the table and began to read the words Matthew Tanner had committed to paper over a decade ago.

Chapter 11

Wolfe and his daughter read the manuscript together, concentrating on the preface which appeared to be a factual record because dates were included in the left margin indicating years of research, more than two decades. The factual record fuelled the narrative.

He began reading a note that referred to a research trip to Eastern Europe in 1985 where Matthew Tanner was given the opportunity to view and reference documents released by the Austrian Authorities. The Central European Historical Archive in Vienna wanted the material cataloguing and cross-referencing to actual events. It was a set of documents found in the basement of a residential property in Budapest, prior to demolition in the late 1960s that aroused his interest. The material, in the form of handwritten notes, in several different handwriting styles, were dated from 1908 to1948, they were personal but contained references to known historical events before, during and immediately after the two world wars, consequently, they were considered to be of historical interest. Matthew was intrigued in particular by one set of notes bound together in a badly stained leather wallet. A description of the wallet stated that damage probably resulted from where it was found in the building next to a wall infested with damp spores from the rising damp eating its way through the structure. Due to the dilapidated nature of the wallet, it was expected that the contents would be illegible; therefore, extracting the contents would need to be done with utmost care. This task was left to the Historical Researcher assigned to catalogue the documents, that person being Matthew Tanner. The note continued:

Taking time to carefully extract the documents from the wallet, I was very surprised to find them in a fragile but legible condition, my patience rewarded by reference to an Austro-Hungarian General, an attaché to the Serbian Minister to Vienna called Goran Sorbrinovic, this name was known to me as one member of the entourage that accompanied the Archduke Franz Ferdinand on his ill-fated trip to Sarajevo in 1914.

The corresponding chapter in the manuscript began:

Sorbrinovic was highly regarded by the Archduke for his loyalty, and his ability to communicate in Turkish, Serbian and Austrian, but what the 'King' of the Austro Hungarian Empire did not know was that Goran Sorbrinovic was a devout and passionate Serbian sympathiser who was biding his time towards what he hoped would be eventual Serbian supremacy in the region.

Sorbrinovic's involvement was in the negotiations with the Turkish Authorities when the Austro-Hungarian Empire annexed Serbia in 1911 from Turkey, in particular the negotiations around the financial settlement with Turkey for the unwanted Serbian state. Many Serbian nationals wanted independence to form their own government and not to be swallowed up by the then huge Austro-Hungarian Empire. They wanted Serbia as a 'buffer state' between them and the Prussians. General Sorbrinovic recognised an opportunity during the compensation negotiations with the Turkish authorities to raise funds in secret, sufficient to arm a battalion of Serbian patriots to fight for independence. His hope was that the rule of the Austro-Hungarian Empire would not last long after annexation, the increasing military might of Germany was beginning to impart influence over Europe, in particular its notion that this latest action by the Austro-Hungarian Empire to expand its influence would inevitably end in conflict. Sorbrinovic's intentions were not officially documented but his views on Serbian nationalism were highlighted in the documents found in Budapest which were contrary to his public image of complicity and approval of the Austro-Hungarian regime, he was, after all, a respected General in the Austro-Hungarian army and fluent in three languages. It was this ability to understand and speak Austrian, Ottoman and Serbian, and his comradeship with one of Franz Ferdinand's most trusted generals that got him a place at the negotiating table at the start of the annexation talks with Turkey in 1908. The nature of these talks was such that talks within talks were taking place and splinter groups were formed to discuss different aspects of the annexation of Serbia, and it was during one of these splinter meetings that Goran made his move.

A Turkish General by the name of Fisal Haquime Masood representing the Ottoman Empire had confided in Sorbrinovic during one of the many after discussion drinking sessions that he had domestic problems that were causing him great financial difficulty. His extra marital dalliance with a married woman needed constant monetary input to keep the matter suppressed but funds were beginning to get low. Sorbrinovic took the opportunity whilst alcohol had loosened their tongues to plant the seed of a money-making scheme into the mind of Fisal, a scheme that would greatly benefit both men.

The final draft of the compensation agreement between the Austro-Hungarian Empire and Turkey for the state of Serbia included a sum of money to be paid in gold bullion. This sum was written into the agreement in two languages, Austrian and Turkish (Ottoman), the name of the overseeing interpreter checking that the documents matched was General Goran Sorbrinovic. The two figures were different, the excess was on the Austro-Hungarian side, and this payment split one third to Fisal and two thirds to Sorbrinovic with his share to be delivered secretly to an address in Sarajevo.

In 1914, as history shows, the city of Sarajevo became host to the flashpoint that would, eventually, lead to World War and, of course, the demise of the Austro-Hungarian Empire as hoped and partially predicted by Goran Sorbrinovic.

A week before the ill-fated visit to the city of Sarajevo by the Archduke Franz Ferdinand, General Sorbrinovic had taken delivery of a large and very heavy packing case. It needed two men with a block and tackle to lift it from the back of a covered trailer truck, and one man, the General himself, to direct the path and progress of the load onto a wheeled boogie that could then be pushed with a modicum of ease. The two men helping were, supposedly, Turkish, but Sorbrinovic knew, via his arrangements with Fisal, they were criminals, petty thieves, promised a full pardon, payment and passage back to their native Kurdistan, if they delivered the crate intact and undamaged to its rightful owner who would pay them on delivery.

To make sure these men weren't tempted to abscond with the load and truck, they were told that the crate housed the putrefied remains of a Serbian dissident who had fled to Turkey to avoid the wrath of the man he had cuckolded, that man being General Sorbrinovic, who had demanded physical proof of this fellows demise, and Fisal unbeknown to the Turkish Authorities was willing to oblige. The delivery drivers were also told that the truck on its travels from Istanbul to Sarajevo would have to pass a number of check points within a certain time frame, otherwise, the men would be hunted down and killed. A story fabricated to reduce the risk of the hoard disappearing and also to involve as few people as possible.

Sorbrinovic knew the risks he was taking in leaving the delivery of the shipment to two untrustworthy vagabonds but with Fisal's help devising the story and convincing the men that payment on delivery would be substantial, the scheme had a good chance of success.

A narrow alley behind the Sarajevo City Library was where the delivery took place at 2am on a wet and windy night in June 1914. Late night deliveries to the building were not uncommon but on this particular night, Goran Sorbrinovic was the only person in attendance. The custodian of the library had willingly handed over the keys to the building to Sorbrinovic after the General had explained security checks must be carried out before the state visit in a week's time and how these were best done at night by the army out of public view so as not to alarm the local residents. This was a plausible story embellished by the General with the statement.

"The Archduke's motorcade is scheduled to pass directly in front of the library, this a very prominent building with views up and down the route, need I say more?" The keys were handed over without further dialogue.

The truck had been reversed into place and the packing case transferred, and once again, with mechanical means was now residing in the basement, some two floors deep below ground level, catacombs actually, foundations for the building above.

"My friends, I am very grateful for your help in delivering the remains of this unholy bastard to my care," Sorbrinovic announced as he handed over a brown paper parcel to one of the men. The men nodded, dumbfounded, they did not speak a word of Austrian. Sorbrinovic repeated the statement in Turkish and then continued,

"My comrade has let me down and now I have no one to secure this coffin of body parts within that opening over there." Pointing to an arched recess where he intended it would remain permanently. The man with the parcel had already torn open a section of it to check the contents, he smiled and looked at Sorbrinovic, and saw him point.

"You want we put crate in there?" said the man with the envelope of money pointing to the same location.

"Yes."

The man then made the universal sign for payment, with his right hand lifted to eye level, rubbing his thumb over his index and second finger.

All was going perfectly to plan, thought Sorbrinovic. He nodded and made a submissive gesture

"I will pay you what I was going to pay my sergeant." He paused. "But I only have Austrian Krone." The driver smiled and started pushing the crate towards the recess, his friend then helped and so did the General. One by one, they began to laugh, heartily as they positioned the crate in its final resting place.

Sorbrinovic had another surprise up his sleeve, well, one of two actually. He walked towards a pile of stone rubble and removed muslin covering a heap of still workable mortar, and then began to start erecting a wall to the front of the recess flush with the neighbouring walls. Still giggling, the two thieves started to help. Sorbrinovic was then suddenly pushed aside as the two men started working, one spreading mortar, the other building the wall. Sorbrinovic surmised that they must be builders by trade and thought they could do a better job.

After an hour, the two Kurds had the wall three quarters built and, once again, money passed hands, before the crate and its contents were fully incarcerated. Sorbrinovic suddenly asked them to stop, a look of desperation on his face. Grabbing a crowbar from a box of tools, he strode towards the newly built wall and squeezing through the narrow gap remaining, he began trying to force the top off the crate. Shaking and cursing, he couldn't get the top off, then he felt a hand on his arm, not an aggressive touch but a supportive one, he turned. The two workmen stood next to him, and he felt that they understood that he needed to see and confirm the contents so he gave the jemmy to the truck driver, and backed out of the nearly constructed tomb. Outside the tomb, Sorbrinovic reached his right hand behind his back and under his trench coat, he pulled out a revolver.

The first bullet hit the truck driver in the left temple, killing him instantly, his body collapsing behind the packing crate, the second bullet caught the other delivery man in the neck, causing him to gag for breath as he dropped to his knees. The third shot impacted the top of his head, forcing him to fall forward. The gun shots would never be heard this far below ground.

General Sorbrinovic frisked both corpses, and collected first his money and then any papers he could find, throwing them on the floor in a pile. Before he finished building the wall, Sorbrinovic had removed one of the gold ingots from the crate, nailed the top back down then the papers removed from the dead bodies were set on fire, he watched as the flames died out leaving a small pile of charred black pieces.

There were two access ways to the basement, one was a manual lift and the other a staircase through a heavy wrought iron door unused for years. Sorbrinovic used the lift to exit the basement, taking with him a toolbox. Two floors up on the ground floor, he cut through the rope holding the counterbalance for the lift, the base of the lift fell back to the basement crashing creating a dust cloud that forced its way up the empty shaft. Sorbrinovic pulled the shutter down before the dust could escape. The newly built wall would be dry long before anyone went near the basement, he smiled. Freedom for Serbia, he whispered to himself as he caressed the weighty cold ingot of precious metal in the inside pocket of his trench coat. 199 gold ingots remained hidden two floors below where General Sorbrinovic stood, there, they would remain until he returned with an army of Serbian nationals.

General Goran Sorbrinovic never saw his dream come true, he died on the 14th June in Sarajevo at the hands of Serbian separatists when a hand grenade thrown at the Archdukes motorcade exploded sending shrapnel into his back and directly into his heart.

'Was this the incentive behind Tanners' trip to Sarajevo with Smythe, Jessop and Watts?' thought Wolfe

The next morning, Wolfe woke with a start. He'd been dreaming but couldn't remember what the dream was about. He looked at the bedside clock, it read 5.50am, ten minutes before the alarm. He lay back in bed and cursed in a low voice, like most people do on a Monday morning. However, the dawning of the first working day of the week wasn't the object of Wolfe's vehemence, it was the fact that he knew he hadn't dreamt about Maria and that worried him. After almost three years, he had grown accustomed to life without her, or had he, in the shower ten minutes later Wolfe stopped weeping and told himself he had to concentrate his energy on the future, without Maria, if not for him then for Isabella.

Wolfe made breakfast for Isabella and he then drove her to school for her 9 am start; they didn't mention the manuscript until Izzy was getting out of the car after kissing her father on the cheek.

"There's another copy of the manuscript in your bag, read it and we'll compare notes this evening," announced Wolfe. "But don't let it get in the way of your studies, your A levels are far more important. However, your take on the story and the historical references would be appreciated, Izzy."

Isabella smiled. "I'll have to tell Proudman Press about the manuscript at the weekend, won't I?"

"Let's not be too hasty to tell them yet. In fact, you might be useful to the investigation by continuing to work there as normal, as if nothing's happened," replied Wolfe. "But, Izzy, that's just between you and me, don't tell any of your friends."

"No, Dad, promise, just you and me."

Izzy closed the door, turned and walked towards the main entrance. Wolfe watched her through the rear-view mirror and noticed how she walked just like her mum, smiling, he drove away.

Arriving late at Holland Walk, Head Quarters of the West Yorkshire Police Force, so called because the water feature and landscaping leading to the main entrance was the work of a Dutch landscape architect who took inspiration for the scheme from the canals and tulip planted banks of his native country.

Wolfe had no sooner arrived at his desk than his phone rang. Having had time only to fire up his laptop, he noticed it was an internal extension number and recognised the number immediately.

"DI Wolfe speaking."

"Wolfe, my office now."

"Sir!" he replied and replaced the receiver as he stood up. Just then, Middleton arrived at his desk.

"Morning, sir. You might want to take this upstairs with you," she stated as she placed a white envelope with his name written on it down on his desk.

"Arnold's preliminary report?"

"Yeah, courier dropped it off five minutes ago."

"Haigh-Watson's mad at you, isn't he?"

"I called him yesterday, left a voicemail, he's cross that all this mayhem has happened while he was on a dirty weekend," answered Wolfe with a snigger.

Chapter 12

Wolfe knocked twice on the door of the office of the Acting Chief Constable, he didn't wait for permission to enter. The uniformed senior officer didn't look away from his laptop screen.

"Carlton moor body investigation!" he announced without any attempt at a personal greeting for DI Wolfe.

"And why the hell are you involved in that car park execution, Wolfe?" he continued. Then as if to emphasise his annoyance he looked at Wolfe over his laptop and slammed it shut with a grunt.

In his mind, Wolfe responded to the curt welcome from his superior: *'Good morning to you as well, sir, did you have a good weekend? The rest will have done you good, I'm sure, calmed your temperament a bit as well, no doubt.'*

But actually, he replied,
"I have the preliminary forensic report here relating to the Carlton moor body, the autopsy is taking place this morning and I expect a statement on that in 24 hours." Wolfe gently placed the report on the desk, purposely to contrast with the slam-dunk attitude of his superior. The smell of cologne invaded his senses. *'Cheap aftershave,'* thought Wolfe, *'bought to mask another's cheap perfume.'*

Haigh-Watson sat behind a large oak desk on a high back leather chair that projected above his head. Wolfe guessed that the seat was probably lifted to its maximum elevation and that meant that Haigh-Watsons little legs, unseen, would be swinging in mid-air. Wolfe didn't show a smirk but he was smiling inside. Opposite the only window in the office on the right, two matching oak cabinets were positioned against the left-hand wall one full of books, the other with police memorabilia, past and present. A smaller cabinet positioned opposite under the large wide window stored glasses and drinks, Wolfe remembered, it was there the last time he visited this room more than two years earlier, when Haigh-Watson's predecessor, told Wolfe in a very sympathetic manner, that he should take sick leave and seek psychological advice to help curb his drinking habit. It had become noticeable to other members of the force to such a degree that official complaints against Wolfe had been received. At the time the office was occupied by a far more professional, experience and personable head of the force, Andrew Hickson.

Haigh-Watson flicked through the report as if he was scan reading it, but all he wanted to do was read the conclusion. However, before he reached it, Wolfe decided to announce the report's findings in person. He'd read the conclusion himself as he made his way to the Chief's office.

"The victim, Matthew Brookes, a known drug user with a record for possession of narcotics, most likely died as a result of trauma caused by two deep stab wounds to his back. These wounds were spotted during a detailed visual inspection of the body prior to removal to the mortuary. Acute kidney failure is expected to be the main cause of the trauma, murder being the conclusion on the basis that he couldn't have inflicted these wounds on himself." He paused, waiting for Haigh-Watson to reply … but nothing, so he continued, "No blood was found at the scene, but autopsy will determine whether there has been serious blood loss or whether the victim has mass internal bleeding. Obviously, if there is a lot of blood loss then the victim must have been killed somewhere else, also leading to the theory that –"

"The murder happened someplace else and moved," Haigh-Watson abruptly interrupted. "Yes, yes, yes, obvious, Wolfe. You say this chap … Brookes … is it?"

"Yes, Matthew Brookes, sir."

"You say he has previous?"

"Yes, possession of low-grade drugs, charge of intent to distribute was dropped shortly after his arrest," concluded Wolfe.

"No such thing as low grade drugs, detective. Scum, all those who have anything to do with them, a scourge on our society." Haigh-Watson stopped there, maybe he thought his tone was a little harsh.

'Fucking hell,' thought Wolfe. *'Obviously, didn't get what he wanted last night.'*

"I assume your team are all over his file and checking up on known associates?"

"Yes, they'll be visiting those known to us today. DC Middleton and I paid a visit to Charlotte Marks, Brookes sister, on Friday, and –"

"Marks, you say?" interrupted Haigh-Watson once again.

"Yes! Her husband, before he committed suicide, was Alfred Marks, a jeweller in Leeds," informed Wolfe.

"Mmm, a jeweller, a shop in Leeds, Victoria Quarter … yeah, about three years ago, wasn't it? Found in a hotel somewhere, left a mountain of gambling debts for her to sort out if I remember?"

"Yes, so I understand, sir," exclaimed Wolfe as he tried to hide his frustration at the constant interruptions.

"Anyway, I digress," replied Haigh-Watson as if picking up on Wolfe's mood. "I'm sure all this will be in your report in due course? Now, why are you working this shooting in Leeds? I assume, you're going to tell me these two victims are linked in some way, Detective Inspector?"

"As a matter of fact, there is a link sir," Wolfe responded with a stare.

"Go on, tell me, but it had better be good because if it's not, I'll order you to hand it over to DI Owen …"

It was Wolfe's turn to cut the Chief off in mid flow, "Sir, at Charlotte Marks house, there's a photo on display and in the photo is Frank Jessop, the victim found shot dead in his car yesterday." Before Haigh-Watson could once more interrupt him, Wolfe continued in a much harder tone than before, "Brookes is Charlotte Marks brother and he used to work for Hennersy Contracting, the MD of Hennersy Contracting is Frank Jessop. No matter how you look at it, that's a solid link … sir!"

"I'll be the judge of that, DI Wolfe." Haigh-Watson then fell silent for a second. "Okay it's convincing enough you continue as the lead on both investigations but you must keep DI Owen informed of progress, just in case the connections you so forcefully explained turn out to lack substance."

"Sir!" replied Wolfe. He turned to leave.

"I haven't finished with you yet, Wolfe," Haigh Watson blurted as he almost dropped off his chair and walked round his desk. Suddenly, the desk appeared much larger by comparison, he handed the preliminary forensic report back to Wolfe, holding onto his end of the report as Wolfe grasped the other and looking up at him said, "Now with everything that's happened to you in last few years, I perfectly understand if you want DI Owen to take over from you, no one would blame you, everyone would understand."

Wolfe clenched his fist but managed to restrain the impulse to send a haymaker in Haigh Watson's direction. "Sir, you know as well as I do that working in the criminal investigation section is where I belong. I have … I mean, I had an exemplary record and I aim to restore that record. I have proven ability, I don't need any more help, I've recruited a good team around me, that I believe will bring results. So can I go now and progress with these investigations …"

"I'm not stopping you, DI Wolfe, just offering my full support," Haigh-Watson said with a smile.

Wolfe decided it was best not to throttle the 'little bastard' just yet, so he smiled and with the report in hand, opened the door to leave the office.

"One more thing, Jac."

'Ah, shit,' thought Wolfe. 'I'm gonna …'

"I have paperwork here for the temporary promotion of PC Middleton to Detective Constable, I'll process it today." Haigh-Watson was by now standing next to Wolfe. "Are you shagging her, Wolfe?" he whispered, "Be discreet, I don't like inter staff relations, it causes unnecessary conflict."

Wolfe left the office and as Haigh-Watson closed the door, he buried his face in the forensic report and screamed into it, 'Ahhhhhhhhhhh'. The Acting Chief Constable smiled as he heard the reaction.

Wolfe called a team briefing for 12 noon but asked Middleton and Halford to chair the briefing, he sat in to observe, to make sure all the necessary items were covered. In truth, he wanted to read more of the manuscript his daughter had acquired whilst listening to all the facts relating to the two murders. Perhaps there was something in the manuscript that would be helpful to the investigation.

The briefing began with a review of the background check done on Frank Jessop. Jessop had been Managing Director of Hennersy Contracting for the past ten years. His wife, Mary, was the only child of Seamus Hennersy, the founder of the company. Mary and Frank Jessop were co-owners of the company, all current shares in the company being split between the two of them 50:50. Mary Jessop stood to benefit financially and would now be sole owner of the company. Mrs Jessop however suffers from bouts of depression and is regularly visited by a care worker and it is she who has confirmed a phone call was received from Mr Jessop at around 10am on Saturday saying he would be attending a meeting in Leeds in the afternoon, around 4pm. She received another call saying he would be having a drink with an old friend and would be home later that night. When the care worker tried to contact the home on Sunday morning the call wasn't answered so she decided to visit the house and attend to Mary Jessop, but there appeared to be no evidence that Frank had returned home. The care worker began to worry because this was not normal behaviour for Frank who doted on his wife. She tried to contact him but with no response, so fearing the worst she reported Frank Jessop as missing to the local police in Carlton. There is no record of who Mr Jessop was meeting. Hennersy Contracting were contacted that morning to establish if Frank had diarised this meeting, no such record existed.

Halford explained, "We have confirmed the whereabouts of Mrs Jessop and the care worker yesterday … err, Sunday morning. Both were at the Jessop's house from early morning. This murder appears professional and calculated, carried out in the style of an execution. Having spoken to the care worker at length and Mary Jessop briefly I doubt either are capable of such an attack. Over to you DC Middleton."

Middleton stepped in and made reference to the photograph obtained from Charlotte Marks and the fact that four of the five men depicted in the photo were dressed in army fatigues. Smythe, Watts and Jessop were all dressed in similar uniforms, and they may have been at the time part of the same Regiment. Tanner at the front was wearing a different style of uniform, was he in the army and the flag emblem needs to be researched to identify the country it represents. Wolfe checked the date on the covering letter for the manuscript written by Cabrinovic that stipulated the conditions for the release of the manuscript for future publication, it was dated 23rd March 2005.

Wolfe stood and walked from his seat at the back of the briefing room to the front, and when Middleton concluded her briefing, he started to speak.

"Thanks, Pam, Team, we need to find the whereabouts of Smythe and Watts, the two uniformed guy's next to Jessop in the photo, check with their families. I will try to find out more about this chap here," he pointed to Matthew Tanner in the photo. "I can't explain at present why these lines of enquiry are important but they could turn out to be critical aspects of this investigation." Wolfe turned to Middleton and said, "Would you finish the briefing then meet me in my office."

"Sir," she replied.

When Middleton walked into Wolfe's office, he was in mid stride, and had obviously been pacing up and down again. The glass partition to his office not providing much privacy, but that didn't seem to bother Wolfe, even though some officers working in the open plan squad room beyond were watching him and sniggering to themselves.

"Sir, you wanted a word."

"Ah, yes," replied Wolfe continuing to walk slowly form one end of his small office to the other, four paces desk to wall and four paces back again. "Two things, Pam. One, your temporary promotion is forthcoming, well done."

"Sir, I haven't applied for promotion, I thought this was a secondment to plain clothes."

"Oh yeah, forgot to tell you, I applied for your promotion, might make it permanent if you wish, in due course."

"I haven't received my detective exam results yet, sir, I can't apply until …"

"That's just procedure and protocol, Pam … rules, that's what they really are and, in your case, you'll have passed the exams with flying colours, I'm certain of that," Wolfe said. Still moving, he continued, "Second, find out what army regiment Smythe, Watts and Jessop belonged to, and in particular see if they all went on manoeuvres together, were they a close-knit group? It could be very important."

"Have you got some new information, sir?" asked Middleton.

"No, not really, just a hunch at present, and Pam … please call me Jac, we're on the same team now."

"No problem … Jac!"

"But if we're on the same team I need to know what you know Jac."

"Yes you're right and you will, all in good time."

Middleton turned to leave the office when Wolfe said, "Oh, just one more thing, our leader thinks you and me are an item."

"An item!" Middleton stopped and turned to face Wolfe. "What the hell does that mean?"

"It means Haigh-Watson believes we're 'shagging' … his words not mine and I wasn't aware you fancied me in any way shape or form," he said with sarcasm.

"Well, I –"

Wolfe interrupted, "Don't say anymore, my ego could be severely dented." He paused smiling, then added, "But don't tell Pete or anyone else what he said. Let Winker Watson think what he wants to think, he's a lusty little letch and it'll keep him occupied. However, if it makes you uncomfortable, I'll put him straight on the issue."

"No, let it run, it'll be interesting to see who mentions it to me first," replied Middleton as she left the office.

Wolfe decided it was time for lunch so he opened the packaging to the roast beef sandwich bought earlier during his journey into the office. Arranging his note pad, pen and the Tanner manuscript in front of him, he began to read once more, and made notes in a word document on his laptop. A few hours later, he finished reading and arrived at a plan for his next move.

Chapter 13

Wolfe had finished work for the day, that is to say, officially, he was off duty but in actual fact, he had arranged an evening interview with Professor Alistair Buchanan Jones, Head of the History Department at the University of Leeds and was now walking towards the university's main entrance. His phone rang and checking the id of the caller, he noted the time, 18.20pm.

"Izzy, hi, sorry, love. I said I'd call ..." he said apologetically, having suddenly realised he'd missed a call from his daughter in the afternoon.

"No, that's alright, Dad," she replied cheerfully. "I just wanted to know what time you're likely to be home for tea."

Wolfe knew this wasn't the only reason. "And isn't there something else you wanted to ask?"

"Well, not really," she hesitated. "Well, yeah ... have you finished reading the manuscript and am I in trouble?"

"Yes and no in that order," he pronounced. "I'm just walking through the main entrance hall at Leeds University, I've arranged a meeting with the head of the History department so ..."

"Oh ... is this to do with the investigations then?"

"Most definitely, but it's not an official interview, I'm just making off duty enquires." Wolfe paused, then continued, "Izzy, are you at home, are you alone?"

"Yes, where else did you think I'd be and who with?"

"No, no. I'm not checking up on you. I want your help, you'll need to access the internet."

"Okay ... Ohh, by the way the head of a department is known as a Dean."

"Yeah, his secretary said that but I thought she'd got it wrong. Seems it's me?"

Wolfe then explained what he needed and with his daughter's help and the internet he hoped to find what he wanted to know. He asked Izzy for a response via text only because he didn't want the forthcoming discussions interrupted by a ringing mobile phone.

The university entrance was more attuned to a grand hall, large portraits of studious looking gentlemen looked down on him from lofty positions opposite the reception area.

"Hi, I'm Detective Inspector Wolfe from West Yorkshire Police. I'm here for a meeting with Professor Buchanan Jones," he announced to the receptionist seated behind an impressive oak finished horseshoe shaped desk that looked like it could accommodate at least six people if required.

Alice, as identified on her name badge, was the only person within the great entrance lobby of this learned establishment and replied softly, "Yes, Inspector, I was told to expect you, please sign here." She opened a leather-bound visitors' book on the reception shelf and pointed to space under the name of the last visitor to arrive.

Wolfe was then directed to the first-floor lobby where, he was informed the professor's secretary would meet him. He climbed the grand marble staircase and reaching the lobby above, he was indeed greeted by a professional looking middle-aged woman.

"Please follow me, Inspector," she said as she turned and walked through an archway, leading, via a short corridor, to a door that she opened.

"Detective Inspector Wolfe to see you, Professor," she announced and kept the door open as Wolfe entered.

The wood panelling that adorned the lobby and corridor continued into the room which was smaller than Wolfe expected, not much bigger than his own office, he thought. A window to his right caught his eye framing as it did an illuminated streetlamp outside but this only emphasised its grubby glazing, making it appear as though it hadn't been cleaned for long period of time. Wolfe then concentrated his attention on the reason for his visit.

"Pleased to meet you, Professor," said Wolfe as a silver haired man with matching unkempt sideburns and beard, wearing a stained olive-green cardigan over a blue shirt reached across the antique desk that separated them.

"Thank you for seeing me at such short notice." The two shook hands. The Professor's appearance seemed as expected. *'A common theme here,'* thought Wolfe. *'Lack of maintenance, human and building.'* Their handshake, however, seemed to contrast with this, being strong and purposeful.

"Your reason for meeting intrigued me, Inspector," Wolfe detected a strong well-educated Yorkshire accent.

"Why so?" replied Wolfe as they sat down on opposite sides of the desk.

"When Matthew Tanner didn't return from a trip to Europe … what, twelve years ago, the University contacted the police and investigations were made but to no avail. It's as if he just disappeared from the face of the earth, and then today, you call and ask to speak to me about Matthew. So, as I said … I'm intrigued."

Wolfe pulled a copy of the photo of the five men from his jacket pocket and placed it on the desk in front of the Professor.

"Do you recognise any of these men?"

"Yes," he replied and pointed to one of the men in the photo. "That's Matthew. When was this picture taken, it doesn't look that recent?"

"That's a copy of the original, dated May 2005, we don't know where it was taken. Do you recognise any of the other men in the picture?"

"No, Inspector, I'm sorry I don't," he replied as he looked closely at the photo. "Identifying this person," he continued as he pointed to the blurred figure in left foreground, "will take a great deal of effort and detection."

"Yes, that person is a mystery to us, however, the other men behind Matthew we can be almost certain are," Wolfe pointed to each of the individuals in turn while the photo was still upside down to him, "Sergeant Thomas Henry Smythe, flanked by Corporals David Watts and Frank Jessop. Are these names familiar to you?"

"No, I'm afraid not."

"Do you recall ever seeing Mr Tanner with any of these men?"

"Once again, Inspector, I can only offer you a negative response. No, I don't remember seeing Matthew with these men, I think I would remember especially if they were dressed in uniform," replied the Professor sarcastically.

Wolfe decided on a change to his line of questioning.

"Did you and Matthew Tanner socialise outside of the university?"

"We hardly socialised inside the university, let alone outside the university," the Professor then took a sharp intake of breath. "I'm still a suspect in his disappearance, aren't I, Inspector?"

"I'm here unofficially, Professor, if you were a suspect, we'd be having this conversation at the police station," replied Wolfe without showing any surprise at the sudden subject change in their conversation. He continued, "However, I understand your comment … I have read the file relating to the disappearance of Matthew Tanner and I noted that you were considered to have benefitted from his disappearance with your promotion to Dean of History here at Leeds."

"Is that written on file?" replied Professor Buchanan Jones in a raised voice. "Because if it is that's a slur on my character, and I may consider legal action to get such comments removed."

"It's implied by reference to your promotion, Professor Buchanan Jones … if it came across as a slanderous statement, I sincerely apologise on behalf of myself and the West Yorkshire Police Force."

"Is this file on Matthew Tanner's disappearance available in the public domain, Inspector?"

"No, it's not, sir, and access within the force is restricted to senior members of the Serious Crime Squad," Wolfe replied with fake embarrassment.

"Alright, apology accepted. Now I'm even more intrigued … serious crime squad?"

"Yes, that's correct."

"I hope this discussion is off the record, Inspector?"

"Yes, but I have to inform you that I requested this meeting because one person in that photograph was found dead in his car yesterday morning and another person not in the photo but linked with the dead man was also found dead last Thursday morning."

"What the hell has that got to do with the disappearance of Matthew? I'm beginning to think I should get myself a legal representative," said the Professor with obvious indignation.

Wolfe had expected this response and with his usual charm, in a calming voice, he replied,

"I believe Matthew Tanner's visit to Eastern Europe in 2005 has something to do with these murders and you professor are the only person that I can contact that knew Matthew before he disappeared."

"Alistair," he interrupted. "I prefer Alistair or Alistair Buchanan … it was my parents' idea to join their surnames … Scottish dad, Welsh mother … so Alistair if you don't mind …"

"Right … Alistair," Wolfe continued. "I've got a few questions to ask about Matthew Tanner, so I'll press on." Alistair Buchanan nodded his approval.

"When did you last see or speak to Matthew Tanner aka Armon Cabrinovic?"

"All Matthew's historical research work is published under the name he was born with Armon Cabrinovic and that's well known, he never kept that a secret. The last time I spoke to him was the day before the Easter recess in 2005 and the reason I remember it so clearly, before you ask, is because I congratulated him on his appointment to Dean. Matthew and I had been interviewed for the position over the previous two months, and the interview board had chosen him over me. He set off for Europe a week or so later and I haven't seen or spoken to him since."

"You were unhappy about the decision?" asked Wolfe.

"Unhappy! I was livid; the board went with the celebrity status of the better-known person, they thought it might encourage more financial investment into the University. Had the board told me they'd decided on Matthew to take advantage of his status, then that would have been okay, but no, their decision was made on purely professional grounds, so they said? Matthew was a 'hands-on' researcher, he made history interesting, palatable and even romantic. That is great for schools and colleges but University educated historians tend to be more circumspect about their advancement in the understanding and relevance of History. I'm an Art Historian, I prefer fact-based investigation not word of mouth historical hit and miss research."

"I think I understand your argument, however, when I mentioned Matthew Tanners' birth name, you said, 'he didn't keep that a secret', implying that there were other things he did try to keep secret. What were you referring to?" asked Wolfe, his phone began to vibrate in his jacket pocket, a text message.

"I heard that, Inspector. Is someone trying to contact you?"

"My daughter, I expect, we usually eat at home together on Monday evenings and she probably wants to know what time I'll be home."

"Ah, I see. Well then, secrets: Matthew would never talk about his personal life, I don't even know if he was married, although, he was always accompanied at official functions by women, many different women, one for each occasion it seemed, some of them students. He was obviously very popular with women, those rugged Eastern European looks, I think."

"Come on, Alistair, you don't strike me as the jealous type, his relationships with women wouldn't cause you concern."

"Very observant of you Inspector, no his philandering ways were of no concern of mine." Wolfe nodded and the Professor continued, "Under the name Armon Cabrinovic, Matthew made numerous trips to Eastern Europe, mostly paid for by the University, but didn't involve students or other colleagues, he conducted his research on his own, which led to questions about authenticity and corroboration of his research. I'm convinced that some of his research was for personal benefit. I'm not alone with that viewpoint; a number of other University colleagues raised these concerns from time to time. However, I didn't kick up much of a fuss in that regard because he would, on most occasions, de-brief me on his return and on a couple of occasions, he returned with artefacts that he would donate, via me, to various museums, so I suppose I benefitted as well in part from his research …" the Professor indicating inverted commas with both hands raised, "Trips to Europe."

There was a lull in the conversation whilst Wolfe openly read the text message from his daughter, the text read:

Dad,
Marks and Son are referred to in several of Cabrinovic's History books as authenticators of artefacts and also co-authenticators with Universities in Israel in connection with historical documents. Alfred Marks is mentioned by name in some

sections of the published works. There's a whole bunch of stuff on the internet about Gen. Sorbrinovic, I've posted some below. Hope this is useful Izzy xx.

He decided now was the time to use the information Izzy had sent.

"Artefacts and other precious items, depending on their age would, I assume, be very valuable, and your expertise as an Art Historian would be helpful in determining the authenticity and value of such items."

"Authenticity, yes, value no. The University has several independent valuation providers who assist in valuing artefacts, fine art, jewellery and precious metals. Now the intrigue has turned to fascination, Inspector. Where are you going with this line of questioning?"

Wolfe realised that Professor Buchanan Jones was beginning to jump to conclusions. The same conclusions he himself had formulated recently.

"You had direct dealings with these independent valuation providers?" he asked.

"Yes indeed, myself and other Art Historians, some university based, some specialist independent valuers."

"Was Alfred Marks ever consulted on such matters?"

"Matthew tended to make direct contact with Alfie Marks and would, more often than not, be visited exclusively by Matthew …"

Wolfe interjected, "Alfred Marks owned Marks and Son they were dealers in precious metals, retained as valuers for artefacts donated to and found by the University. Is that correct?"

"Yes, that is or should I say, was correct. I assume, you realise that Marks and Son no longer exist as a business. Alfie committed suicide, but you know that don't you, Inspector?"

"Mmm, the business folded after his death, no one to hand it over to."

"Very sad," reflected the Professor. "Very sad."

"Alfred Marks committed suicide in December 2015, same month that the University reported Matthew Tanner as missing."

"Wow, that's a long leap, Inspector, are you sure it's not just coincidence?" said the Professor with more sarcasm than intended.

"Yes I agree, it could be just that, which is why I need to know more about the relationship between Alfred Marks and Matthew Tanner, so, Alistair?"

"Any precious metal or jewellery that Matthew returned with from his European trips was immediately handed to Marks and Son to value and authenticate. Alfie would come here to the University, take the items away with him and return them a few days later. He didn't need an appointment to see Matthew, in fact, on numerous occasions in the first semester of a new year, Alfie could be found sitting in Matthew's office waiting to see him. I got the impression they liked each other's company. I saw them walking together from time to time up to the pub on the corner. They never invited me, I'm not a pub type of person, wine and a good meal at home usually, that's me."

"Did Matthew tell you about the items Marks was valuing?"

"Well, most times, yes. Matthew was always very quick to point out an item he had purchased if it was about to render him a profit, but there was never any mention of … duds he'd purchased and there must have been some, he could never be that lucky all the time."

"Lucky, you say, Profess … Alistair," stuttered Wolfe. "What do you mean?"

"If Matthew was buying or acquiring historical artefacts in Europe at the rate he was, then not all of them could have been genuine. For example, during the Second World War, the Nazi's commissioned many budding artists to make copies of masterpieces ransacked by the marauding German army, the original would be sent to Berlin for storage and the fakes would be returned in their place. However, some of the high-ranking Nazi officers had other fakes made and they were forwarded to Berlin instead. The originals were hidden somewhere else entirely, you know, just in case, a bit of insurance, you know, what I mean?"

"So, you think some of the stuff Matthew returned with was fake but also some were real, and he would only mention the real gems and not the 'duds', as you called them?" concluded Wolfe.

"Precisely, like a gambler only tells you when they've won, not when they lose," replied the Professor.

Wolfe thought for a second or two before beginning with the next set of questions, but rather than dance around the subject that had been confirmed by his daughter's text, he decided to aim straight at it.

"Matthew Tanner or should I say, Armon Cabrinovic, was working on a novel at the time of his disappearance."

Buchanan Jones looked bemused and was about to say something but stopped when Wolfe raised his hand in a let me finish gesture.

"We know this for a fact, Alistair, and it doesn't really matter whether you are aware of this or not. However, the subject of this novel relates to an incident not that well documented until recently. The incident I refer to took place in 1911, and involved corruption and fraud at the highest level within the Austro-Hungarian Army. Do you know to which incident I'm referring to?"

"Oh, my God!" exclaimed the Professor. "I'm sorry, Inspector, but if this is the same ridiculous theory, so called Professor Tanner, had been expounding to me for months before his last trip abroad, it's completely baseless, juvenile and laughable."

"Enlighten me, Alistair," replied Wolfe without any hesitation

"Well, if you insist, but this is a waste of time," he replied with a sigh. "When the annexation of Serbia by the Austro Hungarian empire took place in 1911, it was rumoured by those close to the hierarchy of the Austro Hungarian Army and the Army of the Ottoman Empire, now known as Turkey, that some of the money paid to the Ottomans for relinquishing control of Serbia was kicked back to a General in the Austro Hungarian Army who was a Serbian sympathiser. Money has never been found because the General in question was in the convoy of cars attacked in Sarajevo during Archduke Franz Ferdinand's ill-fated visit. The convoy was attacked twice that day and it was the first attack that killed the General, he died taking the location of the money with him. The rest is history, as they say," he concluded, as if that were the end of the matter. Wolfe, however, had different ideas.

"Let's just suppose that Matthew Tanner found evidence for the kickback theory and decided to act upon it, can you remember what the destination of his last trip to Europe was?"

"He kept mentioning Vienna because that was the last known address of General Sorbrinovic, but then kept postponing his departure, cursing the fact that Sarajevo after the siege was still a no-go area, except for the UN of course. I found it all a little confusing," the Professor sighed again as if bored with this subject. He looked at Wolfe and remarked, "You do remember the siege of Sarajevo in the late 1990s?"

"Yes, of course. The Bosnian Army tried to starve and bomb the inhabitants of that city into submission, it was positively medieval," replied Wolfe knowingly.

Buchanan Jones nodded trying to hide his shock at the fact that Wolfe had summed up perfectly the event that took place towards the end of the 20th Century.

"As soon as the siege ended, Matthew was pestering the authorities, British and Serbian, to give him a permit to access the city, he wanted to help with the rebuilding of the university, in particular the library which had been severely damaged by the bombing. He wanted to help assess the damage then use his contacts with other universities to replenish the library."

"That was very noble of him," commented Wolfe.

"Matthew is of Serbian origin so he had emotional reasons, but yes, he threw himself into doing as much as he could to help rebuild the University of Serbia. Then later all he could do was talk about Sarajevo."

"So, the last time you saw Matthew, he was attempting to take a trip to, Sarajevo, you think … not Vienna?"

"Yes, he didn't mention Vienna again. I think he focused on the idea of helping in Sarajevo and forgot all about that ridiculous 'kickback' theory of 1911."

"But you haven't seen him or been contacted by him since then?"

"No, definitely not," the Professor said impatiently.

"I won't take up much more of your time, however, having researched the subject of General Sorbrinovic, using the internet, I can tell you, but no doubt you are already aware, Alastair, that this conspiracy theory has its roots in Serbia in 1912 when an article was published in the SOL newspaper. So, you see, Matthew Tanner may have given the impression that he uncovered or stumbled across the 'kickback theory' but in actual fact, he probably did just what I asked a colleague to do and consulted Google."

"So, you think he went to Sarajevo to find hidden loot, Inspector?"

"I believe, there is a strong possibility that is exactly what he did, but we can't be sure because he's gone missing," answered Wolfe as if stating the obvious.

"Best of luck with that line of enquiry, I believe, it will lead to a dead end," retorted Professor Buchanan Jones.

'An unfortunate choice of words, deliberate or accidental,' thought Wolfe.

Wolfe requested that photos from the university archive be sent to him, together with a list of students that had been tutored by Matthew Tanner during his tenure here at Leeds University up to his disappearance. Wolfe would receive the information in a day or so confirmed the Professor. The two shook hands across the office desk again, Wolfe thanked the Dean for his time and cooperation, as he got to the office door he turned and requested another favour.

"Alastair, do you know if the university still have in their possession any of Matthew Tanners belongings?"

"I'll check with HR and get back to you, Inspector."

Wolfe nodded his acknowledgement, left the office and made his way home to have tea with Izzy.

Chapter 14

Izzy woke earlier than usual the following morning and without hesitation, she got out of bed. Walking downstairs heading for the kitchen in search of cereal whilst wrapping a dressing gown around herself, she noticed a blue light radiating from behind the slightly ajar lounge door. She pushed the door fully open to see her father sat on the sofa, wearing pyjamas and dressing gown. He was staring at the flat screen TV, a laptop on the coffee table was open, the monitor showing the same image as that on the TV, Wolfe didn't avert his gaze.

"Morning, Isabella. Did you sleep well?"

"Dad, have you been up all night?"

"Yeah, I think so." He still didn't stop looking at the big screen TV. The image on the screen was a photo image of the investigation storyboard mounted in the squad room at the police station.

"I know there's going to be another murder and the victim will be one of the men in that centre photo. The body of the guy in the centre left was found yesterday morning and Matthew Tanner in the centre wearing a different military uniform disappeared twelve years ago, I suppose it could be argued that he should now be presumed dead. That leaves two people in the main picture and the blurred figure in the left foreground but I don't know which person is going to be next, and I'm powerless to prevent the inevitable happening. The person or persons indulging in this mayhem are way ahead of me and there's sod all I can do about it," Wolfe's tone was more matter of fact than depressed but Izzy could tell that her father felt helpless.

"Can't you send uniformed police to protect them?"

"No way, the boss tells me we don't have the resources and anyway, he's not convinced about the link between the two murders in the last few days, he thinks it's just coincidence," replied her father rather dejectedly.

Izzy sighed. "Tea and toast?" she asked in an attempt to break his concentration, but it had little impact.

"Yeah, marmite on my toast, please," he replied without looking at her.

She strode over to the audio system positioned on a shelf diagonally opposite the TV and searched through the library of artists and songs, found the song she was looking for and pressed the CD on button.

"This should cheer you up Dad, as you keep telling me whenever this song plays 'it's the best pop song ever written'."

T Rex, Get It On began to play, Marc Bolan at his very best.

Wolfe smiled, "What on earth would I do without you, Isabella?"

Five minutes later Izzy returned to the lounge, "I don't know, Dad, what would you do without me?" she replied, kissed him on his forehead and placed his breakfast on the right hand side of the table, she noticed the image had changed and rather took her by surprise. Both screens were filled with just one image, that of Charlotte Marks. Izzy thought that if Charlotte Marks knew her father was staring at an enlarged image of her on his computer, she wouldn't think so highly of him. A second or two later Wolfe took a half slice of the marmite on toast from the plate and looked away from the screen as he bit down on the savoury slice.

"Dad, Charley? Surely not! You can't believe she's got anything to do with this? You've been out with her … like on a date and everything."

"Well, I don't know what that's supposed to mean?" his gaze finally fully averted.

"It's just that … you two looked like you were enjoying each other's company, you know, like you were into each other."

"You say that as if it's weird?"

"Well, unusual rather than weird, if you now consider that she might be mixed up in this case."

Wolfe's attention was back on the TV screen. "Her brother was found dead on Thursday morning but she was laughing and flirting with me on Saturday afternoon, is that normal behaviour do you think?"

"Flirting! I don't think giving her a full-on snog when she left to go home can be remotely considered just flirting, Dad."

Wolfe felt a little embarrassed but didn't show it. "That's not relevant, Izzy, and anyway, I didn't think you'd noticed that and if you noticed, someone else might also have seen and if the boss finds out, I'll be in trouble."

"You don't think she had anything to do with her brother's death, do you?" Izzy said with surprise, more at herself having blurted out what she was thinking.

"That is not the face of a killer … at least, that's what I think, but maybe I'm too close to her and it's beginning to cloud my judgement," Wolfe replied pointing at the image on the TV.

Wolfe reset the screen so the full investigation board was visible again. Then, he turned his gaze away and concentrated on the breakfast Izzy had made for him. He hadn't been awake all night but had woke up in the early hours, his thoughts rebounding constantly from his interview with Professor Buchanan Jones and Charlotte Marks, his later thoughts not always relating to the two murder cases but intimately personal, he was, without a doubt, very attracted to Charlotte Marks.

Wolfe realised that Isabella wanted to get more involved in the case, she would undoubtedly think it was far more interesting than the A level History lesson that was first on her school timetable so he closed down his computer and insisted that she concentrate on her school work. She accepted her fate, decided to do as ordered and the two eventually left the house together, she to be dropped off at school on his way to Leeds. The traffic was less heavy than of late and he soon arrived at Holland Walk, the state-of-the-art glass cladded steel framed structure some twelve storeys high that dominated the skyline to the northern end of the city. The lowest three storeys of the building were dedicated to the West Yorkshire Police Force, the middle floors to commercial enterprises and the top five floors housing apartments, sold on the open market to those wealthy enough to be able to purchase them. The apartments had been sold off plan before construction had begun and the office space below had also attracted great interest from business's in particular legal firms that found the proximity of new police headquarters in the same building opposite the city courtrooms, too tempting to resist.

Following his interview with Professor Buchanan Jones the previous evening, Wolfe had formulated a strategy to find out as many facts as possible about the disappearance of Matthew Tanner. He had circulated an e-mail invite to all those in the investigation team to attend a briefing in the squad room at 10am. He checked his watch as he entered the lobby from the underground car park, it was 8.50am, time enough to prepare his brief.

"Morning, boss," said Middleton as she placed a cup of tea on the coaster next to his laptop as the desktop image appeared on the computer screen. The coaster was a Christmas present from his father-in-law five years ago, glass with the image of Marlon Brando as 'The Godfather' impregnated into it. The sound of china hitting glass penetrated Wolfe's thoughts.

"Morning, Pam, how are you?" he replied as he swivelled round on his chair.

"Yeah, good, have you got some new evidence on these murders?" obviously, referring to the 10am briefing that had been arranged by him.

"Patience, DC Middleton, all in good time, two bodies discovered in less than 72 hours, both murder victims?" he said nodding towards his computer screen which displayed the preliminary report of the car park shooting two days ago.

"Yes," replied Middleton, "without any doubt, according to the conclusions of both reports. Did you manage to read the e-mail I sent last night? Do you want hard copies?"

"Yes, please," said Wolfe. "Leave them on my desk, I'll get to them later today. Now have we got full attendance for the briefing?"

"All present and correct …" the opening guitar riff to Double Trouble interrupted their conversation.

Wolfe picked up his mobile phone, "DI Wolfe speaking."

"Wolfman," came the reply loud and brash with a West Indies slant.

"Toots! How the devil are you?"

"Don't sound too surprised, Detective Inspector, I might start to believe you didn't know two of your goons were at the airport this morning watching me?"

Wolfe looked straight at Middleton, and silently mouthed to her that she and Halford had been spotted by Toots Mateland.

"Come on, Toots, you know how it is. I have to cover all bases, ya know, corroborate reports if it ever came to court …"

"Court! You didn't mention anything about court. Now I'm definitely gonna employ a lawyer," replied Toots obviously incensed.

"Henry!" In the past, Wolfe used to use his first name to calm Toots down, stop him doing something rash and this strategy returned in an instant, just like old times. "Ease up a minute now and just understand things from our point of view. Now I've had no report yet from my two colleagues, so you tell me what occurred at the airport this morning?"

"Man, it's like you'd never been away, Jac, stringing me along with ya company shpeel, just like the past. Okay, well, no one arrived to take Matt Brookes seat on the plane, the flight took off without incident. Ya know, I cudda gone to Amsterdam then onto the West Indies for less than a 100 quid and me wudda dun five year ago, but me got responsibilities naa, so here I stay."

"Toots, get in touch with your guy in Jamaica and ask him to go to the airport over there as agreed, just to make sure nobody using Brookes name gets off, please, will you do that for me and report back later?"

"Already on the case, boss. I sent an e-mail to my man out there when I got back home, he thinks Matt is on the flight, he'll be a bit pissed off when he doesn't arrive, but I'll sort that."

"Thanks, I owe you a pint, Toots. You knew I'd have my people there, didn't you? And you didn't see them either did you? You just wanted to make sure, you're full of bull sometimes, Henry Mateland," replied Wolfe embarrassed.

"Got ya, Wolfman. Good ta have ya back, don't keep me waiting too long for that drink, call later." And with that, the line was disconnected.

"The pillock … he got me hook, line and sinker," Wolfe slammed the phone down.

"Well, now you know what I was just about to tell you, I'll file a report before the briefing starts," stated Middleton as she walked back towards her desk, not wishing to here Wolfe's reply. There wasn't one.

Wolfe decided to call Haigh Watson, he'd copied him into the invite but hadn't received a reply and he needed to know if he would be attending. Lynne, his PA, answered.

"He's not due in today, Jac," was her response.

"I see," said Wolfe without sounding too pleased.

"I have just responded to the meeting invite you sent last night." Wolfe saw the e-mail received flash on his monitor.

"Yeah, it's just arrived now, Lynne, thanks. If the chief should call, I'll keep the internal phone extension in the squad meeting room open so he can conference in if necessary, okay?"

"Wouldn't bother if I were you, Jac. He's meeting with the Mayor and two high ranking officers from the Met … all day … with lunch," she realised that she shouldn't have confided the whereabouts of the chief to other police staff unless specifically told to but she trusted DI Wolfe and knew he wouldn't blab to others.

"Mmmm. That's come around quick … so it will be official soon then?"

"This goes no further, Jac, or I'll lose my job," she replied in a whisper.

"No, of course, not," now Wolfe was whispering to.

"Word is Hickson has been paid off so they want MHW in post a.s.a.p. official announcement in the next couple of weeks."

"Ah, I see," replied Wolfe still in a hushed tone. Then louder, "Okay, Lynne, thanks." He returned the phone handset to its cradle.

Acting Chief Constable Marcus Haigh-Watson soon to become Chief Constable. *'They'll have to widen the office door just to get his head through'* thought Wolfe. Then his thoughts turned to ex Chief Constable Andrew Hickson, over thirty years on the force and now ignominiously pensioned off due to a lack of judgment, although, he had vehemently defended his innocence in the face of charges levelled at him with regards to gross misconduct. So why had he agreed to take a payoff? Wolfe was now more than a little perplexed at this news. Had he had more time, he might have chosen to research the charges against his former boss, the man who stood by him after his wife had been murdered and Wolfe had almost sunk into the abyss of alcoholism, the only senior officer on the squad who bothered about his wellbeing during his 'dark times'.

Chapter 15

The 10am briefing started on time with all in attendance, except the Acting Chief Constable. Middleton opened the briefing with an update of the post-mortems on the bodies of Matthew Brookes and Frank Jessop. They had been killed within 72 hours of each other and the pathologist report had confirmed that both had been unlawfully killed, murdered. She informed everyone that, at first, the investigations weren't officially linked. This was a careful statement aimed at DI Wolfe and his initial hunch that the murders were linked, albeit tenuously, but unless further evidence to the contrary comes to light, these events are considered to be part of the same investigation as I will now explain. Wolfe nodded and smiled. *'She is a bloody good presenter, another quality hunch'* he thought.

Middleton continued, and confirmed that Matthew Brookes died somewhere between 11pm the previous Wednesday night and 3am Thursday morning. The murder weapon being a 'spear' a very thin high tensile steel skewer approx.150mm long that penetrated the victims lower back in two locations one either side of the torso to a sufficient depth on his left side to cause lethal damage to the victim's left kidney, causing acute trauma leading to heart failure. Middleton also explained that the discovery location of the body was such that it would take more than one person to place the victim's body in the situation where it was found by workmen at 8am on the Thursday morning. The report also concluded the victim was not killed where the body was discovered; however, a statement by the proprietor of the restaurant near where the victim was found does not give any further evidence as to how the body came to be there. However forensic investigation of the wider area, in particular the car park leading up to Blackhill Hide, found scratch marks in the surface consistent with tyre jacks fitted to Ford Transit vans less than five years old. It is possible that the perpetrators were driving the vehicle when it received a puncture and used the car park to make the repair out of sight, less conspicuous than the moor road. Disposing of the body of Matthew Brookes near Blackhill Hide was quite possibly a spur of the moment decision.

Referring to the amount of class A narcotic found in the victim's body, she stated that the amount of heroin found in the deceased's blood would be enough to cause death through organ failure however the report concludes this was administered after death, in an attempt to hide the real reason for the man's demise and due to the heart failure, the heroin hadn't been distributed fully around the body.

As a result, she explained,

"The exact time of death cannot, therefore, be determined accurately. However, the forensic evidence points to death no earlier than 11pm or later than 3am, a four-hour window. Matthew Brookes' whereabouts prior to 11pm last Wednesday need to be established."

Middleton set out a strategy of investigation for each of the two teams of detectives. Enquiries should now concentrate on known associates of Matthew Brookes, known haunts for him and how each pair of two detectives would be expected to focus on Brookes' movements. They would have to be tactful, Brookes is known to have been a drug user but the investigation should not focus on this aspect of his past life, only last known whereabouts and contacts. One of the detectives, DC Harry Fairburn, drafted in two days previously from the South Yorkshire Force without Wolfe being consulted, asked a question almost but not quite interrupting Middleton.

"There seems to be an overriding influence of drug use in this case. Shouldn't this be the focus of this investigation? Maybe this murder is the result of a dispute over turf, Mr Brookes might have been dealing in drugs, he was a user but, perhaps, he was dealing in other narcotics, maybe he trod on another dealer's toes?"

Wolfe stood up next to Middleton.

"That's a lot of maybes, DC Fairburn." A sudden change in the atmosphere swept through the room like a sand storm. "I assume, you've read all the background information handed to you yesterday by DC Middleton?" Wolfe was now staring directly at the newly arrived Detective waiting for a response.

"Yes, sir, I have and it appears to me that drugs …"

"No, Detective, you haven't!" exclaimed Wolfe in a raised voice making sure he had the full attention of all.

"You have been given a precise of this information by another officer in this force whom, I assure you, has a very blinkered view of the direction this investigation is moving in because he has not interpreted the facts accurately."

"But, sir, surely, the facts are open to different interpretations," responded Fairburn, his cheeks visibly blushing deep red.

"Detective Fairburn, Matthew Brookes was the fortunate recipient of a lottery win a few years ago. His most recent bank statement shows more £400,000 on deposit and we have a sworn statement from an associate that he was indeed buying drugs but in quantities that amount to personal use, not dealing, that in itself, though, is not sufficient to rule out dealing. However, if a turf war, was as you suggest, the reason for this poor soul's demise, how do you account for the obvious attempt to mask the real cause of death?" Fairburn stayed quiet.

Wolfe concluded, "Contract killing, perhaps, but not drugs turf war related, Detective, because the methodology of his murder shows a certain amount of finesse, not the rough tough instant spur of the moment killing that you would associate with a drugs related murder. However, DC Fairburn you have the right to question the direction this investigation is taking but if I were you, I'd read the case notes before offering remarks. Shall we continue?" Wolfe scanned the room, there was no response.

Middleton got straight back into her stride. "We can be a lot more accurate about the time of death of the second victim Mr Frank Jessop," stated Middleton with the red beam of the laser pointer positioned in the middle of the forehead of an enlarged driving licence photo of Jessop, not very sympathetic considering how he had died, shot through the head.

"Oops, sorry, didn't mean to be that insensitive," as she turned the laser pointer off. When the sniggering finished, she continued,

"CCTV of the arrival of the Jessop's Range Rover is available on the departments' IT server. However, this still frame photo shows clearly that Mr Jessop was driving the vehicle as it entered the multi storey car park from Horizon Way." Middleton outlined in detail where the investigation was now heading. "Now, I'll hand you over to DI Wolfe to conclude the briefing."

Wolfe stood and took up the place vacated by Middleton, thinking when this investigation was over, he'd fight hard to keep her on his team.

"Thanks, DC Middleton … ah." Wolfe noticed that Haigh-Watson had arrived and was now seated at the back of room listening to the briefing. *'How long has he been here?'* mused Wolfe.

"… A well-presented and concise appraisal of the current status of this investigation. I would like to emphasise to those who are finding it a little difficult to see the connection that both these murders are connected. Matthew Brookes was a previous employee of Hennersy Contracting and Frank Jessop is the MD of Hennersy Contracting, the two men that found Brookes were working for Hennersy Contracting." Wolfe tapped display board, "This photo is a copy of the photo found in the residence of Charlotte Marks the brother of Matthew Brookes. Please note that Matthew Tanner, posing in the foreground, has been missing since this photo was taken twelve years ago. We are not at this time extending these investigations to include Mr Tanner however it is important that we confirm the whereabouts of these two persons, he pointed to the photo again, Thomas Henry Smythe and David Watts as soon as possible as I believe they are in danger. We could be looking at a vendetta and it may turn out that drugs are involved but it does not indicate a dispute over territory, more importantly, in this regard, our contacts on the streets indicate all is quiet." He took a breath and concluded with, "Two teams will immediately be dispatched to the known addresses, home and work, of Smythe and Watts. DC Middleton has the team lists printed out ready for issue, this briefing is now concluded, please be ready to re-convene tomorrow. Thank you for your cooperation." Wolfe immediately started walking towards Haigh Watson.

As Wolfe approached Haigh Watson, he saw him swipe his iPhone and place it in his tunic pocket, then he took his peaked cap from the table in front of him and placed it on his head as he stood up. Wolfe, gradually, purposefully, straightened his back in response.

"Did you wish to address the team, sir?" stated Wolfe with rather more authority than he'd intended looking down on his boss, but Wolfe really couldn't care how his request sounded.

"No, DI Wolfe, I haven't anything to add … it seemed to me your girlfriend covered all the bases quite adequately … rehearsing overnight, were you?"

"There's no substance to your accusations, sir, I should really make an official complaint but that would probably lead to an immediate suspension for me cause you'd deny the accusation and DI Rhys Owen would be installed as lead investigator together with his stooge DC Fairburn, recently drafted into my squad without my approval," parried Wolfe.

Haigh Watson was about to react when he realised that he and Wolfe were not alone. Wolfe had the upper hand here, the superior officer being the one that had to show restraint. Wolfe had taken his opportunity well and wasn't ready to let it rest at that.

"DC Fairburn will report directly to me, isn't that correct, sir? Proper protocol has to be observed at all times, proper line management, can't have a future defence lawyer making propaganda of a lack of procedure within the force, can we, sir?"

"No … quite right, DI Wolfe," replied Haigh Watson, turning to leave and gritting his teeth. "I would like to have a word with you in my office … DI Wolfe, with regard to this investigation."

"Yes … sir … just give me ten minutes to tidy up here and I'll report to your office."

With Haigh Watson gone, striding noisily down the corridor towards the staircase up to his office, Wolfe turned to Middleton.

"Do you want to make a formal complaint about his accusations? I'll support you if you do."

"No, not necessary, Jac. Be careful, he's after you. Is there history between you two because it certainly looks that way?" replied Middleton.

"He didn't want me back on the force, sees me as an accident waiting to happen and probably thinks I've got another agenda … Maria's murder still unsolved … a copper emotionally insecure and working on a high-profile case is a copper who will make mistakes … that's what he thinks anyway."

"So, he links you and me together to make out that I'm your emotional replacement for your deceased wife because I'm more visible, and I'm also dispensable. If you go, he'll get rid of me as well and bring his brown-nosed pals in from South Yorkshire."

"Yep, that's about the measure of it. I'm sorry that you're involved, Pam, you don't deserve it, you're a good detective," concluded Wolfe with genuine concern.

"Don't go soft on me, boss," replied Middleton, stern with authority. "Go in there and take what he has to offer, and then let's get this case solved, that'll shut him up."

Wolfe left the meeting room and headed towards Haigh Watson's office. Halfway up the stairs, his mobile phone rang, removing it from the inside pocket of his jacket and raising it into view, he noted the caller id, Halford.

"Pete, is this urgent or can it wait? I'm just about to meet his majesty."

"Boss, David Watts is missing," Halford said with obvious concern. "The force received a call from his wife and she left a message on my voicemail. I've just finished speaking to her, she says he didn't come home last night and his car isn't on the drive."

"Shit!" replied Wolfe. He was now standing outside Haigh Watson's outer office. "Get over to the Watts place and call me from there."

"Yes, sir," replied Halford. Wolfe put the phone back in his pocket.

Entering the outer office, he walked towards the inner office. "He's expecting me, Lynne, so I'll go …"

"No, Inspector, he's not al–" But before she could finish, Wolfe had opened the door into the Chief's office.

Wolfe was not surprised when he saw DC Fairburn sat opposite Haigh Watson separated by the chief's oak desk. "Oh … you wanted a word with me, sir? Does this involve the Detective Constable here?" he said with mock embarrassment, his question directed at his superior.

"Ah … DI Wolfe … err … no," came the stuttered reply. Silence followed, "I'm afraid, I've forgotten what it was I wanted to speak to you about. You've made a wasted journey up here."

"Oh, well … actually, I haven't … sir," Wolfe stated. "You see, there's been a development." He paused, looked at DC Fairburn and said, "Harry, I need you to report immediately to the squad room and start making enquiries about David Watts, his business and contacts outside his family." Fairburn looked with confusion at Haigh Watson on the other side of the desk. "Now, constable," barked Wolfe, "time is of the essence … it's an order, young man, move yourself."

Wolfe was evoking proper protocol, Haigh Watson had no recourse but to agree. "Go on, Harry, we'll continue our discussion later."

Fairburn stood and walked to the office door, Wolfe held the door open for him and as they passed each other, Wolfe whispered, "If I find out that you've been discussing this investigation behind my back, I'll have you back in uniform quicker than you can say arse licker," he hissed.

When the door closed, Wolfe turned to see Haigh Watson standing behind his desk. Once again, Wolfe straightened his back and immediately stood taller.

"What the fuck was that, Detective Inspector?" he yelled, purposely loud enough so the departing constable would hear.

"Oh no, I'm not raising to your bait, you obnoxious little shit," Wolfe replied in a low tone so only the two of them would catch his reply. He turned in a motion intended to give the impression that he too was about to exit the office.

"Where the hell do you think you're going, Wolfe?"

"As I just informed you, Chief, there's been a development and I have to direct my team."

"We're related, he's my nephew and for your information, he's a good detective, very talented, gonna go far that boy." Haigh Watson sat down, his head beginning to droop.

"What?" said Wolfe, now he was momentarily confused, he hadn't expected Haigh Watson's revelation just yet, he now had to offer some honesty.

"Oh … I found out it was you who seconded him here … sir. I made enquiries when I saw him on the squad list yesterday but I didn't know you were related."

"Well it's not common knowledge."

"Look," Wolfe started as he moved closer to the chief's desk, "I'm also aware of his abilities, he comes highly recommended, however, if you take my advice …" Haigh Watson lifted his head and was about to retaliate at this latest show of, what he saw as insubordination, when Wolfe lifted his right hand in acknowledgement of his boss's thoughts.

"Let him make his own way, he will learn more from making mistakes than you or I could ever teach him." Wolfe sat down at the desk that separated them. "Marcus, you and I don't see eye to eye, I know you want me out, you consider me a liability …"

"DI Wolfe, that is not the case, your past record is impress …"

"That's it right there, my past record, you think that after Maria's death, I'm not focused, alcohol and drug abuse issues, you didn't agree with Andy Hickson's decision to bring me back onto the force after my rehabilitation. Maria is dead, unlawfully killed, the case still open and no one charged with her death. I have to accept that and I have, but yes, there were difficult times for me before I could make my peace with life after Maria. I'm back and I believe I'm a better, a more focused investigator, and Hickson, believed that too." Wolfe took breath as a vision flashed across his mind, the man in front of him flying through the window behind, but that's all it was, a vision, a thought.

"Calm down, Jac, if I'd really wanted you out, you wouldn't be here."

Wolfe decided to leave it there, this argument wouldn't be settled here and besides, Hickson might, one day, with a bit of luck, be back in this office, Wolfe just had to wait and hope.

"You said there had been a development in the Brookes/Jessop case?" enquired Haigh-Watson.

"David Watts, one of the other men in the photo, has disappeared. A message was received by our call centre, and the name registered with our investigation. We called his home number and spoke to his wife, she stated that he hadn't returned home yesterday, out all night. She is very worried, only made worse by the fact that we, the police, made contact, less than hour after she left the message Halford has been dispatched to the family home to interview Mrs Watts. I'll keep you informed." Wolfe stood, turned and began to move towards the door.

"It would appear as though your theory might be beginning to gain momentum, DI Wolfe. What about Tommy Smith? Are you sending a team out to his home?" asked Haigh Watson almost conciliatory in its tone.

"Smythe, sir, not Smith," replied Wolfe. "Yes, that is my next move." And with that response, he closed the office door walked through the inner office, smiled at Lynne and walked into the corridor towards the stairs. Suddenly, he paused, just for a second. "Tommy Smith?" he said to himself, shook his head and continued on his way.

Chapter 16

"Sir, we've located and visited the last known address of Thomas Henry Smythe but there was no sign of Mr Smythe ... no sign of anyone at all," Fairburn reported as they stood in DI Wolfe's office. Wolfe wanted him close, involved but not too involved in the detail or key interviews that way only basic information would get back to Haigh Watson from his nephew.

"Known relatives?" asked Wolfe.

"Son, Paul and ex-wife, Jennifer, now using her maiden name of ..." he looked down at his notebook. "Harrington," he continued without looking up from his notes. "Paul Smythe lives in Carlton at ..." Wolfe heard the constable announce the address and he felt his chest immediately tighten as the DC finished reading it out.

"Moor Top, Panorama Drive, Carlton." He looked up to see Wolfe staring straight past him as if something were happening behind.

'That's where Charlotte Marks lives,' Wolfe was thinking to himself.

The room fell silent for a few seconds before the young DC continued, "Jennifer Harrington lives in Grove House, Carlton, No.6."

"You okay, sir?" he asked.

"Yeah, yeah ... those apartments are luxury abodes."

"I don't know the area that well, sir," Fairburn replied.

"Okay, constable, thank you. Please ask DC Middleton to come into my office, will you?"

"Yes, sir." Fairburn closed the office door on his way out.

Wolfe sat behind his desk looking blankly at his laptop computer screen concentrating only on his thoughts of Charlotte Marks. He realised that since meeting this woman, she had not been very far from his mind, in fact, there had been times, like now, when she was all he could think about.

Middleton knocked and without waiting, entered Wolfe's office.

"Sir, you wanted to speak me?"

She noticed that he looked deep in thought so she sat down in the chair in front of his desk and remained silent.

A few seconds elapsed before Wolfe said,

"This is a Pam and Jac moment, I'm afraid, completely off the record."

"Okay," she replied. "What's the problem?"

"The problem is that I have been socialising with the partner of a man who we will need to interview in connection with the double murder case. Actually, if anyone not involved officially with this investigation had seen the two of us recently, they would probably assume that we were ..." He paused for a thought. "Well, more intimate than just social friends ... if you know what I mean?"

"I don't understand, Jac, you'll have to explain."

Wolfe took a breath. "Charley … I mean, Charlotte Marks, sister of the deceased person we found on Carlton Moor that started this investigation, is the partner of Paul Smythe, the son of Thomas Smythe who we believe may be another target and we're trying to find his whereabouts, so we can protect him."

"Ah … now I understand. Izzy mentioned you were out with someone the other evening that she described as a 'very attractive woman', blonde and tall as well," said Middleton with an inner smile.

"Yes, that's her … but when were you talking to Izzy … no, that's not important … but what is important, is that our meeting –"

"You mean, liaison," interrupted Middleton, this time showing a smile.

"This isn't funny, Pam, me being seen with this woman could complicate at best and compromise at worst, any possible court case … and this investigation hasn't really got going yet but we've got two dead bodies, connected however tenuously to the partner of a woman that I have been seen socialising with."

"Fraternising, I would call it." Now she was wearing a wide smile.

A seemingly dejected Wolfe replied, "He'll use this … will, shiny bollocks to throw me off the case, maybe even demote me, throw me off the force all together, possibly."

"Jac, that's enough," Middleton said with an air of authority that made Wolfe look up in surprise. Middleton realised that Wolfe believed he had made an error of judgement. "It's not that bad. Let's go interview this partner of hers, you introduce yourself as the Detective that came to give the bad news about her brother, he'll know that you've met previously. If it comes out that the two of you were spotted in a more socially relaxed atmosphere, then we'll cross that bridge when we get there, but I doubt she'll admit anything in front of her partner."

Wolfe thought in silence for a while.

"Perhaps you're right, Pam, at least, I hope you're right," Wolfe replied not trying to hide his reluctant acceptance of her summary of the situation. "Get a meeting arranged with Paul Smythe, but in the meantime, make sure we still keep trying to contact his father."

DC Middleton left the office, leaving Wolfe on his own, she came back a few minutes later carrying a cup of tea and a couple of biscuits. Wolfe seemed to be concentrating on typing something, he looked and said, "Thanks Pam that's much appreciated."

A couple of hours later with the meeting with Paul Smythe arranged, Wolfe answered a phone call from Haigh Watson, he required an update on the murder cases prior to his first appearance before the media.

Wolfe went straight to his office sat down opposite him and briefed him regarding the latest aspects of the case. As far as Wolfe was concerned not all facets of the case should be released to the media but it wasn't his responsibility to make that decision, that belonged to the man sat in front of him.

"So, you are suggesting that we tell the media as little as possible, DI Wolfe?" responded Haigh Watson trying to spread the authority between him and Wolfe.

"What I'm suggesting, sir, is that we only release facts to the media, anything that is still under investigation has yet to be confirmed as fact."

"And, Detective Inspector, the facts are …" he replied with a gesture that meant go on DI Wolfe continue.

Wolfe knew this was a test, a report of the case covering both murders was already on Haigh Watson's desk and he could see it resting there next to his laptop, but with much inner reluctance, he decided not to antagonise his boss so replied by explaining that the body of a man had been discovered on Carlton Moor last Thursday morning. The body of another man had been discovered on Sunday morning in a multi storey car park in Leeds. Both victims had been positively identified and can be confirmed as Matthew Brookes and Francis Jessop. The forensic reports for both victims confirmed they were both unlawfully killed. The two killings are being treated as one investigation at present because there is evidence linking together the known contacts of both victims.

"Is that it, Detective Inspector?" responded Haigh Watson without hiding his annoyance. "The media will require a lot more, the papers are already reporting that these murders are the result of some gangland vendetta and that more victims are bound to be discovered."

"Pure speculation, sir, not a shred of evidence exists to imply such a conclusion," retorted Wolfe trying not to sound too indignant.

"But we have evidence to prove otherwise, don't we DI Wolfe?" Haigh-Watson was by now thumbing through the report. "We have names linking the two and oh, what's this …" he continued mockingly, "Brookes, a known drug user and it even states he was arrested on suspicion of possession with intent to sell, a matter of public record that most ordinary hacks can access, so there you are, Inspector." He paused for effect. "Evidence," he stated.

"All charges were dropped, also a matter of public record," said Wolfe. "But perhaps, we should let the media run with the story, it might give our investigation space to pursue the actual cause and effect of these murders."

"Cause and effect, Wolfe, have you been reading police work text books?"

"Sir, I have an investigation to lead, your comments are imperceptive, I'll leave you to work on your report to the press." He stood up, pushed the chair further away from the desk and left Haigh Watson's office leaving the door open.

In the office beyond, he said to Lynne, "And he's gonna be our new leader … God help us."

The door to the corridor closed behind him, he didn't hear a response. "Fucking idiot," he mumbled to himself.

On the floor below, he walked past Middleton, tapped her on the shoulder.

"You and me to Jennifer Harrington's house now, we'll call her on the way if we can find a phone number," he said in a voice louder than he had intended. Then he looked over the partition of Middleton's desk towards Halford's workstation

"Pete, find an address for a Mr Matthew Tanner, Professor of Modern History at Leeds University but he hasn't been seen for twelve years or so, try passed electoral registers."

Halford looked up from his desk and started to write, then looking at Middleton whilst Wolfe headed towards his office. "What?" he mimed as she looked at her boyfriend.

"Just do as he says," replied Middleton. "I think he's pissed off with a certain someone upstairs but I have a feeling, he's onto something, see you later." She blew him a kiss and put on her jacket.

Five minutes later, Wolfe and Middleton were on the road, Wolfe driving his roadster towards Carlton. He'd calmed down a little but said to Middleton whilst they were parked at traffic lights in Leeds City Centre.

"I hope you don't mind, but there again, it doesn't matter if you do, I'm going to play some Sleaford Mods at high volume, they're up front and proud … oh and they swear a lot."

"Play who … what?" said Middleton, confused.

"Philistine," he replied with a grin. "They're a two-piece electronic punk band from Nottingham and they vent their frustrations with life and politics in music … this track is called Jobseeker."

Middleton decided not to reply, the traffic lights changed to green and Wolfe accelerated away with tempered aggression.

By the time they'd arrived in Carlton, the Sleaford Mods had been replaced by a Tom Waites track 16 Shells from a Thirty Ought Six, a connection not lost on Middleton. The sound system in Wolfe's Z4 had been emitting uninterrupted rigorous hard music for forty minutes, Middleton was surprised by the fact that she quite liked Wolfe's taste in music.

Chapter 17

The Grove is the busy main thoroughfare in Carlton, a tree lined avenue with shops facing south, old-fashioned display windows shaded by an array of awnings. The centre of attention on this street is, undoubtedly, Betty's. Great business is obviously still to be had providing that most English of pastimes, afternoon teas, and selling home baked bread, cakes and pastries. The Parish Church and bandstand concourse are the focal points on the opposite side facing north. The late spring captures the best The Grove has to offer under afternoon sunshine, the Cherry Blossom trees are at their most vibrant, it's a joy to behold but now in late winter, the cloud cover dulls everything down to a grey colourless shroud, depressingly bare branches sag lacking the enthusiasm to do anything else.

Middleton and Wolfe arrived at a car park entrance serving a large multi storey block of mock Victorian apartments at the west end of The Grove in Carlton where Jennifer Harrington lived. On this cold drab weekday, the building looked heavy and overbearing like the sky above. Wolfe pressed the button to apartment No.6.

"Hello," was the response over the intercom.

"Jennifer Harrington?"

"Speaking."

"I'm Detective Inspector Jaxon Wolfe, I'm accompanied by DC …"

"Yes, I'm expecting you, park in visitors if you would." And with that the line went dead and the wrought iron gates began to swing open.

"… Middleton," he said to himself as he drove through the car park into a space-marked visitor.

"Good job we found her phone number and called ahead, I don't think we'd have got past those gates without an appointment," stated Middleton.

Wolfe was out of the car and at the main entrance to the apartment block before Middleton. He was about to press the button marked 'Apartment 6' when he heard Jennifer Harrington's voice, "The door is open, Inspector, I'm on the second floor." She'd obviously seen him approaching. *'Mmmm video entry, very security conscious,'* he thought.

The two detectives walked up four flights of stairs to the second floor that coiled their way around the lift shaft; the communal areas were fitted with expensive carpet, flowers and mirrors occupied the focal points.

"I'll bet you need to be well off to live here," commented Middleton in a low voice just before they turned the corner to the final flight of stairs up to the second floor. On reaching the second floor, Jennifer Harrington was waiting at the entrance to her apartment.

"Please, come in," she said. They followed her over the threshold into what immediately struck Wolfe as a very spacious apartment. The two detectives followed her from the entrance hall into the lounge through a pair of glazed double doors.

"Please, seat yourselves where you wish. Would you like a drink?" she asked. "Tea or coffee, being as you are both, I assume, on duty?"

"Tea for me, Mrs Harrington," said Wolfe as he relaxed into a large easy chair, immediately realising his error he was about to correct himself but was interrupted by Middleton.

"Me too," she announced from one side of the sofa.

"Harrington is my maiden name, Inspector, as I'm sure you are aware."

"Yes, I …"

"An easy mistake, just call me Jennifer, but not Jenny if you don't mind. Oh, and please don't use the term Ms, I'm far too advanced in years for such a title." And with that, she walked out of the lounge, to the kitchen.

"This place is a bit posh," Middleton said in a whisper.

Wolfe ignored her remark, "Pam, I want you to start this interview, ask about her ex's whereabouts and then try to get an insight into the reason for their split."

"No problem, gov."

A few minutes later, Jennifer Harrington was back, carrying a tray with a teapot and three cups, saucers, and a plate of biscuits. The tray was placed on the light oak coffee table, and they were served with cups of tea and the biscuits during which time, normal pleasantries were exchanged. Then,

"So, Detective Inspector Wolfe, what can I do for you?"

"Jennifer, we're here to discuss your ex-husband," said Middleton.

"What you're about to tell me must be serious and because you are talking first, young lady, I assume, you are expecting some form of emotional response from me, well, that won't happen."

Wolfe looked at her, a little unsure as to her meaning.

"Jennifer, have you seen Mr Smythe recently?" she asked. Then immediately continued, "We've been to his house at Highton on several occasions but unfortunately, it appears as though he's not in residence."

"The last time I saw Thomas Henry was about two weeks ago." She reached down the side of the chair she was sitting in and from her handbag, extracted a mobile phone. She touched the screen a few times. "Yes, Thursday the 20th in the evening, my son, Paul, Thomas and myself went out for a meal, err … the Kashmiri on Leeds Road, table booked for 7.30pm, it says here."

"Have you any idea where he may be at present?"

"Well, if he's not at his home in Highton, then he's probably in Spain at his place near Marbella," she replied. "And if he's not there, then I've no idea where he is … and quite frankly, I don't care where he might be!"

Wolfe now got the message, there was no love lost between her and her ex-husband.

"Do you still regularly see Mr Smythe, even though you're no longer married?" asked Wolfe.

"No, not really, I only agreed to meet because Paul asked me to. If it had been Thomas only, I wouldn't have gone."

"Was there anything out of the ordinary in his behaviour that night?"

"Detective? …" asked Jennifer.

"Pamela Middleton," replied the DC.

"Detective Middleton, my ex-husband was his usual self and before you ask, he was the same as he was for the last few years of our marriage, that is to say he was his typical arrogant self, conceited and overconfident. We were celebrating our son's success in a business venture, he's in property development just like Thomas used to be. All Thomas could say was that he would have done a better deal and Paul had paid too much for the property, no praise whatsoever. You see, Paul took over the business from Thomas but the business was broke, that self-centred bully had drained all the profits into his own offshore account and left Paul with a ..." She paused for thought. "... What do they call it? A lame duck business? Paul has done really well to turn it around but it took nearly ten years. Anyway, judging by Thomas's attitude towards him, I wouldn't have blamed Paul if he'd punched him—"

Wolfe interrupted, "Did an argument break out between them?"

"No, Paul is far too sensible to act in a way that would cause me embarrassment, Inspector. He's a very restrained and calm man, he just smiled at Thomas and accepted the criticism, although, that just wound that ignorant bastard up even more. He became loud and very opinionated. At one point, the restaurant manager had to tell him to lower his voice, other diners were beginning to complain."

Jumping in with his question, Wolfe asked, "Was your ex-husband's behaviour influenced by alcohol, did father and son argue often?"

"My ex-husband always had a problem with alcohol ... he couldn't get enough." Middleton shot a knowing glance at Wolfe, he came back with a dark scowl.

Jennifer continued, "He's one of those men, they think they can handle drink and they down as much beer as they can at any given opportunity, but, in fact, they just get drunk, loud and obnoxious, a complete turn off." She looked at Middleton. "You know what I mean?"

Middleton smiled in acknowledgement.

"So did Mr Smythe calm down after the manager had a word with him?" she responded.

"Not really. A few minutes later, I asked the manager to order a taxi to take Thomas home, Paul and I stayed on, and as I recall, I finished my bottle of wine. Paul brought me home in his car about half past ten or thereabouts. I haven't spoken to Thomas since then." She paused and stared at her phone. "He sent me a text a couple of days later, apologising for his behaviour, and I sent one back telling him that it wasn't me but Paul he should be apologising to and he could fuck off ... sorry for the language but my ex-husband, really is one of the most hateful of men you are ever likely to meet, although when we first married and Paul came along he was a good husband and father, but for some reason he changed, and it got worse the more wealthy we became."

Wolfe wanted to move on quickly so he ignored Jennifer Harrington's apology.

"Jennifer, I have a photo here." Wolfe placed the photo obtained from Matthew Brookes' sister on the coffee table facing her. "Do you recognise the men in this photo?"

"Oh yes, my son and his partner have a photo just like this in their house, but why are you asking me about ..."

"Please answer my question first and I'll then explain," he interrupted.

"Well, that's Thomas, that's Frankie Jessop, that's Davy Watts and the other one ..." She paused, concentrating her gaze on the image. "... is Matthew Tanner." She kept looking for a moment or two, then looked up at Wolfe, who was staring straight at her.

"He's been missing since not long after this photo was taken," she said looking straight at Wolfe.

"You've found him, haven't you? He's dead?" Tears began to gather in the corner of her eyes, noticed by both detectives.

"Jennifer," said Wolfe in a sympathetic tone, "have a drink of tea."

Whilst Jennifer Harrington sipped her tea, she began to relax and the tears subsided as Wolfe explained two bodies had been found, that Francis Jessop was dead, and their investigations into the two killings meant that Smythe and Watts needed to be contacted but neither could be currently located so a wider circle of friends and family were being tracked down to try to locate them. Wolfe then named the person found on Carlton Moor the previous Thursday morning and confirmed that it was the brother of Charlotte Marks.

"So, my son's partner has a brother who is dead and Francis is dead too. I didn't know Charlotte had a brother, and you think that this photo means that Thomas and Davy are in danger?"

Wolfe could see she was beginning to get agitated and was trying to understand the significance of the photo, so he decided not to mention the fact that Davy Watts was already reported as missing, he was certain she had no concerns for Smythe, just Watts.

"We only want to contact the other two men to confirm their whereabouts and ask them to take care," Middleton explained, "has anything out of the ordinary happened recently?"

"I couldn't give a damn about my ex but Davy is such a nice guy from what I recall. Although I haven't seen him for a long time, probably since this photo was taken, but I do see Sue, his wife, from time to time in Carlton and always ask how he is. I got the impression both he and Francis were doing well," Jennifer sounded as though the initial shock was beginning to wear off.

"You say Thomas Smythe's behaviour changed and got worse a few years ago."

"Yes, our married life for 16 years was good, but when Paul finished his GCSE's at school, Thomas changed, treating me and Paul in particular with utter distain, he wouldn't even eat with us, he started working late at the office and spending time abroad with his friends. Paul had to complete his A levels at a state school because Thomas refused to pay the fees for the private school."

Wolfe interjected.

"What caused this change, Jennifer?"

"I have no idea, Inspector, I tried to discuss it with him but he didn't want to talk about it, he just kept repeating the same thing, 'he'd had enough of married life, and felt choked and constrained by me and Paul, he wanted his freedom back'. I think that was just lies, as I said I think it had something to do with money, the property development business was booming then. Mind you if it hadn't been for those times I wouldn't be living here." She mused as she looked out of the Lounge window which gave an oblique view of The Grove. "Anyway, we divorced a year after Paul completed his degree in Economics, Thomas didn't even turn up to Paul's Graduation at the LSE. I got all I could, citing some tart he was sleeping with, and he didn't contest it so I got this apartment and £1.5million in the bank."

"Jennifer, you say Thomas had run the business down, but, Paul got involved and managed to turn it around, were Paul and Thomas working together?" asked Wolfe.

"Ha! Work together. Paul had far more sense than to work with or for his father." She paused. "No, I think Paul wanted to prove himself to Thomas so he took a job in the city for a year and then made Thomas an offer that he couldn't really refuse." Jennifer paused in thought, then she continued with more than a hint of emotional pride, "He worked so hard that year, eventually, with his own money, a loan from a business investment bank and a push from me on Thomas, I owned 49% of the shares so I told Thomas I'd sell to lowest nastiest investor I could find if he didn't sell his shares to Paul. So the outstanding tax owed to the Inland Revenue was paid off and Thomas relinquished all rights to the company."

"What's the name of the company, Jennifer?" asked Middleton, note pad and pen poised.

"Britannia Limited," stated Jennifer Harrington.

Wolfe decided to bring the focus back to the subject of their visit, repeatedly asking questions about Thomas Henry Smythe's whereabouts but Jennifer Harrington kept answering in the same negative way, she didn't care about her ex-husband's wellbeing at all. Wolfe began to think there was probably more to the acrimonious breakdown of their marriage than was being alluded to.

Wolfe and Middleton began to think that they had exhausted their array of questions, when without really considering the consequences, Wolfe asked Jennifer Harrington if she could explain why Matthew Tanner was part of the photograph, it was still in full view on the coffee table.

"Matthew was one of Thomas's best friends. During the good times in our marriage, Matthew would be a regular visitor to Highton. Thomas and Matthew were always talking about Europe, and making plans to journey to various places. Matthew was a bit of a treasure hunter, you might say and Thomas would be his facilitator, at least, that's what it appeared to be," responded Jennifer, opening up a complete new avenue of questioning for Wolfe.

"What do you mean by … facilitator?" he asked.

"Thomas would sort out the logistics, you know, flight times, mapping routes organising transport, even sorting out mechanical machinery sometimes, you know that sort of thing. They'd been friends longer than I'd known Thomas and even if Thomas couldn't go to Europe with Matthew, he would still help with the planning. This photograph was taken in 2005, I think, Matthew didn't come back from that trip, but Thomas, Francis and Davy did." She stopped again deep in thought. "I haven't spoken to Francis or Davy since this photo was taken, they all seemed in very high spirits, Matthew in particular, going back to Sarajevo to help re-build the national library, you know after the siege."

Wolfe decided to admit that he knew Matthew Tanner had another name that he used in the publication of historical educational texts, Armon Cabrinovic.

"Yes, Matthew preferred to use his English name as a mark of respect to his stepfather, a school teacher in North Yorkshire, who'd treated him as his own son after he and his mother fled Russian occupied Eastern Europe towards the end of the war. From what Matthew told me he was just a baby, not yet a year old when they arrived in the UK."

DC Middleton was frantically writing all this down on her notepad abbreviating where she could and concentrating so hard that asking questions would have to remain with Wolfe.

"How do you know all this information about Matthew … er, Armon, Jennifer?" questioned Wolfe.

"Oh," she paused, "he readily talked about it socially when he visited me and Thomas, he was desperate to find out about his ancestry in Eastern Europe constantly researching, he was born to be a historical researcher, Inspector, and his professorship and employment at Leeds University was the pinnacle of his career."

"You say Thomas was a friend of his before you met Matthew?"

"Oh yes, they met when Thomas first started his property business, converting the old Leeds university library building into a pub. Thomas helped the History Department re-locate their books and research facilities to the new department building. Matthew had no idea how to arrange the move, Thomas stepped in and the two became friends."

"Okay, so Thomas and Matthew went to Europe regularly but since the trip that happened after this photo was taken, Matthew has not been seen again, and now 12 years later, Jessop is found dead, the whereabouts of Smythe and Watts is unknown, and your marriage has ended in divorce."

"Are you implying, Inspector, that these events are linked in some way?" she concluded and then suddenly appeared to understand why the two detectives were asking their questions.

"Oh, you think they are don't you, you think something might have happened after this trip that caused all this acrimony?"

"Anything at all, Jennifer, that you consider might or might not be relevant, please call any of the numbers on this card." Wolfe handed her a business card. "Or contact me personally on this number." He offered another card which she put in front.

Wolfe and Middleton left Jennifer Harrington a few minutes later, and exited the car park in Wolfe's car.

"Wow, I didn't expect that, Jac, did you?" asked Middleton.

"No, not at all," replied Wolfe. "Her lack of concern for her ex-husband was startling. I can't help thinking that something serious must have happened, she doesn't have a good word to say about him, wow what an attitude."

Chapter 18

"Shall we get a cup of coffee, Pam?" asked Wolfe as he drove along The Grove.

"Are you buying?" she replied in hope rather than expectation.

"Of course, if I ask a woman to accompany me for a drink then I'm buying."

"Ooo you are so chivalrous, Detective Inspector Wolfe, you do realise that we are living in the 21st century and there's no need or requirement for a man to buy a woman a drink," she responded with a smirk on her face.

"And in the 21st century, there's no need for a woman to embarrass a man if he wants to purchase a beverage for said woman," retorted Wolfe. "And there's no intention on behalf of the man that the buying of a drink for the woman will mean that the favour is reciprocated in other ways by the woman ... you know, such as –"

"Yea, yeah okay, Jac," interrupted Middleton. "You win ... yes I'd love a cup of coffee." Wolfe was still smiling as they pulled into a parking space on Brooke Street that had just been vacated.

Having found a table in a chic emporium recently opened, simply called Ellie's Coffee House and with cups of coffee cupped in their hands to warm themselves from the bitter sub-zero temperatures outside, Wolfe decided that the next 'port of call' should be the home of the Watts family on the outskirts of Carlton. However, he made the point to Middleton that they should be aware that members of the Watts family, upon seeing even more detectives turning up on their doorstep, might get upset believing that bad news was coming, which, to some extent, was correct because the whereabouts of Davy Watts were still unknown.

Middleton opened her e-mails on her iPhone. "Sir, I have an e-mail from Pete, after he and Fairburn had interviewed Mrs Susan Watts." She looked up from her mobile phone.

Placing his coffee cup on the table onto its saucer, he replied, "Okay, what's the gist?"

"She says that she expected her husband home last night, but he wasn't there this morning and he's not answering his phone. She's concerned that he might have had an accident because he was due to drive home from Abingdon Colliery near Barnsley late last night. She went to bed expecting to be woken up when he arrived but when she awoke this morning there's no evidence of him having come home."

"Similar pattern to Frank Jessop, missing for a whole night then ... we find him dead in a car park in Leeds," remembered Wolfe in a solemn thoughtful tone.

"Was Watts on business ... in Barnsley?" questioned Wolfe.

Middleton paused, scrolled up and down the screen on her mobile device, and then replied, "Yes, Hennersy Contracting have got the contract to demolish Abington Colliery and he was there supervising the installation of explosives, the main lift tower is due to be blown up ... ah ... tomorrow ... early in the morning."

"So Jessop and Watts work for the same company. It's all getting a little incestuous, everyone knows everyone else," Wolfe added. "Okay, that's all I need to know," said Wolfe suddenly revived by the caffeine. "We need to talk to Mrs Watts … now … come on, drink up, Pam."

DC Middleton had called ahead to arrange the meeting and like Wolfe had suggested, she tried not to give the impression that the police were seriously concerned about Davy Watts. It was, however, necessary to move the investigation on. Careful and respectful handling of the situation would be important to get the best response.

The house was impressive, a Victorian style semi-detached dwelling, a full three storey's high, faced in natural stone, tall narrow window frames painted white and a black high gloss solid entrance door with a large glazed fanlight above affirming the high ceilings within, typical of Victorian architecture. Wolfe knew this area of Carlton. Rake Ghyll, as a very sought-after location, property is very expensive.

Wolfe knocked on the door. Waiting he noticed a Range Rover, almost new, different colour but similar to Jessop's vehicle parked in the drive. The door opened and a middle-aged woman stood in the opening, confusion noticeable in her expression.

"Hello, I'm DI Wolfe and this is DC Middleton from the West Yorkshire Police Force," both holding up ID cards as proof, "we called earlier? …"

"Yes," she replied. "I'm Susan Watts, please come in."

The two police officers followed Susan Watts through the hall into the lounge, a beautiful period decorated space with a surprisingly large flat screen TV in one corner, picture perfect, didn't look out of place. A log-burning stove, within a focal point chimneybreast, gradually, almost without effort, emitted a pleasant warmth from gently burning logs within. '*I must get myself one of those,*' thought Wolfe.

Susan Watts was the first to speak as they sat down. "Two detectives came here a couple of hours ago … and now you two," she stated. "What's going on, Inspector? I'm beginning to get extremely worried about David."

"Mrs Watts, we have no further information relating to your husband. As a police force, we are using all the resources available to look for him," stated Middleton with as much assurance as she could offer, which she knew wasn't that much at all.

"David is a grown man, young lady, why would the police force be searching for him with as you say 'all the resources available to us'*,* unless, of course, you think something serious has happened to him or he's mixed up in something." She paused, Wolfe and Middleton glanced at each other, not missed by Susan Watts. "I assume, there weren't any road traffic accidents involving my husband's car, so, Inspector, why are you here?" She looked like she was about to break down in tears or get physically aggressive, Middleton and Wolfe couldn't tell which way this was going to go.

As if by magic, Marcus Haigh Watson appeared on the TV in full view of all, Wolfe and Middleton couldn't help that their reaction gave even more concern to Susan Watts. Haigh Watson's voice could be heard quite clearly. Pam grabbed the TV remote control from the coffee table in front of her.

"May I just turn the …" as she tried to mute the volume, unfortunately Haigh Watson could be heard quite clearly, his face taking up most of the TV screen
"We can confirm that the two deceased persons are Matthew Brookes, aged 31 and Francis Jessop, aged 59. We are treating both their deaths as unlawful. If anyone can

confirm the whereabouts of these two men over the last seven days, please contact the number scrolling across the bottom of the screen ..."

'Ah fuck,' thought Wolfe.

"Oh, my God," shrieked Susan. "That's it, isn't it?" she spluttered. "Frankie is dead, David's missing ... and you're thinking ... oh no, please ... not this ... what is happening, please tell me."

Middleton responded first.

"We came here to inform you ... before this formal announcement, I'm so sorry, it's quite obviously come as a shock to you," Middleton stated in an authoritative manner hoping that would snap Mrs Watts into concentration on what she was about to say next. "We know David and Francis are good friends so can you think of anything that they both might have been involved in recently, anything out of the ordinary not part of their general routine?"

"What? Do you think they are involved in something illegal? I can assure you both these men are law abiding and honest people, their business is correctly managed, they both pay their taxes, they both ..."

"Susan," interjected Wolfe. "We fully believe that to be the case, we are not here because of some impropriety done by either man," he said as he removed the photo from the inside pocket of his jacket. "Susan," he repeated as he placed the photo on the coffee table in front of her. "This photo was taken some twelve years ago and we know that all those pictured in it went to ..."

"What ..." she spluttered still trying to understand what was suddenly happening in her life, thinking more about the children than her husband and then desperately trying to understand why that should be. She looked at the photo.

"What has this got to do with this?" As she pointed at the TV, outside broadcast footage was being shown from Carlton Moor, then the multi storey car park in Leeds.

"Susan! Please, it's important, we need to ask you questions about the individuals in this photograph." Wolfe tapped his forefinger on the photo. "Susan, this is David." Wolfe placed his finger in the appropriate location. "This is Frank, this is Matthew Tanner and this is Thomas Henry Smythe, and this person ... well, we can't tell."

"Tommy Smith is a bastard, I hate that man ... well, actually, he's not a man, he's just a fucking bully. It's like he never grew up, he uses his weight, and fucking loud bastard voice to bully and intimidate people including my husband and Frank Jessop." This venomous response took the two detectives by surprise.

In an effort to calm the situation, Middleton spoke first. "Alright, alright, Susan. Let's just go over why this photo has caused you to react like this ... please, we need to understand what's behind your response because it might help us find David," she implored.

"Smith is behind all of this ... he's a manipulative sod ..."

"Susan, please calm down, this isn't helping," Wolfe raised his voice and looked her straight in the eyes. She looked back at the photo. She sniffed, looked at Wolfe then Middleton, who handed her a tissue from the box on the coffee table in front of her.

"When this was taken, things were good, Davy, Frankie and him ..." she blew her nose then pointed to Smythe, "... they were best mates, inseparable, bosom buddies ... they were in the TA together," she paused, then the hint of a smile lifted the edges of her mouth. "They've known each other much longer than me and David have been married, that's what drew me and Mary, Frank's wife, to David and Frank. You know, the fact they knew what each other would do or say next, Mary and I wanted in, it was a turn on they were relaxed with each other and with us. The first time we met was at the annual TA ball at the Metropole Hotel in Leeds, they made us laugh, I was hooked from the first minute. Davy could have done anything with me, I was more than willing." She sighed, produced another tissue from the sleeve of her jumper and wiped her eyes and nose. "Sorry," she said.

"No, no it's okay, Susan, you take your time," encouraged Wolfe.

"Anyway, a year or so later, Davy and I, and Mary and Frankie got married together at the Catholic Cathedral in Leeds ... that was a day and half, two weddings at once." She smiled and Wolfe saw a glimpse in her eyes of reminiscences that offered her a pleasant feeling. "Yes, life was good, children followed, well for Davy and me anyway, Frankie and Mary found out they couldn't have children. We all worked hard, never managing to keep more than our heads above water ... ya know what I mean?"

Middleton and Wolfe nodded like mechanical toy dogs, both thinking. *'Let's hope she gets to the relevant parts soon.'*

"It was on our wedding day that I first met Matt Tanner and Jennifer, who married Tommy a year after me and Davy." She took breath. "Ya know, even during the Gulf War when our men were called up to assist the regular army, we never worried about them, they returned unscathed." Susan relaxed, as if pining for times passed, caught her breath, "When this photo was taken, the boys were on their way back to a war zone but not fighting, more humanitarian, I suppose, you'd call it, helping Matt ... by the way, he's Serbian by birth ... Matthew is his English name, he was born Arman or Armon, something like that. Anyway, this photo was taken just before they all left for Sarajevo, helping to rebuild the university library as a favour to Matt as I recall." She stopped again. Wolfe was about to say something when Susan continued, "When they came back, everything changed, life wasn't the same, all kinds of shit must have gone on over there. Since then, Davy and Frankie haven't spoken to Tommy shit face, and Matt didn't come back so God only knows what happened but Davy refuses to talk about it and if I ask or mention anything to do with Sarajevo, he just says, 'it's none of my business', and if I mention Tommy ... well, he goes off on one or walks out of the house and doesn't come back until he's had enough beer."

"Susan, this is all relevant, thank you. It would appear as though the Sarajevo trip caused a split ... 'in the ranks' ... if you know what I mean, sorry, poor metaphor ... please excuse me," said Wolfe.

"That's okay," she replied. "I think you're right, even Jennifer was a victim of what must have happened over there. She and Tommy divorced, and Paul, well ... he has done extremely well to make the business work, 'cause apparently, Tommy left it in a right mess ... buggered off with all the profits and left the company in debt. Then Jennifer had to fight tooth and nail to get anything from that git. Mind you, their marriage started to go wrong long before the trip to Sarajevo, whilst Paul was still at school if I remember right."

"What makes you say that?" asked Wolfe.

"Jennifer and I were really good mates. When Mary and I started going out with Frankie and Davy, she made sure we were welcome at all the TA's social events, army men, and even worse, army wives can be very unwelcoming, relationships can be ruined before they start. When Tommy started playing away, she confided in me, she couldn't understand why he suddenly changed, they even slept in separate bedrooms. Then he went to Spain, bought property over there using his company money, couple of years later, employees were made redundant, he'd taken most of the money out by the time Paul stepped in."

"Susan, thank you for being so cooperative, the background you've described to us is all relevant. I'm sure the information will be useful, however," stated Wolfe, "we need to locate Davy as soon as possible to help us with our investigations into what happened to Mr Jessop."

"Inspector …" interrupted Susan Watts. "I hope you're not suggesting Davy had anything to do with Frankie's death? I wouldn't put it past Tommy Smith … Smythe, if you want his pompous git name."

"Why do you say that?" asked Wolfe. "And I don't mean the way his name is pronounced?"

"Davy and Frankie must have had a serious falling out with Tommy because they both told me that they would never speak to him again, and if he was to call, then tell him to go away … or words to that effect … in fact, when I think about it now, that was around the time Mary started to really go downhill mentally, she has periods of serious depression. Takes herself of to bed for days on end, won't even take my phone calls. This all started after Frank and Davy returned from the Sarajevo trip. At the time I thought it was because Frank had told Mary what happened over there but when she's in her better self and we meet up for a chat she denies that and say's her condition is hereditary, her mum suffered in the same way."

"However, you're not sure about that are you Mrs Watts," replied Wolfe in a tone that made Pam look at him and think, '*Wonder what he meant by that?*'

"You think maybe Frank told Mary something about the trip to Sarajevo and that has caused her to worry which sets her depression phases off. Do you think she'll be able to help us with our enquiries?"

"I doubt that Inspector, those anti-depressant's she's on really knock her out."

"Mmmm …" mused Wolfe.

"Well," continued Susan, "Mary always worried about business and money, it seemed to affect her more than Frankie, Davy and me, and it was made worse when Frankie returned because he looked absolutely worn out, he'd had enough of helping out Tommy Smith, he said he would never do it again, that might have pushed Mary over the edge. Then not long after, the two lads joined forces, as it were, Frankie bought Davy's demolition company into his contracting business and now Davy is a Director of Hennersy Contracting. That gave the business a cash injection, more work and they started doing really well, so much so that we moved here, and Mary and Frankie moved in a few doors further up. Unfortunately they didn't manage to have children, not even IVF helped, but they are godparents to our two and we all get on really well. Oh my God, Mary, does she know about her husband?"

"Yes, she was informed yesterday … but she hasn't told you though?" questioned Wolfe.

"Well, that explains it, I tried to contact her yesterday, I should go see her she's probably had another one of her turns … you know," Susan began to weep.

"I'm so sorry, Susan," said Middleton as she moved to sit next to her. "We know you're very upset about Frankie but we now need to concentrate on David, we know he's not at his office, might he be a … er …"

"Abingdon Colliery," spluttered Susan in response.

"Yes … is he likely to be there, do you think?"

"You know that might be it," she started to cheer up a little. "I have known him to stay overnight on similar jobs, to guard the explosives, believe or not people try to steal it, maybe he's there, but he would always call … never hasn't …" Her lighter mood evaporated instantly.

"I'm sure that's it, Susan, we'll send someone out straight away," replied Middleton.

A few minutes later, Susan Watts escorted the two detectives to her front door. Wolfe turned to Susan.

"If you manage to talk to Mrs Jessop and she mentions anything about the trip to Eastern Europe please let us know straight away it could help in our investigations?"

"I'll let you know," she said and watched as they drove away.

Wolfe was the first to speak as Middleton and he accelerated down the hill away from Carlton, "Pam, I know the statements from Jennifer Harrington and Susan Watts need corroborating but there's a lot of information gathered from them that might move this case forward."

"It's gonna take a while to write these notes up though."

"Dictate them into your phone and send them to HQ to get typed, and if you get any grief, let me know," ordered Wolfe.

"Yes, sir," came the sarcastic reply.

"First thing tomorrow morning, you and Pete get yourselves out to Abingdon Colliery, find Watts. Actually, call the local police and get a local patrol car out there soon as, see if they can find him first, if not, then you two get out there at first light tomorrow."

"Jac?"

"Yes."

"You know something don't you? Or at least you have an idea, of what went on with those four guys in Eastern Europe. You think Frank told Mary something about what went on and that's why she gets depressed."

"Oh, you think so do you … well just leave that with me for now and don't mention it to anyone, I'm just guessing."

Pam smiled and let the conversation drop there.

After some thought Wolfe suggested to Middleton that a specialist police liaison officer should interview Mary Jessop. "You never know, that way we might get more of an insight into what Mary knows about the goings on in Sarajevo."

"I'll make a formal request," she concluded.

By the time they reached HQ in Leeds, it was after 6pm. Wolfe dropped Middleton off next to her car and they left separately.

Chapter 19

Tuesday morning arrived far too early for Wolfe, the previous day's interviews kept circling around in his mind, orbiting his head over and over again. He remembered 3am showing up on his alarm clock, now suddenly, it was 6am. He hit the snooze button, at least, he thought he had, but then 7.30am arrived he woke with a start. "Ah, shit," he shouted and jumped out of bed then immediately felt dizzy, and slumped back onto the bed.

Izzy knocked on his bedroom door, then a second later, entered without waiting to be asked. "Are you alright, dad?" she asked.

"Yeah, I'm fine. Just got out of bed too quick, I didn't realise how late it is. I'm supposed to be going to Barnsley this morning. I've probably missed it now."

"Missed what?" she replied a little bemused.

"They're blowing up the lift shaft tower at Abingdon Colliery this morning and I was supposed to be there." He sounded disappointed with a suggestion of guilt.

"So has this something to do with the investigation then?"

"Someone," corrected Wolfe. "Possibly, if that's where we find him, but he might not be there. Anyway, I'm going to get a quick shower." He disappeared through the door into his shower room.

Izzy went downstairs, and made breakfast, tea, yogurt with fruit and a slice of toast for her father, muesli and croissant for herself. She'd turned the TV on whilst preparing the meals and watched the brief live coverage of the explosive demolition of the lift tower on the site of the last coal mine to be closed in Yorkshire, bringing to an end more than 120 years of coal mining in the county. Upstairs, Izzy left her father's breakfast on his dressing table and switched on the TV in his bedroom. Local news had concluded its report on Abingdon Colliery, Izzy retreated to her room. A few minutes later, Wolfe left his en-suite, fastened his dressing gown and smiled as he noticed the food on the dressing table.

"Thanks, Izzy," he announced loud enough to be heard by his daughter. Not waiting, Izzy left her room and knocked on her father's bedroom door.

"Yeah."

She opened the bedroom door. "Dad, that building blowing up you mentioned has just been shown on the TV, so you have missed it," she announced.

"Okay. Pass me my phone from the bedside table, will you?" Izzy retrieved the mobile just as it started to ring.

The opening intro to Lynyrd Skynyrd's Double Trouble erupted in her hand.

"Dad! will you please change that ringtone?" she pleaded as she handed the device to him.

Wolfe swiped the screen without replying, "Morning Pam, apologies, I slept …"

"Boss, you'd better get yourself here as soon as you can. There's something you need to see. Prof Higgins will be the next call I'll be making. We've found another body."

The last few words didn't surprise him, his subconsciousness was obviously working overtime.

"Davy Watts?" asked Wolfe.

"I can see the bonnet of a wrecked four by four pick-up sticking out from the crushed building and it's definitely his registration number … I can see the head of a person inside the vehicle, not moving, the roof of the vehicle has been crushed down so far that it's not much higher than the bonnet … it's got to be him."

"Are you sure he's dead?"

"99% certain. An ambulance is on its way but I'm sure it's not going to be required. We can't get any closer until health and safety say it's clear to do so."

"Oh, for fuck's sake," cursed Wolfe. "Sorry, Izzy," he said into his mobile. "Sorry, Pam! I'm angry with myself for sleeping in."

"Boss, just hang on a second," the line went quiet for a few seconds.

Then, "Hi, boss, it's Pete here."

"Hi, Pete," replied Wolfe.

"With binoculars, I can see that there's a sticker on the door. It reads 'retribution' or something like that."

"Oh shit." Wolfe felt sudden pulse of confirmation hit his thoughts like lightning, "How far are you away from where the vehicle is?"

"A good 150 metres, at least. We're not allowed any closer yet," conceded Halford.

"Pete, I'm setting off now. I'll be there within the hour, text me the postcode, will you?"

"Okay, boss, will do."

Wolfe apologised again to his daughter for his language, she wasn't concerned. She wished she could have gone with him but resisted asking, knowing that revision was her main priority but found her focus being distracted. She'd have to control these emotions.

Almost an hour later, Wolfe arrived at the cordon around the explosion site hazard warning lights flashing on all four corners of his car.

"DI Wolfe, West Yorkshire Police Force," he announced, holding his ID card towards the local constable manning the makeshift gate.

"You're expected, Inspector, please make your way to the left, your colleagues are waiting down there," he responded with confidence.

"Thanks, constable," Wolfe held his position. "Were you on duty here yesterday, constable?" Wolfe asked.

"Yes, sir, double shift up to 10pm then relieved by another constable and back on duty at 6am, in time to see the tower go down."

"When are you off duty again, constable?" requested Wolfe.

"11am, sir."

"Before you leave site, find me. I'd like a further discussion with you."

"Yes, sir."

Wolfe drove down the site to the left.

As he drove down the haul road used by the demolition contractors towards the mound of rubble that used to be the lift tower, he noticed two ambulances, two police cars and Arnold Higgins' Lexus, half a dozen people wearing high-vis jackets and two or three that weren't. He then saw the focus of everyone's attention, the bonnet of a dark grey vehicle protruding from the rubble, the rest of the vehicle flattened by the resultant demolition material. He parked, grabbed his overcoat from the passenger seat, groaned as he manoeuvred his way out of the vehicle and walked towards the spoil mound whilst putting on the overcoat. A mechanical excavator was moving rubble to gain access to the vehicle, large chunks of concrete masonry stacked precariously on top of each other with reinforcement bars protruding, bent at all kinds of angles, were being moved.

Middleton and Halford approached him; Halford was the first to speak.

"A final inspection was done of the site at midnight last night by the demo team; nothing untoward found. The dynamite was detonated at 7.30am this morning, then when the dust settled, the vehicle was spotted. So, between midnight and 7.30am this morning, someone brought it onto site and parked it inside the building. There's definitely a body in the vehicle," stated Halford.

Before Wolfe could respond, Middleton said,
"Sorry to drag you away from the report you were writing, sir, but this situation demanded your direct involvement. Both DC Halford and myself think the person in the car is someone that is involved in the current investigation," stated Middleton as if she were being recorded.

"No problem, constable," Wolfe looked bemused at Middleton.

"Fairburn is here," she whispered. Then, as if on cue, DC Fairburn approached Wolfe from behind Middleton.

"They're about ready to move the rubble from the top and around the vehicle then we can get in," he confirmed straight at Wolfe.

"Good," he replied. "By the way, what are you doing here? Shouldn't you be at Head Quarters?"

"DC Halford and I thought it might be best to have as many eyes in the sightseeing crowd as we could, more chance of spotting Watts, if he turned up," he explained.

"Well, it appears as though you were right, as it happens but perhaps, not in the manner you were expecting, eh, DC Fairburn," Wolfe hadn't intended the cynicism, but he knew that's how it sounded.

"Come on, we'll all go down there together, the more pairs of eyes looking around the better," he said to DC Fairburn with a smile. "Where's Arnold? I know he's here, I spotted his car."

"He's talking to the JCB driver," replied Fairburn. "Probably explaining how he wants him to clear the rubble, to keep the disruption of the evidence to as little as possible."

"That's rather a tall order, I think," Wolfe replied as the team walked towards the demolition site.

When they reached the edge of the mountain of rubble, Wolfe realised that the loose rubble would be dangerous to walk on and that the paramedics who'd made the initial diagnosis of the condition of the person inside the car by climbing onto the bonnet and checking as best they could for any signs of life, had, in fact, risked injury to themselves. One of the paramedics approached the huddle of detectives.

"I assume, you're DI Wolfe?" she asked looking at him across Fairburn.

"Yes, that's correct," he answered.

"The man inside is definitely deceased, so we'll move back now and let the HSE co-ordinate the clearance operation so you guys can access the vehicle in relative safety."

"Yes, I understand. It must have been a bit nerve racking scaling this lot. Please tell me, was it you who checked for a pulse?"

"Yes, it was. He's definitely –"

"Sorry," he interrupted. "No, I'm not questioning your judgement, I wanted to know had rigor mortis set in?"

"Oh … errr … no, it hadn't … ah, I see … no, he hasn't been dead that long. Oh my God, I assumed he'd committed suicide, you know, that sticker on the side of the car, but you're thinking something else, aren't you, Insp–"

"We're not in the habit of assumptions …" Wolfe looked at her badge pinned to her dark green overalls above the left breast. "Laura, but I think, in this case, there might be something in your thinking. However, I'd be pleased if you kept this conversation to yourself … for a while, at least. Is that okay?"

"Yes, of course, Inspector … here," she handed him a business card. "I'm off duty in two hours."

'Strange,' thought Wolfe. 'Business cards for paramedic's, what is the world coming to?'

"Give me a call," she said with a suggestive smile.

"Thank you," he said as he declined the card. "I have someone at home."

'What the fuck was that I just said?' he thought to himself as his face began to redden.

"Oh, that's a shame, she's a lucky one."

"Actually, I'm the lucky one," he added. Then an image of Maria smiling flashed across his mind, he smiled.

"DI Wolfe," came a shout from behind him. "This is becoming a habit Jaxon, you and me at the site of yet another suspicious death," Arnold Higgins announced as Wolfe turned to meet him.

"Arnold," he replied offering his right hand to shake, Higgins duly offered his and the two men shook hands.

"You're right, this has to stop."

"Well, that ball is clearly in your court young man."

Wolfe turned back to the paramedic, "Thanks for your help, Laura," she smiled and walked away.

Higgins and he walked towards an area close to the vehicle where rubble had been cleared. It was now easy to identify the vehicle as a flat back cab up front pick-up truck. The back of the truck was still buried by demolition material but the area was now deemed to be stable. The roof had been crushed so much that the windscreen had popped out, leaving an aperture that Wolfe estimated to be no more than 300mm high; the driver's door had also sprung open, its frame bent and twisted. The left side of the vehicle was also crushed, but unlike the opposite side, it had caved inwards, windows smashed. Wolfe looked at the sticker on the passenger side front door. It was the size of an A3 sheet of paper. He read it out loud, **'retribution'**. It was obvious that the letters had been stencilled on, he could see places where the marker pen had not caught the paper properly.

Higgins was looking at the aperture that used to house the front windscreen through which the paramedic had managed to hold the dead man's wrist in search of a pulse. Wolfe made his way to the driver's door whilst his colleagues gawped at the sticker on the passenger side. He was able to get to the driver's door, he forced it further open, dust and small pieces of fractured concrete and other masonry fell down. He noticed straight away that the man inside was, indeed, Davy Watts, he could see he matched a recent photo displayed at the Watts home

The body initially appeared remarkably unscathed but then he saw the victim's neck had a large bruise on the right hand side, his chin was resting on his chest but the head wasn't bent forward, his torso appeared to have collapsed and his legs were both bent high up, almost meeting his chest.

"I believe, this is Mr David Watts, one of the men we have been looking for," he announced to his team who were now standing behind him.

"Jac!" Wolfe heard Higgins call his name from the other side of the vehicle.

"Yes, Arnold."

"It looks like he has a piece of paper clenched in his left hand, can you reach it?" he asked.

Wolfe reached across the corpse, and managed to prise his fist open and collected the piece of paper, he stood away from the vehicle and carefully unwrapped it. There were words written on it but they were upside down, he turned it so he could read it.

"What the hell?" he pronounced, reading it out. "Tony Chezec knows – they all know."

Middleton was first to respond, "What does that mean?"

"It means it's not suicide," Wolfe replied.

"Who's Chezec?" Halford asked next.

Fairburn didn't say anything he was typing Chezec into Google. "Nothing, it just comes up with Czech Republic."

"Mmm, nice try, Harry, now I want you and Pete to head immediately back to HQ, use all the technology we have available to us to find Thomas Henry Smythe, find his address in Spain, find an interpreter, get local law enforcement out there. If they find him, they are to hold him, he's in serious danger. Also, call ahead and get a couple of uniforms to his house near Carlton, and tell them to stay there until otherwise ordered, get relief if necessary but I want that house guarded 24/7," ordered Wolfe. "Pam and I will track down his son, Paul but first Pam can you send a WPC over to Jennifer Harrington's place. Something tells me we need to protect her as well."

"Okay, boss," replied Halford. Fairburn nodded and the two men walked with purpose back to their vehicle, both were already using their mobile phones.

"Pam, find me an evidence bag for this please," requested Wolfe as he re-read the note taken from Davy Watts. She produced one immediately from her jacket pocket, held it open for Wolfe to drop the piece of paper in, she wrote in the appropriate place, the date, time and location of the find.

"Jac, what the hell is all this about?" she asked.

"Not a bloody clue," he admitted in a whisper. "But that stays between you and me."

"Do you think Thomas Smythe is behind these murders?"

"Anything … absolutely anything is possible," he offered with a conciliatory sigh.

Higgins had walked around to the other side of the car but couldn't manage to gain access to the vehicle so he came back to the side where Wolfe and Middleton stood.

"Arnold, he's not rigid yet," he said nodding towards the victim. "Rigor not set in yet, we know the time of the explosion that brought this building down on top of him." He looked at his watch. "Less than three hours ago, the building was last checked by security at midnight, no sign of a vehicle inside the building; therefore, the vehicle must have been brought into the building after midnight but before 7.30am –"

Higgins interrupted, "Not quite correct, Jac, final security check was conducted at 6 am this morning."

"That makes it more obvious then," Wolfe continued. "Davy Watts might have been alive when the building came down on top of him."

"Yes, I would agree Jac that's a possibility. However, there's a large bruise on his neck …"

"Yeah I saw that."

"I'm hoping he was at least unconscious before this building came down on him."

"We are only a matter of a few hours behind whoever is causing this mayhem and who is this Chezec person?" Wolfe was annoyed with himself, if he'd reacted yesterday evening as he now thought he should have done, this death might have been prevented, he should have insisted on police security at the colliery last night, but the cost was his first thought not the life of someone he has never met until now and now that person was dead, murdered probably.

"Arnold, DC Middleton and I will head back to Leeds, no doubt, you've got a lot to do here. Will you need assistance?"

"On its way, dear boy, ETA half an hour. You get on with finding the bastard that's causing these deaths and I'll have a report ready for you by the morning."

The two men shook hands again. "Thanks, old man, see you soon."

"Not too soon, I hope, dear boy," was the reply as Wolfe and Middleton walked back to their vehicles.

"Pam, we'll meet at HQ, okay?"

"Yes, sir."

Wolfe drove away from the site behind Middleton's car but pulled up when he drew level with the uniformed officer he'd met earlier. Wolfe turned off the ignition and got out of the car.

"Hi, Inspector," was the response from the constable. "I take it the guy in the car is dead?"

"Yep, crushed to death by the looks of it," replied Wolfe noticing that the constable was a little older than he had thought before, well into his thirties, but thick set, tall and broad shouldered, probably works out quite regularly, he assumed.

"So, you saw no one whilst you were here on duty … er, PC …"

"Richardson … Edward, Eddie Richardson," he replied. "Other than Hennersy Contracting placing the explosives and the detonators, and a couple walking their dog being a bit nosey, no one at all."

"Times?" asked Wolfe.

"Yeah, sure." Richardson pulled a small notebook from his tunic pocket opened it and read, "A Mr Coyle and Mr Thornley arrived at 9am yesterday, both from

Hennersy, one vehicle, a Ford Transit Van. I checked the cab and the back, small pallet of explosives packed and tied securely in the back, I checked their explosives licence and let them through."

"How long were they onsite for, Eddie?"

"They left at 15.45 hours," he answered without checking his notes. Then referring, once again, to his notes, he continued, "The couple walking their dog, middle aged, living locally as they told me, came past at 19.20 hours, asked when the lift tower was going to get blown up, I told them what I knew, which was nothing, I watched them go back up the road, didn't see them again."

"Mmmm, who relieved you at 10pm last night?"

"Er …" Richardson had to refer to his notes again. "PC Ian Reece from the Barnsley Division."

"So not someone you knew … not a colleague?" responded Wolfe.

"No, Inspector, I'm stationed at the Sheffield Division. I was ordered to come here because Barnsley had no free uniformed constables due to a protest march going on in Barnsley town centre yesterday, national front supporting their candidate I believe."

"Is PC Reece due back today?"

"No, not as far as I'm aware. When SOCO, and Health and Safety have finished, I'll be off duty, but I could remain if you think I should," he replied with enthusiasm for the task.

Wolfe thought for a second, "I don't think that will be necessary, but please contact Sheffield Division let them know their staff are no longer required West Yorkshire will handle it from now."

"Yes, I'll do that sir." He looked at Wolfe as if he wanted to say something but wasn't sure he should.

"Yes, what is it, have you got something to say Constable Richardson."

Looking towards the demolition site he added, "Why would someone commit suicide in that way? What state of mental health was he in to be able to put himself through that? Ya know, without any guarantee of success?" Questioned the PC. Wolfe hadn't expected this, he was taken by surprise.

"Errr …" he started to reply. "It certainly is an odd situation I've certainly never experienced anything like this before. If I think of any more questions, I'll be in touch via your station sergeant, is that okay?"

"Yes, Inspector, I'm on duty tomorrow, reporting to the Sheffield City Centre Station at 8am," he concluded.

"Thanks PC Richardson … err Eddie," said Wolfe as he turned back towards his car.

Wolfe was impressed by PC Richardson's attention to duty and attention to detail, not that usual for his rank, in fact, so different to many PC's these days.

Walking back to his car Wolfe had a feeling that something wasn't quite right, something just didn't fit. He dismissed these thoughts as a distraction, a reaction to the musings of a detective confused by the clues beginning to seep into this investigation.

As he opened the door, he looked over the roof of his Z4 at the constable manning the gate, he nodded and received the same in return. Wolfe then drove at speed away from Abingdon towards Leeds.

As soon as Wolfe's car had disappeared over the near horizon, Richardson made a casual reconnaissance of the area, made sure he wasn't being watched, he removed his police cap, took off his high visibility jacket, turned it inside out and put it back on inside out, he walked briskly up a nearby banking cloaked in trees and shrubs, forcing his way through the scrub. 300 metres further on the scrub abated and the gradient became flatter. A black Jaguar F type sports car waited for him with the engine running, as soon as he positioned himself in the passenger seat, the car sped off in directly the opposite direction to Wolfe.

Chapter 20

"Okay, let's look at what we've got here." Wolfe, Middleton, Halford and Fairburn sat around a large table in the middle of the incident room, laptop in the centre of the table linked to a projector, a screen hanging down from the ceiling showing the projected images from the laptop.

It was six thirty in the morning, the day after the discovery of Davy Watts' body in the rubble of a dynamited colliery building on the outskirts of Barnsley. The case had taken several twists over the past 18 hours, including a very embarrassing turn of events that if made public would make a laughingstock of all of the West Yorkshire Police Force and by implication Chief Constable Marcus Haigh–Watson.

Wolfe had assembled all the available evidence together in one place in one room, dropped the blinds and shut the door. He wanted to encourage the opinion off the record of the members of his team. Wolfe reluctantly agreed to involve Fairburn in this close-knit group, Middleton had persuaded Wolfe to keep Fairburn close. The family ties he has with Haigh-Watson would allow Wolfe a little more freedom to progress the investigation without constant interference from the head of the West Yorkshire Police force.

"Right, let's start by listing the victims in this case, with the most recent death first," announced Wolfe.

"Davy Watts, 58 years old, Contracts Director for Hennersy Contracting. Found dead in his vehicle, crushed by a collapsed building in the aftermath of the explosive demolition of the lift tower at Abingdon Colliery yesterday morning."

"Francis Jessop, 59-year-old, Managing Director of Hennersy Contracting. Found shot dead in his car in the multi-storey Horizon Centre Car Park in Leeds in the early morning two days ago."

"Matthew Brookes, 31-year-old found dead in a makeshift tomb on Carlton Moor, one-time employee of Hennersy Contracting and a known drug user, but not a dealer."

Then there was a knock on the door. Wolfe looked over his shoulder.

"Come in," responded Wolfe.

"Sir, you asked me to join you," announced PC Andrew Mills.

"Yes, Andy, take a seat, we've just started," said Wolfe. Halford and Fairburn looked a little perplexed, Middleton smiled. She knew about the invite. Wolfe recapped for Mills benefit.

"So, let's look first at what connects these three individuals," Wolfe asked as a request.

Middleton was first to respond, "Brookes worked for a short while for Hennersy Contracting and he was discovered by two other employees of the same company, we have to assume that they all knew each other." Then the room fell quiet.

"Another connection is that Jessop and Watts are known associates of Thomas Henry Smythe, the other person in this photo." Wolfe punched a key on the laptop computer in front of him and immediately the twelve-year-old photo taken before the trip to Sarajevo flashed onto the screen. "Copies of which were on display at Charlotte Brookes' home which she shares with Thomas Smythe's son Paul, and at the homes of Jessop and Watts."

Mills took a deep breath. "These killings don't follow the same pattern, the mode of death is different in all three."

"How's that a connection?" said Fairburn indignantly.

"Because …" Mills paused for a second. Wolfe was about to jump in with a comment, then Mills continued, stopping Wolfe and Fairburn in their tracks, "We now know that to try and stop another murder, there's no point in checking moorland, car parks and demolition sites, it still leaves a myriad of other options but we can at least rule those areas out."

Fairburn stared at Mills. "Myriad? Mills, are you showing off your public school education –"

"That's enough, Harry," interrupted Wolfe. "It's a very plausible assessment and with our resources stretched to the limit, we can better target our investigations." He waited to make sure his statement hit home. "Now what do we know of the last movements of these men?" He tapped a key on the laptop and the image changed back to the original slide, recent photo images of Brookes, Jessop and Watts.

Middleton took the lead, "Watts, an explosives expert together with two other members of his team, were known to have been present on site at Abingdon Colliery 48 hours prior to the demolition. However, it would appear from site sign-in sheets that he didn't report onto site within the 24 hours before demolition. The foreman reported to Hennersy's head office that he hadn't showed up. Staff at head office were also trying to locate Francis Jessop because his whereabouts were unknown, concern then began to build that perhaps they might have been involved in a road accident."

Halford then continued, "Jessop had a meeting arranged with a company called Tribute Noir UK Ltd, according to his PA at Hennersy, for Saturday midday to discuss a building contract, the meeting was due to take place at the Radisson Blue Hotel in Leeds. We've checked CCTV for three hours either side of 12 noon and no one matching his description was spotted. So, either the meeting didn't take place or it didn't take place at the Radisson."

"Or he was hijacked, forced to send a text to his wife stating he'll be out until late and eventually he turns up battered, bruised and shot in the head," claimed Halford.

"Well that fits," offered Wolfe.

"Brookes was last seen four weeks ago, but time of death was a matter of hours before his body was discovered," Middleton once again speaking. "So where was he during the intervening period?"

"We've visited Brookes' apartment," Halford stated. "Found nothing linking him to Jessop or Watts and notably we found no computers, tablets or mobile phone, nothing much at all really. Clothes we searched for evidence and once again, nothing, no car keys. We did, however, find two small pouches containing cannabis, enough for recreational use only. It's almost as if his apartment had been cleaned of anything that you would expect to find."

"Mmmm," responded Wolfe. "And where Jessop was found in the car park, the CCTV camera on that level was conveniently out of order and then where Watts was found the, pre-explosion inspection failed to spot the car inside the building. No mobile phones, tablets or laptops found at any of the murder scenes, Brookes found naked obviously nothing at the scene, but nothing found at his apartment either. All this smacks of premeditation and meticulous planning, someone has spent time and money researching these men before murdering them, and then removing any paraphernalia that one would expect them to have been carrying."

"Jac?" asked Middleton.

"Yeah, what is it, Pam?"

"Well, Jessop and Watts disappear, and within hours, they're dead but Brookes disappears and isn't murdered for a few weeks."

"That's not a certainty though, Pam, he could have been with people we're not aware of for those weeks," replied Halford.

"I agree, but if he was kidnapped and held against his will," stated Middleton, "that again is one of those subtle differences Andy mentioned." She continued, "Thomas Henry Smythe cannot, at present, be contacted. Has he already been kidnapped, is he already dead?"

"Or he's behind all of this," offered Fairburn.

Halford added, "He could be in hiding, maybe he knows who's behind all this and he's gone to ground."

"That's it," pronounced Wolfe. "Brookes apartment cleaned, disappeared weeks before his body was found, no blood at the scene of his discovery ... murdered somewhere else did he have something on the killer. Although the Jessop and Watts murders hadn't actually occurred, did he know what was about to happen ... or did he have something they wanted."

"That adds up, Jac," Middleton said.

"Okay, let's park that thought," announced Wolfe now ready to discuss the embarrassing part of this discussion although he didn't actually think that anyone would want to dwell on it.

"We know, as of this morning when we contacted Sheffield Division that we were duped by a man impersonating a police officer at Abingdon Colliery. The real PC Richardson was on honeymoon in Mexico, again meticulous planning by the perpetrator, actually, perpetrators," Wolfe emphasised. "There must have been an accomplice, someone keeping in touch with him, just in case he had to make a run for it."

"Sir," responded Mills looking intently at the screen of his laptop.

"Yes," replied Wolfe.

"We've heard back from SOCO and forensics," he read from an e-mail, "our impersonator travelled up the hill from the security gate, through fairly dense undergrowth and woodland to a spot where tyre marks were identified next to an unmade road. The tyre tracks are consistent with a car being driven down the road where it stopped and then accelerated at speed back in the direction it had come. This road leads directly onto the A658 within a mile of Junction 31 of the M1."

"Wow, a clean getaway," responded Halford. "It looks like we have a driver picking the police impersonator up and then they got the hell out of there."

"Any idea of the type of vehicle?" asked Wolfe.

"Yes, sir, I was checking that before I came in." Mills looked at his notes. "It's an F type, Jaguar, very new, the tyre tread was deep into the mud at the side of the road, back tyres wider than the front and the tread pattern matches that of the Michelin's used on these cars when they arrive at the showrooms. It's a unique tread pattern made specifically for the F type."

"I suppose, you know the colour and internal trim as well, eh, Mills?" jibed Fairburn.

"PC Fairburn! One more comment like that from you and you're off this case. I don't give a damn that your uncle works for this force, you'll be back in Sheffield on Friday night drunk patrol and there won't be a thing he or you could do about it. Your attitude towards PC Mills is intolerable," barked Wolfe, so loud that other officers outside the room could hear.

"How do you know he's my …"

"By he, I assume, you mean Chief Constable Marcus Haigh-Watson. Well, 'HE' told me and now the whole station will soon know. If you want to continue on this case, shut up and listen, you just might learn something."

"Actually, we do know the colour," Mills stated into the silence that came after Wolfe's chastising, "It's, black and we also thought we had the registration."

"What?" replied Middleton, Halford and Wolfe together.

"A camera at the junction on the A658 with Abingdon Road, set up for red light offences, caught a car turning onto the haul road but the registration is false, it doesn't exist, but visually, the car matches with all the evidence collected at the scene … it's black."

"There can't be that many of those cars on the road, they're expensive and they're new so if it was bought recently, maybe we can trace the purchaser," stated Halford.

"Yeah, we've got people working on it but nationally, there could be, at least a hundred or so of these black models sold in the last year, but we're working on Leeds and Sheffield retailers first." Mills paused.

"Ah, it's probably stolen anyway," sneered Fairburn.

Once again, Mills was ready. "Yes, it could be but it's unlikely because cars of this quality and price have built in tracking systems, and even input codes are required to start the engines, which I'm aware can be overcome with computer software but that is not easy to obtain. No, it's actually easier to buy them under a false name, using a genuine bank account that is closed as soon as the deal is done. It could have been bought second hand through a dealer straight from the forecourt within a matter of hours because there's an eight-month waiting list to buy one of these off the production line. However, buying brand new from a showroom is my guess, paid for by BACS transfer."

"Okay, keep working on this Andy, it might bear fruit but don't get upset if we find this car burnt out in a field somewhere," concluded Wolfe.

"I've also got info on Francis Jessop as well, sir."

"Okay, let's hear it."

Once again, Mills consulted a hard copy e-mail, "A phone message was received late on Saturday from a storage centre called UnLock-NLoad, situated on Whitehall Road close to Leeds City Centre. Three men, one matching Francis Jessop's description and one of similar description to the fake police officer at Abingdon Colliery were recorded entering the storage facility on Saturday at 9.30pm."

"Recorded," repeated Wolfe, Middleton smiled or was it a grin. Halford looked impressed and Fairburn, well, he was pissed off.

"Yes, sir," Mills confirmed. "And a video for the whole day is being sent to us, in fact." Mills paused and looked at his phone that was vibrating, he got up. "Excuse me, sir," he said standing. Walking to the office door, opening it asking, "Upload it onto the case file on the server please, thank you." He closed the door. "Sir, it should be loaded into the case file under Francis Jessop in a minute."

"Well done, Andy, good work," praised Wolfe.

Middleton spun the laptop around to her side of the table, manoeuvred the mouse a little, opened a file and said,

"Here we go; I'll fast forward to 9pm to start with."

The video opened on the large screen for all to see and at the time recorded as 21.28 hours silence enveloped the room, for another 15 minutes or so until;

"What the fuck just happened?" exclaimed Fairburn.

"The last images of the living Francis Jessop," responded Halford.

"Only just alive," Middleton added.

Followed immediately by Mills,

"You saw the guy behind the reception desk pick up the phone, that was the call he made to HQ, but at the time, Jessop wasn't on our radar as a vulnerable person, so a local patrol car was sent in response, but it didn't arrive until nearly 10pm, they took a statement and left the guy on duty to lock up."

Wolfe was still looking at the screen when he said, "I take it you all noticed the metal boxes being wheeled out, obviously what they wanted. A few hours later, Jessop got a bullet in his head." Wolfe paused, he wasn't sure why but something clicked in his mind. He shook his head, Middleton looked at him bemused by his reaction.

"You okay, Jac?" she said.

"Yeah, yeah … er, yeah fine, that's what this is all about. We need to find out what is in those boxes, it's the key to this investigation." His concentration back on track. "Do we all agree that the guy propping up Jessop on his right could be our fake policeman at Abingdon, which means there's three of them one in the Range Rover and two propping up Jessop?" asked Wolfe, everyone except Mills nodded, he hadn't attended at Abingdon. "Therefore, we have a total of three perpetrators involved in the murders of Watts and Jessop, and thereby, implicated in the murder of Brookes as well. Once again, good police work, Andy."

Fairburn in a quiet almost submissive tone asked,

"Boss, three men here." He pointed at the screen. "Two at the site of the Watts murder, is the other guy currently guarding Smythe?"

"That is a distinct possibility, Harry," replied Wolfe. "See if we get better images of the guy in the car because from what I could see, he wasn't wearing sunglasses like the other two. In fact, get close up images of them all, look for any facial or other distinguishing marks and that is where we'll start. Pam, apply for a court order to search Thomas Henry Smythe's home in Carlton on the basis that his life is in danger and we need to find him or evidence of where he might be, we need to protect him."

"Yep, I'll prepare the paperwork straight away."

"Andy, name and security check the officers guarding Smythe's house, make sure they're ours you understand?"

"Yes sir."

"And get onto those enlarged images, search the data base, see if we can find a match."

"Sir. I know it's a long shot, but I'd like to try and track that Jaguar that left Abingdon, it looked from the CCTV, as if it was about to head north on the M1."

"It's worth a shot, Andy, see if there's another PC that could assist."

Wolfe turned his attention to Halford and Fairburn, "Pete, Harry, visit the Jessop household, find out what if anything Mary Jessop knew about those metal boxes, take a still photo of this video." Wolfe pointed to the screen, "Although the last thing she needs to see is him badly injured before he was killed, but that can't be helped now. Don't upset her and in particular make sure a trained WPC goes with you. We need positive ID on Frank. Show them stills of the perps as well, see if they can identify them. Then visit Mrs Watts, go through the same process with her and please be respectful, offer her my condolences, tell her from me we'll get these bastards. Make sure you take someone from family liaison with you."

"Andy and Pam, get the wider team to find out everything you can about Thomas Smythe's son Paul, his businesses, bank statements and more importantly, the people in his life. Contact him urgently, Charlotte Marks, she'll have his mobile number, we need to talk to him pronto."

Middleton nodded her acceptance while she was still staring at the screen.

"Jac?"

"Yes, Pam, what is it?"

"They must have known that the storage facility had security cameras monitoring comings and goings, hence the dark glasses and black clothes, difficult to identify persons dressed like that. They must have known we'd end up with a copy, they're playing games with us, Jac, they're probably watching us."

"Let's not worry about that, be vigilant, be aware of people around you," Wolfe had to be positive, offer encouragement and show strength, he had also come to the same conclusion but hadn't wanted to voice his concern.

"Where does Brookes fit into all this?" asked Halford.

"I think he knew something, maybe who these guys are but Jessop had something they wanted, and maybe that's the same for Watts and Smythe, they have something … but Brookes knew something, that's it, that's all I've got," Wolfe said with a touch of resignation.

"Okay, before we finish here," announced Wolfe. "Pam, bring up the photo again taken before the trip to Sarajevo."

Middleton did as requested, the photo filled the screen.

Using a digital pointer, Wolfe proceeded to confirm what he knew of the men in the picture, "This man here is Matthew Tanner, aka Armon Cabrinovic, a University Lecturer specialising in Modern History at Leeds, but in his spare time, a modern day Indiana Jones and I think, he is the key to understanding the motive behind the recent goings on."

Wolfe continued to impart the knowledge he knew about Matthew Tanner and his journeys to mainland Europe in search of historical artefacts that defined his career, and his thirst for recognition as a historical novelist, he concluded with;

"This photo was taken twelve years ago and shows the four men ready to depart for Sarajevo. A few weeks later, only three men returned, Tanner was never seen again. From what we understand from relatives, Smythe, Watts and Jessop have only ever stated that Tanner remained in Sarajevo, and was expected to return sometime later but he never came back. The question I'm asking is 'what happened on that trip?' because I believe whatever happened has a bearing on what is happening now. Two of these men are dead, murdered together with another man I believe had information relating to this case."

"Are we certain Tanner hasn't come back?" asked Fairburn. "Could he be the one committing these murders?"

"Well, yes, of course, that's one theory. However, we've checked with immigration and they have no record of Tanner or Cabrinovic returning through legal channels, therefore, if he has returned, he's sneaked back in and maybe that's what has happened but we have no way of checking. If he has returned, then we need to know, 'why after twelve years has he suddenly decided to return now?' We know he owned a small terraced house in Headingley and we have requested access to the property through the solicitor acting on instructions left with them by Tanner before going to Eastern Europe. This information was received from Leeds University, Tanner's last employers. We are expecting to be given access to his home tomorrow so Pam and I will meet the solicitor there. I've also requested an appointment with Proudman Press, Tanner's publishers … where have they been sending royalties from the sale of his books over the past twelve years?"

Wolfe adjourned the briefing at this point, thanked them all for their hard work and finally added,

"We have the start of some momentum here, let's push this to a conclusion. These perpetrators have seen fit to show themselves, is that bravado, guile, overconfidence or stupidity, I believe, its arrogance and that's their weak link. I know we have the ability to exploit this weakness, anything at all that seems or looks unusual or doesn't fit, post it on the virtual board on the server where everyone can view it."

Chapter 21

At 10am the following morning, Wolfe and Middleton arrived at the home of Matthew Tanner. Wolfe parked his car on the double drive of the end terrace house next to an Audi that he assumed belonged to the Solicitor from Prime Legal. Headingley is a leafy and affluent suburb of Leeds, the end terrace looked to have been extended recently a substantial two-storey addition gave the frontage an imposing appearance and used up most of the land available at the side of the corner plot.

The front door opened from inside, a woman stood in the doorway ready to greet the two detectives. Her chest was the focal point of her physical presence, her hips offered balance to the top heavy impression given by her breasts, her face was framed by long auburn hair the vision was finished off with brightly coloured high heel shoes on the end of stocking clad legs.

"What the f***?" exclaimed Middleton. "It's a good job you didn't come on your own, Jac, she would eat you alive."

"I'm not sure you being here makes any difference, Pam, she could devour both of us," replied Wolfe as he got out of his car.

"Hello," said the diva holding out her hand. "I'm Andrea, Prime Legal."

"Pleased to meet you, Andrea," Wolfe replied with as much macho indifference as he could muster and shook her hand. "DI Jaxon Wolfe and DC Pamela Middleton." They presented their ID cards.

"Please come in, would you like a cup of tea or coffee?"

"That would be lovely, thanks," replied Middleton on behalf of them both. "Two teas with milk, no sugar."

They followed her into the lounge which was open plan into the kitchen, dining area. Whilst Andrea filled the kettle, Wolfe and Middleton looked around.

"Andrea," asked Wolfe. "This house appears to have been fitted out recently, the kitchen looks brand new and the dining table too. The furniture in the lounge looks like it hasn't been used and the log burner looks brand new. Has it recently been refurbished, has the owner requested this upgrade?"

Andrea walked noisily, high heels clinking on the wood floor then suddenly going quiet as floor covering changed to carpet in the lounge.

"Mr Tanner is a client of long standing with our legal practice and Mr Prime has written instructions on how his affairs should be managed during his long stays in Europe. I've been with the company for three years and this is my first visit to this property but I can confirm that the house has been recently renovated as Mr Tanner has requested."

Wolfe and Middleton looked at each other surprised.

"Has Mr Tanner been in touch with Prime Legal recently?"

"No, no, Prime Legal is undertaking Mr Tanner's long-standing requests. In fact, I have a copy here in my laptop bag." She bent down at the side of the sofa, her skirt rode high on her left leg revealing a stocking topped thigh, unzipped the bag and lifted out a clear plastic wallet, and handed it to Wolfe with a smile. He hadn't been the intended recipient of the stocking top, it was for Middleton's benefit, she too got a 'if you want to see more let me know' smile.

Middleton coughed and looked towards Wolfe, seeking shelter but he was already studying the paperwork Andrea had handed to him.

"So, this was written … in … err 2005," he said scanning the document whilst thumbing through the document. "It appears to give instructions on what to do with his belongings during his absence, but twelve years absence?"

"Well, yes, it does seem a little bizarre but I've discussed it with his employer, Leeds University and his publisher, and in the absence of immediate family or, come to that, any family at all, they are all we can consult with and both are mentioned in the document as persons or organisations that should make decisions on his behalf."

"Okay, so are you telling us that these improvements were made recently and approved on his behalf by Leeds University, Proudman Press and Prime Legal?"

"The University and Proudman weren't interested so we took the decision, all legal and above board as you might say."

"But who financed it?" Middleton interrupted. "Does he send money?"

"Oh, no, no, no," responded Andrea, with another suggestive look at Pam. "It's supported by funds from his royalties. Mr Tanner is a published author and we have power of attorney to access his bank account." Wolfe and Middleton once again glanced at each other. "It's all legal," exclaimed Andrea, she was beginning to look a little worried.

"The legality of all this is not our concern, please sit down, Andrea," Wolfe said as he sat down on the sofa and placed a hand on the cushion next to him. The kettle boiled and clicked off in the kitchen, Andrea looked over her shoulder and was about to raise herself from the sofa.

"Forget the teas," stated Wolfe. "Let me get this straight, this agreement, all legal and above board, as you say, gives Prime Legal the power to spend Matthew Tanner's money whilst he's elsewhere and the money required to add an extension onto this property was paid solely from his royalties entrusted to Prime Legal for this purpose?"

"Yes, Inspector … but, you see, Mr Tanner had specified a date when work should start. He'd already agreed the design, any short fall would be recouped through mortgage, bank account drawdown or cash, and to secure our involvement and commitment, we are also his financial advisors with power of attorney to deal with his financial affairs as we see fit."

"Oh, my God, he wasn't expecting to immediately come back from the Sarajevo trip, was he?" Middleton stated as she sat down in one of the armchairs.

"Mmmm, or he never had any intention of coming back after this particular trip," answered Wolfe as he put the document on the coffee table.

"Maybe he thought something else might happen?" Middleton added.

"Is this agreement strictly legal?" asked Wolfe not wishing to encourage a response, "Sorry, just thinking out loud … I don't expect an answer."

Andrea looked quizzically at him for a moment, "That agreement," she continued, "is a rolling agreement. I haven't brought the previous ones with me, but the original agreement was dated 1990 and until this agreement in 2005, we only handled small sums of money for him, making sure bills were paid and tax affairs sorted, that sort of thing, but this agreement is different and it has a twenty year time clause attached to it. So, in 2025, if Mr Tanner has not made himself known to Prime Legal, we have the power to sell everything, close his banks accounts, re-coup tax, pay our fees etc. any monies outstanding are to be donated equally to Leeds and Sarajevo Universities."

All Wolfe could say was, "Wow, that's what I call putting your house in order. I can't even make a proper list for the supermarket shopping!"

Andrea smiled, "I'll get those teas now, shall I?"

"I think we need them," replied Middleton.

Wolfe and Middleton stared at each other as Andrea walked from the lounge into the kitchen, neither talked. They stared and gazed around the room until Wolfe said in a loud voice that snapped Middleton's attention back to the now,

"Where are Mr Tanner's belongings?"

A voice from the kitchen instantly returned. "In the spare bedroom at the back of the house, clothes, record collection, photos and paperwork, all catalogued and indexed ... all part of our service," stated Andrea as she arrived back in the lounge, carrying a tray upon which stood teapot, cups, saucers and a plate of biscuits.

"Would it be okay for me to take a look?" asked Middleton.

"You're welcome to have a look if you wish." Middleton stood, "Top of the stairs to the left and the door straight in front of you," added Andrea.

Middleton left the room and could be heard walking up the stairs.

Wolfe stared at the biscuits without registering the fact, he was thinking, hoping that Pam could make the next move look natural. It would be a good opportunity to find the right kind of evidence that might move the investigation on but firstly the evidence had to be placed, then found.

Andrea finished pouring the teas. "She's a very attractive woman, isn't she, Inspector? Your assistant, I mean," she added whilst handing a cup of tea on a saucer to Wolfe.

Wolfe ignored the accolade and asked. "Have you met Matthew Tanner, Andrea?"

"No, in my three years at Prime Legal I'm not aware of Mr Tanner contacting our organisation."

"How much money has been spent so far on this property?"

"Well, I'm not sure I can divulge that kind of information," replied Andrea indignantly.

"Andrea, do we have to go through the courts? Because we will if we have to!" replied Wolfe. "Three people have been murdered, two of whom went on the trip to Sarajevo in 2005 with Matthew Tanner."

"I don't understand, Inspector."

"No and we don't either, Andrea, but what I do understand is that other murders may take place and although my question might not appear relevant now, it might become relevant and useful to our investigation."

Without hesitation, she replied, "Currently we have spent £75,000 and we anticipate that the total when the works are finished will exceed £100,000."

"So, he was quite well off."

"Not including this house, Mr Tanner has in excess of £500,000 in bank accounts and investments that we have power of attorney over," stated Andrea.

"He's a very trusting person," responded Wolfe whilst mentally trying to work out how many years he would have to work to earn that amount of money.

Just then, Middleton could be heard calling, "Boss, you'd better come up here and have a look at this."

Wolfe excused himself, left the lounge closely followed by Andrea, they headed upstairs. Accessing the room where Matthews Tanners belongings were stored, they saw Middleton sat on a chair reading a document that Wolfe instantly recognised.

"I've found this in that blue envelope file." She pointed to a file on the desk next to her that had been half emptied. "It's a letter sent to Proudman Press in 2004 and this page corner was folded … see?" She tapped the page on the desk at the side of her. "It describes what the intention of the trip to Sarajevo was for … and … oh my God, this is hard to believe." She stood and handed the page she was reading to Wolfe.

"What is this?" he asked.

"Read these two paragraphs, sir, they give an account of what they were hoping to find," she replied.

Wolfe read the page in his hand, he'd read it before however he needed to act like this was the first time. He read slowly to give himself time to think of his response.

"Well, this certainly gives a reason for the trip and it offers motive for the murders of two of his friends." He paused for a few seconds. "Or does it?" he asked as he handed it to Andrea who stood to the side of him.

"I don't remember seeing this document before," Andrea said out loud. "I'm sure I haven't seen this before," she repeated as she leafed through the pages on the desk and those that she'd snatched from Middleton.

"This is important evidence for our investigation, Andrea. Therefore, we'll be keeping this, but we will give you a receipt for it." Middleton firmly retrieved the document from Andrea and placed it back in the envelope folder where she'd found it.

"But … but, this document wasn't here, it's not part of this collection, it's not supposed …" she stopped herself from saying anymore.

"Andrea, please continue, what were you going to say?" asked Wolfe.

"Oh … err, nothing," she stuttered.

"It's supposed to … what, Andrea?" Middleton interjected.

"It's not catalogued," Andrea said as she reached up to a shelf above the desk and opened a lever arch file, then frantically thumbing through the contents, she removed a piece of paper. "Look, Miscellaneous File 2 … contents listed and no mention of a letter to Proudman Press … it shouldn't be there."

"Are you the only person that has catalogued Mr Tanner's belongings, Andrea?" asked Middleton.

"Yes … well … I mean no it wasn't me that catalogued Mr Tanner's belongings it was Proudman Press. I'm the only person involved with this client at Prime Legal," she spluttered. "But I checked all of these items one by one and I didn't notice that document," she paused and looked hard at the folder now tucked under Middleton's left arm, "maybe I could have missed it I suppose," she whimpered as she straightened her shoulders relieving the tension in her neck and unclenching her fists.

Middleton watched as Andrea de-stressed, *'Wow, she takes things a bit personal,'* she thought then asked, "Who catalogued these items at Proudman?"

"I don't know," she snapped. "I'll have to ask at the office." Then silence.

"Well, you do that, Andrea, and let us know, we might want to interview that person. In the meantime, we need to take this document. Who is your contact at Proudman?"

"Errr … Cynthia Proudman … she owns the company."

"Okay, we'll contact her later today," concluded Wolfe.

Middleton and Wolfe made their way back down the stairs and into the open plan space below, Middleton deciding that events upstairs had left her throat dry so she took a drink of tea from one of the cups standing on the Kitchen worktop. Andrea followed, her attention fixed on the screen of a mobile phone held in her left hand whilst scrolling with her right thumb then she looked up as she leant against the Kitchen worktop,

"Will that be all detectives?"

"Yes, I think we're done here Andrea," replied Wolfe as he grabbed a biscuit from the plate on the coffee table.

"I'll contact my employers now DI Wolfe and explain that a document has been taken. I assume that you intend to send a receipt for this document to our Leeds Office?"

Wolfe was about to eat the biscuit but the request from Andrea made him stop.

"Yes of course, DC Middleton will arrange that on return to our office."

"Thank you that would be appreciated."

Wolfe couldn't see a bin to throw the biscuit into so, without consciously realising, he put the biscuit in the right-hand pocket of his suit jacket.

"Thanks for all your help," he said as Middleton and he left the house.

In the car returning to Holland Walk Middleton made the point that the contents of Proudman Press letter seemed to be a little farfetched.

Wolfe responded with a, "Yeah perhaps, however it's certainly plausible and Andrea didn't really refer to the contents, she seemed to me to be more concerned about it being found and particularly being found by us."

Chapter 22

Wolfe had showered early, and was enjoying his boiled eggs and toast he'd cooked for breakfast. Isabella was still asleep in bed but he'd decided that before he left the house to prepare buttered toast, and a bowl of yogurt and muesli drizzled with honey and a cup of tea. Take it up to her room, because that's what dads do, at least, that what this dad does, he thought to himself, when their daughter doesn't have a mother anymore. Then he choked back a lump in his throat, his eyes began to water.

"Come on, Jac, that's one perfect daughter you have, be strong for her," he said to himself.

Wolfe knocked on the door. "Room service," he announced.

"Orrr ... thanks, Dad. Ya know, none of my friends get this treatment."

"That's cos you have me, the best dad in the world," he said as he put the tray down on her lap as she sat up in bed.

"Yep, I know, Dad."

"How long have you been awake?"

"I was woken by what sounded like an elephant walking around the place."

"Ah, sorry, love."

"No, I set my alarm. I'm going into work early this morning. I'm off in the afternoon, remember? Meeting Pam in Leeds for a coffee?"

"Oh, yes, I remember now," Wolfe paused. "You and Pam seem to be getting on alright?"

"Yeah, she's a good laugh. She gives Pete Halford a bit of stick."

"Yeah and I'll bet you give me a bit of stick as well?"

"Oh, yes. Well, I feel I ought to join in."

Wolfe suddenly released that Izzy was okay, her mum was gone but she was dealing with it, and life in the 21st century with all its technology and social media meant that discussion of loved ones in a sometimes less than reverent attitude was just a modern day release of pent up frustration at life in general, complete normality. Izzy had accepted her mother's demise, why couldn't he do the same?

"Is that your phone I can hear, Dad?" announced Izzy.

"Oh shit," Wolfe rushed across the landing into his bedroom.

"Hello, Detective Inspector Jaxon Wolfe speaking."

"It's Pete, boss," came the reply.

Halford informed Wolfe that Paul Anthony Smythe had called, leaving a message at the station, stating that he had returned from his business trip and was responding to a message to call DI Wolfe. Wolfe told Halford to return the call immediately and arrange a meeting.

Halford had called back and within ten minutes confirmed a meeting at the house on Panorama Drive at 11am that morning.

"I'll meet you there, Pete."

"Okay boss."

Three hours later Wolfe and Halford knocked at the door of the house Wolfe had visited twice before. They were escorted by the frumpy looking au-pair into the lounge, she deliberately but slyly winked at Wolfe as she turned to return back to the hall making him feel a little uncomfortable. A man was standing in the lounge with his back to the lounge entrance looking out onto the rear garden and the extensive views beyond. He was dressed in a salmon pink shirt over dark designer jeans with short, cropped jet-black hair shaved above the collar, the look exuded style and wealth. He turned as Wolfe and Halford were announced.

"Hi, I'm Paul Smythe."

"I'm DI Wolfe and my colleague here is DC Halford," pronounced Wolfe. They shook hands, his handshake was firm without being confrontational then Paul motioned to the two police officers to be seated.

"Mr Smythe, thanks for contacting the West Yorkshire Police," announced Wolfe.

Without hesitation, Paul responded, "Charlotte tells me that her brother has been found murdered on Carlton Moor, it's come as a complete shock to the both of us. He had his problems with drug dependency, I'm aware of that, but murder! Good god, not what I expected to hear on my return. Charlotte wouldn't tell me over the phone about her brother's circumstances only stated that she needed me home. So what can you tell me officers because my partner is distraught and she needs answers?"

Wolfe felt a twinge of guilty embarrassment, 'distraught?' thought Wolfe, 'that's not the impression I got the other afternoon.' Instantly followed by the complete opposite reaction. After all, there wasn't anything to feel guilty about, was there? Wolfe pulled a photo from his inside jacket pocket and offered it to Paul Smythe.

"You know this picture, I assume?"

"Yes, of course, it's a copy of that picture over there," he pointed to the framed version on the shelf adjacent to the chimneybreast. "And I know that because Charlotte told me, you'd taken the original when you came here a few days ago, Inspector Wolfe, and that you returned it a day later."

Wolfe felt a little embarrassed again but decided to brazen it out. "That's correct, so you know those featured in the photo?"

"Frank Jessop, Davy Watts, my dad, Thomas Smythe and Matthew Tanner. It was taken a long time ago, just before they all left for Sarajevo, a mission organised by Matthew to help with the rebuilding of the University after the siege of the city. My dad organised the trip, Frank and Davy went along to help, they treated it as a military exercise, not surprising really, considering they're all ex TA. But what does this have to do with Charlotte's brother."

"Matthew used to work for Hennersy Contracting owned by Jessop and Watts and Mr Smythe we're here to inform you that –"

"Frank and Davy are dead," he interrupted. "I listen to the radio and watch TV."

"We need to find your father, we believe he's in great danger," added Wolfe.

"I appreciate that, your assumptions and mine are the same. The last time I saw my father was a few weeks ago, I don't know where he is now. If I did, I would tell you. You've been to the house, I take it?" asked Paul.

Wolfe nodded and looked towards Halford. "We've been to the house on several occasions and we've now got police officers monitoring the house around the clock."

"Have you checked inside the house?" enquired Paul.

"No, but with your authority, we'd like to."

"Yes, of course, but I don't have any keys, you'll have to force your way in," he concluded.

Following Smythe's permission, Wolfe ordered Halford to organise as soon as possible. Halford left the room, his mobile phone lifted to his ear.

"We've spoken to your mother and she stated the last meeting she had with Thomas was at a restaurant on the Leeds Road, you where there as well?"

"Yes, that's correct, he went home early as I recall, had a bit too much to drink so mum packed him off in a taxi and I haven't seen him since."

"You had an argument with him at the restaurant?" Wolfe stated, then paused as the lounge door opened and Halford entered.

"There'll be someone at Mr Smythe's house in an hour, boss," Halford said into the silence.

"Not an argument as such more a jealous rant, he was upset that I'd managed to do a deal on a piece of real estate in Birmingham next to a development in the city centre that his company Britannia Limited had built seven or eight years ago. He thought I bought the site at a too high a price," Paul concluded.

"Did you?"

"Did I what?"

"Buy the land at too high a price?"

"That's got nothing to do with my father or the police. I bought Britannia Limited from my father and now it is part of my company Andromeda Holdings. We're doing extremely well, thanks to my management, and no, we didn't pay too much for it, we paid the going rate. My father had assumed that Britannia had secured a ransom strip many years ago when he bought the original site, but as usual, someone pulled a fast one on him while he was trying to pull a fast one on them. He always thought he had the monopoly on being a shrewd wheeler-dealer, but in actual fact, he was more vulnerable to the sucker punch than he realised. Anyway, I have the business now, not him."

"So … Britannia Ltd.?" Wolfe looked at Paul then at Halford, "Used to belong to your father?"

"Yes, that's correct," answered Paul wearily, as Halford stood and made his apologies, stating he was going to double check the ETA of the officers arriving at Thomas Smythe's home, once again, he left the lounge. As soon as the door was shut, he was searching the internet for details on Britannia Holdings Ltd.

"When I bought or, more accurately, should I say, rescued the business from my father, it was leaking funds. It was only when I conducted a financial investigation, did I find that the funds were leaking straight into his account in Spain. I liquidated the company immediately, then settled its debts and now it's a dormant company within Andromeda Holdings."

"So, when you bought the company, did you have funds of your own or …"

"Again, Detective Inspector Wolfe that is none of yours or the police authority's business …"

"Well, actually, it is, Mr Smythe. Your father is missing; therefore, my questions are relevant."

"He's a grown man inspector, he can, within reason, do what the hell he likes and that includes going missing. You know he has property in Spain, he's probably sunbathing next to his swimming pool …" Paul didn't get chance to finish.

"We've had feedback from our European colleagues just yesterday Mr Smythe, your father is nowhere to be found, his neighbours haven't seen him for weeks and you are correct he can do what he likes but we are worried about his safety. As a British citizen we have a duty to protect him if we think he is danger and we do Mr Smythe!" Wolfe took a breath, not making any attempt to hide his frustration.

"Okay detective … I understand … you've made your point."

"Now, I can pose my questions here and now or at the police station tomorrow with or without your legal representation, the choice is yours."

"Okay, okay. I'm just a little perturbed about your line of questioning, Inspector, it's almost as if you consider me responsible for his disappearance."

"Mr Smythe, nothing could be further from my mind, however, I have to eliminate possibilities that may appear ridiculous to establish the obvious. Do you understand?"

"No, not really, but it's quite clear I don't have any option but to answer," he replied with more than a hint of resignation.

"Good, now can we proceed?"

Wolfe continued asking questions of Smythe about his time at the LSE, and his contacts with his mother and father, and it became apparent that shortly before Paul turned eighteen, his Father had ceased to communicate with his son and had withdrawn financial assistance for his university education but the LSE had offered Paul a bursary to support his first year at University to study Economics and Business Science. When Paul finished his degree, he was recruited by a commercial bank in the city and within five years, was head of their North America Office until the banking crisis of 2008 caused the bank to cease trading with the loss of nearly 100 jobs, Paul was suddenly redundant. He'd managed in five years to accrue a not insubstantial sum of money and decided to look for investment opportunities of his own. In 2010 whilst visiting his mother he was encouraged to approach his father about buying his failing development company. His father had been siphoning off profits, letting planning approvals lapse and watching whilst other companies took up contracts not exercised by Britannia.

"The company had potential, it was one of the few small development companies operating in Yorkshire that continued to build through the recession and I knew one of the first market sectors to grow after any recession was housing. Therefore, an established company with a small land bank would be ideally placed to take advantage of economic growth that always returns after a recession, but as the economic climate began to improve, Britannia faltered and that's when I decided to step in," explained Paul. Then he continued to explain how his father began to drink more heavily and would go to the company office irregularly, and wouldn't be seen for weeks on end, decisions just couldn't be taken, consequently, opportunities were being lost.

Asked if his father had objected to the takeover, Paul replied,

"He was so drunk the night I suggested buying the company from him that all he could say in response was 'thought you weren't fucking interested in going into dads' business, you spoilt bastard' which took me by surprise because he'd never wanted me to take any part in his business. Then mum started to sob, and then started swearing at him, tried to punch him, in fact, I think she managed to land one on the side of his head before I intervened." He paused, silence only interrupted by another recollection. "Anyway, when it all calmed down, it was decided that I should take over the business, you see, mum owned 49% of the company, thanks to the investment she made shortly after they got married when her father died. So, mum threatened to give her shares to me for nothing, meaning that I could launch a takeover bid if I'd wanted, but it didn't come to that. Although I had to find £500,000 to take the company from him. Thanks to the economic upturn, it wasn't a bad investment at all and that's really why he was so pissed off with me at the restaurant a couple of weeks back."

The conversation was again interrupted by Halford, "Sir, our personnel will be at the home of Mr Smythe in 20 minutes." He confirmed as he sat down.

"Okay you go meet them at the house, Mr Smythe and I will follow soon but don't enter the property until we attend," Wolfe ordered.

"Sir."

When Halford had gone Paul continued with his explanation that his father was still quite well off, thanks to a substantial sum of money he had deposited in the Spanish banking system in 2011, after selling off Britannia assets, just before Paul procured the company.

Asked about the relationship his father had with Alfred Marks, Paul confirmed that his father was a good friend of his and he had regularly put Thomas Smythe in touch with wealthy land owners in the Leeds area whom Alfred had met during his business dealings, many of whom wanted to sell heirlooms to raise cash but Alfred would offer other ways to release capital, for a fee, offering to broker land sales and then cashing in on a finder's fee from Thomas.

Paul explained that when Alfred Marks was found in a Harrogate Hotel having committed suicide, he couldn't believe it, but remorse for a man he hardly knew soon turned to anger when he realised that, perhaps, his father had some involvement in Alfie's death, shady dealings his father had been mixed up in. He confirmed that he had met Charlotte Marks at Alfie's funeral and started talking to her, wanting to know how she knew the deceased only to find out that she was, in fact, Alfie's wife.

"We hit it off instantly when she saw my embarrassment at having not realised that Alfie could have a wife half his age and such an attractive partner at that. A year later, she moved in with me and two years later we bought this place."

Completely without prior preamble, Wolfe asked, "Something went wrong in Sarajevo, didn't it, Paul?"

"What?"

"Come on, you heard me well enough, we know from interviews with the Jessop and Watts families, and more importantly, from your mother, that Frank and Davy didn't communicate with Thomas after they returned from Sarajevo, why, what happened over there?"

"I've got no idea. But now you mention it, I bumped into Davy Watts in the supermarket in Carlton last year, we talked about his kids and Frank, but he didn't ask about my father and when I said without being asked that I haven't seen him for a while, he said he never wanted to see him again as long as he lived, which took me by surprise. However, in answer to your question, Inspector, I have no idea what happened in Sarajevo or afterwards between Jessop, Watts and my father."

"So, no mention of gold bullion then?"

Paul looked aghast at Wolfe. "What? Gold bullion? What the hell are you talking about?"

"How well did you know Matthew Tanner? Like Jessop and Watts, he was a good friend of your father's, so I assume, he must have visited your home and of course, he was known for being a real-life Indiana Jones, wasn't he? Running off in search of historical artefacts, helped in part by your father, Jessop and Watts. He must have made an impression on you, as a young boy he must have seemed like some kind of movie star."

Paul missed most of the last question; he was still trying to digest the previous one.

"Wait a minute, just let me get my head around what you're suggesting, Inspector. You think they went looking for gold bullion in Sarajevo?"

"Yes, and I think they found it, and I also think that is why Jessop and Watts have been murdered."

"That's quite unbelievable, Inspector. And you think that my father is next on the list?"

"Matthew Tanner disappears for twelve years after a trip to Eastern Europe. Then all of a sudden, people directly involved in the trip start being murdered, your father could be next. Paul, he is, in my opinion, in great danger and we need to find him … now!"

"Yes, once again you've made your point inspector but gold bullion, come on that is pure fantasy?"

Wolfe thought it best to leave that part of the discussion until later and asked Paul to accompany him in his car to his father's house a mile or so away rather than taking two cars. Paul agreed.

They were about to leave when Charlotte Marks entered the house and stopped in the hall, in each hand she carried a large full shopping bag of groceries. Paul walked up to his partner put his arms around her waist and pulled her towards him, she held onto the bags, they swayed low down by her sides as he kissed his partner full on the lips, she tensed her upper body. Wolfe watched on and without hesitation, he reached to one side of the couple.

"Here, let me help you with those bags," as he took one bag and then the other.

"Of course, you two know each other, met whilst I was away on business, so no need for introductions," said Smythe with a sardonic grin. Wolfe ignored the comment.

"Shall I put these in the kitchen, Miss Marks?"

Charlotte nodded. "Just through there, Inspector," pointing down the corridor to the left of the staircase.

Wolfe returned to the Hall to see Smythe leaving through the main entrance, he followed. Without words, the two men got into Wolfe's car. They drove in silence towards the home of Smythe Senior. Less than five minutes later, the Smythe residence came into view.

The house held an imposing position high above Carlton and could be seen from the main road which traversed around the front of the house, following a high wall that screened the front garden of the estate. Wolfe turned sharp left onto the driveway which served another house higher up the hill. Wolfe could see the drive to the house which also led to a large detached double garage to the right some 30 metres away from the front of the large glass fronted very modern detached house. Wolfe noticed a police standard issue car and medium-sized, dark-coloured van parked to the left of the drive, and saw five men, Halford with two police officers and two others he assumed were the locksmiths, walking towards the main entrance.

***

Wolfe first saw the bright flash emanate from the garage building then he heard the blast. The noise of the blast hit him like a wall, he saw the large garage door push high away from its housing, then the bright yellow flash became more intense followed by flames that pushed through a large portion of the roof lifting it into the air, the noise seemed to stop everything for a few seconds as the shock wave hit the car and almost pushed it off the drive. Wolfe could see into the garage, it was full of fire and black smoke as the garage door came hurtling, twisting and sluing its way towards him, falling suddenly to the ground, as if it had instantly run out of energy. It landed next to the van in the drive.

"What the fuck!" he shouted Wolfe.

"Oh, my God, his Cobra … it's in that garage," responded Paul.

Wolfe was on the phone before he parked the car well away from the garage that was now completely engulfed in flames. Then another blast almost as loud as the first sent the vehicle inside into the air.

Wolfe yelled down his phone,

"Get the fucking fire service here from Carlton now. Ah shit, I can see a body in the car. What the fuck is happening?"

Within ten minutes, the first fire engine arrived on site closely followed a few seconds later by another. Soon after foam was being pumped out of the tender onto what was left of the burning building. The double garage door had landed some 10 metres away, wires and running gear trailed across the drive, a large portion of the roof had landed half on top of the garage and half hanging down the side. Smouldering residue was forcing its way through the blanket of foam laid down by the firemen, and the smell of damp petrol and timber filled the air around the garage, choking and irritating those nearby.

Paul had jumped out of the car and rushed towards the garage after the second explosion but was stopped from getting too close by Halford who had instinctively run towards the blast after the first explosion.

"No, leave it. I'm sorry but there is nothing you can do," stated Halford as he grabbed Paul stopping him getting any closer to the burning outbuilding. The ease with which Halford had managed to stop him took him by surprise.

"But it's in there. I know it … oh my God."

Wolfe arrived a split second later. "Paul, please step back, it's too dangerous."

"That's my father's pride and joy completely destroyed," he spluttered. He was looking over Halfords' shoulder and noticed, as Wolfe had done, that there was a person sat, strapped into the driver's seat.

"No, no," he screamed. "He's in there, my … my father's in the car … oh my God." Halford continued without difficulty to stand his ground preventing Paul from progressing closer to the building.

"Let the pros do their job," said Halford nodding towards the firemen.

Half an hour later, the fire had subsided, the foam covering the carnage that was the garage, housing Thomas Smythe's AC Cobra, had turned to liquid and was running away from the building down the drive to the road. The beautiful scenery around the house was unaffected but the outbuilding, a single storey ancillary building obviously intended to be functional to store a classic car was now a complete mess, almost levelled to the ground, the back wall and one of the side walls appeared, weirdly, to be unaffected but the roof was non-existent, it lay in pieces on the ground, over and around the front and side of the building.

Almost an hour after the original explosion, Professor Higgins had arrived with his assistant and the two of them were making an initial investigation supervised by fire officers. The building was considered to be unsafe and liable to collapse but Higgins had insisted on getting immediate access to establish whether or not the person in the car was still alive, but all knew that the odds of that actually being the case were highly improbable.

The main house had been forcibly opened and as expected, a search had concluded that the house was empty of persons. Wolfe had contacted Jennifer Harrington, she was now sitting on the sofa in the lounge with her son, he was weeping and sobbing intermittently, watched by Wolfe. He didn't know why but for some reason, he kept thinking that the tears and remorse from Paul sounded false, too much wailing, crocodile tears, perhaps. Wolfe hadn't at all warmed to Paul Smythe, he put that down to his attraction to Charlotte, Smythe's partner. 'Was it jealousy?' He thought, 'if it is, I need to control it.'

Wolfe was then called away by Middleton who'd arrived earlier to co-ordinate the response teams and was now standing in the hallway.

"Boss!" she said as he closed the door to the lounge. "Professor Higgins is on his way from the garage and wanted to have a word with you first."

"Okay but I think I know what he's going to say, that is … or was, Thomas Henry Smythe in the car."

"Yeah, that's what I'm expecting as well."

Higgins walked through the main entrance, he met Wolfe and Middleton in the hall. "Jac, let's have a word in private, can we?"

Middleton opened the door to the dining room. "You should be undisturbed in here, I'll stay outside just to make sure."

"Thanks, Pam," Wolfe nodded his appreciation.

The door closed behind the two men. "Okay, Arnold, initial reaction?" said Wolfe.

"Jac I think whoever is behind this has made their first mistake."

"Go on, I'm listening," said Wolfe.

"I'm convinced it was a remote-control device that set off this explosion."

"Another fatality then?"

"Oh yes, I'm afraid so, but I'm almost certain he was dead before the explosion."

"What makes you think that?"

"He was strapped in so hard, he wouldn't have been able to do that himself. The body has hardly moved from its seating position, bearing in mind that this kind of car has only one seating position, but also the explosion I believe, was under the centre bulkhead, under the drivers feet, both his legs have been severed but the rest of his body is still in the seat. I would have expected the body to have been propelled out of the car completely. Also the ignition key in the dashboard slot is not in the position where I'd expect it to be. When the car is ignited to start, the key needs to click through two positions and then returns back once but the key is in position one not two."

"Meaning?"

"The ignition hasn't been switched, no spark to fire the engine, so what ignited the fuel?" Higgins explained. "So technically, the car engine hadn't been ignited via the key ignition and to add to that, the centre of the explosion is nowhere near the fuel tank, it's centred, subject to confirmation, under the car in the vehicle pit. On top of all that, there's wiring not related to the car or the garages power supply leading back to the vehicle pit. Remote detonation, Jac, I'm almost certain of it."

"Wow, that's quite an assumption, Arnold. But if there's anyone I would expect to be correct in their assumptions, I would expect that to be you. So, if we assume that the explosion was remotely controlled … why?"

"Well, that's it, Jac, and that's where my expertise leaves me high and dry, but what I could surmise is that …"

"All this mayhem is for my benefit … isn't it … that's what you were going to say?"

"Yep."

"Either we're getting close or they're messing with us."

"Either way, Jac, I'm sure you were meant to witness this as it happened."

"Remote, you say, Arnold? How far away … an estimate?"

"No idea, but the experience I gained in the Gulf tells me remote means within 200 metres because of the amount of conflicting radio wave transmittance within a conflict zone, so you get as close as you can before activating the remote." Higgins was almost apologetic, this being the only experience he could offer.

"It was done for effect, that's it. I wasn't in any more danger than anyone else, it's not personal, but someone wanted me to see this. Someone was watching as we drove up the road towards the house," Wolfe was now talking out loud, to himself.

Higgins continued with his description of the scene, "There's not much left of the occupant; however, the person killed is definitely male."

Higgins then made reference to the car, "If that car is an AC Cobra, then it was worth in excess of £150,000 and therefore, I would assume that whoever owned it, must have had the financial wherewithal to maintain such a piece of 1960s' engineering. Thomas Henry Smythe fits that profile, if you ask me."

"Yeah, that's what I think. There's a photo in the lounge, him with the car," Wolfe stated. "It has a caption that says 'before restoration'. It looks like a pet project of his and judging by Paul's reaction after the explosion … it's his father's pride and joy, he said."

"There you have it … unfortunately I fully expect this is the other victim you've been fearing."

"Yeah, the fourth victim Arnold and I'm no nearer to solving this case than I was when we discovered the body on the moor."

Higgins nodded then left the house to go back and continue his forensic examination in the garage, what remained of the body in the car, almost certainly that of Thomas Henry Smythe was collected an hour or so later by two paramedics and taken straight to the mortuary. Wolfe felt in some way responsible for the demise of Thomas Henry Smythe but also frustrated, he had harboured thoughts that it might have been Smythe who was responsible for the murders of Brookes, Jessop and

Watts, now he had to re-think. He decided to take a walk in the surrounding area of the house, give himself some space, space on his own to think.

The house stood within its own grounds, elevated above the surroundings on three sides. The north side faced higher ground, moorland and two more houses that could just be identified to the northeast, smaller older properties connected to farmland, assumed Wolfe. If, as Higgins had suggested, a remote device was used to set-off the explosion in the garage, then north or north east of the property would be the perfect place to monitor all movements to and from the driveway of the house. Ten minutes later, Wolfe was looking down on the Smythe residence from the high ground above, trying to find the best vantage point from where someone could see the driveway without being seen. He found a location that might have been suitable but there was no evidence on the ground to suggest that anyone had been standing, crouching or sitting there recently. Although the sky was bright and rain hadn't fallen recently, the ground was hard but not frozen, a person standing there would have left a mark. Wolfe checked his own footprints confirming that the ground was soft enough to have taken the in-print of an average person's shoes. Wolfe made the same conclusion at two other suitable locations. So, he thought, if there was no evidence of person or persons watching the comings and goings from the Smythe household on high ground, how did the person detonating the blast know when to trigger it. Wolfe was beginning to believe that Higgins may not be correct and that the blast was triggered by a timepiece of some kind. Then he heard someone shouting in a nearby field.

"Hey, you, what ya doing?" said a scruffy looking person on the other side of the road that Wolfe had walked up to get his current vantage point.

"Police," he shouted looking directly towards the person he now assumed to be a woman.

"You here investigating that loud bang then?" she asked.

"Yes, you heard that then?" he responded as he started to walk towards her.

"Course I bloody heard it, scared me and my cows half to death it did."

Wolfe didn't respond but when he crossed the road, he said in a much quieter voice, "Yeah, it was certainly loud and very scary, Mrs?"

"Bradshaw," she stated. "Eve Bradshaw … on my own now. Reg, my husband, passed away three years ago."

"Oh, I'm sorry to hear that," he replied in the best sympathetic tone he could manage.

"Nah it's alright, he was a right bastard. If I'd known what only he and his ponsie quack of a doctor had known 10 years earlier, I'd have given him a heart attack then," she replied without a hint of emotion and without blinking whilst staring longingly at Wolfe.

Wolfe took a breath, a large breath, he was completely taken aback by this person and his only reply, which he had no control over was, "Wow. Oh, so sorry but what you've just said is almost as devastating and as sad as I've just witnessed down there." As he pointed to the house where Smythe lived.

"Oh, don't worry, love. I'm as happy as larry living here on my own, I can't wish for anything else. Six months after Reg died I sold the farm to a property developer who wants to convert it into holiday homes or work the farm into one of those trendy farmsteads that only breed certain types of cattle and grow apples, hops barley, and the like. Ya know, fancy cheese, butter, cider, beer, all that stuff. Great idea if you ask me, he's got the money to invest and the youth to see it through. I'm off to Spain to live out the rest of my life in the …" She looked at Wolfe, his lower jaw had dropped again and he was staring at her, "… the whore house he's set me up in."

"What … the fff …"

"In the sunshine, ya twerp."

"Mrs Bradshaw, I have no idea what you're talking about, I was just taking a look around, and suddenly I bump into you and then you give me …" He stopped, took another breath. "Property developer, you say … who?"

"Paul Smythe, his dad owns that house down there." Bradshaw pointed to the house below.

"Yes, I know. So, Paul Smythe is buying your farm as a business enterprise?"

"Suppose so … I get to end my days in the sun. We're completing on the deal in a week or so. Mind you he's dragged it out long enough, but my solicitor assures me it will happen."

"Seems a big investment?" Wolfe responded whilst surveying the buildings and land beyond Eve Bradshaw.

"Yeah, I know, his dad and I had the same arrangement until he sold his business," Eve responded. "But all his Dad did was talk, and organise surveys and stuff like that but his son has put money where his mouth is, ya know, a deposit, more money than I've ever had in the bank, he's a good bloke."

"I don't know him that well," so I can't comment.

Just then, Middleton came into view, walking up the road. "Sir, you're needed back at the house, forensics would like a word with you."

Wolfe looked at her then at Eve. "Eve, I sincerely hope this deal works out for you, it was good having our little chat." Wolfe nodded and started walking towards Middleton, he turned within a second and looked at Eve Bradshaw.

"Did you see anyone strange up here in the last twenty-four hours or so?"

"No, inspector, not a soul, although I had expected to see Paul, he was supposed to bring a copy of his structural engineer's report for me to read. He and another guy came up here a few times last month looking at the structure, I assumed it related to the conversion plans he had in mind … ya know, that new venture I told you about?"

"Yeah … err … hang on a minute, Pam," he stopped and walked back towards Eve Bradshaw.

"So, you were expecting Paul Smythe to visit recently?"

"Yeah, last week," she responded a little confused.

"What did the other guy look like, did you get a name?"

"No, I didn't get a name he was just the 'structural engineer'," she mused. "He didn't look English though, more east European, ya know, Polish, Albanian, somewhere round there … dark skinned, black hair, shortish … not as tall as Paul, looked quite strong though, seemed a bit moody to me. They spent quite a long time here though, I could see the other guy wasn't happy being around cattle and his mood upset a couple of the girls. Good job the bull was in the field, otherwise, he would have got really pissed off, upsetting his ladies like he did."

"What do you mean by moody, Eve?" questioned Wolfe.

"He was going round kicking everything or hitting walls with a hammer, then grunting … not saying anything, just making grunting noises. I said to Paul, 'what's wrong with him', he said 'nothing, he's just listening to the noise of the walls, it's what they do'."

"Mmmm ... so when was this ... their visit to your farm?"

"Three, four weeks ago ... maybe ... ya know, when we had that cold snap?"

Wolfe was deep in thought. "Yeah, yeah, I remember."

"That's it! I spent the following weekend in Spain, looking at property, so yeah four weeks ago."

"Who looked after the farm?"

"Paul arranged an agency farmer, but the place was in chaos when I got back. The herd were all out of routine, soon sorted though, I think they missed me and they didn't like strangers around ... cows a funny like –"

Wolfe interrupted,

"So, you weren't here three weeks ago then?"

"That's right and Paul paid, and ..."

"Arranged for someone to look after things while you were gone?" Wolfe finished off her sentence, he was getting a little impatient.

"Thanks, Eve. I may be back in touch." Wolfe turned and walked back towards Middleton.

When Wolfe and Middleton were far enough away not to be overheard, Wolfe announced, "We need to question Paul Smythe further, however, I suppose, under the circumstances, we'll have to wait a while, don't you think?"

"Not good to question someone immediately after the death of a close relative," replied Middleton.

"Statements given could be construed as not reliable if those statements were used as evidence in court."

"Yep, that's what I'm thinking ... damn it!"

Walking back down the drive, Middleton returned to the house while Wolfe walked towards the garage intent on finding Higgins. He found him crouched down in the vehicle pit examining wires.

"How's it going, Arnie?"

"Jac, I'm almost certain the receiver that detonated the explosion was destroyed in the blast. I'll take advice on that but I think this was a detonation by a wireless device."

"What a key fob type, battery operated sends a signal that is only recognised by one device, in this case, the detonator," concluded Wolfe.

"That's it, Jac, I'm almost certain of it," ratified Higgins as he climbed the steps out of the vehicle pit onto the garage floor alongside Wolfe.

Wolfe explained to Higgins that he'd looked for evidence on land close to the house overlooking the drive where someone might have waited where it would have been possible to see his car entering the drive and found nothing. That was the frustrating thing about the explosion, who had detonated it and where were they at the time of the detonation?

Chapter 23

Two days later, the identity of the person killed in the explosion was confirmed as Thomas Henry Smythe. A summary report e-mailed to the West Yorkshire Police from the Forensic Laboratory and signed by Professor Higgins concluded the victim was murdered by a remotely controlled detonation of plastic explosive located underneath the car in the vehicle pit, completely destroying the fully restored AC Cobra and its proud owner.

Wolfe was staring at the photo taken in 2005 before the departure to Sarajevo; three of the main characters in the photo were now dead, murdered in different locations and in different ways. The investigation team had, the previous day, conducted an interview with Matthew Tanner's publishers Proudman Press.

In the wider investigation, Matthew Brookes' sister, Charlotte, had been formally interviewed at police headquarters. This, she considered to be a personal affront to her character and as a consequence, her attraction towards Wolfe had waned, so much so that during the interview conducted by him and Middleton Charlotte had made it quite clear that she intended to make a formal complaint against the West Yorkshire Police, believing Wolfe had used her to get information at a time when she was emotionally insecure the day after her brother's death. However, towards the end of the interview, Wolfe had stated West Yorkshire Police were going to re-open the file relating to the alleged suicide of her husband, Alfred Marks. Charlotte softened her attitude slightly. The reason given for re-opening the file was that Alfred Marks was a known associate of Thomas Henry Smythe, whose death was undoubtedly murder and also, Alfred is directly linked to Matthew Tanner whose whereabouts are unknown. Finding Tanner would be the key factor in concluding the current multiple murder investigation and perhaps an examination of the circumstances surrounding the death of Alfred might offer some clues.

What was now apparent was that Smythe, Watts and Jessop had improved their individual wealth considerably after 2005, maybe as a direct result of their trip to Sarajevo. Financial gain was now, in the eyes of Wolfe and his team, the motive behind the series of killings. The murders were bold and precise in their operation, three men directly connected and two more connected indirectly all appear to revolve around an associate of all five men, Matthew Tanner, aka Armon Cabrinovic. What had happened to him, where was he to be found, is he the killer?

"Another aspect of this investigation that we need to focus on," Wolfe stated, "is a person known only as Tony Chezec We have CCTV images captured from the storage facility showing three persons and one of them looks similar in stature to the person who impersonated a police officer at Abingdon colliery. It shows Jessop was forcibly coerced into handing over something to these thugs" Wolfe pointed to each man on either side of Jessop, "we're not sure what but my hunch is gold bullion."

Wolfe was briefing the investigation team in front of the crime board showing the victim's surnames as headings above a montage of images and handwritten notes, it looked clinical, bereft of any human feeling. Words such as 'victim', 'corpse', 'spear entry point /needle entry', 'bullet entry wound', 'bullet exit wound', 'critical impact abrasion', 'torso severed' were clearly visible. Chief Constable Marcus Haigh-Watson was watching from the back of the crime room whilst Wolfe spoke, "The person known as Chezec cited by one of the victims, needs to be located; he could be the connection, the tie that leads us to join the missing parts of this investigation. Finding this person is our priority. Watts had the presence of mind to write the name Tony Chezec on a piece paper before he died." Wolfe then pointed to the central photograph, the one that started this investigation on its current heading. "Smythe, Watts and Jessop, all murdered, Tanner disappeared 12 years ago, is he dead too or is he Chezec? This figure here in the foreground, blurred unrecognisable, unnamed, could be relevant, but who is it, let's also concentrate our efforts on trying to put a name to this person. Thank you, that concludes the briefing."

The crime room emptied quickly, the team members headed back to their desks almost in a procession. Middleton had prepared notes for the team before the briefing on which she had allocated work to squad members. The task ahead of them would involve long hours, internet research, as many social network sites as they could get access to and face-to-face interviews.

"Plenty of information DI Wolfe but still no arrests, and there could be more victims for all we know," stated Haigh-Watson, now standing directly behind Wolfe. "I need to give the press something tomorrow and this chap, Chezec, possibly Eastern European, seems to be the key to unlocking this mystery, but where and who is he? If we don't lock this investigation down soon, I'll have Special Branch hounding me and 'offering their assistance'."

Jac took a breath and thought to himself, '*We're struggling to keep pace with the amount of information that needs processing, a sympathetic reaction from him would help, he doesn't want Special Branch involved any more than I do.*'

"That's the problem, sir," Wolfe began turning to face the Chief Constable. "We don't have the resources to process the facts quickly enough, we'll analyse the intel, eventually, with the staff we have but it will take time, the whole team is working overtime and as you know, those behind all this are using it against us. Other forces have similar issues, South Yorkshire didn't have the resource to properly log one of their staff as being on leave and that was used to dupe us. It seems our every move is being watched."

"Mmmm, embarrassing, however the South Yorkshire Force, not us, were seriously reprimanded over their lack of administration checks," replied Haigh-Watson.

"We've drawn a blank trying to find Matthew Tanner or any evidence of his existence after 2005. However, all the circumstantial material points to there being gold bullion at the heart of this case." Wolfe waited for a response, but Haigh-Watson stayed silent. "We're trying to firm up that line of enquiry by researching the historical facts around Tanner's manuscript held by Proudman Press, but it's so time consuming."

This comment prompted Haigh-Watson to respond.

"Sub that work out, DI Wolfe, don't waste constabulary time on this issue of the investigation, is there anyone you know who you can use?"

"Yes, Leeds University."

"Good idea, use them, reasonable expenses I'll sign off."

Wolfe thought that was the end of the discussion but instead, Haigh-Watson grabbed a chair, spun it round and sat down at the table in front of the crime board and motioned to Wolfe to do the same. "Sit down, Jac. DC's Halford and Middleton, please could you give DI Wolfe and myself a little privacy here?"

"Yes, sir," they replied in unison and left the room. Wolfe thought more accusations were about to be levelled at him relating to the perceived relationship between him and Middleton.

However,

"Give me your off the record scenario of how these murders relate to the seizing of gold bullion," asked Haigh-Watson as he looked up at the crime board.

Wolfe was surprised at Haigh-Watson's sincere and attentive tone.

"Errr ... Okay ... right," he stuttered, "subject to historical accuracy, let's assume, gold bullion as you say was seized some twelve years ago."

"Yep, that's a given."

"Tanner has ideas for the gold bullion, as stated in his manuscript, return the money to its intended recipient, the Serbian Government. However, the other members of the gang are having none of this generosity so they kill Tanner, or at least they think they've killed him. They come back to the UK with the gold and over the next twelve years, enjoy the fruits of their labour in a way that doesn't attract too much attention, in particular that of the Inland Revenue, by investing in their business ventures. Then, without warning, years later three members of the gang are murdered in quick succession, each murder appears to be a product of detailed preparation. Now was Tanner bluffing in the manuscript, was he actually intending to keep the gold or most of it for himself? However, as we know from the experience of other investigations, where money is concerned, gangs more often than not fall out over such matters, so did they argue about the split and Tanner either accidentally or on purpose was killed."

"Mmm ..." mused Haigh-Watson. "Go on."

"The later scenario after the gold gets back to the UK, if that's where it is, is the same for both events ... revenge, vengeance ... whatever you want to call it...oh my god...'retribution'...that's what this is, that word was written on paper at the site of Davy Watts murder." Wolfe paused in silence as he looked directly at Haigh Watson without seeing him. "Tanner is dead, he never came back from Sarajevo because he was murdered." Haigh Watson stared at Wolfe and was about to say something but Wolfe spoke first "That makes perfect sense now so Marks and Brookes were murdered as a result of the heist of gold bullion, not because they might have been involved in Tanner's disappearance, but because they knew or suspected something or someone of involvement in his disappearance...don't you see?"

"Okay, alright, until the last bit, I was with you there, Jac. Why were Marks and Brookes killed first?" asked Haigh-Watson.

"Well, Marks because I think he was involved in laundering or hiding the gold bullion and Brookes because it's possible he may have inadvertently recognised the perpetrator or been innocently involved in the transportation of gold bullion from where Marks had, possibly under torture, indicated where it was being stored, and there may have been multiple hiding places, I mean, you'd be stupid to hide it all in one place, wouldn't you?"

"Yes, I agree with your hypothesis Jac, not sure I can accept all the detail but my God it fits with the murders, but I can't use any of this for the media briefing tomorrow morning."

Wolfe realised there was a hidden reason for Haigh-Watsons' remarks relating to formal confirmation of his impending promotion. Without an arrest soon, his promotion might be put on hold or revoked, but rather than state his thoughts he offered, "You could bring the name 'Tony Chezec' out into the open, if anyone recognises the name or knows his whereabouts to make contact with the police."

Haigh-Watson thought for a second or two. "That could work and if asked where we got the name from, I'll say that its confidential information but a witness to one of the murders has offered that name to us. After all, that's true, the fact that the witness is now dead makes it confidential." He continued, "There will be enough discussion about Smythe anyway, poor sod, what a way to go."

Wolfe took the opportunity to ask a question relating to the last victim that had been niggling him for a while.

"How do you know Thomas Henry Smythe?"

"What makes you think I do?" responded Haigh-Watson in a defensive manner.

"You called him Tommy Smith a few days ago when I reported to you that we were desperate to locate him."

"There must be hundreds of Tommy Smiths in Yorkshire, Wolfe, what makes you think I was referring to him?" he pointed at a photo of Smythe.

"Come on, we were talking about that person." Wolfe paused. "You do know him, don't you?"

Haigh-Watson filled the silence. "Yes, he was my staff sergeant when I joined the army at 17. I hated him then, he'd just been promoted and wanted to prove himself in training new recruits. At the end of my three years training, he told me I'd never make more than corporal because I wasn't tough enough, mentally or physically, he wrote on my final assessment report in large capital letters 'NOT OFFICER MATERIAL'. So yes, I knew him, however, that's all in the past and I think I've now proved him wrong."

"Well, that explains why as a soldier in the TA, Tanner thought him experienced enough to lead a small band of men into a bombed out city, a recently evacuated war zone to extract gold bullion from under the noses of the UN peace keeping force."

Haigh-Watson looked hard at Wolfe, then said, "Jac, I think you are onto something here, it's a very plausible explanation, but this Tony Chezec might be Tanner, that's what you're thinking, isn't it? And that's where the revenge aspect comes into this sorry mess, isn't it? He's back and wants his gold."

Wolfe mussed on these last remarks, he looked at his superior officer. "That's what I thought, you're right, but why wait all these years and why then kill all involved, why not just publish the book, name names, trial by media, ya know, what I mean?"

"The only thing he now wants is the gold, all of it and he's prepared to kill for it, we must find him, Tanner, Cabrinovic, Chezec, whatever his bloody name is," concluded Haigh-Watson.

Wolfe watched him leave in the direction of his office leaving Wolfe to ponder.

"Yeah," Wolfe added.

Haigh-Watson stopped and turned towards Wolfe

"I'm thinking, one of those men on the CCTV at the storage unit is, this Chezec fella, Watts wrote as he was dying." With that he left the crime room leaving Wolfe alone with his thoughts.

Chapter 24

Wolfe left the crime room enthused by the fact that for the first time since the discovery of Matthew Brookes' body on Carlton Moor almost a week ago, there was consensus shared between him and Marcus Haigh-Watson, contentment almost, they were singing from the same hymn sheet.

In the corridor before he arrived at his office, Wolfe was approached by Middleton who informed him he had a visitor waiting in reception who was insisting that he speak with him immediately.

"Henry Mateland," she uttered quietly, "he seems very nervous."

"Thanks, Pam. I'll go straight down there."

On entering the main reception hall, he noticed Toots stood in the most inconspicuous area of the hall, away from prying eyes. "Toots!" he whispered as he got closer. "I can see you feel a bit out of your comfort zone being in here?"

"You can say that again, Jac," Toots replied softly in his Jamaican accent.

"Wait here a second," he said as he walked towards the reception desk. "Angela, is room 1 available?" Wolfe asked.

"Yes, Inspector," she announced. "But only for half an hour."

"Won't need more than that, thanks. Follow me, Mr Mateland." Wolfe gestured towards Toots who walked briskly towards him, hugging the walls as closely as possible.

The desk sergeant watched as Wolfe and Mateland disappeared through the security doors, opened by Wolfe with a touch fob, and into one of the interview rooms beyond.

"So, Toots," Wolfe said as the two men sat down on chairs on opposite sides of the table. "What brings you here, what is so important that you need to enter the underworld of the West Yorkshire Police?"

"This!" announced Toots as he removed an A5-sized brown envelope from under his left arm beneath his leather jacket and placed it the middle of the table. Wolfe looked at the envelope, it had Henry's home address written on it and he could clearly see something inside it.

"That's Matthew Brookes handwriting," he stated as he pointed to the address written on the envelope.

Wolfe didn't say anything but picked up the package gently by the edges and inspected it front and back.

"When did you receive this?"

Toots looked at Wolfe with an air of disbelief, "This morning … it arrived registered post, I had to sign for it."

"Yes, I see … you've opened this, I take it?" Wolfe confirmed, "So, what's in it, Toots?"

"Open it yourself and you'll see."

Wolfe very carefully pulled the sealed flap open and emptied the contents onto the table, out fell another smaller white envelope with the same style of hand writing on it reading: 'Toots, please give this to my sister, Charley, ask her to come to you, she must come to you alone, tell her not to say anything to that bloke she's living with or that nympho au-pair. When I get to the Windies, I'll call her, I intend to stay longer than planned so I'll need to draw more cash out in a few days. C u soon, Chief. It was signed 'Matt'.

Wolfe stared at Mateland, deep into his eyes; he didn't blink,

"You're certain this is Matthew Brookes handwriting?"

"Absolutely, Jac. He's left messages for his sister with me before. But I've always just posted them on, this is different, very specific. Jac, I know this might be important so I crossed over the line to come and hand it over to you, what is going on? He was a good guy, never gave me any hassle and always brought me back some stuff from home."

"Yes, well, I don't need to know about 'stuff from home', Toots, but what I do want to know is if this is genuine –"

"Look, man," interrupted Mateland a little agitated at the inference that the package might, in some way, be false. "That package is as it arrived at my house this morning. If it's fake, it's nothing to do with me. See it for what it is, Jac."

"Okay, Toots, this isn't anything to do with you. I know you wouldn't come here if you thought it was anything but important. However, I can't open it without Charley's consent and what is he referring to in this statement," he said as he looked at and read again the words on the small white envelope. He lifted it from the table by one corner and noticed something slip within. "Mmmm … USB stick, I think," he said.

"Jac, I'm gonna go now, I've been here too long and I feel very uncomfortable."

"Yeah, I understand." Wolfe managed to return the white envelope into the outer brown one holding the corners. He lifted the brown envelope by one corner as he and Mateland stood and left the interview room. As they walked down the corridor and through the door back into the main reception hall, Wolfe said, "I'll contact Charlotte Marks and let you know if this helps."

The two men shook hands and Toots was just about to turn to exit the building when for some reason, he looked up to the first-floor mezzanine and noticed someone.

"Who's that up there?"

Wolfe turned and followed Mateland's gaze towards the first-floor glazed balcony overlooking the lower hall.

"Oh, he's likely to be the next Chief Constable, Marcus Haigh-Watson. Why do you ask?"

"He looks familiar. I'm sure I've met him before."

"Where?" Wolfe asked staring at Mateland for an answer.

"I'm not sure but it wasn't in a police station, in fact, I wouldn't have known he was a policeman at all … until now," he said, confusion etched across his face.

"Strange," Wolfe responded, "are you sure you can't remember where you've seen him before?" His tone made the question seem like an appeal.

"No, I need time to think, Jac … I need to get out of here … I might be mistaken … I certainly don't recognise the name … no, maybe … not him at all."

"See you soon, Jac." Without another word, Mateland turned and left the building in a hurry. Wolfe watched, aghast, he had the feeling that Toots was scared and this was a man who didn't scare easily. As he turned towards the stairs to go back to the first floor, he looked up at Haigh-Watson who was now staring directly at the departing Henry Mateland.

When Wolfe reached the first floor, Haigh-Watson was not to be seen.

'*This can wait*,' thought Wolfe. '*I need to contact Charley.*'

Less than two hours later, Charlotte Marks was seated in the same ground floor interview room where he had met Toots Mateland, this time, Middleton was in attendance.

Wolfe had opened up a laptop before laying two evidence bags containing the two envelopes received by Mateland on the table in front of her face down.

"Interview with Mrs Charlotte Marks," Wolfe stated for the fixed recording device to one side of the table, he tendered the date, time, and his own name and that of his colleague.

"Am I being charged with something Jaaa … err … Inspector Wolfe?" asked Charley a little bewildered she'd been told that she had to attend the police station as a matter of urgency and that a car would collect her if needed, she'd refused the offer.

"No, no, Charlotte, not at all, please let me explain," Wolfe said softly to try and settle her nerves.

"Then what's all this for?" she responded without any change in her attitude which appeared belligerent at best, antagonistic at worst.

"Mrs Marks, this package …" Wolfe tapped the larger of the two envelopes then described it for the recording and explained that it was received by Henry Mateland, an associate of her brother, Matthew Brookes, in the post that morning.

"Do you recognise the handwriting, Mrs Marks?" asked Middleton turning over the clear bag, inside which the large brown envelope was visible and pointed to the script.

Charlotte immediately announced, "That's Matthew's handwriting, I'd recognise it anywhere." Tears began to well up in her eyes. Middleton reached below her chair and lifted a box of tissues onto the table.

"Thanks," she said taking a tissue and wiped under her eyes.

Wolfe took the opportunity to turn over the second plastic wallet on top of the previous one.

"Same handwriting but addressed to you, Mrs Marks. This smaller envelope was found inside the larger one. Your brother has written these comments, what do you make of them?" Wolfe asked.

Charlotte read the statement requiring Mateland to contact her only, she snivelled, then said, "I've no idea what this means, but it clearly relates to Paul and Martha. I know they didn't get on but this isn't right. Paul's a good bloke, he's hard working which gets him a little stressed but that's okay, isn't it?" Neither Middleton nor Wolfe responded.

"And Martha, she's so nice, why would he describe her like this. It's not like Matthew to make these kinds of comments."

"But it's his handwriting?" enquired Wolfe.

"Yes, of course, it is … unless someone has faked it … that's it … it's all faked … what the hell is going on?" She was beginning to weep.

Wolfe freed the small envelope from inside the clear wallet, letting it fall to the table. Middleton put on clear gloves, opened the envelope and let the contents drop to the table. As expected, a USB storage device dropped onto the table. Wolfe positioned his laptop to face Middleton.

"This is your property Mrs Marks," he confirmed as he held the small stick between his thumb and forefinger of his right hand, "I require your authority to connect this to our laptop?"

"Yes of course ... that's okay," she answered dabbing beneath her eyes with the tissue.

Wolfe connected the storage stick to one of the side ports. "Let's see what's on this then."

Jaws dropped soon after the memory stick was opened as a series of Jpeg photos opened in an unnamed folder. The first photos indicated persons, mainly men in dark attire, entering a building, a city centre building, a car parked outside had a steering wheel clearly visible on the left-hand side as did vehicles in other photos. Other images indicated the same men leaving the building, wheeling what looked like a set of portable carrying wheels heavily weighed down, the next series of photos shows the packages, each being lifted by two men into the boot of a black Range Rover.

Wolfe pointed.

"Check that number plate as soon as possible," he commanded.

Other photos showed clear close ups of men that appeared previously in the longer distance images loading a vehicle that matched the Range Rover, they didn't look familiar to anyone. The final series of three photos showed one long range and two closer images of someone different, a man dressed in all black wearing dark glasses, Ray-Ban Wayfarer over a tanned face, medium length jet black hair, goatee moustache and beard, also black.

"Check the descriptions given to us when Jessop was escorted to his lockup, I'll bet one of them matches this fella," Wolfe stated as he pointed to the screen.

"Mrs Marks, does this person look familiar to you?"

"No, I'm sorry, but when I met Matthew a few weeks back in Leeds to countersign a withdrawal of cash from his bank account, he gave me a lift home in a car very similar to that Range Rover. I think Matthew took these photos, every now and again, he'd show photos he'd taken in Jamaica, and like these they were, obviously, taken with a telephoto lens." She paused and then blew her nose. "The handwriting is my brother's and I'm sure he took these photos in Geneva."

"Geneva!" repeated Wolfe. "Are you sure?"

"Certain, because he told me he'd been there, he had to fly out, collect an expensive car for a client and then drive it back a day later. He complained that he had to stay sober ... ya know, off weed for a couple of days and he found it difficult but he was being well paid. When he came back, he wanted to withdraw more money than usual, said he was going to spend longer in the West Indies this time, a few months, I think he said. Now I think about it, he seemed a bit agitated, I just thought he was desperate to getaway."

"Oh, my God ... look at this one," interjected Middleton.

Wolfe and Charlotte turned to look at the laptop in front of Middleton. The image was of a man he was staring straight into the camera lens.

"This fella looks scary and I think he's seen the photographer. Jeez, look at that scar on his face." Middleton moved her head closer to the screen as she grimaced, "Ooh I'll bet that must have hurt."

"Mrs Marks, these images were meant for you and you only to see, and I have a notion that I know what was in those packages placed into the Range Rover. We will need to keep these items."

"Of course. You say you know what's in the boxes?"

"Yes, but I can't confirm my thoughts until the investigation is concluded."

"Do you think these people murdered my brother?"

Wolfe nodded, "Sorry." He put his arm around her shoulder; it was an instinctive reaction, but a bad timed one.

"What's going on here, DI Wolfe?" said Haigh-Watson as he opened the interview room door behind Wolfe.

Wolfe instantly decided that he'd been caught being too familiar with a witness in a murder case, maybe even a suspect in a murder case but it was too late, so he opted for bravado.

"This, sir, is Mrs Charlotte Marks. She's the sister of Matthew Brookes and she just realised that her brother had taken photos of the persons that may have been involved in his death."

"What?"

"DC Middleton, please can you escort Mrs Marks to the canteen? Get her a cup of tea, she's in a state of shock," asked Wolfe.

Middleton was already on her feet and ushered Charlotte into the lobby towards the canteen.

"Investigating officer witness relationships do not aid and abet good convictions, you should know that, Wolfe. Anyway, fortunately for you, the damage is limited, only your girlfriend and I saw that," he said with sarcasm. Haigh-Watson then looked at the screen. "Who's this?"

"Well, perhaps this could be the man known to us as Tony Chezec, but that is all we have. He and his colleagues match the descriptions given to us after the murder of Francis Jessop."

"Well with a scar like that he'd stand out in a crowd, no photos without shades?" Haigh-Watson asked.

"No ... quite," acknowledged Wolfe as he scanned through the series of photos for Haigh-Watson's benefit.

"Where did you get these from?"

"Matthew Brookes sent them for his sister to see. We'll trace the package through the postal system, see where it was posted. However, this could be the information that got him killed. I'm convinced the package was sent before he was murdered. At least we now have more than just a description, we'll circulate a selection of these images throughout the national police forces and the media as well."

"Yep, okay," stated Haigh-Watson. "We'll have to explain how we got hold of these images, or should I say you, DI Wolfe will have to explain at a press conference tomorrow how we got hold of these photos," he turned and left the room.

Wolfe was left on his own, stunned into silence, by Haigh-Watson's insistence he, Wolfe, would have to front the next press conference. A sense of total despair gripped him like a vice, the last time he had to do this was to appeal for witnesses to the shooting of Maria, he'd broken down and sobbed on national TV, and had to be comforted by his daughter who was sat next to him when in fact he'd thought it should have been the other way around. He'd felt embarrassed, futile and weak, a Detective Inspector weeping on national TV, that's what started it, his 18-month downward spiral into depression, alcohol dependency and self-pity.

He looked at the dull grey floor, then took a deep breath. '*Fuck it*,' he said to himself. '*I'm over this*.' Then he made a promise, the same promise he'd made to himself many times before, but this time he said it out loud.

"Maria, I promise, with all the ability I have at my disposal, to find the truth about your death." Wolfe turned off the laptop, pulled the USB stick out and shut the top down with a slam, collected the envelopes and the laptop together under his arm, and left the room.

Chapter 25

Wolfe had a restless nights' sleep, he rose early and arrived very early at headquarters in Leeds on a particularly cold morning. The day before had offered a breakthrough in the investigation and now in a few hours, there would be a formal release to the media of photos showing the image of a man wanted for questioning.

The building was as cold as the air outside, the central heating probably hadn't kicked in yet and it might not for another hour or so. Sitting down at his desk without taking off his overcoat, he noticed a brown envelope on-top of the desk where he would normally place his laptop, an A4 size 'jiffy' bag stared at him, marked for the attention of Detective Inspector Wolfe, West Yorkshire Police. At first, he was reluctant to touch it let alone open it.

"When the hell did this arrive?" he said almost shouting as he stood up, walked towards his office door all the time staring at the package. "It was gone 6 o'clock before I left here last night, how did this get here?" He looked around the open plan space outside his office, but there was no one there.

Wolfe went gingerly back to his desk and sat down, very carefully. "What the hell am I doing? It's nothing, just correspondence that's all," he announced to himself. It was then he noticed the postmark in the top right-hand corner of the envelope, Leeds University, immediately, his apprehension subsided. He remembered Professor Buchanan Jones had stated he would gather some information together, in relation to Matthew Tanner, faculty information both official and unofficial. Opening the envelope, he could see that there were obviously photos inside, together with a letter clearly headed Leeds University.

Wolfe spent the next hour looking at the photos, over thirty of them, some dating back to the mid-1960s. What caught his attention first was the difference in fashions in the '60s through to the present, and the fact that the photos in the '60s and '70s were more regimented, staged, an official catalogue not like today where photos are just a part of everyday life, a social keepsake that more often than not gets erased shortly after the event or circulated on a website for all to see but once seen, instantly forgotten.

Matthew Tanner was featured in all the photos many with people younger, Wolfe turned some of them over to look at the dates. Buchanan Jones had mentioned in the covering letter that dates when taken were written on the back. It was noticeable that most of the people photographed with Tanner were female. Tanner, it appeared, was obviously popular with his female students. One woman repeatedly shown with Tanner looked familiar but he couldn't quite place her, he arranged the photos, initially, three each a year apart but then he noticed two more photos. Tanner was stood next to the same woman and in the latest one dated 1985, he was clearly photographed with his arm around the waist of the same woman but his gaze was towards someone else.

"Of course!" exclaimed Wolfe. "Hello, Ms Harrington, I think you and I need to have another chat."

"Who on earth are you talking to, boss?"

Wolfe looked up from his desk and the photos. "Ah, morning, Pam. Take a look at these."

Wolfe and Middleton studied the photos together, and came to the same conclusion, Jennifer Harrington had known Matthew Tanner from the 1960s to the mid-1980s. It was quite obvious they knew each other but only another interview with her would determine the depth of their relationship.

"I'd been wondering," said Wolfe. "How Smythe and Harrington got together, and now I know, Matthew Tanner, and I think he encouraged their relationship so he could continue with his single life, no permanent commitments. Pam, get in touch with Harrington, get a meeting with her today."

"Shall we bring her in here … a formal interview?"

"Yeah, good idea let's talk to her on our patch."

"Should I explain why we want to interview her, you know, if she asks or resists?"

"Just say we've been sent some information that we need clarity on, and if she wants to know more, tell her that it involves her ex-husband and Matthew Tanner." Wolfe paused. "And if she requires more persuasion, then tell her we'll send a squad car with a policeman carrying a warrant for her immediate arrest for withholding evidence."

"Wow, what evidence, boss? You've got more from these photo's than your letting on, haven't you?" inquired Middleton.

"It's written between the lines but we'll need some factual evidence or a written statement to see if my theory stacks up," he replied with a hint of satisfaction.

Over the next couple of minutes, Middleton tried to find out what Wolfe thought he'd seen in the photos, but Wolfe wouldn't be drawn into explaining, she left without any further insight into his thoughts.

When Wolfe was finally alone, he opened up Google on his laptop after closing the door to his office.

Three hours later, Middleton knocked on his office door, opened it without waiting. "Sir, Jennifer Harrington is in interview room 1 waiting for us."

Wolfe was talking into his office phone, "Yes, thanks. I appreciate your assistance, Doctor, the information you provided is important. Once again, thanks." Replacing the receiver, he stood up from behind his desk. "Okay, Pam." He then grabbed a sheet of paper from the printer as they left his office.

"Here, Pam." Wolfe handed her the paper, she stopped in the corridor and read the printed sheet.

"So, he can't be his –"

"It would appear not," interrupted Wolfe. "But who is … that's the question."

Chapter 26

Middleton and Wolfe entered interview room 1, Jennifer Harrington looked apprehensive; she gave the two officers a confused look.

"Why the hell am I here, Inspector Wolfe?" she said through watering eyes with as much sternness as she could muster.

Wolfe ignored her worry. "Good morning, Ms Harrington, thanks for agreeing to speak to us today."

"I'm not aware that I had a choice, Inspector, in fact, your assistant gave me the impression that if I didn't agree, I would be arrested."

Wolfe and Middleton ignored her comment and sat down opposite her making eye contact, Wolfe nodded and Middleton responded.

"For the record, this interview is being recorded. Jennifer Harrington is attending this interview of her own free will. The conducting officers present are DI Jaxon Wolfe and DC Pamela Middleton as part of an ongoing investigation into the murders of Matthew Brookes, Francis Jessop, David Watts and Thomas Henry Smythe, and the disappearance of Matthew Tanner, aka Armon Cabrinovic. Harrington is not a suspect in this investigation but her answers will be considered in our investigations and she maybe asked these same questions under caution at a later date." Middleton stated this in a calm slightly conciliatory voice.

"On the contrary DC Middleton I was informed that if I didn't attend, I would be arrested," Harrington repeated with obvious irritation.

Wolfe intervened, "New evidence has come to light and we need to formally interview you. If you feel that you have come to this interview under duress, I apologise, but you must understand we are investigating the murders of four people –"

"I'm a suspect then, aren't I?" Jennifer interrupted, her annoyance beginning to rise.

"No, Jennifer, you are not a suspect," replied Wolfe in a matter of fact tone, "but the questions we are about to ask involve you directly and may provide valuable background information important to this investigation."

Silence allowed Middleton to arrange copies of the photos delivered earlier to Wolfe in front of Harrington, she looked at them then looked at the two officers.

"What on earth? What possible relevance do these have to your investigations?"

"Jennifer, please let us ask the questions," Wolfe was calm on the outside but getting very impatient on the inside. Middleton took over.

"For the record, Ms Jennifer Harrington …"

"I hate Mssssss! My name is Jennifer Harrington, drop the Msss or I'll not answer any fucking questions and I'll employ a lawyer, not that that in itself will worry you but it will take time, time you imply is of the essence," Jennifer Harrington lifted a cup of water to her mouth and swallowed hard from the plastic cup.

Middleton continued for the recording, "DC Middleton has arranged several photographs for ..." she paused whilst she finished placing the photos so Harrington could see them. "Jennifer Harrington to see. Do you recognise these five photographs taken in 1972, 1973 ..." She tapped each print as she continued ... 1974, 1986 and 1989?"

"Yes, I have copies of all these at home ... in a box somewhere, but I haven't looked at them for years probably not since they were taken."

"Do you recognise anyone, other than yourself; in these photo prints?"

"Yes, I do, most of them were friends and fellow students."

"Who is this?" Wolfe pointed impatiently to the three earlier dated prints and to the person stood next to her in all three photos.

"That is Matthew, Matthew Tanner," she replied nervously.

"Jennifer, you were a student studying for a degree in Modern History at Leeds University over the period 1972 to 1974 inclusive and the head tutor was Matthew Tanner?"

"Yes, that is correct." Her eyes met Wolfe's for a split second then she dropped her gaze to the table.

"Did you complete your degree?"

"Yes. What does this have to do with these murders?"

"Let us be the judge of that, Jennifer," said Middleton before Wolfe could respond.

"Jennifer, please confirm when you graduated?" continued Middleton.

"Errr ... 1988 ... I think ... it was a long time ago ... yes, '88 or '89."

"You started the course in '72?"

"Errr ... yes, I was eighteen so, yes '72."

"So, it took 16 years to get your degree?" asked Wolfe, he was trying to be polite, understanding, but it didn't appear like that to Jennifer Harrington.

"Yes, 16 fucking years, Inspector Wolfe, and what about it? Is that against the fucking law? And don't look at me like that, I'll say what I like and I hope this recording is played in court because you two will look total idiots in front of a jury."

"Jennifer, please calm down, there is a method and a reason for asking these questions, and it is certainly not our intention to upset you or make quips about your further education, so please can we continue on the basis that you'll answer without making assumptions about our intentions?"

"I took a sabbatical from University to have a baby, my son, Paul, then when the time was right, I returned to finish my degree. Before you ask, Matthew helped me with the modules and shortened the course slightly."

"How did you meet your husband, your ex-husband, Thomas Henry Smythe?"

"Errr ... well, as it happens, it was at a party at Matthew's house in Headingley. Thomas had done some building work for Matthew's mother, we instantly hit it off, a year or so later, we got married," Harrington hurriedly responded.

Middleton asked the next question when Wolfe quietly tapped twice on the desk. "Jennifer, its important background to our investigation that we know exactly what your relationship with Matthew Tanner was?"

"What business is it of yours what my relationship with Matthew Tanner was? What the hell is all this about?"

"Please answer the question, Jennifer," Wolfe interrupted beginning now to show his impatience.

"Okay, we were sleeping together, lovers, at it like rabbits. Matthew was a very attractive man, kind and very strong, all man, if you know what I mean?" she looked directly at the young female DC, who didn't change her expression.

"And you ended this relationship when you married Mr Smythe?" asked Middleton without hesitation.

"Mmmm ... well, yes ... eventually but not straight away, is that what this is about, my promiscuity?"

"No, no, Jennifer, we are not being judgemental," Wolfe was trying to keep himself calm.

"Jennifer, the last time we met, you mentioned that Thomas, your ex-husband, suddenly changed his attitude to your son, Paul, withdrawing him from private school and that you weren't sure why that was, is that correct?"

"Yes, Thomas wanted nothing to do with me or our son and eventually, we split, then we divorced, adultery being the reason, his adultery that is."

"Thomas admitted adultery then?"

"He didn't contest it when my lawyer raised it as a reason for the breakdown of our marriage."

"Jennifer, this document ..." Wolfe placed a single piece of printed paper on the table in front of her so she could read it. "... we have just acquired this as part of our investigations, it's a copy of the results of a semen test that Thomas Henry Smythe requested be undertaken by his GP surgery in 1990."

"It says here that his sperm count is so low that his ability to father a child is non-existent, less than 1% chance."

Jennifer Harrington fell into silence, staring at the page in front of her, then raising her voice, she almost shouted, "Oh my God, this can't be true. There's something wrong here, it's a mistake, someone else's sample this is ridiculous."

"Jennifer, I talked to a doctor at the surgery where Thomas is still registered, the patient notes clearly state that the samples were obtained from Thomas as a direct request from him. We found a copy of the same letter at Thomas's house. We needed to corroborate it and now that has happened."

"Well, I don't believe ..." She paused, looked at the printed page in silence, Wolfe and Middleton, both anxious to push the interview on but understanding that she had to arrive at the obvious conclusion herself without coercion. Eventually, a few seconds later, she announced, "Inspector, I've been stupid ... so fucking stupid ... I can't believe that it never occurred to me that Thomas might not be Paul's father. Oh, my poor son, he ... this will change his life."

Middleton decided it was better if she conducted this section of the interview.

"Jennifer, you need to be concise, it might have an impact on this investigation."

"Well, if Thomas isn't Paul's father then it must be Matthew ... and now that I think about it, it makes perfect sense. Matthew and I were with each other regularly but I was also with Thomas. When Thomas and I got married, I'd stopped seeing Matthew for a few months before, we'd argued, I think. I'd caught him in bed with one of his younger students but for some reason, we arranged to meet up for a drink after Thomas and I had got married, and one thing led to another. I started seeing him again for a few months, only to catch him at it again and that's when I stopped seeing him ... permanently. I suppose, it was during that time that I fell pregnant."

"Okay, Jennifer," Middleton stated. "We don't need to go into any more detail, but it does appear that your ex-husband made assumptions after receiving this letter." She tapped the copy of the letter, "And concluded that Matthew Tanner was your son's biological Father and as a consequence his attitude to you and Paul changed."

"Yes, it all makes sense now," she lowered her head cradled in her hands and began to weep.

The interview was suspended for a short period, Middleton providing a cup of tea and some tissues for Jennifer Harrington whilst Wolfe made notes.

"The time is 3pm and the interview with Jennifer Harrington will now resume," announced Wolfe.

"Jennifer, a copy of a manuscript was found at the last known address of Matthew Tanner, the original belongs to a publishing company in Leeds. In this document, reference is made to the discovery and eventual theft of a large quantity of gold bullion. Are you aware of this?"

"No, I know nothing of this, I've no idea what you are talking about."

"But you were there," Wolfe said trying to hide his exasperation. "At what now appears to have been a farewell party before the trip to Sarajevo and this was the last time you saw Matthew Tanner?"

"Yes, but I didn't know it would be the last time I would see Matthew and … gold bullion … what the hell? This is crazy, why would he steal gold bullion? He's not a thief. He's not here to defend himself, for God's sake. The manuscript … it doesn't mean a thing, he told me he was writing a novel using his European experiences as inspiration and that was twenty or more years ago. Why would it take him so long to write a book? He wrote books for a living, it's not real. He may have wanted it to be real but …" Wolfe saw tears begin to run down her cheeks. Middleton tugged a couple of tissues from the box on the table and handed them to her.

"Jennifer, please don't upset yourself," she softly said.

"The novel took twenty years to write because the research he was undertaking took that long to complete, it's all in the manuscript, the culmination of which is the recovery, theft, of gold bullion," pronounced Wolfe without any hint of sympathy. "So, Jennifer Harrington, what do you know about the disappearance of Matthew Tanner, the father of your son, Paul, the murder of four men and the theft of gold bullion from Eastern Europe?"

"I don't know anything. I would tell you if I did. This is abuse … I want a lawyer … you tell me that my ex-husband, the man I thought was the father of my son isn't, you show me a piece of paper that is supposed prove this, then you accuse me of involvement in the theft of gold … and on top of that, you seem to think I have information relating to four murders … you, Inspector Wolfe, are a deluded bully … I know nothing of what you are talking about …" tears began to run down her face again. "Now let me go home or let me call a lawyer, the choice is yours but I'm not answering any more of your questions, for God's sake, I know nothing of what you are talking, please let me go home, I'm though with all this bullshit!"

Wolfe looked and nodded towards Middleton with what she thought was the hint of a smile. She stared hard back at him, she wasn't happy with the way Wolfe had ended the interview with Jennifer and the smile just made it worse, the cynicism in the expression. As a consequence, Middleton allowed her inner feelings to gravitate towards Jennifer Harrington so much so that she stood up and put her arm around her as she escorted her from the room into the corridor. A taxi was ordered for her then five minutes later Middleton re-entered the interview room.

"Now before you say anything Pam," declared Wolfe pre-empting what Middleton may have wanted to say. "I know I was a little hard on her, however, it was a means to an end and she'll recover …"

"I'm not too sure about that, Jac. She was still crying when I put in a taxi home."

"Never mind that, what do you think? Do you think she's genuine?"

"Yes, I do."

"Mmmm so do I, therefore, we have to consider our next move very carefully, very carefully indeed." And with that comment, he walked past Middleton into the corridor and onwards towards his office.

Middleton stood holding the interview door open, staring at the back of Wolfe as he walked away. Suddenly, she said quietly to herself, "Oh my God, he knows who's behind this, he knows?"

Chapter 27

Wolfe spent the remainder of the day wedged in his office, reading, thinking then pacing up and down. Nick cave and the Bad Seeds – Push the Sky Away Album was playing in the background. Then close to the end of one of his walks to the office door, he stopped and sang along with the lyrics of Jubilee Street, 'I'm vibrating, I'm glowing, I'm flying'. He stopped at the door, opened it and called in a calm authoritative voice, "Pam … Pete, Harry … Andy, meeting in the incident room a.s.a.p. thank you."

Five minutes later, they were all seated in the incident room;

"Okay," announced Wolfe. "Harry and Andy, I want you two, once again, to go back over the port authorities' CCTV records, going back as far as possible, 10 years if possible, quality might be an issue and I know its painstaking but it has to be done. Anyone matching the descriptions, and photos of the person we think maybe Tony Chezec and his two henchmen. Compare with the photo's Brookes took. My hunch is that they were bringing in gold bullion hidden in vehicles, expensive cars sold to clients in this country and before handover, the gold was retrieved and hidden. Andy, I understand that we now have the software that will help."

"Yes, sir," replied Mills. "I've tried it out and it works, it allows you to stop and start instantly without loss of definition, it offers facial recognition but be careful not to request a perfect match, it works better if you expand the parameters because you can skip through the findings very quickly and evaluate them yourself after the obvious none matched items are rejected."

"Excellent, recruit help if you need from the uniform guys. Pete, I'd like you to arrange another visit to the home of Matthew Tanner and contact forensics, get one of their guys to accompany you. I want samples of anything that might offer DNA profiling, hair, nail cuttings that sort of thing. The samples should be accurately located in position in the house and make sure you take samples from the new extension. I want to know if Tanner has been there since the extension was built. We can match his DNA with samples taken from his belongings left in storage at Leeds University. Higgins sent one of his team over to the University earlier today to collect the samples." And with that, he dismissed them all except Middleton.

"Right, Pam, call that Development Company that Paul Smythe owns … Andromeda Holdings? I want you and I to meet him at his offices, see the people he has working around him, you never know someone we see may fit a description we've got."

"Sir, that's a bit of a long shot, isn't it?" she replied, she had expected something more definite than further investigation.

"Well, I know it is but that's not all. I want to talk to him away from Charlotte, I want to find out if he knows about the fact that his parental father is not his biological father. I want to get to know what makes this guy tick because it certainly isn't his home life."

Chapter 28

At 11.55am the following day, Wolfe and Middleton walked across City Square in the centre of Leeds towards their appointment with Paul Smythe at the headquarters of his company; Andromeda Holdings. The doors to Andromeda House opened as they walked under a high glass canopy roof and side panels that shrouded the building's main entrance to a height of two storeys. The glass theme continued into the lobby where two glazed fronted lifts ferried people up ten floors to various businesses within a glass and chrome atrium.

"Wow, this is classy," remarked Middleton with as much sarcasm as she could manage.

"Andromeda Holdings bought this building five years ago, it used to be the Leeds Mutual Building Society office. They folded in 2008 at the start of the last recession and Andromeda bought it, put another floor on top and now they rent most of it out to other companies," replied Wolfe. "Andromeda have the third floor. From what I've managed to find out on the internet Andromeda were in hock to the banks until three years ago when an injection of funds from an asset sale wiped out all their debts."

"Is that unusual?" responded Middleton as they walked slowly towards the reception desk.

"Don't suppose it is, maybe it's me being too suspicious. Where did this injection of funds actually come from, is it on record what asset was sold? I'll bet not"

"Hi," Wolfe said to the smiling young woman behind the central podium signed 'reception'. "We have a meeting with Mr Smythe at …" he continued but didn't manage to finish.

"Andromeda Holdings," replied the receptionist. "Mr Smythe's secretary informed me this morning to expect you. Detective Inspector Wolfe and –"

"Detective Constable Middleton," she interrupted.

The receptionist continued. "Please take the lift to the third floor, someone will meet you there, but before you go, please would you sign the visitor's book?"

Wolfe and Middleton did as requested, then made their way to one of the lifts.

"So Smythe owns all this?" asked Pam Middleton as she surveyed the interior of the atrium as the lift ascended.

Wolfe viewed the atrium with tempered admiration. "Yes that's what the profile search told me … but where did the money to fund this come from?" he asked as the elevator arrived at the third floor.

The lift door opened Wolfe and Middleton stepped out and were immediately greeted by another young woman wearing what appeared to be a corporate uniform of dark blue slim fit jacket and matching fitted skirt, white blouse, and contrasting red and white silk scarf.

"Hello, I'm Sandra, Mr Smythe's PA," she announced as she shook their hands. "Pleased to meet you, DI Wolfe and DC Middleton. Mr Smythe is expecting you, please follow me." She turned and walked elegantly to a pair of stained timber doors that opened automatically. They walked through. "Mr Smythe's office is at the far end of this floor," she remarked, turning just enough to make eye contact with Wolfe as she strode past another reception desk and open plan anti room, offering smart black leather chairs for visitors.

The two detectives walked past glazed fronted meeting rooms, two on one side and what appeared to be a large boardroom on the opposite side of the central corridor leading into a large open plan office where people were working mostly staring at laptops and large screen monitors. Some workstations had three large screens arranged like dressing table mirrors with one person scanning each screen in turn. The office wasn't crammed with personnel but it certainly appeared active and busy.

Large floor to ceiling windows down either side showed the expanse of the office, between the windows was a brickwork finish that appeared to be the original internal wall finish, the mortar joints weren't regular but the contrast of old and new gave the space a comfortable feel, contemporary refurbishment of an old interior space. The wall at the end spanned the whole width of the office space, decorated with a mosaic of colour, corporate advertising of projects completed and new projects under design. A large TV screen to one side with the volume turned down was tuned into the BBC News Channel and this too just added to the feel of productivity.

Sandra opened a door to the right of centre and held the door open as she announced,

"Your guests have arrived, Mr Smythe."

"Thank you, Sandra, that will be all," stated Paul as he stood from his chair behind a huge oak desk. The door gently closed behind the PA. Paul walked around the desk towards a sitting area where a large black leather sofa and two matching chairs surrounded an oak coffee table, it appeared over large for its intended function.

"It's good to meet you again, DI Wolfe," said Paul as he offered to shake Wolfe's hand, Wolfe responded in kind, but deep down he felt a vague hint of reluctance.

"Likewise," he said.

"DC Middleton, it's a pleasure to meet you," Paul shook her hand as well but with a little less vigour and a lot more eye contact.

"Thanks for agreeing to meet us at such short notice, Mr Smythe. May we offer you our condolences for your loss? It must have been a shocking experience for you?"

"Thank you, that's very kind of you detective, yes it was and particularly so for my Mother, despite all that has happened between her and Tommy I think deep down she still had fondness for him."

"Yes quite," offered Wolfe with the snobbishness of a politician, thinking *'That's not how I would explain her feelings towards him.'*

"Before we start, can I offer you a drink … tea, coffee, fruit juice, water?"

"Coffee for me, black, one sugar," responded Wolfe. "Thank you."

"Tea, milk, no sugar," Middleton requested.

To their surprise, Paul walked over to a sideboard, matching oak again, arranged at right angles to the large window, similar to those in the main office. He came back carrying a tray with three cups and saucers, and a plate of biscuits. After distributing the drinks and commenting that the biscuits were homemade, Charlotte had baked them, Wolfe took his chance to start the interview at the first opportunity.

"Mr Smythe, we have discovered something in our investigations into the murders of Matthew Brookes, Frank Jessop, Davy Watts and Tomas Smythe, your father, which directly involves you and he."

"A very polite way to put it, DI Wolfe, if it's what I think you are eluding to, then my Mother or should I say …" He continued not trying to hide his sarcasm. "… The person I believe to be my mother, informed me yesterday evening of the fact that the man I have called father since childhood is not my biological father." Silence hit Wolfe, it was for effect reinforced by Middleton's silence, just as they had rehearsed. "You look surprised, did you not think she would have told me?"

"Your mother was very upset when she left the Police station yesterday, we assumed she would talk to you but we weren't sure," admitted Wolfe. "It must have come as a surprise to you."

"Not really, I'd had my suspicions for years, it was the only explanation that seemed to fit why my father suddenly changed his attitude towards me, around my sixteenth birthday as I recall." He took a sip of tea. "However, to be told Matthew Tanner is possibly my biological father is taking some getting used to."

"The conclusion I came to many years ago was that Tommy Smythe was not my biological father and mum confirmed it last night." He paused. This made Wolfe uncomfortable, now he had a choice, continue with questions that could be considered too personal or change the subject, give the impression that this line of questioning had little relevance to the investigation.

"Do you have a financial interest in the farm close to Thomas Smythe's House?"

"Er … yes, but what relevance does that have with who my real father is?"

"None," responded Wolfe with an apologetic look, "however, we are interested in why you have a financial interest in the farm and land surrounding it because it may have a bearing on our investigations."

"Eve Bradshaw … now the sole owner of the farm, accepted my offer to buy the farm. I intend to convert it into a local produce outlet and brewery. It's a good investment, an excellent opportunity so I approached her a few months ago with my ideas, and was hoping she'd want to stay and manage the new venture but she had other ideas."

Wolfe got the impression Paul was being very circumspect in his disclosures. Wolfe reached for his cup of coffee and raised it to his mouth as he looked at Middleton, she took the hint.

"Other ideas?" questioned Middleton.

"Yes," he answered with a sigh. "Eve has always wanted to go to Spain. Her husband, when he was alive, would never go on holiday, difficult owning and running a working farm, I suppose. But when he died, she spent what small amount of money she had in the bank on a two week holiday in Spain, and low and behold, she fell in love with the place so she's going to use the money from the sale and buy a villa over there, moving there permanently, she tells me."

"Who's the Structural Engineer that upset her cattle?" snapped Wolfe as he returned his empty cup to the coffee table.

"What?" Paul replied. "How did you know ... you've interviewed her, haven't you?"

"Mr Smythe, we ask the questions," Middleton said with the perfect amount of authority.

"Okay, okay. Bartek Wharzowski is an Associate Engineer working for Lupton and Poole in Leeds. They are an engineering consultancy that Andromeda use for its developments. I paid for his time myself, it didn't go through the company books ... am I in trouble, DI Wolfe?"

"Oh, no, we're not interested in that, Mr Smythe," answered Middleton while Wolfe shook his head in agreement. "And is the building structurally sound?" she continued.

"There were signs of structural fatigue, yes and some reinforcement works were undertaken a month or so ago."

"Yeah, that's what Eve Bradshaw said," interrupted Wolfe. "You paid for her to go to Spain for a week whilst you undertook those works, isn't that so?"

Paul looked straight at Wolfe, eye contact was made, neither man blinked until Paul smirked and followed it with a childish grin. He blinked and said, "I'd promised Andromeda work to a contractor but it had been delayed so I got them to undertake the structural reinforcement works instead , I was worried that the structural fatigue might have been worse than we'd thought and if that had been the case, I would have pulled out of the deal. As it happens, all was okay."

"You wanted Eve Bradshaw out of the way, didn't you?" retorted Wolfe.

"Its business, that's all, Inspector. I wanted to make sure I was buying a sound building not something that was going to disappear down the hill in year or two. So yes, I 'got her out of the way', as you put it."

"You don't actually own the farm yet though, do you, Mr Smythe?"

"No ... but we have a –"

"Contract, yes, we are aware of that, Mr Smythe," interrupted Middleton. Then she continued whilst looking at her notes she'd been compiling during the interview, "Bartek Wharzowski. Can you describe him for us, Mr Smythe?"

"What?" he said with petulance.

"Come on, Mr Smythe," Wolfe responded with a sigh. "You heard what DC Middleton asked, answer the question please."

"No, I want a lawyer," he said as he stood up. "In fact, I'm going to call one now." He walked over to his desk and pressed a button on the phone.

"Yes, Mr Smythe," Sandra's voice could clearly be heard by all.

"Please call Mr Blackmore for me, tell him it's urgent that I speak to him," then for effect, he said, "you know who he is, don't you, Sandra?"

"Yes, Mr Smythe. Harrison Blackmore at Blackmore Law and Co.," she replied with all the efficiency of a good PA.

"Okay, detectives, I think that's the end of this interview so if you wouldn't mind leaving, any further questions you have will have to be asked of me in the presence of my lawyer."

Wolfe and Middleton stood, then Wolfe bent back down and instinctively collected their cups, and walked towards the sideboard where the drinks had been made.

"Harrison Blackmore, now there's a top-notch lawyer, please give him my regards when he calls back." Wolfe was by now stood at the sideboard looking out of the full-length window that had a good view over Park Place. He looked down to the street, then up and across the road. Middleton came to stand by him. "Good view from up here, Mr Smythe." But there was no response so Wolfe focused his eyes on the reflection in the window from inside the office. Smythe was staring at his mobile phone, concentrating on finger punching the screen for what appeared to be a text message. Wolfe turned and repeated, "Good view from up here?"

Paul Smythe finished punching the screen with his right index finger and threw the phone flat down onto the writing mat on his desk next to his open laptop. "Errr, yes, I suppose, it is, that's why I bought the place."

Wolfe felt a sharp nudge in his side, he turned, Middleton was waving at someone through the window. "Look, it's Izzy over there with her friend." Wolfe looked down to the street. "No, in the coffee shop up there, across the road," she said in a voice intended to be a whisper but turned out to be loud enough for Paul Smythe to hear. Wolfe waved and smiled as he saw the reflection of Smythe in the window, he was stood right behind him looking over Wolfe's right shoulder.

"Orrr, that's sweet, your daughter, I assume, DI Wolfe. I was going to say is she out shopping with your wife, but that person with her is, I assume, not your wife?"

"No, that's my daughters' friend." His right fist clenched hard, he could feel his finger nails digging into his palm. "My wife is dead, Mr Smythe. Ask your friend, Harrison Blackmore, about that, he has all the details."

A buzzing noise came from the office desk it was Paul's mobile phone. Wolfe caught the reflection again in the window, and as clear as day, he could see the screen to the phone and a large V shape with a line horizontal in the middle joining splitting the V shape. Then it was gone as he rejected the call.

"Is that all detectives? Can I get on with my work now please? Thank you. I'm sure you'll be in touch," he said as he opened his office door. "Oh, and Harrison Blackmore represents my partner, Charlotte Marks, as well, DI Wolfe, so stay away from her unless she is represented as well."

Wolfe turned to face him as he walked through the open door, he looked slightly down at him but straight in the eye. "I assume your structural engineer to be a thick set man who takes to wearing dark glasses and dark suits, and drives a very new Jaguar F type, also black. At least, that's the description we have from Eve Bradshaw, and that matches the description of a man and a vehicle leaving the Davy Watts murder scene. Goodbye, Mr Smythe, we'll be in touch. Don't forget to mention me to Harry Black."

The door slammed behind them which shocked Sandra, the PA, but just made the two detectives smile.

"Okay, fancy another coffee in the company of the most beautiful young lady in the world?" Wolfe said with glee.

Chapter 29

Wolfe and Middleton left the foyer of Andromeda House, and walked out into Park Place together. They looked up to the highest part of the building opposite and the café on the fourth floor, neither could see Izzy or Jemma, but a text message confirmed they were there waiting. The buzzing in Wolfe's jacket pocket announced that his mobile had received another text, removing the phone from his jacket, he said, "Arnold Higgins wants a call back. You go ahead, Pam, I'll catch you up."

"Hi, Arnold, it's Jac. You got something for me?"

"Arrr, Jaxon, ma boy, well, yes I have, I hope you're sitting down?"

"No, Arnold, I'm not, but you've got my full attention."

"Okay here goes: three of the six DNA samples we got from the house in Headingley recorded a match with a sample retrieved from Matthew Tanners' belongings sent to us from Leeds University, let's call this the base sample."

"Great that means …"

"Hold on Jac, first I have to tell you that the house has been doused, bleach sprayed everywhere. The only samples we could obtain were deep in the trap of the shower waste, the plastic wallet inside the folder you described as being handled last time you were there, one window handle and cup in a wall unit in the kitchen. The cup, a fingerprint from the plastic wallet, and hair from the shower waste proved to be identical. The folder cover and another clear plastic wallet inside offered further prints and a partial print from a window handle, none of these matched or was a match with the other three samples. Therefore, three different profiles from six different locations."

Wolfe thought for a second. "So the three that matched?" he was by now, on the third floor of the John Lewis store, one floor below the café, home furnishings all around him, "Are they a match for Matthew Tanner?"

"Yes … but it's not what either of us was expecting," Higgins replied apologetically.

"Okay, go for it, Arnold," he said as he found a display sofa to sit on.

"The matching samples found in the house match as a progeny of Tanner's. No DNA evidence of Tanner in the house that we could find but there is a DNA match for a daughter."

"A daughter?" shouted Wolfe into his phone startling a couple walking past.

"No doubt about it, Jac," replied Higgins. "There's still a due diligence process to go through before I can officially confirm our findings but at this moment in time the finger print from the cup and plastic wallet, and hair follicle from the shower waste definitely offer a link to Tanner."

"Arnold, this throws the whole investigation into turmoil. I never expected a daughter." Wolfe paused, took a breath, let this latest news whirl around in his head for a few seconds. "This doesn't mean that Tanner doesn't have a son, in fact, all it confirms is that he has a daughter."

"All this evidence isn't worth anything without actual DNA samples taken from a possible match, which you haven't got, Jac. Tanners' base sample could be argued as not conclusive in court."

"Yeah, I know, Arnie, it's all circumstantial," concluded Wolfe with more than a hint of resignation in his voice.

"Call me later with an update?"

"Will do ... oh, Jac?"

"Yes, still here."

"Don't let this get you down, you can solve this and I'll do everything I can to help."

"Thanks, Arnold, see you soon, in The Unicorn?" he disconnected the call without waiting for a response.

The feeling of satisfaction that Wolfe felt following the interview with Paul Smythe was now starting to recede as he stood up from the display sofa in John Lewis and walked towards the escalators leading to the café on the fourth floor. The escalator was positioned against the glass curtain wall, a feature of the building design and as he rode the moving staircase, he looked out of the window to see Paul Smythe standing on the pavement four storey's below in the street outside Andromeda House at the right-hand corner of the building. He was looking directly up towards Wolfe as he got to the top of the escalator, Wolfe stopped and stared directly back. Smythe made a mock salute towards Wolfe, and then extended his right arm and pointed his index finger at him in a, 'I'm watching you cause I know you're watching me'.

"You arrogant bastard!" Wolfe shouted as he looked out the window and again caused passing strangers to give him a curious look. Smythe turned left and walked down the street to the right of Andromeda House, and disappeared from view.

Wolfe stood staring for a few moments then shrugged his shoulders and continued his way to the cafe.

He found Izzy, Jemma and Pam sat at a table overlooking Park Place in deep conversation about something, pointing at Andromeda House, on the opposite side of the street.

"Hi," Wolfe said to announce his arrival.

"Hi, Dad," Izzy said, as she pulled out a chair next to her between herself and Pam. "I saw you at that window over there." She indicated towards the second window in from the right on the third floor one storey down from their position.

"Surely, you mean that one," Wolfe pointed to first window from the right.

"No, it was definitely that one," repeated his daughter, pointing again to the second window from the right.

"Yes, it was that one," said Jemma. "You were stood to the left in front that cabinet thing."

"Oh yes, I can see that sideboard now," confirmed Middleton, "it was that window –"

Wolfe interrupted, "Pam, do you remember seeing a door out of his office towards another room and there wasn't another window either, was there?"

"No, no other window … there was a wall, wood panelled to half height with wall mounted prints above. I didn't see a door but maybe there was one blended into the wall giving access to …" she paused.

"To what?"

"Well, err … an en-suite bathroom, perhaps."

"If that's the case, why hide an entrance to a bathroom?"

After some thought, she responded, "You're right, Jac, there appears to be a room beyond his office but without any recognised access, it's hidden from view on the inside but very openly on show from the outside."

"He's hiding something, Pam, but what?" Wolfe stood up, and looked out of the window and pointed. "I've just seen him outside the building on that corner, not a care in the world, he watched me ride the escalator up to this floor, he's a cocky sod I'll give him that. Bloody hell, what's she doing there?"

"Who?" responded Middleton.

"That legal rep. that showed us around Tanners' house."

Pam stood and looked out to where Wolfe pointed. "You mean, Andrea … err … oh yeah, I see her now."

Andrea was walking in front of Andromeda House, she walked past the main entrance and then around the corner of the building in the same direction as Paul Smythe.

"Ahhh … for fuck's sake," pronounced Wolfe, chastising himself as he strode away from the window overlooking Park Place. After 5 paces, he turned back, Pam, Izzy and Jemma stared.

"Dad, what's up? What's happened?"

"Are you okay, Jac?" Middleton looked concerned.

Wolfe stopped again overlooking the street below. "We've been had, Pam, those two," he pointed towards Andromeda House. "They've been one step ahead of us all the time."

"Sorry, Jac, but you're going to have to explain what the hell you are talking about," beseeched Middleton as she stood next to him, both now looking to the street below.

Wolfe sighed and quietly explained to her what Professor Higgins had found from the DNA samples he'd taken from Tanner's house to check against Tanners DNA from hair follicles collected from his belongings stored at Leeds University.

"A daughter …" she replied not trying to hide her frustration, "Tanner has a daughter!"

Wolfe explained that no proof was found linking Paul Smythe to Tanner. So, no evidence that they are father and son but considering that his mother was in an intimate long-term relationship that ended just before she married Tommy Smythe, and given that he wasn't capable of fathering a child it was quite possible, but only circumstantial, that Tanner is Paul's father.

Middleton looked confused, dismayed and quite clearly trying to work out what all this DNA profiling was telling them.

"Okay, Pam, hear me out," Wolfe asked as he guided Middleton to an empty table where they could better speak without being overheard.

"Just give us a minute girls Pam and I need to discuss something," he warned as they stepped away to a quieter part of the café.

"So, Tanner we think is Paul Smythe's biological father, no proof ... yet. However, a DNA match to Tanner's base sample taken from Tanner's items that are at least 12 years old has been confirmed with samples taken yesterday from his house in Headingley. The match is for a female, a daughter. Now we met Andrea from Prime Legal a few days ago at the house, maybe she is Tanners daughter ..."

"Well it certainly puts her in the frame," considered Middleton, "of course she might not be aware of this, she could be blissfully thinking someone else is her father."

"But Paul may have thought for some time that Tanner probably is his biological father. Add that to the fact that we've just witnessed Paul and Andrea in the same area at similar times."

Middleton surmised where Wolfe was heading with this scenario,

"Jennifer Harrington told us she stopped her relationship with Tanner before Paul was born, therefore it's possible they have the same father but different mothers."

"Maybe ... at least I'm willing to run with that possibility at the moment however in order to add another layer of proof we need to get back into Paul Smythe's office ... now!"

"Jac ... without a warrant?" Pam replied a little louder than she anticipated.

"Dad, what are you two discussing? I thought we were going to Roberto's for lunch."

"Ahhh ... yes," hesitated Wolfe. "That's just down there, isn't it?" He looked at Middleton, "A good view of Park Place and that road over there," he said pointing to the pedestrian precinct that Paul and Andrea walked down.

"No, Jac ... sir ... any evidence found will not be admissible in court ... you could get thrown of the force, Jac ... don't do it."

"Needs must, Pam. We're so close to solving this now."

"Ah, shhhit!" exclaimed the young DC, "You're not going in there without me, anyways, you'll need support and a lookout if you're to blag your way into his office."

Wolfe turned away from the window to speak to his daughter. "Izzy, Pam and I need to go back over to that building because," he paused. "... –"

"I left my notebook over there," interrupted Middleton. "If your dad doesn't help me find it, I'll be disciplined, could be back in uniform tomorrow."

"Yeah," said Wolfe looking at her. "So, if you two want to get a table, we'll join you in five or ten minutes, okay?" The two detectives weren't waiting for a response, they were already walking towards the escalators.

"Oh okay, Dad," Izzy replied as they disappeared from view.

Wolfe and Middleton soon arrived back at Andromeda House, and the reception area of Andromeda Holdings on the third floor, having walked straight past the sign on the ground floor reception desk that said 'back at 2pm'.

"Hi, Sandra," announced Middleton. "If you remember, I and my boss came to see Mr Smythe." Wolfe stood behind with a thunderous look on his face. Middleton leaned forward and lowered her voice. "I left my notebook in Mr Smythe's office and if I can't retrieve it ..." she looked around at Wolfe. "... He's going to give me the sack. Please can you ask Mr Smythe if he has found it?"

"But Mr Smythe isn't in; he's gone out to a meeting."

"Oh, no. When will h ... h ... he be back?" sniffled Middleton giving the impression, she was going to cry.

"Sorry, he's not expected back until tomorrow," Sandra replied as Middleton reached for a tissue out of the box on her desk.

"Oh no ..." Middleton blew her nose as loud as she could muster into the tissue. "Unless I find my notebook, I'm out of a job."

"Are you sure it's in there?"

Middleton realised she was now on the home stretch, just a matter of time and they'd be in the office.

"What? Err, yes, he's the only person I've interviewed today so it must be in there, in fact, he is the first person I have ever interviewed. I'm in the middle of my probation period and it's been ..." she leaned in again towards Sandra after another sniffle. "... a fucking disaster ... sorry but I'm so upset."

Wolfe coughed loudly and impatiently.

Sandra looked around the office. It was quiet, lunchtime for other employees. "I'll let you in," she said as she stood and walked towards the entrance door to Paul Smythe's office. "But I'll have to stay with you."

"Yes, of course, I'm so grateful," she replied as Sandra opened the door. Middleton touched her on the shoulder to stop her as the door swung fully open. "Has he broken into a smile yet?"

Sandra looked at Wolfe, he was directly behind her, he smiled sarcastically and he pressed the phone symbol on his mobile phone clutched in his right hand held in his trouser pocket. A few seconds later the phone on Sandra's desk rang.

"I'll go get that." She let go of the door. "I'll be back in a minute." Wolfe put out his left arm to keep the door open. As Sandra walked back to her desk, Wolfe and Middleton disappeared into Smythe's office.

"Hurry up, she'll be back any second," stated Middleton as she whipped out her notebook from her handbag and threw it on the floor under the coffee table.

"Not necessarily," Wolfe replied confidently as he redialled the last number. He moved to the sideboard and grabbed the unwashed coffee mug that he recognised as the one that Paul Smythe drank from, it had No.1 embossed on it. "I'll have that." He placed it in an evidence bag, using a pen lifted from the inside pocket of his jacket threaded through the handle.

Middleton was, by now, tapping the wall thought to be the party wall between the office and the hidden room behind. "I don't know, Jac, I can't tell if it's' hollow behind here."

Wolfe walked quickly towards her, as he stood next to her, he said, "Shah ... what's that noise? It's a rumble, sounds like an elevator moving ... shit, let's get out of here!"

Middleton noticed the office door open. "Ahh, there it is, sir, under the coffee table."

Sandra said, "Sorry about that, wrong number, I think, twice, that's strange, isn't it?"

"Ohh, I'm so glad I found this," announced Middleton as she picked the notebook up. "Thank you so much, Sandra." Grabbing and hugging her.

"Oh that's okay, please, can you leave now?" she replied as she freed herself from Middleton's hug.

Wolfe was out through the door first. "Yes, thank you, Sandra. Come on, get a move on, DC Middleton, we've got work to do, we've wasted far too much time here."

Middleton winked and blew a kiss at Sandra as they left the office, and made their way down the stairwell as quickly as possible. At the ground floor, they exited the building but Wolfe held onto Middleton's arm restraining her from walking towards the restaurant where they were to meet Wolfe's daughter and her friend.

Wolfe lifted his phone so he could see the screen. "One more time for luck," he said pressing the phone icon. "Wait till I hear it ring ... now let's walk quickly, don't run."

Middleton got to the restaurant first, closely followed by Wolfe. They sat in the centre of the ground floor on a table with the two teenage girls, then after a couple of minutes, Wolfe stood up and walked to a window where he could just see the third floor office window to Paul Smythe's office, his curiosity rewarded when he saw Paul was stood at the window looking out across Park Place towards John Lewis. He was mouthing something, then a woman came to stand next to him, he recognised her as Martha the au-pair. At first Wolfe was perplexed but then suddenly he realised,

"Ha ... another piece of this puzzle has just been put into place."

"What was that Jac?" asked Middleton now standing next to him looking in the same direction as Wolfe.

"Well, I'll tell you ... Martha is Andrea and Andrea is Martha," he said as he raised his phone to take a photo Smythe uttered something, and pushed the woman away from view, but it was too late.

"Got ya!!" Wolfe turned and walked back to the table followed by Middleton and announced

"In the words of the late Charles Barclay. 'You Think I Don't Know (But I Know)'!" Wolfe sang silently to himself as a satisfying smile spreading across his face.

Chapter 30

Wolfe and Higgins sat side by side in the Crescent in central Carlton at 7pm the next evening, drinking pints of Carlton Rock Gold beer, a drink brewed on the premises. The log fire was burning with steady force, the mirrors at either end of the room were actually TV's switched off, a music background chosen from the barman's iPhone could be clearly heard but not so loud that patrons couldn't talk to each other. Slim Smith and The Uniques were singing My Conversation, Wolfe was singing along in his mind to the classic reggae track whilst listening to the forensic scientist explaining the latest DNA results.

Wolfe had delivered the coffee mug taken from Paul Smythe's office to Professor Higgins pathology lab in North Leeds just after 4pm the previous afternoon. Higgins team had got to work immediately and a positive DNA match had been confirmed between Paul Smythe and Matthew Tanner, proving indeed, that Matthew Tanner was now known to have fathered two offspring with different mothers. Wolfe was not surprised by the findings, however, to now have undisputable scientific proof would allow him to push forward with his theories.

"Arnie, thanks for agreeing to attend the investigation meeting tomorrow morning."

"Yeah, well Jac I might have reconsidered, had I known you wanted me there at 8am," Higgins replied with a grin. "Have you decided on your next move yet?"

"Not quite, the DNA might not be considered substantial enough in court because the base sample could be contested, it was never held in a secure situation it could have been tampered with at any time during the last 12 years. We need to catch them together ... all of them, the two Tanners and the thugs. Once that happens one of them will blab." Wolfe raised his pint glass from the table to his mouth. "This will help." He took a mouth full of the amber liquid. "I'm struggling to find a way that will make sure when we show our hand to these two, we stay one step ahead of them."

"You may have a definite link back to Tanner but that doesn't prove murder, does it?"

"No, we need to find the evidence." Wolfe looked around the bar, to see if anyone could overhear their conversation. He lowered his voice slightly, "Evidence in the shape of gold bullion."

"And you believe you know where that might be hidden?" whispered Higgins.

"Oh yes, I'm very confident I've got that location sussed," Wolfe replied. "But that in itself doesn't prove murder either, it just offers a motive. So that's the dilemma, how can we prove murder, no witnesses, no admission of guilt, no DNA, nothing and I'll bet they'll both have cast iron alibies for all the murders."

"Well, that's why you're the detective and I'm just forensics."

"We'll need you later because, I reckon, there'll be more DNA than you can shake a stick at all over that gold, but before we get to that point, I still have to find a way to put them in the frame. However I think, the killings have stopped. If you think about it, they have the gold, Smythe has his revenge over his patriarchal non biological father."

"Do you have anything that puts him in the frame for Smythe senior's murder?" asked Higgins.

"Circumstantial that's all …" Wolfe left the answer there.

"Jac, don't be coy, come on, explain yourself."

"I think he set off that explosion using an electronic signal, like a car plip key. He was taking a risk but I think he did it when we drove up to the drive of Tommy Smythe's house. It seems to be the only explanation that ticks all the boxes anyway."

"Well, of course. That explains it and it was probably exactly that … a plip key! That answers it … of course, it does." Wolfe looked quizzically at Higgins, "That car was built in the sixties but it was fitted with an electronic ignition, probably by Smythe senior to get insurance, the plip ignited the fuel and with a little help from a detonator linked to the ignition … boom! As you say, such an explanation would certainly tick all the boxes," concluded Higgins as he raised his pint glass to his mouth.

No further conversation was had on the subject, instead, the subject turned to rugby league and the forthcoming season, new players and which teams are most likely to have a good season. The conversation revolved around the three first team players that had recently retired from the sport and finished their careers on a high, helping the Rhinos to a memorable treble. Behind all the conversation about sport, Jaxon Wolfe was doing what he does best, thinking of ways to break the case and running over scenarios.

On the walk home, the three pints of beer helped him perfect his next move, but booze also dulls the senses, so he didn't notice the black Jaguar F Type parked in the side street next to the Crescent. The car moved slowly away a few seconds after Wolfe had passed the end of the street. He walked to the kerb, looked up and down the street, saw nothing and stepped into the road on a diagonal heading to the other side of Town Street. Three steps into the road, the powerful roar of the Jaguar's engine erupted into the night air, it sped at increasing speed directly towards Wolfe.

"Look out!" shouted someone stepping out of the convenience store whose young attention had been drawn to the throaty sound of the accelerating sports car. Wolfe turned and seeing the danger, started running, he ran over the opposite kerb as the car mounted the pavement 10 metres behind him. The young man who'd shouted darted back into the store, Wolfe dived for the safety of the set back entrance of a jewellers' shop, his head hit hard against the security screen protecting the entrance door knocking him out whilst the passenger side of the car hit the panel under the glazed shop front, immediately setting off the security alarm. The car roared away from the scene as the young man and others came out of the store drawn by the commotion. It turned left at the top of Town Street without slowing down and headed southeast through Carlton in the direction of Leeds.

It was a few minutes later when Wolfe regained consciousness to hear an ambulance siren loud in his head and getting louder, then a voice he recognised,

"Jac, can you hear me? The paramedics will be here any second now." Wolfe opened his right eye to see Higgins leaning over him, the noise of the sirens was deafening. Suddenly, the glass around and above him reflected the flashing blue light of the ambulance, the siren stopped. Wolfe sighed, then passed out again.

He awoke in strange surroundings, his head above his left eye ached like a bad hangover and his neck felt restricted. He looked around as best he could and realised that he was in a hospital bed, in a room on his own, then he noticed the door open.

"Dad, you're awake, thank God," Izzy came towards the bed, and kissed him on his right cheek and held his right hand squeezing gently with warmth that made Wolfe smile.

"Yes and so pleased to see you, darling, you look more like your mum every day," he said in a deep crooking voice with an emotion that belied his current state, neck brace, stitches to a wound above his left eye that continued around his eye socket curving for another two cm, his left eyebrow had been shaved off. A dark red and blue bruise surrounded his left eye, it blended into his cheek. "What time is it, Izzy?"

Isabella looked at her mobile phone. "10 to 9," she replied.

Wolfe looked around as much as the neck brace would allow. "Morning or afternoon?"

"Oh sorry, Dad. Morning, you've been here since 9 o'clock last night. Do you remember what happened?"

"Errr, someone driving a very powerful car lost control at the same time that I was crossing the road. I had to get out of the way fast. Lucky, I guess."

"Well, yes, you were very lucky, dad, but we both know that some bastard tried to run you over and I know you're trying to protect me! Dad, because of what happened to mum, but I'm a big girl now, so don't lie to me. We had these issues a few years ago, let's not go back there." Izzy leaned forward and kissed him again, on his forehead.

"Okay, love, point taken." Wolfe paused for a second. "How do I look?"

"Well, you've looked better."

By 3pm, some eighteen hours after the incident, Wolfe had had the drip removed from his left arm and his headache was starting to reduce, thanks to the painkillers he'd been prescribed. An X-ray of his neck had shown no problem with his upper vertebrae so the neck brace had been removed. In addition to Izzy, Middleton and Halford were visiting mainly to let him know what was happening with the investigation.

"An APB went out at midnight. At 1am the car was spotted in a long-term car park at Leeds Bradford Airport. We're checking CCTV from the arrivals and departures hall but we reckon that if the person, or persons driving were flying out, then there were only three flights leaving after 9pm, the time at which they tried to run you down in Carlton. All the flights before had been called to departure by 8pm. The last flights of the day were to Malaga, Alicante and Faro and they all left before midnight," reported Halford and continuing he stated "we doubt they went into the airport concourse, no CCTV of anyone matching their descriptions. Likelihood is they rendezvoused with another vehicle out of range of cameras and scarpered"

"And the car?" asked Wolfe.

"Registered to a Mr and Mrs Jones at an address that doesn't exist. The postcode exists but the house number doesn't, simple but effective. We're checking where the car was bought and asking for descriptions but we think the trail will go cold there," stated Middleton.

"Yep, I'm sure you're right but complete the search anyway and file a report," Wolfe said as he swung his legs out of the bed.

"Where do you think you're going, dad?" asked Izzy.

"Yes Jac, where do you think you're going?" repeated Middleton.

"I'm getting out of here. This case is almost broken and I don't want you lot claiming all the glory."

"I told you, Pam, he wouldn't want to stay in here long. Jac, can you see out of your left eye?" asked Halford.

"Oh yes, perfectly. 20-20 vision, no problem," declared Wolfe with glee, although, he knew no one believed him.

"Yes, Dad," Izzy said cynically, "but until that bruising goes away, I think you should wear this." She produced a black eye patch suspended on black elasticated string and dangled it in front of her father with a smile. "It'll look so stylish, there's not many women could resist that look," she said with a giggle.

"Oh, my God," Wolfe responded, "she is constantly trying to get me hooked up with a woman … any woman."

Not trying to hide their amusement, Halford and Middleton laughed. Pam winked at her boss, her arm around Halford. Wolfe looked around the room, with his one good eye, smiled, then to everyone's surprise, announced that when his wife died, he thought that continuing life without Maria would be impossible at worst and a chore at best, but he was glad he had family, friends and colleagues surrounding him now to make life just that little bit more bearable. Isabella was right to make fun of him because that's what Maria would have done.

Wolfe stood up from the bed without a shake, taking the eye patch from Isabella's hand and turned to the single wardrobe to get hold of his clothes that he assumed were within, forgetting that in hospital, unless you wear your own pyjamas, you get standard issue, a light blue cloak worn back to front which more often than not meant a full open back. Wolfe grab some underclothes, a shirt and a pair of jeans turned to face his audience, who began sniggering for some reason unbeknown to him, and walked towards his en-suite bathroom. More sniggers.

"Nice arse for a forty-two-year-old," announced Middleton as he entered the bathroom. "None of that ugly black hair that some men have," she shouted out loud as Wolfe shut the door behind him. The sniggering was now full-blown laughter.

Wolfe began to smile to himself as he closed the door, realising his mishap, then he shouted his reply, "Oh my god they've shaved my eyebrow off, what the …" The last word was drowned out by loud hoots of laughter.

Two hours after discharging himself from hospital, Wolfe was at home sitting on the couch in the lounge, laptop on his lap, typing out his thoughts into a word document. An hour later, an e-mail with the attachment password protected was sent to Marcus Haigh-Watson. Two minutes later, he sent the password to Haigh-Watson's mobile phone, the password would allow him to open the document in his e-mail inbox. Wolfe had put together a very strong case for search warrants to be sanctioned for three separate properties, two in Leeds and one in Carlton. The applications for all three addresses were enclosed in the encrypted e-mails, each quoting the relevant section of the Police and Criminal Investigations Act (PACE) with a statement explaining that the same applications had been sent direct to the High Court for processing. Wolfe knew that this process would take at least two days and at the end of this bureaucratic procedure, the villains may have left the country, never to be seen again.

Chapter 31

Two days later at 9.30pm, Detective Inspector Wolfe walked into the briefing room to chair what he hoped would be the final team briefing of this investigation.

Before he could say anything a round of applause broke out from the gathered police officers and detectives. Wolfe smiled and mouthed his appreciation. The eye patch had been discarded he was making a strong recovery from the effects of concussion, a stick-on bandage contrasted with the now yellow bruising around his left eye. His sight was very slightly blurred but the prognosis was no lasting damage.

"What's the other guy look like boss?" asked Halford when the applause had subsided.

"Don't know, DC Halford, the bastard got away," replied Wolfe with a smirk, "but when we find 'em, and we will, with the help of this team of fine law enforcement professionals gathered here, I'm sure we'll find out what they really look like. Now let's get down to business."

Wolfe began the briefing stating that they would be arresting at least two individuals the very next morning in connection with the investigation into the murders of Matthew Brookes, Francis Jessop, David Watts and Thomas Henry Smythe and for the plan to be successful it had to be followed to the minutest detail.

"Forensic evidence gathered from Matthew Tanners home in Headingley and a cup used by Paul Smythe taken from his office in Leeds have confirmed that Paul Anthony Smythe and Andrea Cathcart are related, they have the same Father, Matthew Tanner, aka Armon Cabrinovic. We know that Andrea Cathcart also goes by the name of Martha Styles due to matching DNA samples obtained from Paul Smythe's home in Carlton and Prime Legal offices in Leeds. We also know that Paul and Martha teamed up some 18 months ago, when Martha was employed by Paul Smythe as the family nanny for his partner Charlotte Marks and her young daughter, Samantha.

"It's possible they've known each other longer but we are not able to confirm this yet."

Wolfe was reading from an extensive list of bullet points he'd put together previously and copied to his officer team. Continuing to work through his notes, he detailed his thoughts and where the evidence, albeit circumstantial, had been obtained. He detailed the manuscript found in the house that used to be occupied by Matthew Tanner, and that the person whom he and Middleton had met at the house acting for Tanner on behalf of Prime Legal, was Andrea Cathcart aka Martha Styles. Andrea Cathcart is a genuine employee of Prime Legal, but not in a legal capacity, she is an office administrator and receptionist.

Wolfe added, "Andrea's mother was a student of Matthew Tanner and research has shown that Mary Stoppard married Robert Cathcart, a successful investment banker, shortly after receiving her History degree from Leeds University but the marriage only lasted three years and Mary raised Andrea as a single parent. We can only surmise that over the years, Andrea must have found out who her biological father was. It is important to state at this point, that despite all the surveillance we have conducted over the past few days Paul and Andrea aka Martha have not been seen." Wolfe then handed over the briefing to Middleton.

She outlined the basis of the link between Tanner and the murder victims and how the common denominator connecting them was gold bullion. Confirming the evidence used to establish this link is the manuscript left with Proudman Press in 2005, only circumstantial evidence but without it there is no other link.

"There are two other persons we are seeking who we believe are involved in the murders of Jessop and Watts. In the case of Francis Jessop directly involved as observed on CCTV from the Unlock'n'Load storage facility and in the case of David Watts witness descriptions from the murder scene. In particular, the man impersonating a police officer at the scene, witnessed and described by DI Wolfe, DC's Halford, Fairburn, Mills and myself."

A subdued whooping cheer from the wider investigation team invaded the briefing, Wolfe and Middleton smiled, Halford nodded and spread his arms in an adoring fans gesture.

"Okay, okay, let's calm down," Wolfe announced to break the reverie.

Middleton continued, "The impersonator is described as male, thickset approximately 5ft 10ins tall, spoke English with a slight Eastern European accent. Photo fit descriptions have not yielded a match. European agencies have been contacted with photos and descriptions but, currently, we have received no positive responses."

Wolfe took the lead again to explain the theory he and his team had considered to be the most credible reasoning behind the murder of Thomas Henry Smythe, how the murder was committed and by whom. He initially explained that Thomas Smythe was assumed to be the team leader and possibly the mastermind behind the logistical arrangements for the recovery of gold bullion taken from a building in the Bosnian city of Sarajevo in 2005. Smythe, Jessop and Watts all had military backgrounds with the regular army and the TA. Smythe being the highest-ranking officer of the three and with Matthew Tanner a civilian, it is likely Smythe gave the orders.

"Thomas Henry Smythe died when explosives placed in the vehicle pit underneath his AC Cobra were detonated by a nearby electronic signal. Knowing what we now know, Paul Smythe has a credible motive for murdering the person he once thought to be his father. When Paul turned 16 years of age Tommy Smythe completely changed the way he treated had Paul. It must have been around this time when Smythe senior found out that biologically he could never father children. We believe the animosity towards Paul over many years was returned to Smythe senior in a revenge killing that destroyed him and his classic car." Wolfe paused before explaining more about how the electronic detonation of the explosives under Tommy Smythe's AC Cobra was from a source no more than 100 metres away.

"… And what makes it more galling is the fact that Paul Smythe detonated the bomb using a plip key device in his pocket whilst sitting in my car." Wolfe let this statement hang for a while and then asked DC Mills to take over the briefing for the next segment.

Andy Mills rose a little nervously from his seat and in his well-spoken middle England accent explained, "We have reason to believe that the person in the foreground of this photo," he pointed to the copy of the 2005 print of Jessop, Watts, Smythe and Tanner taken before the trip to Sarajevo, "is most likely Paul Smythe, based on digital imaging of several other photo images we have of him from the early 2000s using comparison software to compare height, bulk, stature and more importantly in this case distinguishing marks." Mills took breath whilst pointing to the close-up image of a person copied from a photo taken by Matthew Brookes in Geneva. "This distinctive looking man appears to bear no resemblance to Paul Smythe, but closer examination shows that the scar, which looks real, is in fact fake. It's beginning to peel away from his skin as is the beard under the chin. This in itself is not conclusive but when we zoomed in we saw these two puncture marks to the left ear lobe and when we zoomed into the left ear of the person in the foreground of the 2005 photo," he pointed to an enlarged extract of the photo, "we see two earrings in the same place as on this image taken in Geneva. Not conclusive but close enough to believe we are looking at the same person."

To Mills surprise several of his colleagues broke into applause, including Middleton and Fairburn.

"Thank you, I'll hand you back to DI Wolfe."

"Bloody hell he gets applause for being a 'whiz kid' with technology, I have to get myself run over!" responded Wolfe with a proud smile. Laughter rang out across the gathering. '*Good,*' thought Wolfe, '*we're acting as a team, this bodes well.*'

"Thanks Andy, okay let's continue. We are not sure whether Tanner ever returned from the Sarajevo trip, if he did, he's living under another name. My assumption is that the four men argued over the gold after the Sarajevo heist and Tanner was killed. If Paul Smythe made the same assumption and then found out the secret of his real parentage, well it's not a huge leap to assume revenge comes into play and I believe that's what we have here, plain and simple, with the added bonus of a large amount of gold bullion at stake."

Middleton took over the briefing again to outline the next item of accrued evidence, and the link between the photos received from Matthew Brookes and the name written on paper clenched in Watts' hand inside his crushed vehicle. She pointed to a photo on the case board with the name Tony Chezec written under it and the adjacent photo received from Brookes.

"This person may be Tony Chezec, however we have no knowledge of this person, no national insurance number, nothing on the national data base, no criminal record. However, thanks to Andy Mills we are confident that when you remove the facial hair and the rather menacing scar on his face, this person is in fact Paul Anthony Smythe. It appears as though the ability to disguise one's appearance runs in the family like brother like half-sister." As she spoke Middleton tapped the photos of Paul Smythe, Andrea Cathcart and Martha Styles. Middleton then continued with her final statement. "Finally, during our investigations into the murder of Francis Jessop we were informed that Mr Jessop had arranged to meet someone from a company call 'Tribute Noir' only a few hours before he was murdered. Well 'Tribute Noir' don't exist, it's an anagram," she announced pointing to the photo of the word stencilled on paper stuck to one of the doors of David Watts crushed vehicle, "this word 'RETRIBUTION,' when re-arranged spells out TRIBUTE NOIR, the murders of Jessop and Watts are most definitely linked." Middleton paused, she wanted to refer to another aspect of the case recently uncovered.

"Once again DC's Mills, Fairburn and Halford have worked hard trawling through years of digital footage obtain from our colleagues in the port authority and we can confirm that Matthew Brookes was indeed a delivery driver of expensive vehicles ordered by garages and individuals in the UK. Whether these vehicles were carrying hidden gold bullion is not confirmed. All we know is the registrations were false, all trace of the vehicles vanished after they left port. Was Matthew Brookes involved voluntarily or was he an innocent protagonist, we may never know. DI Wolfe will now conclude the briefing."

Wolfe continued with the final stage of the briefing, he proceeded to outline, and then reiterate where he wanted staff to be and what he wanted them to do, and that the whole process would start at 6am the following morning, with squads being allocated to various addresses in Leeds and Carlton, the search warrants sanctioned by the High Court were complete and ready to be used. Surveillance officers were already in position and reporting regularly from the three addresses.

"There are however no reports of any suspicious goings on at any of the addresses which could mean that our suspects resident or having access to these properties are aware of our intentions and they've evaded us." Despite this there was no hiding his excitement; it was quite obvious that Wolfe was confident that the case would conclude very soon.

"To clarify, the intention is to find hard evidence that will lead straight to the arrest of the two main suspects. We are convinced that evidence does exist in the form of gold bullion hidden at one of the addresses which are the subject of the search warrants, these addresses will be revealed tomorrow morning. Thank you for your attendance, please rest well tonight. Tomorrow, we will conclude this investigation."

The investigation team broke muster and quietly left the room. As usual, Marcus Haigh-Watson revealed himself at the back of the room immerging from the shadows walking towards Wolfe.

"So, Detective Inspector, cometh the hour, cometh the …"

"Well, let's see what tomorrow brings, sir. In fairness, I'm backing a huge hunch here and the whole investigation is reliant upon it."

"Oh, I agree with that, Inspector, I certainly do." Haigh-Watson moved in close and whispered into the base of Wolfe's neck, "I didn't sanction this operation for you to fail, Wolfe, so beware the consequences if you do."

"Sorry, sir," responded Wolfe in a loud voice designed to grab the attention of those around him. "I thought you just said my career in the force hangs upon the success of this operation." He paused and Haigh-Watson backed sheepishly away. Wolfe thought he'd got the better of him, once again, but he was wrong.

"No, Detective Inspector, you said that … not me!"

"Sir, I have a job of work to do here and my senior team need to be briefed which I intend to do now. Would you like to stay and listen? Maybe offer comment, given the circumstances leading up to the attempt on my life in Carlton four days ago should make it easy for you considering that I'm a risk to myself, my colleagues and therefore this police force, tell them all I'm still an alcoholic."

"Okay, Inspector, have it your way, I was actually impressed with your briefing and I hope it all goes according to plan tomorrow … so good luck, keep me posted on events." He turned and left the room striding purposely towards the main entrance.

"You may have been a little harsh on him, Jac," said Middleton in low voice.

"Yeah, maybe, but I don't want him thinking I'm his friend, there's skeletons in that guy's cupboard and one day, they'll be exposed and I don't want to be there trying to catch them when they fall out," Wolfe concluded. Middleton knew not to respond any further.

Whilst they were packing up, shutting down laptops and unplugging chargers, Wolfe asked,

"Have you spoken with Charlotte Marks? Is she safe?"

"Yes, she's staying at the Albany near Skipton, plenty of space around the Hotel, two security officers one in each room either side of hers. A WPC also staying in the same suite with her and her daughter. Anyone comes within a quarter of a mile of the place will be stopped and searched. Three times we changed vehicles, one escorted train journey and a blacked-out police transit finally ending up with an ambulance taking the final journey from Skipton station to the Hotel, then in through the kitchens."

"Very thorough … well done," complemented Wolfe, "what about Eve Bradshaw?"

"She's on a flight to Spain" stated Middleton with quiet satisfaction "at least that's what we put out there in the form of a letter sent from her solicitor to Paul Smythe's legal team in which confirmation is also stated regarding completion of the sale of Bradshaw Farm to Smythe. However she too is staying under surveillance at the Albany."

"Good, let's hope it's not all a waste of time" reflected Wolfe.

Chapter 32

All personnel involved in the investigation and several seconded officers convened as arranged, 6am Holland Walk, Leeds City Centre. Forty-five minutes later, a squad of uniformed and plain clothes detectives arrived at Andromeda House less than half a mile away, search warrants in hand. Using unmarked police cars, they surrounded the building able to monitor all comings and goings to and from the building. At this early hour of the morning all was quiet. DC Peter Halford was in charge of this section of the operation code named 'Armon 1' for all radio transmissions.

At 7am, just as the concierge was opening the building, Halford announced over the airwaves.
"Go! Go! Go!" he shouted with authority over the radio link.

The front entrance self-close doors hadn't had time to close behind the entering employee before the foyer was filled with half a dozen flack vested uniformed police officers who burst their way into the building. Behind them, Halford walked purposefully towards the reception desk the caretaker now standing in front of it, shaking with shock.

"Sir, we have a warrant to search the premises in regards to an on-going investigation into unlawful behaviour of persons who occupy and use these premises. Please open the office on the third floor. Your cooperation would be appreciated and reported upon favourably in any subsequent court proceedings." He paused. "Do you understand the seriousness of this request?"

The man nodded without uttering a word, he looked scared as he rummaged in a drawer within the reception desk to find a set of master keys. A few minutes later, the third-floor entrance to Andromeda Holdings was opened, Halford, flanked by two uniformed fire arms officers sporting un-holstered hand guns, led the way into the open plan office. They switched the lights on, empty work stations arranged methodically made the space look much larger than Wolfe had described but Halford wasn't interested in the outer office. The three men walked with purpose towards the inner office with another PC escorting, almost pushing, the caretaker close behind. The master keys wouldn't work; the concierge apologised nervously and dropped the keys on the floor. For a split second, Halford was frightened about what might happen next but before he could even think about taking evasive action, an extremely burly PC, gripping a door ram, pushed his way through to the door.

"Let me at it," he announced.

One move of the ram backward then forward, it connected with the door halfway through his forward swing. The door swung violently open, the inner room instantly filled with policemen but like the outer office the inner room was empty.

"Over here," shouted Halford as he walked towards the far wall. In his right hand he carried a photo. "Right here." He pointed to a spot on the wall that corresponded with a mark Wolfe had added to the photo, Halford was staring at the area. There was nothing visually confirming the existence of a door but Wolfe had taken the photo during his and Pam's unlawful visit to Paul Smythe's office having noticed two joints in the skirting board.

Once again, it only took a three-quarter swing to break through the door.

There was nothing, the further room was void of all but carpet, it was obvious from the depression marks that a desk and a freestanding storage cabinet had recently been removed. Another door was clearly visible; an emergency quick release bolt confirmed it as a fire escape door. On the same wall, a pair of steel doors identified that a passenger lift was also available for use from this room, confirming Wolfe's suspicion. He'd heard what he assumed to be an elevator, again when he and Pam Middleton blagged their way into Smythe's inner office. Halford pressed a button next to the right-hand door, a humming noise announced movement. A few seconds later, the elevator could clearly be heard arriving at the third floor. Halford was pushed to one side by the two firearms officers; they crouched at 45 degrees to the lift entrance pointing their weapons at the doors in readiness, but the elevator turned out to be empty. Halford nodded towards the fire escape door, one of the firearms officers moved to the door, hit the quick release handle and moved through.

"Nothing here," he stated.

"Radio, PC Broughton," ordered Halford. "Check that no one has entered or left the building through the fire escape."

Broughton was stationed outside the street level entrance door to the fire escape and his response was negative on both accounts, Halford hissed his disappointment.

"Shit, I chose the wrong one. I was convinced it would be here."

"Sorry, sir, I didn't catch that," Broughton replied.

"This raid has been a waste of time, what we were looking for isn't here," said Halford disappointingly as he turned to a uniformed officer standing at his side, "search the rest of these offices just to make sure, I'll contact Detective Inspector Wolfe, let him know the outcome."

Squad code Armon 2 raided Matthew Tanner's house in Headingley, DC Harry Fairburn in charge of a six-man team, they too had to force their way in and once inside, they also found nothing, literally nothing.

"Hi, Harry," announced Wolfe, as he connected with Fairburn's mobile phone. "Any joy?"

"Nothing, sir, in fact, nothing at all. The house is completely empty, no furniture, no fittings other than kitchen units and bathroom suites, it's as if …" he paused.

"It's been abandoned," Wolfe added.

"Yes, that's it … abandoned," confirmed Fairburn. "But we had this property under surveillance for the last five days, no reports of any movement in or out, when and how was stuff removed without us knowing?"

"Before we started watching the place, probably the very day that forensics left the property," Wolfe replied.

"We'll run another visual check and scan for any under floor voids that may be capable of being used to stash contraband, but I don't think we'll find anything here, sir," concluded Fairburn.

"Mmmm, two down, one to go. Pete Halfords team have drawn a blank in Leeds City Centre as well, so finish there Harry and we'll catch up for a de-brief later today."

"Okay, boss," the discussion ended there.

"Unless I've got it completely wrong, Pam, this is the place we'll find what we're looking for," Wolfe said calmly to his colleague sat beside him in the warmth of Wolfe's car. "Call 'em in, Pam."

"Do you want me to scramble the call?"

"No, I want them to know we're on our way," he confirmed.

"All units, Armon 3 is a go. Eye in the sky, what is your ETA?"

"Two minutes, Armon 3," replied the helicopter pilot almost immediately.

"Armon 3, all ground units stand by its go in two minutes and counting."

A few seconds later came the response, "Armon 3, all ground units ready for a go 'T' minus two minutes."

""Sirens and headlights, noise and visibility" replied Middleton.

Gradually with increasing volume, the helicopter could be heard approaching Bradshaw's farm. Wolfe and Middleton looked at each other. "15 seconds," said Middleton. Wolfe started the car engine.

"All teams go, now!" commanded Middleton.

The silhouette of a large SUV appeared in Wolfe's rear view mirror approaching at speed, then manoeuvring to overtake, it sped past his car closely followed by another identical vehicle. Wolfe accelerated his car away from its standing start to following the pair of SUV's. Wolfe approached the farm at a steady pace. As he reached the farm driveway, he saw one of the large vehicles drive across the lawn to the West. He knew the vehicle with its passengers was heading towards the rear of the farm it turned right across the front lawn heading for the back where a pair of patio doors, and another access door were known to exist. The far side of the building was not visible so it was important to block any escape routes from that side. The second vehicle headed east towards the main farm entrance and stopped abruptly some 10 or 15 feet from its target.

The helicopter made its first low pass the floodlight fitted to the underside illuminated everything its beam touched.

The occupants of the SUV at the front of the farm building exited the vehicle immediately after it came to a halt. Three armed police officers escaped from within, one holding a small battering ram the others sporting semi-automatic weapons. Wolfe and Middleton could only see that one vehicle now and as soon as the main farm entrance door was within striking distance of the armed officers the one holding the battering ram swung the heavy implement hitting the door lock first time. The door swung brutally open, the officer with the ramrod stood back for a second then speedily followed his two colleagues inside.

The helicopter was by now making a 180-degree turn behind the farm, ready to make another low-level sweep of the exterior of the building, but before it had completed its manoeuvre, a flash of light came from within the building closely followed by the sound of an explosion. Then the garage doors over to Wolfe's right blew open and a second later a vehicle came speeding out from the opening, it drove straight across the lawn heading towards a five-bar gate in the boundary wall approximately 250 metres away. Wolfe and Middleton watched as the vehicle, an SUV, ploughed through the timber gate that offered no resistance to the charging vehicle, the gate, in one piece, flew into air then smashed into the drystone wall on the other side of the road and broke into large splinters.

"What the fuck?" shouted Wolfe.

The helicopter was now flying over the building, the pilot had seen the incident unfold from his elevated position and was closing in on the vehicle, illuminating the back of it with the floodlight as Wolfe and Middleton saw it turn left, spinning its rear wheels and creating smoke from the rear tyres as they tried to grip the hard road surface.

"That's Paul Smythe's Porsche! He was driving but there was someone else in the passenger seat," exclaimed Middleton.

"Yeah and I'll bet its Andrea, Martha or whatever the fuck she calls herself." Wolfe had already turned his car almost a full 360 degrees within the driveway of the farm and was now accelerating towards the driveway entrance intent on following the escaping vehicle. "They're not going to get away this time, not like at the colliery, no fucking way."

The helicopter was now above the Porsche, its floodlight engulfing the vehicle completely.

"Anyway," announced Wolfe as he hit third gear and almost sixty miles an hour. "They've got a surprise waiting for them as they drop down the other side of that brow in the road." Then with a smile on his face he added, "Hah! I love surprises, don't you Pam?"

Middleton knew exactly what Wolfe was referring to. He had mentioned it in the car whilst they were waiting for the helicopter to arrive overhead, a roadblock called in as a favour from one of his long-time pals, a fellow Rhino's supporter who'd stood by Wolfe during his depression and addiction times after Maria had died.

"Like I said, two traffic police cars primed and ready for action, they're not going to move."

"How did you know they'd turn left and not right onto the road?" asked Middleton, raising her voice above the scream of the straining engine in Wolfe's car.

"It leads the backway over the tops to Otley and if they needed it, the option of Harrogate as well as leading to the A1, that's the way I'd make a break for it. But if they'd turned right, Mills and another PC in two squad cars were ready to intercept on the road back to Carlton."

"Hell Jac, you're throwing everything at this," shouted Middleton as she held onto the grab handle above the passenger door.

The Porsche hit 75mph as he reached the top of the gradual hill climb almost half a mile from the farm, Paul cursed as he looked at the speedometer. "If it wasn't for all that shit in the back weighing us down, we'd be away by now and that fucking helicopter would have no chance once we hit the forest." The floodlight from above bathed his vehicle in bright white light which hindered visibility in front of the beam, he could only see blackness, his eyes couldn't react normally under the extremes of bright and dark.

"Slow down, Paul," screamed Andrea as they hit the brow of the hill. From that height they could see the red morning sky in the distance across the Wharfe Valley now adding to the driver's problems, to make the confusion worse, two sets of vehicle headlights switched to main beam in front of them on the downside of the hill. The lights blinded Paul as his vehicle dropped down from the high point on the road.

"Shit!" he shouted as his instinct took over his actions and his right foot stamped hard on the brakes.

Two traffic police cars were some 500 metres down the hill, spaced evenly across the road between the one-metre high drystone walls either side. The four police officers manning the cars were a safe distance behind their vehicles having seen the helicopter floodlight in the distance.

"Just like Jac had predicted," PS William (Bill) Mason said with glee as he instructed full beam lights to be switched on giving time for them to retreat to safety.

"What happens if this nutter tries to break though and wrecks our vehicles?" a worried new recruit had asked.

"Well, we'll have to leave it to the fly boys, but he'll make a mess of his vehicle and it won't get far after that. Also, Jac informs me that there could be enough contraband in that vehicle to pay for fifty more new cars like these," responded Bill as the SUV reached the high point in the road. Then he announced, "Here we go, boys, hang on t'ya hats."

The Porsche Cayenne swerved violently to the left, highlighted by the helicopter floodlight then it veered to the right as Paul wrestled with car under heavy breaking. He regained control then in a fit of rage he screamed as the vehicle turned left again under acceleration. Paul had spotted a section of drystone wall just in front of the blockade that appeared quite low. He aimed the vehicle at the weakness in the wall.

"What the fuck are doing Paul, turn around let's try another …" Andrea shouted.

Seconds later the Porsche climbed at speed up the grass bank at the base of the wall, the bonnet hitting the wall as the front wheels climbed the bank below. The sound of the over revving engine, the shattering of glass from the headlights, metal and plastic being ripped away from the front of the vehicle, and the bonnet sluing to the left away from the driver's side could be heard over the drone of the helicopter above and in the midst of all this noise, the driver's side front tyre blew out, instantly shredding the rubber. However, despite the damage, the SUV managed to break through the wall into the open field beyond. The terrain though didn't ease the situation for the occupants as the ground dropped steeply but uniformly away. The vehicle suddenly disappeared from sight but the overhead floodlight moved in the same direction as the Porsche.

Wolfe's Z4 screeched to a halt close to the demolished drystone wall, he and Middleton jumped out, and were met by Bill Mason who'd ran towards the incident when he realised what the driver of the SUV was trying to accomplish.

"Crazy bastard," he shouted as he ran towards the two detectives through the gap between the two police vehicles blockading the road. "There must be some fucking expensive booty in that vehicle, Jac, for him to try that stunt?"

'Well, they'll all know in a minute or two,' thought Wolfe.

"Gold bullion," he said.

"Are you fucking serious, Jac?"

"Oh yes, Bill, oh yes."

A split second later, another loud crunch was heard from the direction the Porsche had been travelling in, the helicopter drone changed, they looked up, it was now hovering. "He's had it, Jac, probably hit a tree."

"Okay, let's go down and see," pronounced DI Wolfe.

The first man to step up over the banking and through the wall was Bill, his yellow high visibility tunic making him an easy target. A sharp crack was heard as the bullet hit Bill below his right shoulder, he let out a muffled scream and dropped where he stood.

Another of the traffic officers was about to tread the same path intent on pulling him back.

"No," ordered Wolfe. "Keep down! Grab his legs and pull him back. You," he said to another traffic policeman. "Call for an ambulance, now!" he commanded as Bill was pulled through onto the road.

"Bloody high vis jacket made me a sitting duck, Jac … fucking schoolboy error," he remarked as he was laid on his back in the road.

"Nothing of the sort, Bill," responded Wolfe as he crouched over him. "Don't forget we've got a five-a-side game on Monday, don't for one moment think that this will stop you playing," he said with a wry smile. "The bullet went straight through, I heard it ricochet of the wall, we've ordered a chauffeur driven vehicle to take you to a nice warm bed, plenty of nurses ready to make a fuss of ya, imagine that, ya lucky sod."

Wolfe then ordered the younger traffic officer to take his jacket off, roll it up and place it under Bill's shoulders. "Get something to support his head and keep his shoulders off the road surface, don't want that wound getting infected."

Wolfe whispered to the young traffic constable, "Keep him talking, the ambulance will take at least 15 minutes to get here, he needs to stay awake. If he starts nodding off, put a bit of pressure on the wound, he'll swear and curse but he'll thank you for it later, okay?"

"Yes, sir."

"Jac, come on, can't you ask your DC to do that?" asked Bill, his voice slightly slurred.

"Sorry Bill, Pam is going to have to help me track down the bad guys, see you later, pal."

Bill couldn't resist making another comment, "Jac, keep ya head down pal, that shiner of yours is glowing like my hi-vis jacket."

"Very funny," whispered Wolfe whilst Middleton sniggered.

Chapter 33

Wolfe and Middleton were walking down the road behind and away from the road block, trying to make steady progress whilst crouching down to keep below the wall and not in line of sight from where the Porsche had appeared to stop. Wolfe was thinking they'd have a better chance apprehending the couple if, as he expected the vehicle had been abandoned, he and Middleton could circle around in front of them, he had no idea if this was a plan worth pursuing or if it was just stupidity. Maybe, they should wait until armed officers from the farm could get to the scene, but by then, it could be too late, they'd be away, gone to who knows where. No, it's better trying to follow them rather than just waiting for help to arrive.

The helicopter was still hovering over the incident near the roadblock, its jet engine droning loudly, its floodlight continuing to shine brightly illuminating the ground in the early morning as the darkness of night started to wane. Then another gunshot rang out and the floodlight was extinguished, the two detectives stopped in their tracks and turned towards the noise.

"Damn it I wondered if that would be their next move," cursed Wolfe. As they looked up, the helicopter banked to the right away from where the bullet had been fired, it was the pilot's instinctive response to protect the most vulnerable element, the rotor blades.

"Call the chopper off, Pam, there's nothing more they can help us with, besides, if those guys fire another round, it could bring it down creating more mayhem."

They crouched down behind the stone wall providing them with cover. Middleton ordered the pilot to leave the scene immediately, and then thanked him and his crew as sincerely as she could for the assistance they'd given.

As the helicopter sped away from the scene, noise levels dropped so much that an eerie silence filled the gap the chopper had left.

"Okay, boss, now what are we gonna do?" asked Middleton.

"Start by whispering, now that the chopper has gone," Wolfe replied in a low voice. "We'll walk down the road, it bends to the left, stay close to the wall and keep your head down below the parapet."

"We haven't seen any traffic on this road, Jac, why is that?" she queried in a tone that made it quite clear that she knew the answer but just wanted confirmation.

"PC Broughton came straight over from Leeds when the raid there amounted to nothing, he's down at the junction of this road and Timble Lane about a half a mile away with a road closed sign, that's why," admitted Wolfe.

"They have a gun, Jac … we don't and neither does PC Broughton."

"Yeah and I've also got jack shit which means, Jac could be in the shit if he's not careful. But you've got your Taser…yes?"

"Oh, very funny, a Taser's no fucking use unless you're stood virtually next to the person, you're aiming it at," whispered Middleton almost spitting out the statement, "and no, it's in your car, no use there, is it?"

Wolfe suddenly stopped again, turned and fanned his right arm up and down, then crouched down against the wall, "There's someone, some … thing moving further down there, can you hear it?"

"Yes."

Then unexpectedly, the sky lit up above immediately followed by the sound of an explosion causing a blast wave that could be felt against the wall they'd taken shelter behind. When the blast wave receded, Wolfe took a risk and lifted himself up to gaze carefully over the wall.

He saw the Porsche Cayenne 100 metres or so away, halfway down the steep slope at a slightly lower level to where he was. It was rammed against a large tree trunk, the drivers' side crushed to a point where it appeared as though the bonnet of the vehicle was completely gone, parts of the engine suspended by wires and tubes was hanging down almost touching the ground, black smoke emanated above the flames. The driver's door was open, as was the passenger door. From his angle, Wolfe could see straight through the vehicle, both air bags had been activated. The boot was open but Wolfe couldn't quite see into it. Looking to his right, he saw two figures, a good distance below his position, one holding up the other, staggering through the trees, they appeared to be constantly losing their footing and making slow progress. Wolfe was sure he heard them speaking, one of them seemed to be lambasting the other. He dropped back down behind the wall.

"They're both out of the vehicle walking through the trees away from us but I think one of them is injured and my guess is that it's Paul Smythe, that Porsche took a lot of damage on the driver's side of the car."

"Ah shit, I can hear the ambulance siren now," said Wolfe. "No, no, it's travelling up Timble Lane towards the junction with this road … oh shit, shit." Wolfe started running down the road. Middleton couldn't quite understand what was happening, however, she too started running but Wolfe had already disappeared round the left-hand bend before she managed to increase her pace. Then the reason for Wolfe's reaction suddenly hit her like a smack in the face. Wolfe was concerned the ambulance might get hijacked.

As Wolfe rounded the left hand bend, he knew he had three or four more bends to run round and the right hander he was now heading towards would, to his frustration, take him away from the escaping pair, they were walking in a straight line over treacherous irregular ground towards the Timble Lane junction, he was running down a road snaking its way to the same junction. Wolfe could hear Middleton running behind him, she was catching him up. He had to make another decision that would cover more bases, more eventualities. He stopped, inhaled hard, and as Middleton stopped, he said,

"Look, we know what could happen now," he said breathlessly, he inhaled again and coughed. "You run back to the blockade, get my car, not a traffic police car and follow me down here. I'll see you at the junction." Middleton looked hard into Wolfe's eyes she knew he had the right idea.

"Be very, very careful, Jac." She leaned towards him, aimed to kiss him at his left cheek but missed and planted the kiss directly on his bruised eye. Not waiting for a response, she set off running back up the road. Wolfe winced as the pain shot down his cheek into his jaw.

He turned and started running again, he knew he had half a mile to cover to the Timble Lane junction but could he get there in time, and if he did, what would he do. The sound of the ambulance siren was getting louder.

Wolfe thought he had speed on his side, he was running quicker on an in-direct line but the fugitives were making slow progress in a direct line through dense woodland although they had a head start. He'd slowed down to a steady jogging pace to conserve energy, confident he'd get to the junction before them. The siren was getting louder, the oncoming ambulance was getting closer. Wolfe smiled as he thought to himself *'Creedence, Run Through The Jungle ... haven't heard that in ages'*

Middleton was finding it tough going, trying to run up hill against a steep gradient. She'd decided whilst running, jogging then walking up the hill she'd call for another ambulance, and request this second one make its way to the scene via Carlton and not through the Wharfe Valley from the station in Menston. Then as the roadblock came back into view, she noticed one car was missing, she couldn't see Bill Mason at all. The other two traffic policemen were stood by the one remaining vehicle. As she got closer, she heard one man on the phone and the young officer who'd been taking care of Bill was leaning against the car.

"Where's Bill gone?" she asked.

"When the chopper got hit, we decided it was best to get him to the hospital as quick as possible, he kept drifting in and out of consciousness so Ray put him in the back of the SUV, and is now on his way to A and E in Otley."

"I've just contacted the ambulance service and they said they'd call their vehicle back," said the other officer as he placed his mobile phone in his jacket pocket.

"Okay, okay," said DC Middleton as she ran towards Wolfe's car. "Call the armed response unit at the farm, tell them to get down here pronto."

The car was unlocked, the electronic key fob resting in the centre console she climbed in and started the engine. A few seconds later, she was speeding back down the road towards the Timble Lane junction. Natural daylight was beginning to gain supremacy over the darkness; the shadows cast by tree canopies offering the most resistance, the headlights were switched on but perhaps not needed, however, they were helping with judgement and that gave some confidence to Middleton as she drove as fast as she dared.

Wolfe was walking, trying to keep up a constant pace, his thoughts, muddled darting from one thing to another, when would Middleton catch him up? Would Broughton try and be a hero, take on the villains on his own, get himself shot? What about the crew of the ambulance ... Wolfe suddenly stopped in his tracks, he'd just heard a crack, a gunshot, he was certain?

"Why is there no siren anymore?" he said out loud to himself. He heard a car approaching before he saw it, as it rounded the corner, he recognised the car and the driver. It pulled up next to him, he opened the door and entered sitting down breathlessly.

"Get us to that junction as quick as possible, Pam, a couple of seconds ago, I heard a gunshot, I can't hear the siren from the ambulance anymore," Wolfe stated.

"It's been called back, Bill's been taken to the nearest A and E, his condition was getting worse," replied Middleton

Wolfe didn't reply, they rounded the next corner, the T-junction with Timble Lane came into view. There were two people in the road just before the two roads connected; the one standing over the other was wearing green overalls, the one on the floor was wearing a yellow hi-vis jacket.

"Oh no, not another cop down! That's Broughton," said Middleton, anger tinged with dismay.

"I hope he hasn't done anything stupid," Wolfe said as their car drew up next to the two figures. It became instantly apparent that Broughton was lying down and the figure stood over him was a paramedic.

"What happened?" asked Wolfe.

Broughton was the first to answer, "Shot in the leg; I didn't even see them till after the shot was fired, came over the wall. Laid me in the fucking road, Jac, ambulance had to stop, then she brandished the gun and forced this guy out of the drivers' seat."

"What about the man with her?" Wolfe asked.

"He was in a bad way," the paramedic responded. Wolfe noticed his name badge T Walker.

"T?" asked Wolfe pointing to his badge.

"Trevor," stated the paramedic.

"What's happened, Trevor? Have they got another paramedic with them?"

"Yeah, Sara. Sara Wade, she's only six months into the job, the women threatened to shoot this PC in the head." He turned and looked at Broughton. "She said she would if I didn't hand over the ambulance, she stood over him with the gun pressed to his head. The man was handed over to Sara, she looked at him and had to prop him up and help him straight into the back of the ambulance. He was very badly injured."

"Which way'd they go, Trevor?"

Trevor and PC Broughton pointed towards the route leading to Harrogate.

"Come on, Pam, we're going after them."

Wolfe was now driving his own car, he knew its capabilities, it gave them the best chance of catching the ambulance, although, catching it up wouldn't be beyond many sports cars or their drivers, but what would he do when he caught up to it?

Middleton was already on the phone to Halford, explaining the events of the last fifteen minutes. Halford and Fairburn were now on their way in one car having heard all about the incidents at Bradshaw's Farm. One of the armed response units had left the farm ready to offer assistance if required.

"Pete, divert towards Otley, take the Harrogate Road," she ordered, then for some reason, she instantly felt guilty issuing orders to him, but needs must.

Within a few minutes, the Z4 was within sight of the ambulance on the road linking Harrogate with Carlton. Climbing at a constant rate to the summit of the moorland, catching up to the ambulance now wasn't going to be difficult.

"Now what are we going to do?" Middleton asked.

"Just what I was going to ask, Pam."

"I hope they send reinforcements?" Middleton asked in reply.

Wolfe let out a snigger. "We'll need more than three and four pence."

"What?"

"A joke my dad told me, many years ago." He looked at Middleton. Blankness filled her gaze.

Wolfe knew that his actions, under most circumstances, were instinctive. This next action, however, would be calculated and refined. Wolfe wanted to know where Halford and Fairburn were.

"Otley, driving over the tops towards us on the Harrogate Road."

"Are they driving a squad car?"

"Yes, I'm sure they are."

"Tell them to make as much noise as possible, let these two in front of us know that we aren't the only ones chasing them, I'm gonna get closer."

"Watch out, Jac, they're not bothered about using guns."

"Yeah, I know, but I'm betting those shots were fired by Andrea, he's in no fit state and I think she's driving, I hope she can't multitask too well." Wolfe replied as the revs of the engine under the Z4's bonnet increased. They hit the summit of the moor road a matter of seconds behind the ambulance which managed to increase its pace now that the terrain became flat.

"Look!" pointed Middleton towards the half-right horizon. Wolfe eased off the accelerator. His gaze followed Middleton's direction and he saw blue lights flashing.

"Good, now let's see what reaction this brings, however ..." Wolfe eased off the accelerator again and just in time.

"Ah, fuck!" Wolfe shouted as he swerved to avoid the ambulance which had suddenly braked hard in front of him. Wolfe turned left then right and managed to accelerate past the now almost stationery vehicle that had turned slightly right to try and broadside the chasing sports car. Wolfe was now in front of the ambulance, which he rapidly realised was not a good place to be. The ambulance straightened and began chasing the BMW.

"Get down, Pam!"

The first bullet was high and missed Wolfe's car all together. The second bullet pierced the rear windscreen, hit the head restraint behind Wolfe's head and ricocheted through the front windscreen close to the rear-view mirror. Head lowered as much as possible, Wolfe shouted

"Okay two can play that game! Brace ya-self." Wolfe hit the brakes hard. The ambulance driver couldn't react quickly enough and rammed into the back of Wolfe's car.

The resulting collision stopped both vehicles, the front of the ambulance smashed and creased, it bounced off the back of the sports car its boot crumpled to less than half its original size. The air bags blew out in both vehicles, preventing more bullets being fired. After the hideous sound of fibreglass, metal, glass and engine parts smashing into one another, came silence. Wolfe's Z4 was trapped against the front of the ambulance and a drystone wall.

Everything was still for several seconds; Wolfe turned his head as best he could to look at Middleton,

"Pam, are you okay?"

She coughed a little. "Yeah, I'm okay ... you?"

"Think so," he replied as he looked out of the door window, the collision had spun his vehicle round towards the ambulance, he was staring at the radiator grill, steam hissed as it escaped and smoke was billowing from below the vehicle. He could see movement around the vehicle.

"On my mark, we'll roll out together ... keep low, on the ground, I'll call when it's safe ... okay?"

"Yep."

"Go … now." Wolfe fell out of his car and rolled as quickly as possible towards the front of the ambulance, safety under the cover of what was left of the ambulance bonnet. Looking to the left, he noticed the ambulance drivers' door was open and then he heard the rear door open. He pressed his head to the ground so he could see under the vehicle to the back. He saw black boots beneath green trouser hems. Paramedic, he thought. Then he heard a police siren approaching

"Sara? Sara Wade? Is that you … at the back of the ambulance?" Wolfe shouted as he watched for a reaction.

"My name is Wolfe, Detective Inspector Wolfe."

"Yes, I need to get this guy in the back to a hospital; he has extensive and severe injuries."

"Where's the driver?"

"I don't know, straight after we crashed, she jumped out," Sara replied.

Wolfe decided to stand up; he used the bonnet of the ambulance to lever up his aching body. Once up, he could see into the cab of the ambulance and through into the back section and out of the vehicle. The paramedic had her mobile pressed against her right ear. Wolfe could see the lower half of someone lying on an accident trolley to the right of the vehicle, the top half was hidden behind the bulkhead behind the passenger seat. He assumed it was Paul Smythe.

"Where's she gone?" asked Middleton as she peered above the boot of Wolfe's car.

"Don't know, can't see her," responded Wolfe.

Halford and Fairburn screeched to a halt in the middle of the road near to Wolfe's Z4. As soon as their vehicle was stationery, both men got out.

"What the hell has happened here?" asked Halford as he ran around the passenger's side of Wolfe's car towards Middleton. "Are you okay, babe?"

"Yeah, I'm fine, Pete, don't fuss."

"Are they bullet holes?" Halford pointed to hole in the back windscreen.

"Pete, I said don't fuss."

"Careful Harry, they're not shy about using guns," said Wolfe to Fairburn as he shuffled around the open driver's door and then down the roadside of the ambulance. Before he'd reached the rear of the vehicle, the paramedic appeared from the back.

"Who's DI Wolfe?"

"I am." Wolfe walked towards her.

"He's asking for you," she nodded towards the patient in the back of the ambulance.

"Yeah the ambulance is a wreck on a wreck," she said into her mobile phone. "And my patient is in need of serious medical care, he's not in pain because he's on a morphine drip but that'll soon run out, get someone here as soon as … well, get the air ambulance here then, he's not going to survive long without specialist care." She ended the call.

"What are his injuries, Sara?" asked Wolfe.

"Well, where do I start? Compound fracture of his left leg, bandaged but needs resetting soon or it will get infected. Multiple rib fractures both sides, internal bleeding, punctured internal organs, a collapsed lung I think on his right side but what's worse than all of that is a ruptured spleen, all the symptoms are there. He's dying, Inspector and the best I can do for him is to make him as comfortable as possible. I don't think he has long … sorry."

"Thanks, Sara." Wolfe moved to go to the back of the vehicle but he stopped and turned back towards her. "Are you okay? Bit of a traumatic morning for you but you seem to be coping with it though."

"My nerves feel like they're having a party, they're at an all-night rave, but apart from that, I'm fine. She didn't have to shoot that policeman in the leg though, I hope he's gonna be okay."

"He'll be fine," replied Wolfe, "which way did she go?"

"I didn't see where she went … coz when I heard the first gunshot … I … I crouched down on the floor and then fell back when the crash happened, when I got back on my feet, she'd gone. She's a maniac … what she do … breakout of prison?"

"No, she's suspected of murder, as is the bloke in the back."

"Surprised about him but not her," Sara said with indifference that Wolfe thought only presented itself in the police force.

"Did she say anything to him whilst she was driving?" Wolfe asked trying to appear blasé about the question.

"Oh yeah … she was giving him hell … called him a snivelling little wanker … told him she'd have done better on her own … or words to that effect. Don't you think you should go see that guy … er, his name is Paul, he was asking for you, don't forget."

"Yeah, yeah … okay … we will need a formal statement from you later … okay?"

"No problem, I ain't going nowhere … at least till the air ambulance gets here."

As Wolfe entered the rear of the ambulance, he was shocked at the state of the person he saw inside laying on the trolley. Paul looked grey, weak, drawn and fragile in complete contrast to the person he'd interviewed a few days earlier.

"Mr Smythe, where's your sister, half-sister, gone … where's she heading for?" asked Wolfe as he sat down next to Smythe.

"Lift the back up a little if you wouldn't mind, Inspector," Paul responded coughing and wheezing, the pain making him wince. Wolfe did as he was asked as gently as he could but Paul let out a groan that Wolfe realised was a helpless reaction to severe pain.

"I've no idea what her plans are now, Inspector," he agonisingly replied. "She's on her own, I think she believes I let her down."

Wolfe looked quizzically at Paul,

"This whole thing was her idea, she contacted me a few years ago …" He coughed, blood trickled from the corner of his mouth. "She approached me about this gold, I didn't believe her, even when she gave me a copy of Tanner's manuscript. Only after she said she'd got Alfie Marks to talk, did I consider getting involved and then she eventually persuaded me to get rid of the man that murdered my father." Wolfe looked at him quizzically. "He admitted it as well, when I was strapping him into the Cobra, the bastard spat in my face." He stopped for a few seconds to lift his right hand clenching a tissue and wiped the blood from his mouth, but this time, there was no coughing, just a gargle and rattle in his throat.

"I can taste blood … I know I'm bleeding to death … and by the look of your expression, I think you know the same thing."

"We're expecting the air ambulance soon," Wolfe confirmed.

"Well, that just might finish me off." Spluttering again, he said, "Plip key in my pocket set off the explosion in Tommy's garage. I didn't feel anything, no remorse, no sorrow, just relief, retribution if you like … for the ill he'd done me and for the cold-blooded murder of a man I barely knew … a man I never got to know." Paul spat into his tissue, white turned red instantly. "Shot him in the head and buried him … somewhere in Bosnia after they'd found the gold." He paused; his throat rattled again, another globule of dark red fluid dribbled from his mouth.

"Watts and Jessop told her as well, she fucked 'em both, then blackmailed them, threatened to tell their wives. Jessop broke easily enough, Watts held on a lot longer, he didn't care at first but then she found out that he'd been shagging his secretary for years and when she threatened to tell his wife, that was when he broke … she has a way of getting to people, men in particular." His eyelids began to close, Wolfe decided that pain might have an effect on Paul's concentration so he lent on his fractured leg, the response was immediate.

"Ah!" Paul let out a muffled groan. Wolfe knew the pain must have been excruciating, but he didn't really care, he needed Paul to continue talking.

"Expensive cars …" Wolfe stated not as a question, more as a remark to force a response.

"Yeah …" spluttered Paul. "Most people just look at them, in awe, especially at border controls, they never once suspected gold bullion stashed in the boot or under the seats, it was easy, bringing the stuff in from Geneva. That bank vault was less secure than Jessop's lock up or Tommy's vehicle pit in his garage."

"So, you organised and took part in bringing in the gold from Geneva?"

"Oh yeah, thought I'd do what Tanner wanted to do, give it back to the Serbian Government … she had other fucking ideas though."

"Watts and Jessop gave up all their security numbers?" Wolfe asked trying to inject some urgency into the discussion; he was getting a little agitated because he knew his mobile phone, he was using to record the conversation might soon run out of charge.

"Oh yeah, Antonia took Jessop to a swingers party in Harrogate. After that, he was putty in her hands, especially after she'd shown him photos of what he got up to."

"Antonia?" Wolfe looked curiously at Paul.

"Yeah, my half-sister," Paul answered, then paused before stating, "you didn't know her name?" he tried to smile at the sarcasm behind his comment.

"Yeah, we knew about her but her Christian name is Andrea."

"Ah, it used to be, she changed it to match our Grandmother's Christian name."

"Toni Chezec … not, T O N Y … Dave Watts spelt it wrong, didn't he?"

"Not sure what you're referring to, but I can tell you she's a real bitch," he coughed just as Middleton and Sara, the paramedic, accessed the rear of the ambulance. Sara checked the monitor displaying her patient's vital signs and Middleton stood where she could eavesdrop on the conversation between Wolfe and Smythe.

"Just curious Paul," Wolfe started to ask in manner seeking to be educated, "how did you get Watts' pickup truck into the building without security noticing?"

"Marko," replied Paul without hesitation.

"Who?"

Paul coughed sending a few specks of blood into the air that landed on his chest. "He's our Serbian muscle, scares the heck out of people but he's actually dead soft. It's his younger brother Luka you need to be worried about, he's a convicted criminal and would slit your throat as soon as look at you." Paul's recent memory kicked in then, "You met Luka … he was dressed as a policeman."

"Yeah … that was embarrassing," replied Wolfe, wanting to forget all about that. "Marko was disguised as security then, but how …?"

"Ha … night shift guy had a few laxatives slipped into his coco, while he was gone we manoeuvred Watts pickup into the building, same guy still feeling sick the following morning, Marko stepped in."

"Easy as that," admitted Wolfe, "so, the vehicle sales were legitimate?"

"We … Andromeda Imports which I registered in the Cayman Islands bought cars in from Europe, we were acting as agents, delivery agents for main dealers, ten to twenty gold bars hidden in each one way trip. Did a couple dry runs first. Didn't take long to get all the bullion from the bank in Geneva over here." His speech had begun to slur. Smythe's responses were getting more laboured.

"How many bars did you bring in, Paul?"

He tried to clear his throat, but the blood in his throat just gargled, "A hundred or so, that's all that was stashed in the Swiss bank, she's got two in her backpack and there's twenty or so in the back of the Porsche. Ha! Bet your colleagues have nabbed them by now," he tried to laugh but he coughed instead and blood spat from his mouth.

"Did Tommy Smythe hand over his security code for the bank?"

"Antonia blackmailed the numbers out of Alfred Marks, but he was going to tell Tommy so she got rid of him," groaned Paul.

"You need to rest, sir," interrupted the paramedic as she pushed in front of Wolfe to check his monitor and the drip bag hanging from the ceiling. She wiped his lips. His eyes were closed.

"He's not well enough to answer any more questions, inspector," she looked straight at Wolfe.

Middleton gently took hold of the paramedic's arm and guided her to the back of the vehicle.

"Four murders we know of," she whispered. "A possible fifth and two persons this morning suffering from gunshot wounds, and it's not eight in the morning yet. We need to know what he knows and we need to know it now, we have to put a stop to this or others might get hurt, do you understand?"

"Yeah, I suppose so; I'll have to monitor him though."

"Okay, but you can see the monitor from here, right?" Sara nodded and pulled a seat down from the ambulance side panel.

Middleton moved next to Wolfe, she put her right arm around his waist and slipped her mobile phone into his right hand. "It's recording," she whispered.

Wolfe passed her his phone with his left hand.

Paul was beginning to slide once again into sleep; the heart rate monitor indicating this was noticed immediately by the paramedic.

"Where's that bloody air ambulance?" she said as she moved back towards her patient. Middleton was the first to respond.

"Oh yeah and they almost managed to down a helicopter as well this morning."

Sara was now increasing the adrenalin being pumped into Paul's body, he immediately opened his eyes.

"That was me," he said proudly. "Good shot, eh?"

"You could have killed someone," Middleton pronounced in a raised voice. "You could have hit the pilot."

"No, you misunderstand, if I'd wanted to kill the pilot, I would have done," replied Paul like a pompous school teacher. "But I just wanted to disable the search light."

Wolfe looked surprised, "You made that shot?"

"Yep, fortunately, my right arm seems to be functioning okay, which is more than I can say for the rest of me." He coughed, once again, blood was visible around his mouth as the paramedic helped him sit further up in the bed.

Sara then stepped onto the road from the back of the ambulance responding to a request from DC Fairburn to take her statement as Halford arrived at the back door of the ambulance. "More officers including armed response have arrived, we're organising a search."

"Be careful, she's got a firearm and she will use it," Middleton responded as Halford turned to leave.

"You'll need a description from the paramedic," Wolfe added.

"Yeah, Harry is with her now getting a statement."

"What about Charlotte's brother?" Wolfe asked Smythe.

"That was a terrible accident, he was given a sleeping drug but he must have had an allergic reaction to it. We were just keeping him locked away in the farm because he'd taken photos of Luka, Marko and me, and wouldn't tell us where he'd hidden them or who he'd sent them to."

A bemused Wolfe looked deep into Paul's eyes.

"Are you telling me the truth?"

"Yes … why … why would I have purposely killed Brookes? He's Charlotte's …" he coughed as the realisation of Wolfe's question hit him.

"That fucking bitch!" he shouted, blood oozed in a large globule from the left corner of his mouth. He coughed and wiped the blood away with the back of his right hand.

"Please tell Charlotte that I had no idea. As far as I knew, it was an accident, that's what she told me …" Paul paused his face warped by pain, an inner pain. "She's heading for Harrogate," he spluttered. "There's a car parked on the Stray near The Yorkshire Rose Hotel, a Range Rover, we have a ferry to Ireland booked for this evening, get her, Inspector! Stop her killing again, she loves it, she's got a taste for it."

Wolfe looked towards Middleton but she was already stepping out of the ambulance.

"Paul, Matthew was murdered, two-minute puncture wounds were found in the small of his back, made by a –"

"A spear," interrupted Paul. "Luka has two of them sawn into the lining of his jacket, he'll show them off if you ask him, he's a maniac … that poor boy, he didn't deserve that."

"Your sympathy comes far too late," Wolfe was trying to control his reaction. Inside, he was ready to burst and if he did, Paul would be dead in seconds, he took a deep breath.

"Where are Luka and err …?"

"Marko," said Paul.

"Dunno, I'm sure they left the farm before me and Toni … and there's more … more stuff at the …" Paul let out a breath that was followed by more loss of blood, his head dropped.

The noise of a helicopter could now be heard from inside the ambulance. The paramedic entered and immediately reacted to Paul's condition. Within seconds, she had deployed an automatic defibrillator device.

"Stand clear!" she shouted as the device shocked through Paul's chest, the response from her patient was negligible so she hit the device again. This time his eyes opened, but the pupils were dilated and he looked vacant, very unaware of his condition.

"Go and bring that helicopter in, Inspector, this man is dying, he needs to get to a hospital immediately."

The air ambulance landed noisily with a thud onto the road 50 metres from the ambulance. Within seconds, Sara and the paramedic from the helicopter were transferring her patient into the air ambulance. Wolfe accompanied them during the transfer still talking to Paul, he wasn't responding, although Wolfe was certain that he was trying to say something. He groaned and coughed, his skin was grey, eyes black and sunk deep into his skull: lost, life was ebbing away. As the trolley carrying Paul was being pushed into the air ambulance, he raised his right arm, he looked at Wolfe a sudden brightness in his eyes.

"Look after Charlotte, tell her I'm sorry, tell her …" A spluttering cough sent him back into semi-consciousness. The trolley locked in place as Sara handed over her patient to the air ambulance crew. She and Wolfe retreated to a safe distance, and watched as the helicopter lifted itself above the ground, then when high enough, the nose dipped the helicopter banked to its right and began its journey back to Leeds.

"I don't think he'll make it," commented Wolfe. Then Sara's phone rang.

"Wade here," she answered and whilst listening intently she beckoned Wolfe over towards her. "Okay, some good news then, I'll tell him … thanks, bye."

"Your constable shot in the leg is okay, flesh wound only, a clean out and stitches, and he'll be sent home later today," she stated, "and the other policeman is in a stable condition, he will need an operation so they are preparing him for theatre at present, prognosis is positive, full recovery is expected."

"Excellent, thanks for all your help, Sara, sorry you had to experience all of this," replied Wolfe as he surveyed the scene which now included more and more vehicles, constables with dogs, SOCO had just arrived and were beginning to cordon off the scene, another helicopter could be heard in the distance. '*TV,*' thought Wolfe, blue flashing lights on the far horizon in the direction of Harrogate and a full 180 degrees to his right the same on the near horizon back towards Carlton, the search for Toni Chezec was well underway.

Chapter 34

Wolfe went back to his car, initially to inspect the damage but he soon realised there was no point in cursing or wondering if there was anything he could have done that wouldn't have resulted in his car being wrecked. He retrieved a few personal belongings and his laptop bag, he suddenly remembered the flask of coffee Izzy had made for him earlier that morning, he'd put it in the boot. Examining the extensive damage to the rear of his BMW, he wondered if the flask had also fallen victim to the collision but to his surprise, having managed to force the boot lid open, he saw the silver flask stood defiantly upright protected by two overcoats and two sterile packs of blue overalls. He grabbed one of the overcoats and the flask which he shook, all he could hear was liquid sloshing about within, then unzipping his laptop shoulder bag he placed it inside.

Opening the door to the squad car driven to the scene by Halford, he gently placed the laptop bag on the rear seat.

"Jac?" shouted Middleton from the other side of the drystone wall on the opposite side of the road to where the collided vehicles had stopped. "Pete and Harry are each supervising a search team but there is no evidence, no foot prints, the dogs haven't picked up a scent, she's completely disappeared," she declared in dismay.

"Okay, okay, Pam, spilt into three groups and you take the third team, widen the search area. I'm going to take a walk around."

A car drove over the brow of the hill behind Wolfe and pulled up next to him.

"What is it with you, Jac? Mayhem wherever you go these days!" announced Arnold Higgins from behind the steering wheel of his SUV and looking over towards Wolfe's car, he continued, "Ouch, that's gonna hurt ya no claims!"

"Perfect timing, Arnold, you can help with our search of the area, we're looking for a murderer … a woman in her mid-thirties … long dark hair, but that's probably a wig, so possibly short blonde hair. Her most distinguishing feature is her bosom, to say its ample is under stating the visual impact of those puppies on the rest of her figure. Seen anyone fitting that description?"

"Nope! Sorry, Jac. If I'd have seen someone fitting that description, I would have asked where she was going and offered to take her there."

"Had you done so, you'd probably be face down in the road with a bullet wound in the back of your head?"

"Paul Smythe's half-sister?"

"Yep … got it in one," replied Wolfe

"How long has she been gone?" asked Higgins as an unmarked white van drew up behind him, Wolfe knew it to be the rest of the forensic team.

"Say 20 minutes, half an hour tops, she's dangerous, Arnold … very dangerous."

When Higgins had set his team to collect and catalogue any forensic evidence, he found Wolfe crouched down behind the drystone wall on the blind side of the ambulance.

"Have you found something, Jac?" he asked.

"Heel prints here on the ground and …" Wolfe paused as he examined the wall above the depressions in the ground. "Fresh marks on the wall, looks like something has scraped along the lower level of the wall. A rucksack, I'm thinking."

"You think she hid here then went where?"

"She jumped over this wall, crouched down …" Wolfe mimicked the description. "She walked staying very close to the wall, footprints here against the base of the wall, crouching down all the way." Then he stood up, looked over the wall towards Higgins and the ambulance behind him, only his head was visible. "She wouldn't have been visible from the back of the ambulance or my car and we'd all assumed she'd jumped over the wall on the other side of the road because that was closer to her point of exit from the ambulance."

"She's a slippery one, that's for sure," replied Higgins.

"Yes, but how did she manage it so swiftly? That's what's concerning me, I find it hard to believe that she was able …" Wolfe stopped mid-sentence. He scaled the wall, jumped down the other side and ran across the road, looked over that side and shouted, "Pam bring your team and a tracker dog up here." Middleton called her team and within minutes she had them organised, the tracker dog excitedly pulling its handler along the route used by Chezec.

Higgins walked away from the ambulance to a high point in the road to see if he could spot anyone running or walking in the distance.

Wolfe approached Sara Wade as she sat on the back step of the ambulance looking down at her mobile phone.

"She didn't leave by the driver's door, did she, Sara?" asked Wolfe looking straight into her eyes.

"Sorry … what was that, Inspector?" she responded as she looked up from her mobile phone.

"You heard me very well, Sara, where did you hide the bar of gold she gave you?"

"I'm sure I don't know what …"

"Don't bullshit me, Sara, I'll get the forensic guys over here in seconds, they'll be like a swarm of ants all over the inside of this ambulance, and when they find it, I'll charge you with aiding and abetting a known criminal, and I'll make sure those charges stick."

"Shit! I nearly got away with it, they're in my rucksack next to my jacket on the passenger seat." Sara looked down at the floor in despair. Wolfe retrieved the rucksack and handed it to Sara.

"She gave you more than one bar?" he asked.

"There are three in here," she said without a hint of emotion.

"Paul told me she only had two bars, did you see how many she actually had?"

"No, but I got the impression she had enough left for herself and of course, she left here a little lighter, she leapt out the back, jumped over the wall and that was the last I saw of her. She just handed them to me, didn't say a word and didn't even look at Paul. What will happen to me now, Inspector?"

Wolfe opened the rucksack, the dull yellow shine of the gold bullion burst out from within. For the first time, he realised the story told in manuscript form by Matthew Tanner was real. He took hold of two gold bullion bars, one after the other and stacked them on top of each other on the floor of the ambulance. Each bullion bar was approximately 150mm long by 25mm thick and 100mm wide. He zipped the bag back up, and then he sat down next to the paramedic and dropped the bag in Sara's lap.

"You ever speak a word of this to anyone and I'll make sure that charges are brought against you, okay?"

Sara looked up at him, tears welling up in her eyes, she leaned into him and kissed him on his cheek.

"Thanks, you're a good man, Inspector," she sniffed back to clear her nose.

"I love happy endings, Sara and you've been through a lot this morning so I think that today you deserve just that." Wolfe smiled, stood up, took hold of the two gold bullion bars and shoved one in each outer pocket of his overcoat.

Wolfe left Sara holding her rucksack containing one gold bullion bar tight to her chest, he walked towards Higgins who was staring at scenery that unfolded below his elevated position, now bathed in low full morning daylight.

"Any luck, Arnold?" he asked.

"No sorry, Jac, these old eyes of mine are not offering any assistance at all, what was all that about with the young paramedic?"

"Oh well, I suppose, it was about these." He took a gold bar out of each of his overcoat pockets and held them up for Higgins to see.

"Oh my God! They are a thing of beauty. Can I hold one, dear boy?"

"Be my guest," Wolfe handed one of the bullion bars to his friend. He held the gold bar in both hands, caressing it like a lost pet that had just been found, rubbing it softly. Turning the gold bar over, he looked at the indented marks on the underside.

"I'm no expert, Jac, but this looks like a hallmark, it might confirm country of origin and this part here" he turned towards Wolfe pointing to a section of the marks "could be a date" Handing the bar of gold back, Higgins patted Wolfe on the back. "This proves your theory, Jac, well done."

Wolfe looked at his friend. "Well, all it proves is that Tanner was reporting the truth in his manuscript, and thereby offering motive for his murder and the actual murders of four people and the possible murder of Alfred Marks."

"Where do you suppose she is heading, Jac? Just anywhere or is it an attempt at a permanent disappearance?" Higgins muttered more to himself than Wolfe.

"What's in that direction anyway?" Wolfe responded not really thinking as he returned the gold bars to his overcoat pockets.

"Well, back to Carlton via the moor top," offered Higgins as an explanation.

"That's it ... of course ... stupid bastard Wolfe," Wolfe said as he turned aiming to run towards his car, then he suddenly realised his dilemma. He grabbed Higgins by the arm, "Arnold, come on, we need your car."

"What? Why? Where are we going, Jac?"

"Back to Smythe Senior's house, her plan B ... C or fucking D ... I don't know, come on we're running out of time ... either she's lucky or she's so intelligent she has contingency plans for all eventualities, probably somewhere in between."

As soon as they were underway, whilst Higgins drove, Wolfe called Middleton on his mobile phone, "Yeah, leave Harry in charge, you and Pete follow me a.s.a.p. to Tommy Smythe's place, call out an APB for all major routes out of Carlton."

"I don't suppose you have any idea of vehicle type or better still a registration?" Middleton asked as she ran back to the collision location.

"I'm working on a hunch again …" he took a breath, "remember earlier this morning on the way to Bradshaw's farm?"

"Yes."

"There was a car parked in the driveway of Tommy Smythe's house, a golf I think?"

"Same as the one we saw at Paul Smythe's house?"

"It's possible."

"Okay, see you there," the discussion ended.

Higgins drove as quickly as he could and within 10 minutes, he and Wolfe arrived at Bradshaw's farm, but they drove straight past. Wolfe and Higgins noted that SOCO were on site as they drove past, their destination was a little lower down the hill. When they arrived at Tommy Smythe's house, the place looked abandoned and what was left of the double garage and all the related debris was cordoned off with temporary metal fencing. Wolfe told Higgins to park on the road, he noticed tyre tracks on the drive and on the road.

"Sod it!" cursed Wolfe as he and Higgins walked from the car to the driveway entrance. "We've missed her, these tyre tracks look very fresh to me."

"Yeah, you're right," agreed Higgins as he scraped a small amount of black rubber residue off the road and rolled it between his thumb and forefinger of his left hand. "Still pliable, 10 minutes, quarter of an hour? That's all, I reckon."

"Travelling at speed," Wolfe remarked as he walked to the opposite side of the road. "She caught the underside of the car on this grass bank, there's a deep rut in the turf." He turned and walked back across the road to the car.

"Well, nothing we can do now, just hope they can get a helicopter in the air to keep track of her," Wolfe stated as he got back into the car, his mobile phone clamped to his left ear. Within seconds, he was speaking with Middleton.

"Meet at the farm, Pam …"

"No one there?"

"No she's gone … in the direction of Carlton … onto Harrogate perhaps? We have to assume it's the same car, Charlotte Marks will have the registration … can we get an eye in the sky?" Wolfe added.

"Requested it, Jac, but no confirmation from HQ yet."

"A known killer on the loose and still money is the deciding factor over community safety," Wolfe responded dejectedly as Higgins turned left into the drive at Bradshaw's Farm.

Two uniformed officers were on duty at the gated entrance to the farm. Higgins pulled up next to one of them and lowered the driver's door window.

"Arnold Higgins, county forensics and this is …"

"Hello, Inspector," said the uniformed officer bending down to see through the window.

"Good morning, PC Morgan, what's happening within?" asked Wolfe as he bent his head slightly towards the main farm building.

"All I know, sir, is that SOCO have restricted access to all but authorised persons, but I'm told it's an absolute mess in there." He waved them forward as Middleton and Halford pulled in behind them. They too were ushered through. The two vehicles parked next to each other facing the farmhouse.

"Shoe covers and overalls please," announced Higgins as all four of them alighted from their cars. He distributed the clothing from his stock in the boot of his car.

The building cast a dark foreboding feel over the immediate surroundings, deep black stonewalls and small unkempt timber window frames surrounding unwelcoming black windows panes. The dark green garage doors lay splayed open bent and hanging loosely on their damaged hinges about to fall over at the merest touch. The main entrance door to the farm seemed to lack any sense of style or reception, there was a feeling of trepidation from all four as they crossed the threshold into the bleakness of the inner building.

"ID please," was the request made by a burley Scene of Crime Officer wearing full-length white overalls. When he'd accepted and scrutinised their IDs, he remarked, "All the interesting stuff is down the stairs, please stay inside the taped areas, thank you."

Wolfe led the way closely followed by Middleton, the stone steps appeared cold as they reflected the arc lights that had been erected giving the appearance of a wet sheen to the treads. As they reached the bottom, a sharp left turn was required and then a more intense array of floodlights lit up the open area beyond, the bright glow of two other persons dressed in white overalls focused their attention and as they entered the windowless catacomb like space, the full horror of what had happened below ground hit them like arctic ice.

Wolfe was the first to speak, "Okay, let's see …" he fell instantly silent, in fact, the humming of the floodlights was all that pierced the silence. Then as he moved closer to focus his attention he said,

"What the hell has happened here?"

"Two men found dead by police firearms officers they called us in immediately," replied the SOCO. "Is one of you DI Wolfe?"

"Yes, that's me," stated Wolfe.

"We tried contacting you but your phone wasn't being answered and then we were informed that you were giving chase to persons that fled this building so we decided to secure the scene and wait," he confirmed.

"Okay, well, firstly," asked Wolfe, "is the scene we see here as you found it?"

"Yes, sir, we cordoned off the scene, moved nothing; although we did check that they're both dead."

"Who are they?" asked Middleton.

"I think they're Marko and Luka," replied Wolfe with calm confidence.

"Who?" replied Higgins.

"That's exactly what I said less than an hour ago to Paul Smythe," responded Wolfe trying to bring a ray of light-heartedness into the gloom. "They are the two henchmen Smythe and Chezec recruited for muscle … at least, that's the impression I've been given," Wolfe stated with obvious knowledgeable insight. "So, we know who Chezec is?" questioned Halford.

"Yes Toni Chezec ... Toni with an I ... she's Andrea, Martha and now Toni and as we know Smythe's half-sister."

"Toni! where'd you get that info, sir?" asked Halford, his tone a little more abrupt than intended.

"Paul Smythe," he answered, "gave me loads of intel. He knew he was dying, wanted to get stuff off his chest I assume. Arnold are you ready?"

"Yeah, yeah, one step ahead of you, Jac," responded Higgins as he stepped forward reaching once again for his badge ID.

"Professor Higgins, forensic examiner," he stated as he thrust his ID card under the nose of another white clad SOCO official. He was allowed forward to examine the two corpses, he was already opening a pack of sterile synthetic gloves and pulling them onto each hand in turn.

Strewn like discarded garbage on the cold concrete floor of the cellar, one man lay face down, the other on his back, a single bullet wound clearly visible in the centre of his forehead. Examining more closely the corpse laid on its back, Higgins said, "Shot through the back of the head, very close range, there's a pressure ring around the wound. I'd say a silencer was used."

"That tallies," responded Wolfe. "Smythe thought they'd left the farm before he and Chezec, at least, that's what Chezec probably told him."

"No one upstairs would have heard a thing if a silencer was being used down here," commented Middleton.

"Precisely," replied Higgins as he moved onto the next corpse. With a groan, he turned over the second body. "This fella weighs a ton ... oh my God," he uttered more to himself than anyone else. The others a few feet away, however, could also see that this man had been shot multiple times, at least, three times in the head. Blood, sticky like half set glue and sinew of muscle spread over what was left of the man's face, resembling the makeup used on graphic horror films.

Higgins let out a long breath to calm his nerves. "Okay, at least, three bullet wounds to this man's face, not fired from as close range as the other guy. Other wounds over the man's torso and one, no, maybe two, impacting his crotch, blood still discharging from these wounds, turning him has probably caused more body fluid to escape."

Upon hearing this, the SOCO standing next to Halford began to sway and would have fallen had Halford not managed to hold onto him and lay him gently down on the cold floor. Middleton ran to the foot of the stairs and shouted,

"First aider needed down here now ... a person has collapsed."

A few seconds later, another scene of crime officer came down into the basement and crouching down next to his colleague, he loosened the man's clothing around his neck, felt his pulse and checked his breathing.

"He's okay, I'll put him in recovery, ah, he's coming round now. It's okay, Ben, just lay here for a minute or two then we'll sit you up."

"Jac?" Higgins asked. "I reckon this guy put up a bit of a fight, got shot a couple of times in the testicles, and then, at least, four times in the gut and chest, then to finish him off, he was shot in the face, probably as the person with the firearm stood over him, perhaps with time to reload the firearm"

"Wow, I think we can assume this is Toni Chezec's work, she's a real mean SOB, that's for sure," replied Wolfe. "I'm assuming she caught the first guy unawares then the big guy tries to stop the same happening to him but in the struggle, she manages to get off several rounds then finishes him off."

"Yep, that about sums up my theory as well," Higgins replied as he checked the fingers on both hands of the corpse. "There's hair and what I think might be skin under his right finger nails, we should get some good DNA from this fellow." He stood up. "But we both know, who is behind these two deaths and the DNA results will just prove us right." Higgins turned to walk back to the others.

"Arnold, can you check the lining of the other guys jacket lapels please, cause if I'm right, you'll find a couple of lethal looking close combat weapons?" asked Wolfe.

Higgins felt around the collar, right hand lapel, then the left and when he turned it over, two rings of bright metal could clearly be seen protruding from the lining, he pulled one out.

"Well, what d'ya know, a spear," he announced. "Look at this," he said admiring the instrument as one would a highly engineered ornament, but this was no piece of visual art, it was a weapon of devious callousness.

"That's why she killed him first, if he'd have fought back, he could have done some serious damage with two of those," Wolfe coldly added.

"Matthew Brookes' killer?" Higgins concluded.

"Think so, Arnold, think so," Wolfe replied with melancholy that seemed a little irrelevant now.

Wolfe then decided further investigations were needed within the basement but needed SOCO out of the way for a while.

"Officer, why don't you take your colleague upstairs for some fresh air?"

"Yeah, let me help," said Halford crouching down as the recovering officer put his arm around Halford's shoulder.

When the three men were halfway up the stairs, Wolfe asked if Higgins had any more gloves in his pocket.

"Yep, another two pairs, 'be prepared' that's my moto."

"I thought that was the 'Boy Scouts' moto, Professor?" responded Middleton.

"I used it first," he replied with a wink.

"Look at that wall at the back," Wolfe pointed to the wall to the left of their position, Higgins and Middleton followed his direction. "Does that look recently built to you?" he asked.

"History repeating itself? Is that what you're thinking, Jac?" asked Middleton.

"That is exactly what I'm thinking, Pam."

"Jac, are you referring to gold bullion, you don't actually think …" Higgins paused, then with a slight grin he said, "It's hidden behind that wall, isn't it?" suddenly enthused by Wolfe's fervour.

"We're going to need a couple of lump hammers … this is a farm, I'm sure, there's something lying around that we can use."

Middleton was already on her way to the stairs before Wolfe had finished talking. Five minutes later, she returned with an 8lb hammer while Halford carried a crowbar.

Middleton took the crowbar from Halford at the bottom of the staircase. "You wait here, Pete, shout if anyone comes down those stairs."

Ten minutes later, after intermittent loud banging of steel hitting masonry and the noise of stonework hitting the basement floor, Middleton pulled one of the stands supporting an arc light over to the hole in the wall that had been knocked through by Wolfe and Higgins.

"There it is," announced Wolfe with a self-satisfied look on his face. The hole was big enough for all three to see through, the light flooding a small chamber behind the wall and there in the middle, neatly stacked on a timber pallet, were numerous gold bullion bars.

"That's a neat looking stack of precious metal, Jac," stated Higgins as he patted Wolfe on the back. "Well done, Jac."

"Thanks, Arnold. Pam, get photos on your mobile, will you? We'll use them as a record of numbers, don't want anyone getting light fingered now, do we?"

***

Three o'clock in the afternoon, a press conference was held in the foyer of Holland Walk in Leeds, a large sign behind the podium proudly confirmed that this was the headquarters of the West Yorkshire Police Force. Acting Chief Constable Marcus Haigh-Watson, Detective Inspector Jaxon Wolfe and Director of Forensics Professor Arnold Higgins, occupied the podium; Wolfe in the middle was the main focus of attention. DC's Middleton, Halford and Fairburn together with PC Mills were seated on the front row facing the podium. Pam's smile glowed white like a beacon. Isabella was in the audience with her friend, Jemma, having not gone to school that day, she'd arranged with her dad that she would spend last night at Jemma's house, her parents had agreed to let her stay for safety reasons, two constables keeping watch throughout the night. Izzy had an earworm of a Dr John song in her head that reflected just how proud she was of her dad, Big Shot.

Wolfe knew that a dangerous person was still at large, however, the investigation could be concluded and the team disbanded to allow officers to pursue other on-going investigations. Asked about the person still being sought in connection with 'The Gold Bullion Murders' as they were being tagged by the media, Wolfe had a reply ready but Haigh-Watson jumped in with his response before Wolfe could take breath.

"We have an APB out with all the UK force networks and European networks, we are confident of an arrest very soon."

'That ain't gonna happen,' thought Wolfe.

Chapter 35

The White Rose Hotel in Harrogate looked imposingly splendid in its location overlooking the Stray: an area of public open space bequeathed to the Borough Council in the early 1900s by a Victorian philanthropist for the inhabitants of Harrogate to use in perpetuity for recreational pursuits. The history around the hotel and the neighbouring open space was not uppermost in the minds of the four plain clothed police officers sitting in unmarked cars, watching the hotel car park and the black Range Rover parked on the road outside. No one had approached or seemed to be interested in it within the last five hours. This was the third shift of a 24-hour rota police stake out that had been on-going for three days. Traffic wardens had affixed several notices of breach of parking regulations on the vehicle but still the vehicle stayed put. A DVLA check on the registration had drawn a similar blank to the Jaguar F Type: registered to a Mr and Mrs Jones, using a postcode that exists but a house number that doesn't. PC Mills had confirmed that although the number didn't exist, the car was bought online, the purchasers stating the house was a new build and the post office had registered it but their database hadn't been updated yet.

The ferry terminals at all major ports had received orders to carry out stringent passenger security checks, descriptions of Antonia 'Toni' Chezec had been circulated citing several alternative physical descriptions of disguises that she might be wearing and pseudonyms she might be using. Once again, three days had gone by and no report of a sighting.

Paul Anthony Smythe had died three days earlier, time of death recorded meant life had left him during the flight back to the Leeds Infirmary, just as he himself had predicted. The cause of death was given as multiple internal injuries but a ruptured spleen was stated as the fatal wound.

DI Jaxon Wolfe was piecing together a few loose ends of the investigation, the most relevant being, the house in Headingley that belonged to Matthew Tanner, aka Armon Cabrinovic, used to belong to Paulette Cathcart, aka Pauletta Chezec, a Serbian political refugee who had been granted asylum to stay in the UK in 1974 when she was 19 years of age. It was Tanner's evidence that convinced the UK Government that Chezec would be in danger of losing her life if she was sent back to Bosnia. Tanner and Chezec had started an affair that resulted in the birth of a daughter, Antonia, in 1976 but as political tensions grew between Bosnia and Serbia in the late 1990s, Pauletta Chezec changed her name to Paulette Cathcart and her daughter to Andrea Cathcart, and moved into the property in Headingley until Paulette secured a job in London working for the RSC as a make-up artist becoming Director of makeup before retiring. It turned out that Tanner bought the property in 1992 with the intention of adding to its value by extending it and then selling the property when the extension works were completed with all the proceeds going to a hospice in Headingley that specialised in the care of Alzheimer's patients. One of which is Paulette Cathcart.

Another loose end Wolfe realised may never be tied up related to the whereabouts, dead or alive of Matthew Tanner. The mobile phone recorded testimony of Paul Smythe in the back of the ambulance shortly before his death had led to the likely conclusion that Tanner had been killed, his body dumped somewhere deep in the heart of Eastern Europe. It would, however, be very difficult to prove or disprove this possibility, so Wolfe left this as an open explanation on file.

The gold bullion found at the farm had been counted to compare with the 200 bars seized by Tanner, Smythe Senior, Jessop and Watts from the old library building in Sarajevo in 2005. A very basic calculation was undertaken to try and quantify the bullion recovered from the original assumed haul in 2005. Sixty bars recovered from Bradshaw's farm and twenty bars form the back of Paul Smythe's Porsche Cayenne, assume ten bars retained by Toni Chezec amounted to ninety bars therefore Smythe senior, Jessop and Watts must have sold approximately one hundred and ten bars through Alfred Marks' connections to enhance their individual wealth and businesses. Wolfe, however, knew this was only an exercise done for the Serbian Authorities and he wasn't convinced the numbers stacked up, he couldn't accept Alfie Marks was that involved in fencing the bullion, not one hundred and ten bars anyway, Marks' bankruptcy seemed to contradict such a theory.

'There are some bullion bars still out there somewhere!' he thought to himself.

That left one further loose end, Toni Chezec, where had she disappeared to and was she still dangerous, would she return to avenge the death of her half-brother? Wolfe thought that was unlikely, given the evidence of overheard conversations between the two and Paul Smythe's willingness to accuse her of murder whilst he lay dying. The gold she so obviously desired was no longer hers to covet. The gold bullion bars recovered, would soon be transported back to Sarajevo on the quiet with diplomatic secrecy for the Serbian government to deal with as they thought appropriate on the understanding this remain a diplomatic secret.

Charlotte Marks was completely devastated by the events that had led to her partners' demise but it was the fact he had been indirectly involved in the murder of her brother that caused her the greatest sorrow. Her brother, Matthew, was a beautiful human being but his vulnerability and wanton instinct to protect his sister had led to his murder, she sobbed and sobbed until tears ran dry. Wolfe wanted to keep his distance from Charley, feeling somehow that he was responsible for her discomfort, however, a message taken by Izzy whilst he was on duty, the timing purposefully intended, three weeks after Paul Smythe's death asked Wolfe to call at Charley's house on his way home from work.

He arrived at the house as requested in the evening: a low full moon bathed the front of the house in soft blue light and when Charley opened the door, her tall beauty framed in the doorway immersed in moonlight made Wolfe take a deep loud breath, one of the most beautiful sights he had ever seen in his life. He sighed and when she saw his reaction, she moved forward arms wide open, the two embraced with such intensity that one could be forgiven for believing these were two long lost lovers brought back together by some intensely personal tragedy, which to some extent was true.

"I'm so sorry for every …" but Wolfe couldn't complete his sentence as Charley gently pressed her right forefinger to his lips.

"Shhhh ... you have nothing to be sorry for, Jac, you were right all along." Their embrace broke, she held on to his left hand and walked him into the house.

"Sit down with me, I don't want to talk, I just want to feel you next to me, the quiet company of a man is what I need." She wasn't being in any way seductive, she wasn't being coy she just wanted to be with him.

Wolfe smiled but it was Maria uppermost in his mind as they cuddled up together in silence on the sofa. Wolfe didn't feel any pangs of guilt, just comfort and momentary contentment, 15 minutes later, Charley and he fell asleep.

At the same time that Wolfe and Charlotte Marks were asleep in Charlotte's house in Carlton, a stylishly dressed woman walked elegantly through the foyer of a five-star hotel on the Mediterranean coast of Spain. She entered the residents lounge, strode through the centre of the open plan area. Turning to her right she sidled up to a handsome man who was nursing a gin and tonic as he stood at one end of the bar. Everyone in the lounge, male and female alike stared at the vision of confident feminine beauty, most of the men looked jealously at the man as she leant into him and whispered in his ear,

"I told you I'd get you noticed. Now hold my waist and kiss me gently on the lips then order me a vodka martini, you beautiful man."

The man in his mid-fifties, a millionaire chief executive of a large UK import company whose wife had just divorced him on the grounds of adultery, looked lustfully at the woman he'd met only five hours earlier whilst he was trying to drown his sorrows at the pool side bar. What he didn't know was that the woman now cuddling up to him, waiting for the barman to complete the vodka martini he'd just ordered for her had recently had surgery to remove the implants of her previous incarnation. She wasn't sure how long this soon to be affair would last but what she did know was that stage one of her plan to snare this man was complete. Stage two would begin in Madrid where she was certain to be invited to stay with him at his villa on the outskirts of the city.

The End?